MAGNUS

MAGNUS

Sigmund Brouwer

VICTOR BOOKS

A DIVISION OF SCRIPTURE PRESS PUBLICATIONS INC.
USA CANADA ENGLAND

Copyediting: Carole Streeter and Barbara Williams
Cover Design: Scott Rattray
Cover Illustration: Kazuhiko Sano

Library of Congress Cataloging-in-Publication Data

Brouwer, Sigmund, 1959–
   Magnus / by Sigmund Brouwer.
      p.   cm.
      1. Knights and knighthood—England—Fiction. 2. Druids and
   Druidism—Fiction. 3. Young men—England—Fiction. I. Title.
   PS3552.R6825M3   1995
   813'.54—dc20   94-13611
                                                               CIP

---

1 2 3 4 5 6 7 8 9 10   Printing/Year   99 98 97 96 95

Chapter One

Northern England
March 1312

Since dawn, three ropes had hung black against the rising sun. Enough time had passed for a crowd to arrive and develop a restless holiday mood.

"Hear ye, hear ye, all ye gathered here today." The caller, short and stout with middle age, made no effort to hide the boredom in his voice.

His words had little effect on the restlessness of the people crowded in front of the crude wooden gallows platform. Their eyes were on one who soon would die.

"Get on with your blathering, you old fool!" The shout came from a hungry-faced woman near the back of the crowd. A skinny child held her hand.

The caller scratched at a flea beneath his dirty shirt and ignored her.

"This punishment has been ordered by the sheriff under authority of the earl of York," he continued in a listless tone. "The crimes to be punished are as follows." He unrolled a scroll and held it in front of him at arm's length.

"Andrew, you dimwit! We all know you can't read. Don't be putting on airs for the likes of us." This from a fat man with jowls that shook as he yelled.

The crowd hooted with appreciation, even though none of them realized the scroll was upside down. They grew quiet again, as all stared at one soon to die.

Six burly soldiers stood behind the man with the scroll, holding three prisoners. Too often, even the most weary prisoners made a sudden struggle for freedom when finally facing the thick rope which hung from the gallows. It was such a struggle the crowd hoped for. A hanging was now as common as a wedding or funeral; without a final bolt to escape or howlings of despair, it would be a dull event. Indeed, this hanging drew as many as it did because one of the prisoners was an unknown knight.

"John the potter's son. Found guilty of loitering with the intent to pick the pockets of honest men. To be hung by the neck until dead."

Most of the people in the crowd shook fists at the accused boy. He grinned back at them. Ragged hair and a smudge of dirt covered the side of his face. "Intent!" he shouted in a tinny voice at their upraised fists. "Intent is all you can prove. I've always been too fast to be caught!"

The hangman waited for the noise to end and then droned, "The unknown girl who does not speak or hear . . . theft of three loaves of bread. To be hung by the neck until dead."

The crowd quieted as they stared at her. She in turn stared at her feet. High cheekbones and long dark hair hinted at a beauty to flower. That tragic air about her forced a mumble from the middle of the crowd. "The baker could have easily kept her for kitchen work, instead of forcing the magistrate on her."

The baker flushed with anger. "And how many more mouths should I support in these times? Especially one belonging to a useless girl who cannot hear instructions?"

Behind all of them lay the town known as Helmsley. Although it was important enough to be guarded by a castle, the town was little more than a collection of wood and stone houses along narrow and dirty streets. The stench of rotting mud and farm animals filled the air. Few of the people gathered on the rise even noticed anymore.

Now, the crowd fell as completely silent as the town. The strange knight was about to be formally accused. "Finally," the hangman in the dirty shirt felt their growing excitement and his voice rose beyond boredom, "the knight who claims to be from a land of sun. Found guilty of blasphemy and the theft of a chalice. To be hung by the neck until dead."

The babble of the crowd renewed itself as the people

strained to watch for reaction. The knight did not acknowledge any curiosity. He had been stripped of all the wealth of his apparel except for his trousers, tunic, and a vest of chain mail. The bulges of his muscled arms and shoulders showed a man who had lived by the sword. He stood with bowed head that hid the features of his face.

Having read all the charges, the hangman intoned, "This on the twenty-eighth day of March in the year of our Lord, thirteen hundred and twelve."

Finished with the memorized words, the hangman scrolled the useless paper back into a roll and nodded at the soldiers.

To the crowd's disappointment, none of the prisoners provided entertainment through resistance. Without any visible excitement, the crowd grew restless. Some had neglected a day's work and traveled as far as six miles. Others had brought their entire families. With all attention focused on the three figures slowly climbing the gallows, none in the crowd saw a figure approaching from behind the town.

Not until he strode amid the crowd did anyone notice him. Then, the awed silence was immediate.

As it should have been.

No man in the crowd stood higher than five feet and nine inches. This figure was a giant, four hands above the tallest.

His attire sent a chill among them. The black cloth which swirled around him gleamed with richness and flowed like a heavy river. A hood covered his face; his hands were lost in the deep folds of his robe. He projected nothing less than the shadow of death.

He did not break stride until he reached the gallows. Only then did he stiffly turn to face the crowd. The specter let the silence press down upon the people before uttering his first words.

"The knight shall be set free." His voice was unearthly, a deep rasping evil that sent the crowd back even further. "He shall be set free immediately."

With those words, he extended his arms toward the crowd. One of the children keened high with terror.

The black specter hissed, and blue and orange flames

shot outward from the right sleeve of his robe.

The silence was such that the entire crowd seemed frozen. Then, as if time had resumed, voices broke out.

"Return the knight!" someone shouted, "before we all die!"

"Andrew, save us now!" pleaded another voice. "Set the knight free!"

The hangman blinked twice, then pointed at the figure. "Seize the stranger!" he ordered the soldiers. Two reluctantly stepped forward and drew their long swords.

The specter turned slowly toward them. "For your disobedience," he rasped, "you shall become blind as trees."

He waved his left arm as if invoking a curse on the soldiers. Both fled the gallows, screaming and pressing their faces in agony.

"Do others dare?" the specter asked the crowd, as the soldiers' screams faded.

Andrew was brave and not entirely stupid. He issued fumbling orders to the remaining soldiers to cut the ropes binding the knight.

The specter held his position without motion, his hooded face directed at the crowd.

Before the knight was fully free, a bent, white-haired man in faded rags stepped forth. He limped steadily until he faced the specter with an unfearing upward gaze.

"Your name is Thomas. You are an orphan, reaching manhood," he whispered, staring into the deep shadows of the black cowl. "And you shall give the crowd *my* instructions as if they came from your own mouth."

The specter did not reply. To the crowd, it was as if each figure were made of stone.

"Do you understand me?" the old man whispered calmly. "Nod your head slowly, or I will lift that robe of yours and expose the stilts upon which you stand."

The nod finally came.

"Good." The old man whispered, "Order the release of the other two prisoners."

Silence.

The old man smiled. "Surely, lad, you have no acid left

to blind me. Otherwise you have would done so already. With nothing left to bluff the crowd, you must listen to me." His whispered intensified. *"Order their release!"*

The specter suddenly spoke above the head of the old man. "Release the others or face certain doom," his harsh voice boomed.

The old man chuckled under his breath. "As I thought. You are poorly equipped."

"Release all three?" the hangman protested, "The sheriff will hang *me.*"

"Do as I say," the specter thundered.

Not a person moved.

"You are out of weapons," the old man cackled quietly. "How do you expect to force them now?"

The hangman dared his question again. "All three? Impossible!"

Murmurings came from the people as they too began to lose their edge of fear. A rock, thrown from the back of the crowd, narrowly missed the giant specter. He roared anger, but without flame or the cast of blindness, it was a hollow roar.

Another rock sailed dangerously close.

"Old man," Thomas hissed from the cowl's black shadow, "this is your doing. Help me now."

The old man merely smiled and looked past the specter's shoulder at the sun. "Raise your arms," he commanded.

One more rock whistled past and struck the ground. The murmuring grew.

"Raise them now," the old man repeated with urgency, "before it is too late!"

The specter raised his arms and the crowd fell silent as if struck.

The old man continued quietly, "Repeat all of my words. If you hesitate, we are both lost. There is less time remaining than for a feather to reach the ground."

The black hood nodded slightly.

"Tell them, 'Do not disobey,' " he whispered.

"Do not disobey." The heavy voice rasped with renewed evil.

"Say, 'I have the power to turn the sun into darkness.' "

"Impossible," Thomas whispered back.

"Say it! Now!" The old man's eyes willed him into obedience.

So the specter's voice boomed in measured slowness. "I have the power to turn the sun into darkness."

A laugh from the crowd.

The old man whispered more words, and the specter repeated each one slowly.

"Say, 'Look over my shoulder. I have raised my arms and even now you will see the darkness eating the edge of the sun.' "

Another laugh, this time cut short. Sudden gasps and assorted fainting spells in front of him startled the specter. He fought the impulse to look upward at the sun himself.

The old man gave him more instructions. The specter forced himself to repeat his words. " 'Should I wish, the sun will remain dark in this town forever.' "

He nearly stumbled at the words given him, because already the light of day grew dim. "What kind of sorcerer are you?" he demanded of the old man.

"Say, 'All prisoners shall be released immediately,' " the old man replied in a hypnotic whisper. "Tell them now, while they are in terror."

Thomas did as instructed. In the unnatural darkness, he heard the hangman and the soldiers scurrying into action. Then he repeated the final words given to him by the old man. " 'Send each prisoner from town with food and water. Tonight, at the stroke of midnight, the town mayor shall place a pouch of gold on these very gallows. The messenger I send for the gold will appear like a phantom to receive your offering. Only then will you be free of the threat of my return.' "

As the specter finished, trying hard to keep the wonder and fear from his own voice, an unnatural darkness covered him and the gallows, the crowd, and the countryside.

"You have done well. Go now," the old man spoke. "Drop from your stilts and wrap your robe into a bundle and disappear. Tonight, if you have any brains in your head, you will be able to retrieve the gold. If not . . ."

In the darkness, the orphan named Thomas could only imagine the motion of the old man's hunched shrug.

"These prisoners?" Thomas whispered back. He wanted the knight more than he wanted the gold.

"You desired the knight. As you planned, he will be yours . . . *if* you prove to him you are his rescuer."

As I planned? How did the old man know?

In his confusion of questions, he blurted, "Why release the others?"

The old man answered, "Take them with you. The boy and girl will guarantee you a safe journey to Magnus. You *must* succeed, to bring the winds of light into this age of darkness."

"You cannot possibly know of Magnus."

"Thomas, you have little time before the sun returns."

"Who are you?"

Later, Thomas wondered if there had been a laugh in the old man's reply. "The answer is in Magnus. Now run, or you shall lose all."

Chapter Two

For a man so big, thought Thomas, *the knight cuts through this forest like a roe deer.*

In contrast to the stiffness of the stilts Thomas had discarded less than an hour earlier, he now moved lightly on the leather soles strapped to his feet.

His crudely sewn tunic fit him almost as tightly as his breeches. Normally that double reminder of poverty — clothes he must wear long after outgrowing them, and the brown of monk's charity cloth — irritated Thomas. But today, while silently dodging branches as he moved from tree to tree, he was grateful for the brown which blended him into the background.

Thomas glanced up, seeking the sun's position by the light which streamed dappled shadows onto the moss of the forest floor. He made a rough calculation.

Already they were five miles east of Helmsley and the abandoned gallows. Shortly the Sext bells would mark midday. The halfday of light remaining was ample to continue north and return to the abbey. But were there enough hours left to secure the gold at midnight?

Thomas decided he could not risk a delay in his plans. He reckoned the knight's forward progress and began a wide circle through the falling slope of the forest to intercept him.

The deep moss absorbed his footfalls; he was careful to avoid the scattered dead and dry branches which might crack beneath his weight. Around him, sounds of birds echoed against the hush of the forest. The splashes of green on trees tired of winter gave the forest an air of hope.

Thomas did not pause to enjoy the beauty. He concentrated on footstep after silent footstep, hoping he had remembered the lay of the land correctly. Fifteen minutes later, he grinned in relief at the expected wide stream at the bottom of the valley. While it blocked him, it would also block the knight. And a thick fallen tree appeared the only way to cross the water.

Thomas reached the tree and scrambled to its center above the water. He sat cross-legged and half hidden among the gnarled branches that reached down into the stream, and he waited.

The knight merely raised an eyebrow when he reached the bank of the stream and noticed Thomas on the fallen tree. His face, once hidden by a bowed head at the gallows, now showed clearly in the midday sun. His brown hair was cropped short; his blue eyes were as deep as they were careful to hide his thoughts.

He kept his eyebrow raised. "For a forest so lonely, this appears to be a popular bridge."

Thomas smiled at the irony in the knight's voice and added a touch of his own. "A shrewd observation, sir." Then he stood and balanced in the middle of the fallen tree. "I shall gladly make room for you to pass, sir. However, I beg of you to first answer a question."

Most men who had fought long and hard to reach the status of knighthood would have been enraged at such insolence and would have responded with a menacing steel blade. This knight simply permitted the slight curl of a grin to cross his face.

"You are an unlikely troll." The knight set down a leather food bag he had been carrying over his shoulder and contemplated Thomas. "That *is* legend in this country, is it not—the troll beneath a bridge with three questions to anyone who wishes to pass across?"

"*I* am not a legend," Thomas answered. "But together, *we* may be."

They stared at each other in a silence pleasantly broken by the burbling of the stream between them.

The knight saw a square-shouldered young man dressed in the clothing of a monk's assistant, who did not flinch to be examined . . . ragged brown hair tied back . . . high forehead to suggest strong intelligence . . . a straight noble nose . . . and a chin that did not quiver at a strange knight's imposing gaze.

The knight almost smiled again as he noted the lad's hands. Large and ungainly, they protruded from coarse sleeves much too short. *A puppy with much growing to do,* the knight thought with amusement. *At that awkward age before maturity.*

What checked the knight from smiling was the steady grace in the boy's relaxed stance. And the depth of character hinted by gray eyes that stared back with calm strength. *Does a puppy have this much confidence?* the knight wondered. *This much steel at such a young age?*

Then the knight did grin. This puppy was studying him in return with an equal amount of detached curiosity.

"I presume I pass your inspection," the knight said with a mock bow.

Thomas did not flush as the knight expected. He merely nodded gravely.

Strange. Almost royal. As if we are equals, the knight thought. He let curiosity overcome a trace of anger and spoke again. "Pray tell, your question."

Thomas paused, weighing his words carefully. He knew the future of his life depended on his words.

"Does your code of knighthood," Thomas finally asked, "make provision for the repayment of a life saved and spared?"

The knight thought back to his tired resignation in front of the gallows, then to the powerful joy which followed as he was spared by the miracle of the sun blotted by darkness.

"If there is nothing in this code you speak of," the knight said slowly, as he pictured the heavy ropes of his death hanging against the dawn sky, "I assure you there certainly should be."

Thomas nodded again from the center of the log. He

fought to keep tension from his voice. Never would he have this opportunity again. And the childhood songs from a tender nurse haunted his every dream. . . .

"Sir William, it was I who saved you from the gallows." Thomas cast his words across the water, "Consider me with kindness, I beseech you, in the regretful necessity which forces me to ask repayment of that debt."

On a normal day, the knight would have merely chuckled at such an absurd claim. But this was not a normal day.

Only hours earlier, Sir William had prepared himself to die with dignity, and such an effort was not easy. The mix of emotions he had been holding inside after the sudden escape from death needed release, which they now found in white hot rage.

"Insolent whelp!" he roared.

In one savage movement, he surged onto the log and lunged at Thomas. As his bare hands flashed, fingers of iron tore into Thomas' flesh.

"I'll grind you into worm's dust!" the knight vowed, as he tightened his fingers around Thomas' neck. "To follow me and lay such a pretentious claim. . . ."

Rage prevented Sir William from continuing his words. Instead, his biceps bulged with quick hatred as he began to lift Thomas by the throat with his war-hardened hands.

Unable to speak, Thomas did the only thing he could do. Eyes locked into eyes, he waited for the knight's sanity to return.

The knight only roared an animal yell and lifted Thomas even higher.

Blackness began a slight veil across Thomas' vision. He brought a knee up in desperation. It only bounced off the chain mail stretched across the knight's belly.

Still, Sir William squeezed relentlessly.

The blackness became a sheet. *I . . . must . . . explain,* Thomas willed to himself. *One . . . last . . . chance.* He reached for one of the gnarled branches of the fallen log. *If . . . this . . . breaks . . . I . . . am . . . dead.*

He did not waste energy to complete the thought. The knight's rage had already drained too much life from his bursting lungs. With his final strength, Thomas pulled hard on the branch. It was not much, but it was enough.

Already in an awkward position with Thomas held extended in midair, Sir William did not anticipate the tug on his balance. Both men toppled sideways into the stream.

Thomas bucked against the water and fought for the surface. He reached his feet in the waist-deep water, and sucked in a lungful of air.

Looking for the knight, he prepared to scramble for land. Instead of a charging bull, however, he saw only the matted cloth of the knight's half-submerged back. Thomas reacted almost as swiftly in concern as Sir William had moments earlier in anger.

He thrashed through the water and pulled the man upward. Immediately, the reason for the man's lethargy became obvious. An ugly gash of red covered the knight's temple.

Thomas winced as he noted a smear of blood on a nearby boulder. He dragged the man to shore, ripped a strip of cloth from his shirt, and began dabbing at the blood.

Within seconds, Sir William groaned. He blinked himself into awareness and looked upward at the boy.

"By the denizens of Hades," Sir William said weakly, his rage vanished. "This cannot mean you now have *really* spared my life."

As their outer clothes dried on the branches, they began to speak.

"You left the pickpocket and the girl at the road." Thomas made it a statement. "And you seek to hide in the forest."

"You followed me," Sir William countered, as he hopped and slapped himself with both arms against the cold. "And don't think that because I am not strangling you again, I accept your story about the rescue at the gallows."

Thomas moved back to place several more cautious yards between them.

"I *was* that specter," he said.

Sir William laughed. "Look at you. A skinny puppy

drenched to the bone. Barely my own height. And you claim
to be the specter who brought darkness upon the land.''

"I was that specter," Thomas persisted. "I stood on stilts,
covered by a black robe, and . . ."

The knight moved to a patch of sunlight. His white legs
gleamed. "Don't bother me with such nonsense," he
growled. "I heard the specter speak. Your voice is a girl's
compared to the one that chilled the crowd."

Thomas hugged himself for warmth. A complete silence
seemed to swallow them as they shivered in the depths of
the forest.

"I spoke through a device that concealed my voice,"
Thomas began to explain.

Again the knight waved him into silence. "I see that none
of these inventions are with you."

"I needed to find you quickly," Thomas protested. "I
barely had time to hide my bundle."

"You stated you followed me."

"Yes."

"To lay this claim," the knight repeated darkly. His voice
rose. "Impossible!"

Sir William paused to let his anger grow. "You try my
patience, puppy. No man, let alone a half-grown man, has
the power to shoot flame from his hands or cast blindness
upon the sheriff's best men."

The knight drew himself up. "And no man," he said with
renewed anger, "has the power to bury the sun." He
touched his forehead and brought his finger down to examine the blood, then scowled. "If you continue to insist upon
these lies, I shall soon forget you pulled me from the
stream."

Thomas paused halfway through the breath he had drawn
to reply. The forest was silent. Hadn't the muted cries of
birds been a backdrop for most of their time among the
trees? He held up a hand and cocked his ear for sound. Any
sound.

"Did the hangman make any suggestion that you would
be followed?"

Sir William shook his head in irritation, then scowled

again at the renewed burst of pain. "None. The man was as cowed as any of the villagers. He fairly cried with relief to see me on my way."

They stared around them. Thomas hugged himself harder to fight the chill of wet skin against spring air.

"I promise you, Sir William," he said in a low voice, "I was that specter. And I beg you to give me the chance to prove it."

"For what reason? I don't even know who you are."

"My name is Thomas. I was raised north of here, in Baxton's Wood, at a small abbey along the Harland Moor."

The knight snorted. "A stripling monk."

Thomas shook his head. "Never a man of the church. And with your help, something much more. The help, I humbly add, that you have already promised to the person who saved you from the gallows."

Sir William waved a fist in Thomas' direction. He dropped it in frustration.

"Thomas of Baxton's Wood," he announced heavily, "here is my word. Show me the pouch of gold to be taken at midnight from the gallows—which I assure you will be heavily guarded—and deliver it to me tomorrow in the guise of the specter. Then I shall be in your debt. Failing that, as you surely shall, give me peace."

Thomas grinned his elation in response. In his careful planning of this day, he had never expected to be shivering and waiting for his clothes to dry as he heard the words he wanted so badly. Still, his quest was about to begin, and only a fool looked a gift-horse in the mouth to check for worn teeth.

His thoughts turned, as they always did, to the childhood songs repeated evening after evening by the one person at the abbey who had shown him compassion and love.

So much to be fulfilled . . .

A giggle interrupted his thoughts.

Sir William reacted again with swiftness and sprang in the direction of a quivering bush. There was a flurry of motion and a short struggle.

Then Sir William straightened. He held the pickpocket

and the mute girl by the backs of their shirts.

Thomas reached for his damp shirt to cover his naked chest from the girl's dark eyes. Then he wondered suddenly why he wanted to stare back in return. He had seen many of the village girls before, always ignoring their coy glances as he accompanied the monks to market. Fourteen was an age when already some began to consider marriage. Thomas had a future to find, the one given to him during his childhood songs and fables. No girl had tempted him to look beyond that future. But this one . . .

He shook his head at the distraction and fumbled to pull his shirt on. There was barely time to return to the abbey, and he had much more to accomplish by midnight.

Sir William walked forward, carrying his double burden. Disgust was written plainly across his face.

The dirt-smudged pickpocket shook trying to free himself. "People, they shouted curses at us along the road. Threw stones and called us devil's children," he said mournfully from his perch in the air. "What had we to do but come follow?"

Sir William sighed long and deep and set them down with little gentleness.

Chapter Three

"A witch! A witch!" John, the pickpocket boy, scarcely touched ground as he dashed between trees and skimmed over fallen logs. "An ugly, flesh-eating witch!"

From where Sir William enjoyed drowsiness in the afternoon sun with his back against a tree, he opened his eyes and grimaced. This portion of the forest was far from the road, and, alongside the stream and deep among the trees, it was unlikely to be visited by superstitious peasants. Yet if the boy cried any louder, even the village bells would be put to shame, and seclusion might soon become a lost luxury.

He glanced at the girl to see if she felt the same disgust. After all, she too was a fugitive, and who could predict how long until the hangman reconsidered his decison to set them free?

The knight shook his head in self-disgust. *You are growing old. First, a young man defeats you so soundly he must save you from drowning, and then he places an obligation on you that forces you to wait here. Now, you expect a deaf girl to hear the boy's cries.*

Sir William rose. He grunted with the effort. *Was there once a time when my knees did not pop? That the chain mail across my belly had no more weight than a fly? Yet once a man passes his thirtieth year . . .*

"A witch! With giant claws and fangs for teeth!"

As the boy plunged into the small clearing, Sir William extended his arm.

"Oooof." The boy slammed into the knight's arm.

"What is this nonsense you wish to share with the entire

valley?" Despite his determination to be angry, Sir William smiled, for the boy had forgotten his panic and now lifted his feet to hang from the knight's arm as a way to test both their strengths. "And why did you wander far enough to find the witch?"

The boy dropped and grinned.

"You slept, and . . ." he motioned with his head at the girl, ". . . she doesn't speak and barely moves. Was I too supposed to act as if dead?"

"You have a sharp tongue, lad," the knight warned. "Perhaps I shall cut it loose and serve it as supper to the witch, if indeed she exists."

The boy's eyes widened as he nodded. "She appeared from behind a bush! And it is not my flesh she seeks, but yours."

"Mine?"

"She clutched my arm and pronounced it too skinny."

"I suppose you informed her that you knew of fatter game and pointed down the hill to where I slept?"

"She was horrid. How else could I seek freedom? She said your flesh would prove tasty enough."

Sir William returned to the tree, then slid down so that his back leaned squarely against the trunk. "A witch indeed," he yawned. "More like an old crone who wanders for herbs and even now cackles at your terror. Hmmph. Fangs and claws. What thoughts will you entertain next?"

The boy squatted beside the knight. "Thoughts of money well spent." He held out a grimy palm for the knight's inspection. "I removed this from her pocket."

Sir William leaned forward for closer inspection. Sunlight gleamed from a silver gold coin thick enough that it represented a month's wages for any peasant.

The knight opened his mouth to admonish the boy, but the bushes parted beside them and before either could react, a heavy wooden cane slashed down at the boy's hand. He pulled away, but not quickly enough, and the tip of the cane slapped his open fingers, spilling the coin to the ground. He danced back, hugging his stung hand under his arm and biting his lip to hold back a cry of pain.

Sir William began to roll to his feet to face the unexpected intruder, but he stopped as the cane stabbed downward into the ground between his legs.

"Move again," screeched a voice, "and you will be less of a man."

Sir William wrapped one hand around the cane and ignored further screeching as he grabbed the intruder's wrist with his other hand. "Much as I admire your bravery, milady, it is wasted here. The coin is yours, and it shall be returned with no fight."

He looked upward, but against the sun he saw only darkened outlines of the old woman's face.

"Very well." The screech softened. "As it appears I have no choice, I shall trust you."

The crone lifted the cane, but Sir William did not release his grip until he was standing and able to ensure that he would wake as much a man tomorrow as he had been the previous morning.

He could now see her without the glare of the sun. Black eyes glittered beneath ridged bones plucked free of eyebrows. Her face was greasy, her filthy smudged cheekbones like lumps of blackened dough. Under her ragged shawl were straggles of oily gray hair. A worn cape covered her entire hunched body, shiny where the cloth swelled on her back over the giant lump that marked her deformity.

"Shall I be in your dreams tonight?" she mocked, in response to the knight's studying gaze. Then she leered, showing darkened teeth. "Or is there a reason you travel with the young wench?"

Sir William glanced at the mute girl, who was watching the entire scene with disinterest.

"The girl, it appears, travels in her own world," Sir William replied. "As to my dreams tonight, if you appear, I shall crack that cane across your skull."

"Such a brave man," she crooned, "to bully a helpless old woman."

At that, Sir William laughed. "So helpless that I still tingle to think of that cane."

"My hand," moaned the boy. "It more than tingles."

Sir William frowned. "Give this woman her coin. You were nearly hung for your thievery earlier. A sore hand is hardly enough punishment now."

The boy bent to pick the coin from the dirt, and the old crone cuffed him across the back, then threw her head back and laughed a hideous shriek of delight. John held out the coin for her and glared.

She pocketed the coin, then pointed a bent finger at the knight. "You are an honest man," she said. "Many others would have killed me for much less silver. I shall favor you then with a gift. But you must follow."

Sir William shook his head.

"It is not far," she said. "Humor an old woman."

With that, she moved to the edge of the clearing and pushed her way through a screen of shrubbery.

Sir William shrugged. "Stay with the girl," he told the boy. "I shall return immediately."

When he stepped beyond the clearing, the old crone had moved deep enough into the forest that he could barely see her in the shadows beyond.

"Come, come," she beckoned. "Quickly follow."

The knight grinned at his own curiosity. The gift, he was certain, would be of little value. But the old woman showed spirit, and how much harm could there be in a short walk?

When he reached the shadows, she was not to be seen. He paused as his eyes searched the trees.

Her shawl was hung from a branch. A few steps farther, her cape covered a small shrub. And past that, her shabby skirt.

Sir William scrunched his face in puzzlement. Surely the old woman was not coyly disrobing herself as she walked. Surely, her promised gift was not herself.

Hearty laughter greeted his puzzlement.

Sir William tensed. The laughter came from a deep male voice. The voice's owner stepped out from a nearby tree.

"William, William," the visitor chided. "To see your face as you contemplated the old woman's favors nearly makes our long absence worth the while."

Sir William stared in disbelief. Not at the wig of horsehair that the man held in his left hand. Not at the wax he was pulling from his face. But at the man himself.

"Hawkwood!" Sir William said. "My lord and friend!"

"Whom might you expect? For the prescribed years have passed. As promised, you made your return. Is it not fitting that I too keep my promise?" Hawkwood grinned, then raised his voice to the screech he had used earlier. "Shall I be in your dreams tonight?"

"Scoundrel," William replied. "Few are the hags uglier than you."

"I shall accept that as flattery, for if you can be deceived, then I have retained some skill in the matter!"

They moved toward each other and briefly clasped arms in deep friendship. Then each stepped back to study the other.

The silver-haired Hawkwood was slightly shorter than the knight. Although older, his face had seen less sun and wind, and his lines did not run as deep as the knight's. It was a lean face, almost wolflike, but softened by his smile. Stripped of the old crone's clothing, he wore simple pants, and a light vest, which although not tight, still gave ample indication of a body used to physical labor. His voice was gentle and low. "It has been far too long, William. The years have treated you well."

"We are both alive," the knight observed dryly. "Anything more is a gift, is it not?"

Hawkwood nodded. "In our fight against the enemy, yes."

The knight watched in silence as Hawkwood removed the last traces of disguise from his face. Hawkwood winced as he plucked at the wax imbedded in his eyebrows, wax not smudged with dirt like the false cheekbones, but shinier white to resemble the bony ridges that had fooled the knight minutes earlier.

"Would that we had the time for me to cleanse at the stream before we speak," Hawkwood said. "And would that we had the time to converse over an ale at a tavern, like the old friends we are. Such luxury however . . ."

"Who is there to hinder us?" William asked. "The forest

has no ears. And we have much to discuss."

Hawkwood shook his head in disagreement. "You must return to your young companions shortly. They cannot suspect I was anything other than a wandering old woman."

"They are children!"

"Look more closely at the girl, William. She is almost a woman. And, I'm afraid, more."

"More?"

"More. But hear me later on that subject." Hawkwood began to pace a tight circle. "Were your travels difficult?"

"No, milord. Exile still provides the secrecy and refuge we cannot have here. And in the southern half of England, none questioned me." Sir William shrugged. "I knew, of course, as I traveled north, that word of my arrival would reach the enemy. But also that it would reach you, that you would thus seek me, as you have. This far from Magnus, I thought myself yet safe from the enemy."

Hawkwood spat. "Nowhere in England is it now safe."

"With the gallows rope around my neck, the same thought occurred to me. For too much time, I wondered if perhaps the plan we laid those years ago had failed, and that you might be dead by now."

Hawkwood spat again. "There have been moments, William. Our enemies' power grows. It was child's play for them to hide the chalice in your horse's saddlebag."

"And child's play for *you* to arrange the time of the hanging?"

Now Hawkwood laughed. "The years haven't dulled you."

The knight sighed as he recalled his fight with Thomas. "Perhaps. Perhaps not. But I find it difficult to believe that the eclipse occurred when it did because of happenstance or because of a divine miracle that presumes any importance for my scarred hide."

"Tut, tut, William. We are not without our allies among the powerful. As you surmised, I did indeed arrange the time of the hanging based on our ancient charts. But is it not God who arranges the stars? A century will pass before the sky darkens again. We could not have asked Him for more in the spring of this year."

Sir William waved away the protest. "You would have found another method, had there been no eclipse. Perhaps *you* would have arrived as a specter. . . ."

Hawkwood resumed his pacing. He stepped in and out of the shadows, so that the dappled outlines of leaves played across his lean face. "Sarah trained the young man well, did she not?"

The knight nodded. "It took all my willpower to pretend surprise when he found me earlier this afternoon. Thomas has grown much since I last saw him."

"Grown enough to topple you into the stream?" Hawkwood laughed at the knight's sudden coughing fit, then moved to a log and sat. The laughter ended and his voice became heavy, much heavier than his years. "Yes, against all odds, the boy has grown to manhood."

Sir William studied Hawkwood's face. "Your countenance suggests a sorrow I do not understand. For I have returned safely, you are here, the boy appeared as Sarah told him to, and Magnus awaits its delivering angel."

Hawkwood closed his eyes and winced in pain. "Sarah is gone. She died four years ago, at Harland Moor."

The knight placed a comforting hand on his friend's shoulder. They remained in silence for several moments before Hawkwood continued. "Because of her death, William, we cannot know whether the enemy has reached Thomas and converted him to their cause."

Sir William raised an index finger, as if to emphasize his next words. "Is it not significant that he sought me out at the gallows? Only Sarah could have instructed him to expect me."

"I have wondered the same. Yet Sarah died when he was only ten, his teaching barely begun, and him far too young for the passage of rites where a boy is trusted with knowledge of our cause."

William closed his eyes in thought. "If not from her, then, how could he know of me? Magnus fell long before his birth."

"I pray, of course, that he acts upon Sarah's instructions," Hawkwood agreed. "Yet the enemy plays a masterful game. It is equally conceivable that Thomas has been sent forth to lure us out of hiding, that he is one of them. Did you hint anything of our plan to him?"

William shook his head. "I played the fool. As further demonstration of my ignorance, I told him I needed proof he was the specter."

Their conversation was interrupted by a high-pitched cry several hundred yards away. "Sir Wiiiillllliam!"

"The pickpocket," Sir William said. "We *do* have little time."

"He is a bright one," Hawkwood said. "It served my purpose to let him steal the coin, for I then had reason to visit you. But his fingers are so light I almost did not detect his actions. He is crafty and has spirit. If this were the old days, we could consider teaching him in our ways."

"I have affection for him too," Sir William said. "Except for now, because he searches for me, and it seems you have much to say. What of Thomas? What of the girl?"

"Wiilliaammm!" came the boy's voice.

Sir William paused. "Will we meet again soon?"

"In Magnus. I suspect Thomas will take you there. I shall go ahead and wait for your arrival."

"The girl? You said the girl—"

"Watch her closely, William. Would not the enemy expect one of us to have you rescued from hanging?"

"Yes."

"Would it suit the enemy's purpose more to guard against the rescue and have you killed, or to let you escape and see where you lead them?"

William took a breath and said in rueful tones, "I am more valuable to them alive and in flight. Thus, they would need some method to track my flight."

"Yes, William. Is it the pickpocket boy who watches you? Or the girl? Or Thomas? That is why I spent long hours waiting for the proper moment to appear as an old hag. I cannot afford to be seen."

"Wiillliamm!" Now the boy was near enough that they could hear the crashing of underbrush.

"Guard yourself, and do what Thomas demands," Hawkwood said with urgency. "If he is not one of the enemy, he will desperately need our help."

"I will guard myself carefully," Sir William vowed, "and wait for you to greet me in Magnus, in whatever guise you next appear."

Hawkwood began to edge into the shadows.

"My friend," Sir William called softly, "what if I discover Thomas belongs to the enemy?"

"Play his game until you have learned as much as you can," Hawkwood whispered back. "Then end his life."

Chapter Four

As Thomas reached the summit of the final moor before the abbey, bells rang for None, the service three hours past midday. If one could fly with the straightness of a crow, the Harland Moor Abbey was barely six miles due north of his meeting place with the knight. Winding footpaths and caution against roaming bandits, however, had made his travel seem more like twelve miles. Despite that, he had moved with a quickness driven by urgency.

Below in the valley, Thomas could see the stone walls of the abbey hall through the towering trees. The valley itself was narrow and compressed, more rock and stunted trees on the slopes than sweet grass and sheep—probably the only reason it had been donated to the mother abbey by an earl determined to buy his place into heaven. The mother abbey at Rievaulx, just outside of Helmsley, was part of the large order of Cistercian monks, and had always accepted such gifts. With this one, Rievaulx had quickly established an outpost designed to earn more money for the church. Time had proven the land too poor, however, and barely worth the investment of abbey hall, library, and living quarters made from stone quarried directly from the nearby hills.

Thomas moved quickly from the exposed summit toward the trees down near the river which wound past the abbey. Years of avoiding the harsh monks had taught him every secret deer path in the surrounding hills. At times, he would approach a seemingly solid stand of brush, then slip sideways into an invisible opening among the jagged branches, and later reappear quietly farther down the hill.

His familiarity with the terrain, however, did not make him less cautious, especially since his first destination was not the abbey itself, but a precious hiding place.

Several bends upstream from the abbey hall, comfortably shaded by large oaks, was a jumble of rocks and boulders, some as large as a peasant's hut. Among them, a freak of nature had created a dry, cool cave, its narrow entrance concealed by jutting slabs of granite and of bushes rising from softer ground below.

Thomas circled it once. Then he slipped into a nearby crevice and surveyed the area.

Count to one thousand, he said to himself, echoing the instructions given him time and again. *Watch carefully for movement, and count to one thousand. Let no person ever discover this place.*

Thomas settled into the comforting hum of forest noises, alert for any sign of intruders, as he pondered the day.

First, he would need the power of knowledge hidden within the cave. Then, time to assemble that power. Thomas smiled. So much was waiting for him inside among the books. . . .

Enough time had passed. He circled slowly once more, remembering the love someone had given him with the instructions he had repeated back endlessly.

"Never, never speak of the existence of the books. Always, always, be sure beyond doubt no person sees you slip into the cave. The books have the power of knowledge beyond price. Take from them, and never, never speak of their existence."

As Thomas entered the coolness of the cave, sadness overwhelmed him, because the place never failed to remind him of the one who had so patiently taught him.

He stood motionless until his eyes adjusted to the gloom. He waited another fifteen minutes. Then he moved forward to the shaft of sunlight that fell in a large crack between two slabs leaning crookedly against another.

Thomas pulled aside a rotting piece of tree that looked as if it had grown into the rock behind it. Dragging out a chest that was as high as his knees and as wide as a cart, he opened the lid, reached inside, and gently lifted out a leatherbound book the size of a small tabletop.

He searched page after page, carefully turning and setting down each leaf of ancient paper before scanning the words before him. Nearly an hour later, he grunted with satisfaction.

Without hurry, he returned the book into the chest, then the chest into its spot in the stone, then the lumber in front of the chest.

He silently counted to one thousand at the entrance of the ruins before edging back into the forest.

"No supper for you tonight," wheezed Prior Jack with vicious satisfaction, as he pinched Thomas' right ear between stubby thumb and forefinger.

Thomas did not move. The only sound in the abbey hall was a slight scuffling of Prior Jack's feet as he balanced his huge bulk on the stone floor.

Prior Jack was disappointed not to find immediate fear in Thomas.

"I've changed my mind on your punishment." Prior Jack's eyes became pinpoint dots of black hatred almost hidden in rolls of flesh. "You're finally to the age which lets us consider flogging, you ignorant peasant orphan."

Thomas closed his eyes and fought pain and anger. *Today is my last day here. It will be fortunate if I don't murder this man. . . .*

Prior Jack's permanent wheeze was the result of the gross fatness which also forced him to waddle sideways through the abbey's narrower doorways.

Once, on a sweltering summer day, Thomas had heard splashing in the pond behind the abbey. He'd crept closer and seen Prior Jack in the water. So wide and blubbery were the rolls of white fat that Thomas could barely recognize the shape of a man beneath the round, boulder head.

Not that fatness was unfashionable. On the contrary, it was a status symbol that only the rich could afford. Most peasants suffered from continuous hunger, and considered themselves fortunate each day to eat more than a bowl of thin cabbage soup and some slices of black wholemeal bread, never with butter. Yet Prior Jack took advantage of the distance of Harland Moor Abbey from the mother abbey of Rievaulx, becoming a tyrant in relentless pursuit of his gluttony.

Because of that gluttony, it had angered him immensely to see Thomas slipping through the back hall of the abbey, because it meant that once again, Thomas had neglected his work in the garden. The soil was poor enough to irritate a man of Prior Jack's girth. Without the boy's constant work, the fall harvest would last only until January.

Worse, no one knew where the boy went. Often Prior Jack or one of the other three monks had tried following him, but it was as useless as tracking smoke from a fire. All they could ever do was to punish him on his return.

Not once did they guess how badly the method had back-fired. In efforts to escape over the year, Thomas had learned secret ways through the old abbey and hidden paths on its grounds. He had been forced to learn how to move quietly. The continuous punishment had made him the perfect spy and had toughened him to endure anything.

Within the abbey itself, Thomas did not always escape Prior Jack's quick mean hands and silent padding feet. This was not the first time the monk had managed to sneak close enough to grab his ear.

But it *will* be the last, Thomas vowed to himself.

"Prior Jack," Thomas said through gritted teeth, as he reached into his shirt for a hidden knife, "you are a fat, obscene pig." Thomas pulled his hand free. "If you don't let go, this knife will slice lard off you in strips."

Prior Jack rattled a gasp from his overworked lungs. "How dare you threaten me? I am a man of God!"

Regardless of his claim of status, the monk dropped his grip and stepped back. Thomas took a deep breath before he finally spoke the words he had been rehearsing.

"You? A man of God? First convince me that God exists. Then convince me you're a man, not a spineless pig of jelly. And, if God does exist, prove to me that you actually follow Him, instead of preaching one thing and doing another."

The fat monk's cheeks bulged in horror. For years, the boy had responded with defiant silence. It curdled his blood to suddenly hear this, and then to realize that the scrawny boy and his corded muscles had grown close to manhood without his notice.

Resolve had changed Thomas' eyes, the monk decided in fear. The gray in them had become ice and the knife in Thomas' right hand did not waver.

"Philip! Frederick! Walter!" Prior Jack bellowed into the empty stone corridors. He took a step back from Thomas and dropped his voice to its usual strained wheeze. "Put the knife away. Immediate penitence may spare your soul after such blasphemy."

Dust danced between them, red and blue in the glow of the light beams from a stained-glass window on the west side of the corridor. It reminded Thomas that the sun was indeed at a sharp angle. Eventide would be upon him soon.

My plan must work, and there is little time to complete it. First I must get past this detestable bully and the three other monks.

They arrived almost immediately, shaved heads faintly pink from exertion.

"The boy has lost his mind," Prior Jack whined. "As you can plainly see, he is threatening to kill me."

Brother Walter, gaunt and gray, frowned. "Put the knife down, boy. Now. And you will only be whipped as punishment. If not, you will lose your hand."

Thomas knew this was no idle threat. Peasants *had* lost their hands for a simple crime like theft. To threaten members of the clergy was unimaginable.

"Tonight," Thomas said calmly, instead of dropping the knife, "is the night you set me free from this hole that is hell on earth. Furthermore, you will send me on my way with provisions for a week, and also three years' wages."

"Impertinent dog," squeaked Brother Philip. Tiny and shrunken, he quickly looked to the others for approval. "You owe us the best years of your life. Few abbeys in this country would have taken in scum like you and raised you as we did."

"As a slave?" Thomas countered. He lifted his knife higher, and they kept their distance. "Since I was old enough to lift a hoe, you sent me to the garden. When I cried because of raw blisters, you cuffed me on the head and withheld my food. Your filth—dirty, stinking clothing and the slop of your meals—I've cleaned every day for seven years. I chopped wood on winter mornings while you slept indoors, too miserly to give me even a shawl for my blue shoulders."

Brother Frederick rose on his toes and pointed at Thomas. His greasy face turned red with indignation. "We could have thrown you to the wolves!"

Thomas spat at their feet.

"Listen to me, you feeble old men." In saying that, Thomas felt a surge of hot joy. The moment was right, he knew without doubt. The hesitation that had filled him with agony for six months had disappeared.

Yes, he had been ready to leave for some time. The words of his childhood nurse had echoed softly during the dark hours as he lay in bed, night after night, dreaming of this moment. But he had waited and endured until, as his nurse had promised, the day arrived when he could make best use of all the weapons of intelligence and strength she had given him before her death.

With news of the scheduled hanging of a knight, a vision of his future had filled him. During the busy hours of daylight over the last week, the words of his childhood songs had echoed as he had prepared carefully to ensure the moment would indeed belong to him.

"Listen," Thomas repeated, "you did not take me here as charity. You took me because the prior at Rievaulx ordered that you take me and the nurse. He did so because my parents were not peasants as you have tried to lead me to believe. My father was a mason, a builder of churches, and he left behind enough money to pay for my education among the clergy. Yet you took advantage of the distance from the abbey at Rievaulx; instead of providing education, you used me as a slave."

Brother Philip glanced wildly at the other three. "He cannot know that," he sputtered.

"No?" Thomas' voice grew ominous. As he spoke, he began to see by the reactions of the monks how much strength he had carefully hidden from them and, to his surprise, from himself.

"No?" Thomas let his tone grow cold, and he spoke quietly enough to make them strain for every savage word. "The letters you leave carelessly about speak plainly to me. I've read every report—every false report—that you have sent to the prior at Rievaulx, including the first one in which you promised to do your Christian duty to me. Bah!" Thomas spit at their feet. "Would that I were half as content as you have made him believe."

Brother Walter shook his head. "You cannot read. That is a magic, a gift the clergy give to very few."

Thomas ignored him. "Furthermore, I have written in clear Latin a long letter which details the history of this abbey over the last years. To be certain, I have also transcribed the letter into French, with that copy reserved for the earl of York."

"Thomas writes too?" gasped Brother Philip. "Latin and French?"

"These letters are in the hands of a friend in the village. Unless I appear tonight to ask for them back, he will deliver them to the mother abbey. All of you will be defrocked and sent penniless among the same peasants you have robbed for years without mercy."

"It's a bluff," Prior Jack declared. "If we all move at once, we can lay hold of him and deliver him to the sheriff—for hanging."

Time ebbed heartbeat by heartbeat in the stillness of the abbey.

Thomas waved his knife and the sudden motion checked any rash action. "Brother Frederick. Your accounting of the wool taken from the sheep that I guarded night after night . . . will it bear close scrutiny when the prior at Rievaulx sends men to examine the records? Or will they discover you have been keeping one bag of wool for every ten sold, and turning the profit into gold for yourself?"

Frederick's face grew white.

"Don't worry," Thomas said. "The strong box you have hidden in the hollow of a tree behind the pond is safe. But empty of your gold. That has already been distributed among the villagers as payment to hold my letter."

The other monks swiveled their heads to stare at Frederick.

"I see," Thomas said. "It is a secret guarded from the others."

A growl from the prior proved the statement true.

"Prior Jack," Thomas snorted, "the menial tending of dishes after each meal you forced upon me made my task very easy. For that letter also details the food you consume in a single month. I'm sure the prior at Rievaulx will be disappointed to discover that you slobber down nearly four hundred eggs from full moon to full moon. Over fifty pounds of flour. Three lambs. And a side of beef. It will explain, of course, why this abbey has not made a harvest contribution to the mother abbey in five years."

Prior Jack's cheeks wobbled with rage.

"Tut, tut," Thomas cautioned. "Anger, like work, may strain you."

"Enough," Brother Walter said.

"Enough? Is it because you dread to hear what that letter reports of you?"

The lines of Brother Walter's face drew tight. "You shall get your provisions."

"This means, I take it, that your fellow monks don't know *your* secret vice?"

"You will also receive three years' wages," Brother Walter said.

"He's a male witch," Thomas said simply to the other three. "A practicing warlock. Potions, magic chanting, and the sacrifice of animals at midnight."

The three monks recoiled from Brother Walter.

"Oh, fear not," Thomas said. "He's quite harmless. I've heard the man sobbing into his pillow from failure more times than I care to recall."

In the renewed silence, they could only stare at each other. Four monks in shabby brown and a grown boy with enough calm hatred to give him strength.

"I will take my wages in silver or gold." Thomas was the first to break the impass. "Have it here before the sun is down, along with the provisions. Or I shall demand *four* years' wages instead."

They hesitated.

"Go on," Thomas said. "I'll keep my word and have the letter returned to you tomorrow, when I reach the village safely."

They turned and scurried, but even before rounding the corner of the hall, they had already begun heated arguing and accusations.

Shortly after the last rays of sun warmed the stained glass, Brother Walter and Brother Philip strode back to Thomas.

Brother Walter held out a oily leather bag. "Cheese, bread, and meat," he said. "Enough to last you ten days."

Brother Philip tossed Thomas a much smaller sack. "Count it," he said. "Two years in silver. Another year in gold."

Thomas regarded them steadily. *Where is the fear with which they departed barely a half hour earlier? Why the gleam of triumph behind Brother Walter's eyes?*

"Thank you," was all Thomas said, as the comforting weight of both sacks dragged on his arms. Yet he waited before leaving. An unease he could not explain filled him.

"Go on, boy," Brother Walter sneered in the gathering darkness of the hall.

Still Thomas waited. Unsure.

Brother Philip gazed at the rough stones beneath his feet.

"In the letter," Brother Philip mumbled, "what have you to tell the prior at Rievaulx about me?"

Thomas suddenly felt pity. The tiny man's shoulders were bowed with weariness and guilt.

"Nothing to damn you," he said gently. "Nothing to praise you. As if you merely stood aside all these years."

"You show uncanny wisdom for a boy," Brother Philip choked, his head still low. When he straightened, he made no effort to hide his tears. "Perhaps that is the worst of all, not to make a choice between good or evil. I'm old now. I can barely hear, yet the slightest noise wakens me from troubled sleep. My bones are brittle, and I'm afraid of falling, even from the steps to the chapel. The terrifying blackness of death is too soon ahead of me, and all I am to the God who waits is an empty man who has only pretended to be in His service."

"Quit your blathering," Brother Walter said between clenched teeth. "Send the boy on his way. Now!"

Brother Philip clamped his jaw as if coming to a decision. "Not to his death. Nor shall I go to meet God without attempting some good." He drew a lungful of air. "Thomas. Leave alone the—"

Brother Walter crashed a fist into the tiny man's mouth. The blow drove Brother Philip's head into a square stone which jutted from the wall. He collapsed to his knees without a moan.

Brother Philip smiled once at Thomas, struggled to speak, then toppled from his knees and did not move.

Thomas felt a chill. What had Philip been trying to say?

"Spawn of the devil," Brother Walter hissed at Thomas. "Your soul will roast in hell."

Thomas said nothing and rested the bag of food on his shoulder. He took a half step away, then turned to deliver a promise.

"Brother Walter," he began with quiet deadliness, suddenly guessing the reason for Philip's death. "If indeed there is such a place as hell, your soul will be there much sooner than mine. And your own death shall be upon your shoulders as surely as the death of your brother here."

Thomas then left the hall as silently as a shadow. He paused outside until the noises inside told him that the three remaining monks were struggling with Brother Philip's body. Then, to fulfill his parting promise, Thomas slipped to the rear of the abbey into the cool storage room below the kitchen.

He departed shortly after into the darkness, climbing the valley hills with one sack fewer than he had planned.

Chapter Five

Compline. Every three hours the small village church rang its bells to let the people mark the passage of time. Each new ringing from the church marked a different devotion for the clergy. Matins at midnight, Lauds at three A.M. and so on. The eighth ringing of the bells meant the last service of the day, Compline, at nine P.M.

That clanging of bronze clappers against bronze bells reached Thomas where he sat, arms hugging knees, beneath a tree halfway between the village and the gallows.

Compline. Already.

Three bundles now lay beside him. One, a small sack with gold and silver given by the monks. The second, from his efforts in the Roman ruins that afternoon. And the third, the bundle of stilts and cloth he had recently recovered from its earlier burial place near the gallows.

Thomas could do no more to prepare himself for his next test. Yet the waiting passed too quickly.

He merely had to turn his head to see the distant gallows etched black against the light of moon when it broke through uneven clouds.

If I could pray, Thomas thought, *I would pray for the clouds to grow thicker. Clear moonlight will make my deception more difficult.*

The mayor had not yet deposited the gold beside the gallows. That Thomas knew. He had chosen this place to hide because it was near the road that wound out of Helmsley. It would let him see how many men the sheriff sent from the village to guard the gold on its short journey.

Not for the first time in the last few cold hours did Thomas wonder about the mysterious old man. In front of the panicked crowd in the morning, he had taken great pains to force Thomas to demand gold that was more money than five men could earn in five years. Enough to provision a small army.

Almost as if the old man had read Thomas' mind. Thomas shivered, but not because of cold.

How did he know I was not a specter, but an impostor on stilts? How did he know what I wanted? And how did the old man deceive them all with a trick of such proportion that the sun appeared to run from the sky?

But the question that burned hottest—Thomas wanted to pound the earth with his fists in frustration—was one simple word. *Why?*

If this unknown old man had such power, why the actions of the morning? He could have revealed Thomas as an impostor; yet he had toyed with him, then disappeared. Why would—

Thomas sat bolt upright.

Will the old man suddenly appear again to recapture the gold?

With that final question to haunt him, Thomas discovered that time could move slowly. Very slowly indeed.

"I'll not rest until this gold has been safely borne away by the specter."

The voice reached Thomas clearly in the cold night air. By reflex, he put his hand on the bundles. Reassured by their presence, he listened hard.

"Fool!" a harsh voice replied. "The sheriff has promised a third of this gold to the man who brings down the specter. I, for one, have sharpened my long sword."

"I'm no fool," the first voice replied with a definite tremble. "I was there when the sky turned black. The ghostly specter is welcome to his ransom. I only pray we never see him again."

"Shut your jaws!" commanded a third voice. "This is a military operation. Not a gathering of old wives."

Thomas counted eight men in the flittering moonlight. Eight men!

As much as he might take joy in the way his muscles responded more and more to hard work during the day, he swallowed fear to remind himself that he had yet to shave a full growth of beard.

Am I a village idiot to think I might overcome the odds of eight well-trained sheriff's men? And if I do succeed, what will I face in the months to come?

Again, Thomas regretted briefly that he could not pray.

Instead, he silently sang lines from a chant that had so often comforted him in his childhood.

Delivered on the wings of an angel,
he shall free us from oppression.
Delivered on the wings of an angel,
he shall free us from oppression.

In the play of moon and clouds, Thomas snatched glimpses of men setting themselves in a rough circle around the gallows.

The bells for Matins began to ring from the village. Exactly midnight.

The promised phantom did not keep the sheriff's men in suspense. It appeared as if from the ground, not more than a stone's throw from the men circling the gold.

Ghostly white, the phantom moved serenely toward the gallows. It was merely a full hand taller than the largest of the sheriff's men, not four or five hands taller as the black specter had been.

In the dim moonlight, it did not show arms. Nor a face. A motionless cowl covered its head.

"All saints preserve us!" screamed the first soldier.

"Advance or you'll lose your head!" countered the commander's voice. "Move together or die in the morning!"

After some moments, all eight men began to step slowly forward with swords drawn.

The phantom stopped and waited. It did not speak.

A cloud blotted the moon completely. The men hesitated, then gasped as an eerie glow came from within the pale body of the phantom. Some stumbled backward on the uneven ground.

"Hold, you cowards," came the tense voice of the commander. The retreating men froze.

"A third of the gold to the one who defeats this apparition!" from someone in the pack.

Still, the phantom said nothing and held its position.

Finally, just as the cloud began to break away from the moon, the one soldier with the sharpened long sword began a rush at the phantom. "Join me!" he shouted. "Show no fear!"

The point of his outstretched sword had almost reached the outline of the phantom when a roaring explosion of white filled the soldier's face and etched sharply for one split heartbeat every ripple of the ground for yards in every direction.

"Aaargh!" the soldier screamed, falling sideways as his sword clattered uselessly to the ground.

No one had time to react.

The phantom moaned as it became a giant torch of anger. Flames reached for the soldier on the ground, and he crabbed his way backward, screaming in terror.

The other soldiers finally unfroze. They stepped back to huddle in a frightened knot, staring wild-eyed at the flames which outlined the figure of the phantom. They whispered hurried prayers and crossed and recrossed themselves in the anguish of fear.

"A spirit from the depths of hell," one soldier groaned, "spreading upon us the fires which burn eternally."

In response, the flames grew more intense, still clearly showing the shape of the phantom. And it said nothing.

The men stood transfixed. Nearly half an hour later, the last flame died abruptly and the phantom collapsed upon itself. The men did not approach.

One soldier finally thought to glance at the gallows. The large bag of gold no longer rested in the center of the wooden structure.

Sir William stirred as a figure shaded his face from the early morning sun. He had not slept well anyway; the ground was lumpy and cold, and both the pickpocket and mute girl had pressed hard against him to seek warmth during the night.

He blinked open his eyes at a mountain of black which filled the entire sky above him.

"Mother of saints," he said with no emotion. "If you are not the boy Thomas, I am a dead man."

"Your control is admirable," breathed the specter in low rasping tones. "It makes you a valuable man."

With a slight grunt, Sir William sat upright. His movement woke the pickpocket and the girl.

Her hands flew to her mouth, and she bit her knuckles in terror. The pickpocket tried to speak, but no sound came from his mouth.

"Send them down to the stream," the cowled specter said in his horrible voice. "Our conversation must be private."

Sir William waved the two away.

Neither needed a second invitation to flee, and they were far from sight long before the bushes in their path had stopped quivering.

Sir William stood and measured himself against the specter's height. His head barely reached the black figure's shoulders.

A twisted grin crossed Sir William's face. "May I?" he asked, motioning at the flowing robe.

The specter nodded.

Sir William pulled back the robe. He snorted exasperated disbelief. "Stilts indeed."

Thomas leaned forward, and as the stilts fell free, hopped lightly to the ground. He peeled back the ominous cowl. Strapped to his face was a complicated arrangement of wood and reeds that looked much like a squashed duck-bill.

He loosened the straps. The piece fell into his hands, leaving behind deep red marks across his cheeks.

"Much better," Thomas said in his normal voice. He rubbed his cheeks, then grinned.

In that moment, the knight saw the unlined face of a puppy; but he quickly swore to himself not to forget the puppy had sharp teeth.

The knight shook his head again and gruffened his voice

to hide any admiration that might slip through. "And I suppose you can equally explain the fire from your sleeve."

Thomas pulled his sleeves free from his arms to show a long tube running from his wrist up to his armpit. "A pig's bladder," he explained, as he raised one arm to show a small balloon of cured leather. "I squeeze," he brought his elbow down and compressed the bag, "and it forces a fluid through this reed. I simply spark it," he flicked something quickly with his left hand, "and the spray ignites."

Sir William nodded, simply because he could think of nothing to say.

"Unfortunately," Thomas mumbled, as he remembered how helpless he had felt when the old man challenged him in front of the crowd, "it works only once. Then the bag needs refilling."

"The fluid?"

Thomas shook his head. "I need to keep *some* secrets."

"How did you blind those sheriff's men?"

Thomas lifted his other arm to show a small tubular crucible of clay strapped to his left wrist. The crucible had a long, tiny neck that pointed almost like a finger.

"Another fluid," Thomas explained. "I sweep my hand and it spews forth. It burns any flesh it touches."

"Another secret, I suppose."

Thomas shrugged. He then said, "I also have the gold from the gallows. Is that enough proof that I was the one who saved your life?"

The knight reminded himself that he must play the role of an unsuspecting skeptic. He must make Thomas work to convince him. "Perhaps it is enough proof. Did you use more trickery?"

"*Simple* trickery. Shorter stilts and a white cape around me, supported inside like a tent by a framework of woven branches. The cape was waxed and oiled. I lit a candle inside, stepped back through a flap, and let it burn itself down. It was enough distraction to sneak to the gallows."

Thomas did not mention the mixture of charcoal, sulfur and potassium nitrate—which men in later centuries would call gunpowder—that he had exploded in a flash of white to temporarily rob all the sheriff's men of their night vision. It was another secret which might lead to questions about the precious books.

"You think you have great intelligence," the knight observed dryly.

Thomas thought of the endless hours his childhood nurse, Sarah, had spent coaching him through games of logic, through spoken and written Latin and French, through the intricacies of mathematics. Thomas thought of his greatest treasure—the chest filled with books. But Thomas did not think of his intelligence.

"I have been taught to make the most of what is available," he replied without pride.

Suddenly, the knight sprang forward with blurring swiftness, reaching behind his back and pulling from between his shoulder blades a short sword.

Before Thomas could draw a breath, Sir William pinned him to the ground, sword to his throat.

"You are a stupid child," Sir William said coldly. "Not even a fool would disarm himself in the presence of an enemy."

Thomas stared into the knight's eyes.

Sir William pressed the point of the sword into soft flesh. A dot of blood welled up around the razor-sharp metal. "Not even a fool would walk five miles into a desolate forest with a king's ransom in gold, and offer himself like a lamb to a man already found guilty of stealing a sacred chalice."

Thomas did not struggle. He merely continued to stare into the knight's eyes.

"And," Sir William grimaced as he pressed harder, "lambs are meant for slaughter."

The dot of blood beneath the blade swelled to a tiny rivulet.

"Cry you for mercy?" Sir William shouted.

Neither wavered as they stared at each other.

"Blast," Sir William said, as he threw his sword aside. "I feared this."

He took his knee off Thomas' chest and stood up. Then

he leaned forward and grabbed Thomas by the wrist and helped him to his feet. Sir William gravely dusted the dirt off himself, then from Thomas.

It was his turn to grin at Thomas. "The least you could have done was prove to be a coward. Now I have no choice."

Thomas waited.

"For saving my life," Sir William said, "you have my service as required. I ask of you, however, to free me as soon as possible, for I have urgent business."

"Agreed," Thomas said.

Each refrained from showing a secret smile. Yes, Thomas knew that only a fool would have brought a king's ransom in gold to a stranger, so he had not done so. Instead, Thomas had hidden the bulk of it with his precious books. And, of course, the knight did not need to know of the books.

The knight also smiled inside. If Thomas was of the enemy, the bluff with sword against throat would have been the action of a man totally unsuspecting any intrigue. Thomas now had no reason to believe he was detected.

In the quiet of the woods, they clasped hands to seal the arrangement. Left hand over left hand, then right hand over right hand.

"Now what service do you want of me that was so important to risk your life first as a specter, then a midnight phantom?" Sir William asked.

Thomas let out a deep breath. "We shall conquer a kingdom," he said. "It is known as Magnus."

Chapter Six

The wind blew strong, as it always did in the moors. Above them, the blue sky was patched with high clouds. Sir William led the way along a narrow path cutting through the low boughs of heather. They had traveled across the top of the moors. The valley bottom offered too much cover for bandits.

Behind the knight, Thomas and Tiny John—as they now called the grinning pickpocket—followed closely. The mute girl, farther back, meandered her way in pursuit, stopping often to pluck a yellow flower from the gorse or to stare at the sky.

When their journey had begun, the knight had explained that he was not cruel-hearted enough to force those two to follow. Thomas, of course, had his own silent reasons for allowing the girl and the pickpocket to remain. *"Take them with you. It will guarantee you a safe journey to Magnus."* Thomas remembered the old man's whisper each time he looked back at the girl.

But, distracting as the mystery in her face might be, Thomas had other matters to occupy his mind.

"This must be the valley," Thomas said for the fifth time in as many minutes. "I am certain the last moor was Wheeldale; as marked on my map, Wade's Causeway led us there."

"A remarkable map," murmured Sir William. "Few have the ancient Roman roads so clearly shown."

As Thomas knew from Sarah's patient teaching, Wade's Causeway—a road sixteen feet wide which trailed across the desolate moors from Pickering to the North Sea coast—

had been laid by Roman legionnaires. The speed of movement the road allowed them had made them a formidable
occupying force.

A thought struck Thomas. "How is it you know Wade's
Causeway was Roman built and so very old? You profess to
come from far away."

His local knowledge was not the only thing strange about
the knight's observation. Because so few could read, most
barely knew their family history. To show awareness of the
Roman invasion so far back . . .

Silently, Sir William cursed himself. Every second of every
minute in the presence of this young wolf demanded vigi-
lance. If Thomas was what he appeared, Sir William could
not let him suspect that he was anything more than a
knight, for that would lead to questions. Yet if Thomas was
of the enemy, he would know Sir William's role, but could
not know of the suspicions outlined by Hawkwood. It
meant that the knight's every action and every word had to
reflect nothing more or less than a fighting man under obligation to Thomas.

So Sir William swung his head slowly to survey Thomas.
"England was only a barbarian outpost to the Romans.
Where I come from, there are many similar to this."

End of discussion, the knight's face warned.

Thomas decided to look across the valley again.

"Where *is* Magnus?" Thomas spat out the words at the
endless valley.

Sir William sighed. "Three days of hard travel. Three days
of rough cold meals, and nothing but silence from you.
Now you dance like a child the night before Christmas." He
paused to wipe sweat from his forehead. "With the impossible task you have set for us, I should think you would be in
no hurry to arrive at Magnus."

"It's far from impossible," Thomas said. As if to confirm
this, he shifted the bundle packed across his shoulders.
*Such simple material inside, but enough to conquer a
kingdom.*

The knight did not disguise his snort of disbelief, for as a
simple fighting man, he would be skeptical. "We are not

much of an army. Only in fantasies do two people find a way to overcome an army within a castle."

"I have the way," Thomas replied. *Given to me by the nurse who served as both mother and father before her death.*

"Thomas, you have much to learn," Sir William said with exaggerated patience. "You must see the world as it is. Castles are designed to stop armies of a thousand. Soldiers are trained to kill."

" 'Delivered on the wings of an angel, he shall free us from oppression,' " Thomas said.

Sir William squinted. "Make sense!"

Thomas smiled. *How many times did Sarah make me repeat the plan? How many times did she promise it would take only one fighting man to win?*

"There is a legend within Magnus," Thomas said. " 'Delivered on the wings of an angel, he shall free us from oppression.' I have been told each villager repeats that promise nightly during prayers. It will take no army to win the battle."

Sir William did not interrupt the rustling sound of the heather for some time. He had questions now, questions that only Hawkwood could answer. The nightly promise had not, of course, existed in Magnus when he was a knight of that kingdom. Had Hawkwood, who foresaw so much, decided long ago that this was how Magnus would be reconquered? But Hawkwood could not foresee Sarah's death; and now, Thomas might be a double-edged sword. Or perhaps not. How should he now react to Thomas' certainty? As one who knew little?

"You presume much," Sir William finally said, in a gentler voice that did not suggest mockery. "Is there oppression within Magnus? And where do you propose to find an angel?"

Thomas plucked a long stem of grass and nibbled the soft, yellowed end. "I know well of the oppression." He paused to think of a way to phrase it. "It was told to me by someone who escaped from there. She was like a mother and a father. In fact, I believe my parents arranged to send her with me, when they knew the pox had taken them and there was no hope from the dread disease."

He pulled the grass from his mouth and stared into Sir William's eyes. "Her name was Sarah. She was my teacher and my friend at the abbey. The monks endured her presence only because it was stipulated by the money my parents left for my upkeep. She taught me how to read and write—"

Sir William shook his head in the postured amazement such a statement required. "Latin?"

"And French," Thomas confirmed. He said nothing about the necessity of reading the books in a chest hidden in a faraway valley. "Sarah told me it was the language of the nobles and that I would need it when . . ."

"When?"

"When I took over as lord of Magnus."

"You sound so certain," Sir William said. "What right have you to take this manor and castle by force?"

"The same right," Thomas said, suddenly cold with anger, "that the present lord had when he took it from Sarah's parents."

During the next half hour of walking, Thomas repeatedly asked one question to break the noise of the wind across the heather. "Where is Magnus?"

The knight remained in front, seeing no need to answer. The girl still trailed them. Only Tiny John showed enthusiasm, as if they were on an adventure.

"Let me get on the man's shoulders!" Tiny John finally piped, in response to the question. "I'll get a good see from there."

Sir William groaned. "I feel like enough of a packhorse without my steed." A cloud of anger passed his face. "First to be arrested falsely for a chalice I didn't steal, and then to lose my horse and armor to those scoundrels . . ."

The knight sighed. "Tiny John, get on my shoulders, then. *Without* taking a farthing from my pockets. I've had enough trouble with you already."

Tiny John only widened his eternal grin and waved a locket and chain at Sir William, who felt his own neck to reassure himself that it was not his.

"It's the girl's," Thomas said. "Tiny John took it from her this morning. I didn't have the heart to make him give it back yet. And she hasn't noticed anything all day."

Sir William kept his face straight. *The only reason Thomas saw the theft was because he spends so much time glancing at the girl,* he thought. *It is almost as if she has riveted his heart, and without a word between them.*

Tiny John tossed the locket to the knight. He glanced at it idly, then felt as if a hand had been wrapped around his throat. *The symbol! The locket shows the symbol!*

Sir William knew now who had been sent to spy. The question remained—was she a partner with Thomas? Or was he ignorant of the danger?

"A peculiar cross emblem," Sir William mumbled as thoughts raced through his mind. He too had learned acting skills. "Nothing I've seen before."

Tiny John did not give him time to finish wondering. He darted to the knight's back, then scrambled up the broad shoulders and shaded his eyes with his left hand to peer northeast into the widening valley.

Tiny John whistled. "I've caught the spires! Far, far off! But we can make it by eventide."

"Only if I carry you, urchin," Sir William grunted. "And already you're far too heavy for a knight as old as I."

Tiny John dropped to the ground lightly and kept pointing. "That way, Thomas!" he said. "I'm sure I saw the castle that way!"

Thomas said nothing. His eyes showed that he was deep in thought.

Sir William glanced at the girl, still several hundred yards back. "Rejoin our silent friend," he told Tiny John as he handed him the thin chain and locket. "Return this to her. Yet do not let her know that it was on my instructions or that I have seen it." The knight searched for an insignificant reason that would not give Tiny John reason to think any more of the incident. "It will appear to her that you have honor, you scoundrel. Then, Tiny John, keep pace! We will do our best to reach Magnus before nightfall."

Tiny John had been right. With the easy downhill walk, it took them less than four hours to reach the final crest which overlooked the castle of Magnus. They heard the bells inside the castle ringing to celebrate the church service of None only a few miles before that crest.

They paused, not in need of rest, but to comprehend Magnus as it stretched out before them.

"All saints preserve us," breathed Sir William in awe, as if he had never seen Magnus before. "Our mission is surely one of suicide."

Even Thomas faltered. "I have been told the army is not large."

Sir William laughed a strained whisper. "Why maintain an army when you have a fortress like *that?*" He spread out his arms to indicate the situation. "From afar, I wondered about the wisdom of a castle which did not take advantage of height to survey the valley. Now I understand. A force as large as a thousand might be useless in attack against Magnus."

The valley around Magnus differed little from those they had been seeing for the previous three days. The hills were steeper, perhaps, but the grass and woods in the valley bottom were equally rich, and dotted with sheep and cattle.

But there were two differences: There were no farmers' huts anywhere in the valley, and there was water.

Magnus stood on an island in the center of a small lake. High, thick, stone walls ringed the entire island and protected the village inside.

The keep of the castle, home of the reigning lord of Magnus, rose high above the walls, but safely inside and away from the reach of even the strongest catapults.

At the north end, a narrow finger of land approached the island. Just before the castle walls, however, it was broken by a drawbridge no wider than a horse's cart. Even if an army managed to reach the lowered drawbridge, soldiers could only advance three or four abreast—easy targets for the archers on the walls above.

Water, of course, was available in almost infinite amounts to those behind the wall. Lack of food, then, might be the castle's weak point, because siege was obviously the only way to attack Magnus. With the foresight to store dry foods, however, the reigning lord of Magnus would never suffer defeat.

For several minutes, Thomas could only stare at his impossible task. He forced himself to remember and believe the plan given him by Sarah.

He hoped the doubt in his heart would not reach his words. "If it is so obvious to a military man like you that a host of armies cannot take Magnus by force from the outside," Thomas said, "then the way it must be conquered is from the inside."

Although Sir William told himself not to sigh, he did anyway. "That's like saying the only way to fly is to remain in the air." He frowned at Thomas. "Of course, it must be conquered from the inside. That's the only way to conquer any castle. Our first question is how to get an army. Then we can face the usual question of how to get that army inside."

Thomas ignored him. "There is something wonderful about a castle this impossible to overcome. Once we have it," Thomas smiled, "it will be that much easier to keep."

He marched forward.

After hiding the bundle he had carried for three days, Thomas returned to the others near the north end of the lake.

"I think," Sir William said in greeting, "it would serve us well to conceal any signs of my trade."

"Can it be that serious?" Thomas asked.

"More than you might imagine. Whatever your nurse said in that hermit's abbey could not have taught you how drastically the earls and lords of any land guard against threats to their power."

"But against a single man? I would have thought rebellion in the form of a peasant army or a even a gathering of knights—"

Sir William shook his head grimly and lowered his voice. "Now is not the time to explain. Suffice it to say that serfs and peasants have so little training and so little weaponry that they are considered harmless. So harmless that one man with training or weapons can rise far above an entire village in potential for danger."

Sir William paused. "Aside from the expense of a warhorse—five years' wages—why do you think it is so difficult to reach the status of a knight? And why there are so few in the land? Those in power limit the number of knights for their own safety, should the knights rebel."

Thomas considered this and drew a breath to speak.

Sir William waved him quiet, and then reviewed himself.

On foot without lance or horse, without full armor or following squire to tend his gear, Sir William did not at first glance appear to be a knight. After the rescue at the gallows, the sheriff's men had given back to him only his chain mail and one of his swords. Sun's disappearance or not, no sheriff would dare risk an earl's displeasure by sending a knight with unknown allegiance forth into the land with full fighting gear.

He smiled a tight smile of irony. And much as he had regretted the absence of the rest of his equipment, this was one moment he did not mind to be without it. When approaching the castle of a strange earl or lord, a knight who did not declare himself as such could expect immediate death if discovered.

Even without his usual full range of war gear, however, Sir William did not feel safe from notice. He knew that the guards at the gate would be trained to search for the faintest of military indications in any approaching stranger.

The chain mail covering Sir William's belly, of course, was an immediate giveaway, should it be found. Sir William drew his shirt tighter and checked for any gaps which might betray the finely worked iron mesh. To be totally risk free, he should have abandoned the chain mail miles before the castle. But then he would have been as vulnerable to the thrust of a sword as a piglet before slaughter.

His own short sword, of the type favored for close combat since the time of the mighty Roman legions, hung in a scabbard tightly bound to his back between his shoulder blades. Once again, it would have been much safer to leave the sword behind, but next to impossible to find a weapon inside the castle walls. Sir William would have to risk being searched.

And he could lessen the chances of search. Sir William dropped his cloak onto the ground. He wrapped himself in it again without shaking it clean. He smudged dirt into his face and ran debris into his hair.

"Show no surprise when I become a beggar," Sir William warned. He turned to Tiny John with a savage glare. "Stay behind and hold the girl's hand. One word, urchin, and you'll become crow bait."

Tiny John gulped and nodded.

The four of them—a full-grown man, a half-grown man, a small boy, and a slave girl—made a strange procession, as they moved from the cover of the trees to the final approach into Magnus.

"No castle is stronger than its weakest part," Sir William grumbled, as they reached the finger of land that stretched from shore to the castle island. "And generally that is that gatehouse entrance. This does not bode well for your mission."

"Expert military advice?" Thomas bantered. Almost within the shadows of the towers of Magnus, he could not be swayed from his high spirits.

Tiny John remained several steps back with the girl, head craned upward to take in the spires. His grin, unlike Thomas', was finally dampened by those same cold shadows.

"Not advice. Sober fear," replied Sir William. "Unless a man can swim," Sir William snorted, "which is unnatural for any but a fish, the lake is impossibly wide."

"Nobody *swims* across," Thomas argued. "That's why the drawbridge."

"Not swimming *toward* the castle. *Away.* Defenders often force attackers into the water. Those steep banks make it impossible for a man to get out again." Sir William shuddered. "Especially one weighed down with the iron of armor."

Sir William pointed farther. "Worse. This road is the only approach to the monster castle, and I've never seen a barbican which stretches an entire arrow's flight from the drawbridge to the gatehouse. And nearly straight up!"

Lined with small stone towers on each side—small only in comparison to the twin towers of the gatehouse itself— thick walls guarded a steep approach to the castle entry.

"If this gives a hint of the defenses, I can only guess at the treacherousness of the gatehouse itself," Sir William said. He opened his mouth to say something, then paused as a new thought struck.

"Not even Vespers, the sixth hour past noon. Yet this road is as quiet as if it were already dusk. No passersby. No farmers returning from the fields. No craftsmen to or fro. What magic keeps this castle road so quiet?"

"What does it matter?" Thomas shrugged. "All we need to do is get within the walls as passing strangers seeking a night's rest. From there, we shall find the weakness of Magnus and complete my plan. It only makes me happier to see how difficult it is to attack. Once we have this, it will make it easier for us to keep—"

"Don't be a blind fool," snapped Sir William. "I am bound to you by a vow, but I will not follow you to a certain death. Lords of manors like this have power and wealth beyond your imagination. You think there is no reason he has remained lord since taking it? Inside those walls are soldiers to jump at his every whim. It is a rule of nature that when men have power, they use it to keep it."

"Sir William," Thomas said, unperturbed by the knight's sudden anger, "not once have I given you an indication that I expected you to fight any soldiers. I simply need your military knowledge."

Thomas thought of his books, hidden safely three days to the southwest. "With you as adviser, I have ways of using my own powers. . . ."

Sir William checked his objections. For a moment, his military background had caused to him to forget his true purpose for remaining with Thomas.

"We shall proceed to the gatehouse," Sir William said.

"But slowly. I do not like this situation at all."

As they began the journey across the narrow finger of land to the drawbridge, Sir William began to drag one foot, and he worked enough spit into his mouth so that it drooled from his chin.

A latticed wall of wood meshed with iron bars hung head-high above the first opening past the drawbridge. Each iron bar ended in a gleaming spike.

"Not good," Sir William whispered. "Someone cares enough to maintain those spikes in deadly order. An indication of how serious they are about security." He motioned his head briefly at the shadows of two men standing against the sunlight at the next gate, at the end of the stone corridor that ran between the portals. "All those soldiers beyond need do is to release a lever, and those spikes crash down upon us like hammers of the gods."

Thomas held his breath. The gate remained in place as they passed beneath.

Sir William maintained his whispered commentary as he leaned heavily on Thomas. "Look above and beside. Those slots in the stone are called murder holes. They are designed for spear thrusts, crossbow arrows, or boiling liquids from hidden passages on the other side."

Thomas tried not to wince.

With his dragging foot, the knight tapped a plank as wide as two men, imbedded in the stone floor. "It drops to a chute, I'm sure, straight to the dungeon."

The knight took two more slow and weary steps, then paused as if for rest, just before earshot of the two guards. He spoke clearly and softly from the side of his mouth in the dark corridor as he wiped his face of pretended fatigue.

"Thomas, the outside defenses of this castle are as fiendish and clever as I've seen. It does not bode well for any man's chances on the inside. Something impossible like this. . . ." Sir William hesitated. "You may still turn back with honor. And live."

Thomas felt very young as he stared at the broad shoulders of the first soldier at the gate.

How could he really expect his fantasy to come true? Night after night, on the straw bed during his waking dreams of glory in the darkness of the abbey, it had seemed so easy. Now, in the harshness of the sunlight and the dust and the noise of the village beyond the stone-faced soldiers, it seemed impossible. Not even the solid presence of Sir William helped.

The guards blocked a narrow entrance cut into the large gate. Dressed in brown, with a wide slash of red cloth draped across their massive chests, they stood as straight and tall as the thick spears they balanced beside them.

"Greetings to you," Sir William said in a hopeful, almost begging tone.

The guards barely grunted to acknowledge the arrival of the newcomers.

Thomas forced himself to look away from the cold eyes of the soldiers. They were so fierce, so dominating.

Suddenly, the guard on the right whirled! He tossed his spear sideways at Sir William!

"Unnnggghh," the knight said weakly. He brought his left hand up in an instinctive and feeble motion to block the spear that clattered across his chest. The effort knocked him back, and Sir William sagged to his knees.

"I beg of you," he moaned, as spit dribbled from the side of his mouth. "Show mercy."

The soldier stood over him and studied the dirty cloak as Sir William cowered.

Even as Thomas held his breath in worry, a thought nudged the back of his mind. A thought from one of his precious books. A thought written by the greatest general of a faraway land who had lived and fought more than fourteen centuries earlier. *"One who wishes to appear to be weak in order to make his enemy arrogant must be extremely strong. Only then can he feign weakness."*

For his unlettered knight to know such wisdom by instinct was truly more amazing than the cowardice he feigned.

Thomas grinned inside. He felt a fraction more confident than he had upon approaching the gate.

Finally, the soldier sneered downward at Sir William. "Mercy, indeed. It's obvious you need it. Get up, you craven excuse for a man."

Sir William wobbled back onto his feet. The spit on his chin showed flecks of dirt.

"Lodging for the evening, good sir," the knight pleaded. "We are not thieves, but workers seeking employment."

Sir William fumbled through his leather waist pouch and pulled free two coins. "See, we have money for lodging. We ask no charity of the lord of the manor."

The second soldier laughed cruelly. "Make sure it is cleaning and slopping you seek. Not begging as it appears."

The first soldier kicked Sir William. "Up. Get inside before we change our minds."

Sir William howled and held his thigh where the soldier's foot had made a sickening thud. He hopped and dragged his way inside the gate, without looking back to see if Thomas and the two children followed.

Thomas pushed Tiny John and the girl ahead of him.

Not until they had turned past the first building inside did Sir William stop. He waited and watched Thomas with a proud chin and guarded eyes.

Thomas did not let him speak. "Artfully done," Thomas said quickly, before the knight might decide to explain his cowardice. "By using your left hand instead of the right when he threw that spear, you made it impossible for them to guess you are an expert swordsman."

Sir William grinned as a warmth of loyalty toward the boy surprised him. The grin then faded as he motioned for them to continue walking.

"I like this less and less," he said in a low voice. "When I showed those coins, I expected greed would force the soldiers to demand the normal bribe for our entry. They did not."

Thomas raised a questioning eyebrow.

"Corruption shows weakness, Thomas. We are now inside, and everything points to unconquerable strength."

Chapter Seven

Thomas usually slept lightly. Years of constant awareness in the abbey had taught him to do so. Here, in strange lodgings, with a fortune in gold hidden in his leather pouch, he expected that even the slightest shifting of movement would have pulled him from deep slumber.

When he woke as first light nudged past the wooden crossbeams of the crude windows high on the dirty stone wall, he was surprised to discover the girl gone.

Thomas did not stop to wonder why his first waking thoughts—and glance—had turned to her. He had not spoken more than a dozen words to her over three days.

The knight could have explained with a knowing smile. At least a dozen times each day, Sir William had hidden his amusement over Thomas blushing at eye contact with the silent girl. With manhood came powerful and befuddling emotions, especially when one finally noticed the curve of a girl's smile, and other equally distracting curves.

The knight, familiar with ways to make a woman laugh with joy in his presence, had early decided only the girl's poor rags hindered grown men from staring at her now with unhidden admiration. In a few years, even the coarsest of clothing would not be able to keep that beauty from shining. Much of it came from the mystery of thoughts hidden in a flawless face. The rest, from the grace of her slim body as she moved effortlessly in a walk that suggested the confidence of royalty.

Yes, the knight had judged each time Thomas blushed, *the girl will be a woman for whom men become glad fools.* And each time Sir William had made that bittersweet judgment over the last few days, he was torn. *If Thomas makes himself a fool for her, he is not one of the enemy, but will be helpless in their claws. If Thomas is of the enemy, then little sympathy need be wasted upon him.*

This morning was the beginning of the fourth day together for Thomas and Sir William. The knight's thoughts were interrupted by slight scufflings as Thomas rose to his feet.

"She's gone," Thomas blurted.

"She is, indeed," Sir William replied. *Is Thomas an actor beyond parallel? Or truly bewildered?*

"We don't even know her name. So many times I wanted to speak, yet . . ."

"It happens that way."

Silence.

Sir William stretched away his sleep.

Thomas adjusted his clothing as a way to struggle through an ache he couldn't explain.

Tiny John merely sat up, hunched against his knees in his corner position, and grinned at the world.

I'm in Magnus, Thomas thought, *with a task that threatens my life, that will test everything I have been taught and demand that I use every power available to me. Yet my mind turns to sadness. How could that have happened simply because of . . .*

The girl pushed open the door by walking backward through it. When she turned, the bowls of steaming porridge in her hands gave reason for her method of entry.

She looked shyly at Thomas. For the first time since the gallows, she smiled.

I shall conquer the world, Thomas finished in his mind. *Lead me to the lord of Magnus.*

"The walls of Magnus contain no mean village. There must be nearly five hundred inside the walls," Sir William said. "I'm surprised it has no fame outside this county."

And I'm more alarmed, he thought anxiously, *that there was so little traffic on the road during our approach. Towns this size draw people from two and three days travel in all directions. Has the enemy so thoroughly taken Magnus that the entire countryside is in his power?*

He did not voice his worry. It would not have mattered anyway.

Thomas was too busy staring in all directions to reply. While he had occasionally visited the village near the abbey on market days, it was nothing compared to this.

Already the clamor in Magnus was at a near frenzy.

"Fresh duck!" a toothless shopkeeper shouted, as he dangled it by the feet in one hand, and with the other waved at Thomas. "Still dripping blood! And you'll get the feathers at no charge!"

Thomas smiled politely and followed closer behind the knight. He could only trust that Tiny John and the girl would do the same.

Shops so crowded the street that the more crooked buildings actually touched roofs where they leaned into each other. Space among the bustling people between the row of shops was equally difficult to find.

Thomas scanned the buildings for identification. "Apothecary," he mumbled to himself at a colorfully painted sign displaying three gilded pills. He made a note to remember it well. The potions and herbs and medicines inside might be needed on short notice.

He mentally marked the signs of each shop, even as he enjoyed the feeling of a crowd after so much silence in the abbey.

A bush sketched in dark shades—the vintner, or wine shop. Two doors farther along, a horse's head—the harness maker. Then a unicorn—the goldsmith. A white arm with stripes—the surgeon-barber.

There was a potter. A skinner. A shoemaker. A beer-seller. A baker. A butch—

Butcher. How could I have been so careless?

Thomas grimaced and pulled his foot away from the puddle of sheep's innards that had been thrown into the middle of the street. Butchers did their slaughtering on the spot for customers and left behind the waste for the swarms of flies.

"Where is it we go?" Thomas called to the knight's broad shoulders which cleared room, step by step, in front of him.

"A stroll," Sir William said. "I have a few questions which simple observation should answer."

They continued. At the end of the first street, they turned left, then left again to follow another crooked street. It took them away from the market crowd, and past narrow and tall houses squeezed tightly together.

The girl caught up to Thomas. He remembered what Sarah had taught him about manners and quickly moved so that he walked on the outside, to ensure the girl stayed on the inside nearer to the houses. Thus, if a housewife emptied a jug of water or a chamberpot onto the street from the upper stories, Thomas would suffer, not the girl.

She seemed content to stay beside him, glancing over to smile whenever Thomas stared at her for too long.

In contrast, Tiny John burned with energy and scampered in circles around them, first ahead to Sir William, then back to Thomas and the girl.

"Check his pockets," Sir William said, without breaking stride. "Make sure they're empty. If that little rogue so much as picks a hair from a villager, all of us are threatened."

Tiny John stuck out his tongue at the knight, but quickly pulled his pockets open to show he'd managed to remain honest.

As they walked on, Thomas began to sniff the air with distaste. He knew they were approaching the far edge of the town—the traditional location of a tannery—because of the terrible smell of curing hides.

Thomas knew the procedure well. How many times had one of the monks at the abbey ordered him to scrape away hair and skin from the hide of a freshly killed sheep? As many times as they had then ordered him to rub it endlessly with the normal amount of cold chicken dung. That ingredient, plus the fermented bran and water which was used to soak hides, made it a terrible task.

As they quickly walked by the tannery, Thomas felt sympathy as he watched one of the apprentices scraping flesh, mouth open to keep his nostrils as useless as possible.

The street turned sharply, and they were soon back within earshot of the market.

"Stay with me," Sir William said. "We need to learn more."

Just before reaching the market area, Sir William held up his hand.

"Thomas," he said with low urgency. "Look around. What strikes you?"

Thomas had a ready reply. "The crippled beggars. The men with mutilated faces. Far more than one would expect."

The knight's eyes opened wide. "My mind was on military matters. I had not noticed. Surely the lord of Magnus hasn't . . ."

Thomas shrugged. "I have been told many stories of the evil here." And in his mind, Thomas heard Sarah singing gently, *"Delivered on the wings of an angel, he shall free us from oppression."*

Sir William said, "Scan the shop signs. Tell me what's missing."

"Missing?"

The knight only frowned in thought. Thomas began to study the busy scene ahead.

Finally Thomas answered. "I see no blacksmith."

"You speak truth. Why is that significant?"

More waiting. This time, Thomas shook his head in apology.

"Don't bother yourself for missing the answer," Sir William said. "You have not developed your thinking to a military level."

Sir William then pursed his lips sternly and added, "Horseshoes and hoes are not the only items a blacksmith will make."

"Swords," Thomas said after a moment. "Blacksmiths also forge swords. Without a blacksmith, there are no weapons. No armor. Whoever controls Magnus takes few chances."

"Well spoken." The knight *was* impressed. Thomas showed a rare mind. One which grasped simple facts and drew them together for meaning.

Before Sir William could comment farther, a small man broke toward them from the fringes of the crowd.

His shoulders were so insignificant they were nearly invisible under his full-length brown cloak. A tight black hat only emphasized the smallness of his head. His wrinkled cheeks bunched like large walnuts as he smiled.

"Strangers!" he cackled. "So brave to visit Magnus, you are! No doubt you'll need a guide. No doubt at all!" He rubbed his hands briskly. "And I'm your man. That's the spoken truth. No doubt. The spoken truth."

Thomas made a move to step around him.

Sir William shook his head at Thomas, then addressed the small man.

"What might be your name, kind man?"

"Ho, ho. Flattery. Always wise. Indeed, you are fortunate. I *am* a kind man." He paused for breath from his rapid fire words. "And I am called Geoffrey."

"Hmmm. Geoffrey. You are a merchant here?"

"Indeed I am. But strangers are wise to engage a guide in Magnus. And I make a fine guide. A fine guide, indeed."

"Any man can see that." Sir William smiled. "What is it you sell when you are not a guide?"

"Candles. Big ones. Little ones. Thick ones. Skinny ones. The finest in the land. Why, the smoke from these candles will wipe from a window with hardly any—"

"Sold." Sir William jammed his single word into the pause that Geoffrey was forced to take for breath.

"Sold?" Geoffrey's confidence wavered at this unexpected surrender. "I've not shown a one. How can you say—"

"Sold," Sir William repeated firmly. He pulled a coin from his pouch. "Maybe even as many as we can carry."

He peered past Geoffrey's shoulders. "Where might your shop be?"

Geoffrey opened and closed his mouth, again and again, like a fish gasping for air. He did not take his eyes away from the coin in Sir William's palm.

"My . . . my shop is away from the market. I only bring enough candles for the morning's sales. I . . . ."

"Lead on, good man," Sir William said cheerfully. "It's a

pitiable guide who cannot find his own shop."

"He's a blathering fool," Thomas whispered to Sir William, as soon as it was safe. "What do you want from him?"

"Certainly not candles," Sir William whispered from the side of his mouth. "I want a safe location to ask questions."

Thomas could not fault the knight his strategy. Yet, must the information come from an empty-headed babbler like this one clearing a path for them through the crowd?

Every five steps or so, Geoffrey rudely pushed people aside—despite his runtlike size. The resulting arguments proved to be a humorous distraction.

Too much of a distraction. Otherwise Thomas or Sir William might have observed the three soldiers who followed them from the simple distance of a stone's throw back in the crowd.

Just as Thomas began to see clearly the jumble of vats and clay pots in the dimness of the candlemaker's shop, a ghostlike bundle of dirty white cloth rose from a corner and moved toward him.

Thomas brought both of his fists up in protection, then relaxed as he noticed that the worn shoes at the base of the ghost had very human toes poking through the leather.

He backed away to make room, and the bundle of cloth scurried past, bumping him with a solidness that no ghost could give. Moments later, it squeezed past Tiny John and the girl.

"That's Katherine," Geoffrey the candlemaker said. "Daughter of the previous candlemaker. Ignore her. She's surprised because I've returned early from the market, and she's afraid of people."

Thomas watched her shuffle past a curtain and out of sight in the back of the cramped house.

"The bandages around her head?" Sir William asked.

"It's to keep people from screaming at the sight of *her*. When she was little, I am told, she reached up and grabbed a pot of hot wax. No mind that she'd been warned a hundred times. No mind at all. She learned the lesson, she did. It poured over her face like water. The foolish child jumped blind into the flame warming the pot. Yes, indeed. As bright as a torch she became. And with half the customers standing in your very spot. The business that was lost because of her screaming!" The candlemaker waved his hands as if dismissing the importance. "It's a curse she did not die. I was stuck with her as part of the arrangement to take over this shop on the owner's death. Who might marry her now? And I'd get no price for her if she did, that's the truth." The candlemaker shrugged before moving on to business. "The will of the Lord, I suppose."

Year after year at the orphanage compressed into a single moment for Thomas. He turned on the candlemaker with a bitterness he did not know he possessed. "How can you say there is a God who permits this? How can you give that girl less pity than a dog?"

"Thomas." Sir William's calm rebuke drew Thomas from his sudden emotion.

"I give her a home," the candlemaker said in a hurried voice. "It's much more than any dog gets. You've seen the beggars and cripples who gather around. She could be cast loose among them."

Thomas told himself he had no right to interfere. "I ask your forgiveness," he said coldly. "For a moment, her situation reminded me of someone I once knew."

Thomas did not explain that he meant himself and his lonely aching years as an orphan freak in the abbey. His heart cried for the pain he knew Katherine suffered; yet moments later, his brain sadly told him there was no use in caring. The candlemaker was right. In this town alone, there were dozens of beggars and cripples who had less than Katherine.

Thomas added silently to himself, *Such evidence of pain is all the more reason to be angry at this God the false monks so often proclaimed.*

Thomas spoke to move from the subject. "We came for candles."

Relief brightened the candlemaker's face. "Yes. I'll bring my finest."

He clapped his hands twice.

Immediately Katherine appeared with a wooden box.

"She must earn her keep," Geoffrey said defensively, as he glanced at Thomas.

Thomas said nothing. He looked away from the bundled clothes with outstretched arms. The wrap around Katherine's head was stained with age, almost caked black around the hole slashed open for her mouth.

"I'll take the entire box," Sir William said. "You've made mention this is not a town for strangers."

"These are my best candles," Geoffrey said. "I'm surprised you don't know the reputation of Magnus."

Sir William wanted Thomas to believe he knew little about Magnus, and he chose to barter as a way of showing a need for local knowledge.

"Perhaps these are the best candles you have. But compared to London . . ." Sir William shook his head to reflect doubt. "In London, the name Magnus stirs no fear into the hearts of good citizens."

"I've not been to London," Geoffrey said, as wistfulness momentarily sidetracked him. "Few of us ever leave Magnus."

He coughed quickly to hide embarrassment at his ignorance, then grabbed the box from Katherine and shook his head as she cowered and waited for instructions.

Thomas felt a comforting hand on his shoulder, even as he winced to see Katherine's fear. The mute girl had seen the pain on his face and moved beside him. Tiny John also seemed subdued at the horror of Katherine's primitive mask. He clung to the edges of the mute girl's dress.

The three of them stayed in a tight cluster, and Thomas felt a great sadness to know their instinctive joining resulted from the status of outcast they all shared.

"I apprenticed from the best master for miles around. I don't need to see London candles to know these burn as bright as any in the land," Geoffrey said, as he forced his voice back to a bartering tone. "And I don't need to see London to know the reputation of Magnus."

"A farthing each dozen," Sir William offered. "And hang this reputation at which you hint of this place."

"Two farthings and no lower," Geoffrey countered. "And

strangers as good as you have said less about Magnus and died for it."

Thomas gave the conversation full attention.

"Two farthings for a dozen and a half." Sir William lowered his voice. "And who might be doing the killing?"

Geoffrey shook his head and held out his hand. "The color of your money first. This box holds three dozen candles."

"Four farthings, then. You drive a hard bargain." Sir William counted the coins. "About this fearsome domain . . ."

Even in the dimness, Thomas could see the eager glint of a born gossip in the candlemaker's eyes.

"A fearsome domain, indeed," Geoffrey said. He looked around him, even though he knew every inch of his own shop. "Ever since Richard Mewburn disposed of the proper lord."

"Surely the earl of York would not permit within his realm such an unlawful occurrence as murder."

"Bah." A wave of pudgy fingers. "That happened twenty years ago. Ever since, murder is the least of crimes here in Magnus. The slightest of crimes results in hideous punishment . . . men with their ankles crushed for failing to bow to Richard's sheriff . . . faces branded for holding back crops, even though the poor are taxed almost to starvation."

Geoffrey lowered his voice. "The earl of York is paid rich tribute to stay away. It is whispered that some evil blackmail prevented his father from dispensing justice after Magnus was taken from the rightful earl. A blackmail that still holds his son long after his own death from—"

Katherine gasped. She had not moved since delivering the candles. The first sound of her voice, eerie and muffled from behind the swath of dirty rags around her head, startled Thomas.

"You cannot reveal this to strangers," she protested. "It is enough to sentence them to death!"

Geoffrey brought his hand up quickly, as if to strike the girl.

She stepped back quickly and bumped a table. Two clay candle molds teetered, then fell to the ground and smashed into dust.

"Clumsy wretch!" the candlemaker snarled. He grabbed a thin willow stick from the table beside him and whipped it across the side of her head.

Had Thomas paused to think, he would have decided it was her complete acceptance of the cruel pain that drove him to action. She did not cry, merely bowed her head and waited for the next blow. It tore at his heart to see someone so defenseless, and so less deserving of more pain.

The animal struck her face. What more cruel reminder of her deformity could exist? And how many times has he done exactly the same?

Holy rage burst inside Thomas. As the candlemaker raised his arm to strike again, Thomas roared and dove across the narrow space between them. He crashed full force into the candlemaker. Both fell with the blow. Before the candlemaker could react, Thomas pounced on his chest.

Berserk fury possessed Thomas, and he grabbed the candlemaker by both ears. He pulled the man's head inches from the floor and held it. His arms shook as he fought an overpowering urge to dash the candlemaker's head in one savage motion.

"Foul horrid creature," ground Thomas between clenched teeth. "You shall pay dearly for the abuse—"

He did not finish his threat.

Sir William pulled him upward, and during that motion, the unthinkable occurred.

Soldiers burst into the shop.

Had not Sir William been so helpless with both his arms around Thomas, he might have been able to reach between his shoulder blades and pull the sword free.

Instead, less than a second later, three soldiers had him pinned against the wall.

Two other soldiers grabbed Thomas.

"You hail from the abbey at Harland Moor," the soldier said. It was not a question. "Four monks have been found dead there. One by a blow to the head. Three by poisoning."

The soldier grinned evilly. "You and your large companion here will hang. You for murder. Your companion for aiding a murderer in escape."

Chapter Eight

Late morning heat baked the bandages that covered Katherine's face. In heat like this, it always seemed that she could not draw enough air, no matter how she strained her lungs. Yet it was more than the heat outside which made her long for the cool shadows of the candle shop. She hated crowds. She hated the mockery and taunting of children. She hated the unexpected jostlings; the small holes left for her eyes gave her little vision except straight ahead, and most sounds which reached her were muffled and displaced.

So she walked with hesitation through the marketplace, holding her basket as close to her side as possible, and hoped Hawkwood might find her soon.

"Fresh bread! Fresh bread!"

Katherine turned her head to seek the source of the cries. These were loud enough and insistent enough that . . .

No. It wasn't Hawkwood. This seller of bread was a man with only one arm. The other arm, ending at his elbow, tucked a long loaf of bread against his ribs. Hawkwood was a master of altered appearances, but even he could not give the illusion of a stumped arm.

"Potions! Healing potions! Love potions!"

Katherine turned her head in the opposite direction. It was an old woman, face half hidden in the shadows of a bonnet, leaning over a rough table covered with dried herbs.

Inside her bandage, Katherine smiled. Hawkwood would enjoy the irony of posing as someone with knowledge of herbs and potions. Passersby would never realize how fitting the pose might be.

Katherine moved closer to the old woman and pretended to scan the table.

"Potions!" the old woman screamed again, to be heard above the din of the market. "Healing potions! Love potions!"

Katherine waited. Would Hawkwood give her the phrase?

"Scat, girl," the old woman hissed. "You'll turn others away. I've nothing to restore a face like yours."

Katherine hesitated. There might be someone standing right behind, unseen to her, and Hawkwood would have no choice but to react thus.

"Scat! Scat!" The woman's voice rose to a strained screech. "No love potion would earn you even a blind fool!"

Katherine backed away. Why did people who were weak and hurt take satisfaction in showing cruelty to those even weaker?

Something bumped her ankle.

It was awkward, bending over so far to crane her head that she might be able to see the ground through the eye-holes of her bandage.

The object at her feet was a red ball. Before she could puzzle further, a second ball, blue, rolled past the red one. Then a green ball.

"Ho, ho fair lady! A tiny farthing is all I require." A man danced in front of her, scooped the balls into his hands, and began to juggle. "One farthing and laughter is yours."

Katherine shook her head. Whatever reason Hawkwood had for arranging the three lit candles at the altar of the church to wait her morning prayers, it was important enough to have summoned her forth. She could not dally, not even for a jester with a bouncy, belled hat, twinkling eyes, painted face, and ridiculous red and green tights.

The jester spun the balls in a tighter circle so that it was almost a blurr. Blue, red, green. "Come, come, fair lady. The Lord loves laughter. Heaven stands open at the sound!"

Heaven stands open.

Katherine did laugh. Again, Hawkwood had managed to arrive unexpected, even as she searched for him. "One farthing then. For when heaven stands open, only fools turn away."

Hawkwood nodded, satisfied from her answer that it was indeed Katherine beneath the bandages. They both knew that should she ever be discovered, two things were certain: her death, and then someone put in her place behind the bandages, to capture Hawkwood.

"Arrange to deliver candles to Gervaise," he said in a lowered voice. "I shall be in the church when the midafternoon bells ring."

Katherine set her basket down and clapped in glee as his juggling continued. Appearances might be important.

The jester bowed, then reached into a bag at his feet, pulled out a short straight stick, tilted his head back, and balanced the stick on his chin. He began to juggle again, stick tottering, as he walked away from Katherine to cajole others in the marketplace.

The stone walls of the church provided coolness, and as Katherine entered, she set down the cloth bag which held the candles. She pulled her clothes away from her body to enjoy the relief of that cool air against her hot and sticky skin.

"Welcome, Katherine," were the words that greeted her from the shadows of a large pillar. "I trust these candles are the same fine quality that our father priest has come to expect."

"Yes, Gervaise," she answered, as her eyes adjusted to the dimness. "Geoffrey complains, of course, that for what payment he receives, he should call the candles a contribution of charity."

Gervaise was an elderly man, gray hair combed straight back. A plain cassock covered his slight body, and he stood with his hands in front of him, folded together.

"Please, Katherine, let me help you with that bundle."

"Thank you," she said.

As he stooped to take the candles, he said, "Will you bring these to the nave? I'll set the others in storage."

Again Katherine nodded. The elaborate acting, she felt, was rarely necessary, but Hawkwood insisted on behaving as if enemy ears were always nearby and open. And, although she didn't know whether to believe him, he said the island was riddled with enough hidden passages that those ears could very well be there.

In the nave, she began to remove from the candelabra the stubs of burnt candles to replace them with new. Not for the first time did it anger her to see the fine wrought gold of the candelabra gleaming in the light which poured in through stained glass high above. How many mouths could this gold feed? How fat must the clergy become?

Something bumped her ankle and rolled over her foot. A red ball.

She smiled, a movement that scraped her skin against the tight bandages. When she turned, she saw the outline of a figure in the shadows behind the beam of light.

Wordlessly, she moved closer.

She saw Hawkwood as he usually was, an old man bent beneath a black cape. "Milord," she whispered, "fare thee well, here where heaven stands open for those who believe."

With this proof that she was behind the mask, Hawkwood relaxed. He pressed farther back, so that he stood in a recess of the wall, invisible in deep shadow. Katherine moved in front of him and bowed her head. Any unexpected visitor would see only her, deep in meditation.

"Katherine, I fare well. Magnus, however, may not."

"Milord?"

"In the candle shop, you were visited yesterday by two men, each now in the dungeons."

"Yes. They were strangely familiar."

Hawkwood wanted to smile. Strangely familiar, indeed. Later, if they lived, he would explain, for to tell her now, with their fate uncertain, was far too cruel.

Instead of smiling, he nodded. "The older is one of us."

Katherine drew in a startled breath, loud enough in the cool silence of the inner sanctum of the church that it echoed slightly from the far stone walls.

"The other," Hawkwood continued, "is one I had hoped long ago might take Magnus from the enemy."

"Then if we release them from the dungeon . . ." Katherine began.

"We must, yet the knight is well known to them," Hawkwood said. "He fought hard when Magnus fell, and he was barely able to escape with his life. We must find a way to let them escape without revealing how we have hidden ourselves in Magnus all these years."

"If he is well known to them, why did he return to certain death?"

"Because of the other," Hawkwood replied. He took a moment to gather his thoughts. Katherine did not interrupt. She rarely did.

"We play a terrible cat-and-mouse game with the enemy," he said with a grim smile. "And we are the mouse. They know, as do we, the knight's purpose here. They can afford to let him live while the rest of the game is played. What we do not know is the heart of the other, Thomas."

"Thomas? He is a good man," Katherine said quickly.

Again Hawkwood smiled. This time less grimly. Her defense had been too quick.

"Katherine," he said gently, "do not let his countenance sway you."

She stiffened. "Hardly. Do I forsake what little teaching I have received?"

"My apologies," Hawkwood said.

"He defended me," she said. "A man comely enough that he could chose among maidens fought for a freak behind bandages. What says that of his heart?"

"Would that I could believe it," Hawkwood said. "For in this game, none could suspect that you are of us. Thomas, then, had no other reason to defend you than for what lay in his heart."

"He too is part of this terrible game?"

"Yes, Katherine. As you were hidden here since childhood, so was Thomas hidden in an abbey several days away. He was to be taught in our ways, and given the plan to take Magnus."

"Was?" Katherine said.

Hawkwood smiled at her. She was bright. In happier

times, she would already be the best of a new generation.

"Was," he repeated. "The one who was to teach him died. We do not know what happened in the years since. He appeared at the gallows to rescue the knight, and I fear he was sent by our enemy in hopes that we would trust him completely."

"Yet," Katherine said, "he may *not* be the enemy."

"Is it hope that you express?"

She said nothing.

"Yes, Katherine, he may not be the enemy. And if he acts on his own, he needs our help until we are certain he can be trusted."

"If he acts on his own, he knows nothing of us, or of them," she protested. "It is like sending a sheep into battle against ravenous wolves."

"This too I have considered," Hawkwood said. "Yet, who shall we risk to deliver the knowledge? For the enemy still searches, and if Thomas is one of them, the deliverer is doomed. We are so few that we can spare none."

Katherine sighed. "Yes, milord."

"However," Hawkwood said, "it does not mean we shall abandon him or the knight completely. It is fortunate indeed that Thomas defended you as he did."

"Milord?"

"You now have ample reason to befriend him."

Chapter Nine

"Jailer!" Sir William shouted at the rusted iron door in frustration. He did not expect an answer. "Two days have passed. Surely the lord of this manor must appear to us soon!"

"Shhhhh!" hissed a man hunched in the corner of the cell and pointing at a tiny hole.

Sir William groaned and looked to Thomas for sympathy.

Thomas shrugged and grinned. Since the man had said nothing since they had been flung into the cell, there was little else to do.

What light appeared in the cell came from oily torches outside the grated opening in the door. It took Thomas two large steps to reach from side to side of the clammy stone walls, three steps to reach front and back. It was so cramped that had the fetters on the walls been used, one of his wrists could be on either side. Yet there were three of them in this small space, sharing the bedding of trampled straw that soaked up the wet dungeon filth.

Thomas dug inside his shirt, searched quickly with his fingers, and snorted triumph.

"Found it."

He withdrew his hand and squeezed the flea between the nails of his thumb and forefinger until he felt a tiny snap.

"Spare me the battle glories, Thomas," Sir William said. "We have greater concerns. If we are able to meet the lord of this manor—although I am prepared to believe he is a myth—we can present our case. He will see there is no injustice in the fate of those monks and then release us."

"I regret not sending that letter to the mother abbey at Rievaulx," Thomas said almost absently, as he scratched himself again. "We might have been spared this."

Sir William did not have to ask which letter. In the two endless days of darkness and solitude, interrupted only by the bowls of porridge shoved between the bars of the grate twice daily, he had learned of Thomas' final day at the abbey, including the letter of evidence against the monks.

"How often must I tell you?" Sir William said with gentleness. "They are dead. It makes no difference to our fate how little virtue the monks had. Unless the lord of Magnus learns who truly did poison them, we will hang. He must appear to accuse us so that we can defend ourselves."

Then William grinned. "As I've also told you many times since our arrest, there is justice in that the monks poisoned themselves."

Thomas grinned back, but without much feeling.

It gave him little consolation that he had guessed right in his final hour at the abbey. As he had done countless times during the slow passage of time in this dungeon cell, Thomas replayed in his mind the moments before Brother Walter had lashed out with a heavy fist.

"Quit your blathering," Brother Walter had said between clenched teeth. "Send the boy on his way. Now!"

Brother Philip clamped his jaw as if coming to a decision. "Not to his death. Nor shall I meet God without attempting some good." He drew a lungful of air. "Thomas. Leave alone the—"

Leave alone the *food*, Thomas had realized, as Brother Philip died. It could be nothing else. The monks knew Thomas would immediately retrieve the letter of condemnation upon leaving the abbey. By inserting a slow-acting poison into his requested provisions, he would die later and never reveal their crimes.

For that reason, his last act at the abbey had been to replace the food among the other provisions in the kitchen storeroom. If his guess was correct, he would let the monks bring punishment upon themselves. How could he have known that the act would send him to a dungeon?

"The lord of Magnus will never appear," crowed the man in the corner.

"Ho, ho! After two days, the man of silence speaks," Sir William observed. "Have you tired of your scavenging friends?"

"My good fellow, in my time here I have seen many like you come, then go to the hangman," the man said, unperturbed by Sir William's jesting tone. "I learned early not to befriend any. It proves to be too disappointing."

He gestured at the corner hole with his hands. "These furry creatures which make their visits, however, are not so fickle. They require little food and their gratitude is quite rewarding. And *they* always return."

Thomas shuddered. He did not need a reminder of the noose awaiting him. He also hoped he would not remain so long in the cell that rats would be more attractive than human company. Not when he had the means to conquer Magnus. If only he could escape! All it would take is one clear night and . . .

The man dusted his hands of the last of the bread crumbs he had patiently held in front of the hole.

"The lord of Magnus will never appear?" Thomas prompted.

The man did not rise from his squatting position. He merely swiveled on the balls of his feet to face them.

"Never. It is obvious you know nothing of Magnus."

His cheeks were rounded like those of a stuffed chipmunk. His ears were thick and flappy. Shaggy hair fell from the back of his head to well below his shoulders; his patched clothing was as filthy as the straw which clung to his matted chest hair.

"It is time to introduce myself," he said, with a lopsided grin that showed showed strong teeth. "My name is Waleran."

He stood, shuffled forward, and extended his empty right hand in the traditional clasp that symbolized a lack of weapons.

"Generally, visitors hear nothing from me," Waleran said, after Sir William and Thomas had shaken hands with him. "Unlike you, they arrive alone and learn to ignore me after several days. Thus, I am allowed my peace. With two of you, however, the constant talking has given me little peace, and finally I am driven to break my silence."

"Two days of waiting shows remarkable patience," Sir William said.

Waleran shrugged. "I have been here ten years. Time means nothing."

Water trickled in a constant drip from the roof of the dungeon cell to the floor.

"Ten years!" Thomas examined him again. Although pale, Waleran seemed in good health.

"You wonder what crime sends a man here?" Waleran replied to the frank stare. "Simply the crime of being a villager in Magnus. My son, you see, went to the fields outside the castle one harvest day. Instead of threshing grain, he departed. London, perhaps. I am held here as hostage until he returns. And I am held as an example."

Sir William frowned. "How are you an example?"

"To the other families in Magnus. As long as I am here, they know the lord is serious in his edict. No man, woman, or child may leave the village, except to work in the fields and return before nightfall."

"That's monstrous!"

Waleran smiled wanly at Thomas. "Indeed. But who is to defy the lord?"

Sir William began pacing the cell. "It is a strange manor, this Magnus. The lord murders its rightful owner, yet the earl of York does not interfere. Entire families are kept virtual prisoners inside the castle walls, yet the village does not resist."

"Strange, perhaps, but understandable," Waleran said quietly. "You've seen the fortifications of the castle and outside walls. The moors make it unapproachable by an army of any size. Even a man as powerful as the earl of York knows it fruitless to attack. Besides, the lord of this manor is shrewd enough to give no cause for the earl's anger."

Sir William raised an eyebrow.

Now that Waleran had decided to talk, it seemed as if a flood poured forth. "Because the entire village is in vassalage, this manor is extremely wealthy. The lord gives ample homage to the earl of York in the form of grain, wool, and even gold. Simple, don't you see?"

"I do see," Sir William said thoughtfully. "The earl of York is bribed not to attack a castle in his kingdom which he could not successfully overcome anyway."

"Yes, yes!" Waleran nodded quickly. "And with enough soldiers within the gates, the villagers are powerless. Those who do leave to till and harvest the fields know they must return each night, or members of their family will be placed in these very cells. Richard Mewburn may be hated by those inside Magnus, but all are helpless before him."

"What I don't see," Sir William said in the same thoughtful tones, "is why this lord has not appeared to formally accuse us. Strangers that we are, we deserve the justice which must be granted anywhere in the land."

Waleran only shook his head. He returned to his corner, found a crumb to hold above the rathole, then squatted in his former position.

Minutes passed, broken only by the never-ending drips of water onto stones not covered by straw.

Thomas could not stand it any longer. "That is all?" he cried. "You are choosing silence again?"

Waleran slowly craned his head upward and measured his words.

"My silence would be better for you." He sighed heavily. "Remember, I tell you this with reluctance."

Sir William thought of the empty road leading into Magnus. Strong premonition told him he did not want to hear the next words.

"Magnus has around it a black silence," Waleran said. "Traders and craftsmen learned long ago that they risked freedom and all they owned to visit. Whispers of death keep them away. And for good reason."

Waleran looked back to the hole and spoke as if addressing the wall. "Had there not been convenient charges against you, you would still have found yourselves within this dungeon. There are dark secrets in Magnus. Secrets only hinted even to villagers. Secrets which must remain hidden from the entire land."

He paused, and the deadness in his voice spoke chilling truth. "Once inside these walls, strangers are never permitted to leave."

Thomas woke with the sour taste of sleep in his mouth. *Fear and worry must be exhausting me,* he decided, as he rolled into a sitting position and wiped straw from his face. *The nights pass without dreams. And how is a person to mark the passage of time in this dark hole? No bells to mark the church offices, no sun to mark dawn or nightfall.*

In the dull flickering of torches, Thomas could see that Waleran lay huddled motionless on one side of the cell; Sir William snored gently in his corner. Neither hidden sword nor concealed chain mail seemed to hinder his sleep.

Because he knew the boredom which stretched ahead, Thomas concentrated on a routine to delay his restlessness. Any thoughts other than questions tortured him with reminders of his helplessness. *My bundle lies outside the castle walls and is capable of winning me a kingdom; yet I am trapped with no hope of leaving.*

So Thomas plucked from his mind the first of many well-worn questions, determined to gnaw it yet again, like an animal searching for the tiniest shred of undiscovered meat.

It demanded patience to turn first one question, then another, over and over in his mind, to approach them from every angle, striving to fit different facts into place. In the four days of captivity, Thomas had concluded nothing new from all his questions. However, all he had was time, and the questions would not leave the cell.

Who is this knight? Thomas asked himself, as another snore reminded him of Sir William. *A man of honor, he has fulfilled his pledge by entering the castle walls of Magnus. He has become a friend, yet he speaks nothing of his past, nothing of his own quest.*

Thomas suddenly realized something he had missed in all his previous thoughts about the knight. *Can the man fight with skill?* Certainly, like any knight, he could easily defeat a dozen unarmed and untrained peasants. That assumption had lulled Thomas into a sense of security. But a new question disturbed him. *Is Sir William man enough to fight boldly against other armed and trained men?*

Thomas pondered the sword and chain mail that the knight refused to hide beneath the straw, then decided yes. They had not been searched before being thrown in the dungeon. Sir William could then have removed the uncomfortable chain mail, but he chose not to. Any man who would endure discomfort day and night to be constantly prepared for any brief chance at escape would be a man to have as an ally.

Thomas then moved to his next question. *Tiny John, no doubt, can well find a way to survive. But is the mute girl withstanding the terrors of being alone and friendless in Magnus?* Thomas regretted again not even knowing her name, and he let worry fill his hunger-pinched stomach. It had been four days. The girl could not speak. *What work will she find to sustain her? What stranger will treat her with kindness? Or, will she simply flee Magnus and disappear from my life forever?*

Thomas smiled at his foolishness. Barring a miracle which would give him the chance to use his secret knowledge to win Magnus, he and the knight would never leave this cell for anything but death by hanging. Searching for the girl should not even be a concern.

Stubbornly, despite the only future he could see, Thomas moved to his next question. He was not dead. Yet.

Thus, the next question followed naturally, as it had every time over the last four days. Thomas closed his eyes and pictured himself in the panicked darkness in front of the scaffold.

Again and again, Thomas replayed those few minutes of terror beneath a blackened sky. The old man had known it was Thomas beneath those robes. The old man had known how Thomas had given the illusions of power. And the old man had known of his desire to win Magnus.

How did that mysterious old man know so much—even of my search? And who is he to have the power to block the sun?

Thomas attacked that problem with such intensity that Sir

William had to clap hands to get his attention.

"Thomas, you scowl as if we have lost all hope."

Thomas blinked himself free from his trance and answered the knight's easy smile.

"Never!"

In the warmth of their growing friendship, Thomas ached to confide in the knight.

There is so much to tell, Sir William. The chest of books, a source of power as great as any in the land. The gold I have concealed in the cave beside them. The means of winning Magnus. And the promise made at Sarah's deathbed never to reveal these secrets.

Sir William yawned. "My mouth is as vile as goat's dung. Even the water from this roof would be better."

With that, Sir William moved beneath one of the eternal drips and opened his mouth wide. After several patient minutes of collecting water, he rinsed and spit into a far corner of the cell.

Waleran unfolded from his motionless huddle and grumbled. "Must you be so noisy? My friends will never venture forth."

Sir William merely yawned again and said, "Precisely."

Before Waleran could retort, the door rattled.

"A visitor," droned the jailer.

"Impossible," Waleran said. "Not once in ten years has a visitor been permitted to—"

The door lurched open, and the jailer's hand appeared briefly as he pushed a stumbling figure inside.

Thomas tried not to stare.

Caked and dirty bandages still suggested mutilated horror. A downcast head and dropped shoulders still projected fear. *Katherine.*

"Who is this wretched creature?" Waleran demanded.

Again, it hit him, the instant fury that someone so defenseless might suffer insults. Thomas spun, shoved his palm into Waleran's chest and drove him backward into the filth.

"Another word and you shall pay—" Thomas began in a low tight voice.

Sir William stepped between the two. "Thomas . . ."

Thomas sucked air between gritted teeth to calm himself as Waleran scrambled backward into his corner.

"Please do not hurt him," Katherine said clearly. "To be called 'wretched creature' is an insult only if I choose to believe it."

Thomas turned to her. She stood waiting, hands behind her back. She was only slightly shorter than he. Her voice, still muffled by the swathed bandages, had a low sweetness.

"I beg of you pardon," Thomas said. It pained him to look at her. Not because she was a freak, but because he remembered his own pain and loneliness. It tore at his heart to imagine how much worse was her private agony.

"How is it you are allowed to visit?" Sir William asked.

Katherine's head nodded downward in shyness. "Every day since your capture, I have brought hot meals to the captain of the guards. I have washed his laundry, cleaned his rooms."

"Bribery!" Sir William laughed. "But why?"

Katherine took a small basket from behind her back. "Because of the candle shop. Not once has a person defended me as you did," she answered. "Prisoners here do not fare well. I wished to comfort you."

She pulled the cloth which covered the basket.

Juices flowed in his mouth as Thomas smelled cooked chicken.

Bread. Apples. Chicken. Cheese.

"These luxuries are more than you can afford," Thomas protested.

She ignored him and offered the basket and held it in front of her until finally he accepted.

"I have little time," Katherine said. "If it pleases you, Thomas, I wish to speak alone."

"You know my name," Thomas said, as he handed the basket to Sir William.

"Your friend, Tiny John, told me."

Sir William retreated with the basket to a corner to give them privacy.

"Tiny John! He is well?"

"As long as he continues to avoid the soldiers. Many of the shopkeepers take delight in helping that rascal. They like to see the soldiers made fools of."

Thomas pictured Tiny John darting from hiding spot to hiding spot, never losing his grin of happiness.

"And the girl?"

Katherine caught the worry in his voice. She drew a quick breath and turned her head away as she spoke. "The girl truly is beautiful. And you are very handsome. I understand your concern." Katherine faced him squarely again, but her voice trembled. "She has disappeared. But if you ask, I shall inquire for you and search until she is found."

Thomas silently cursed himself. *How little affection must be in this poor girl's life if a few moments of kindness from a passing stranger kindles the devotion she now shows. Here she stands, knowing her hideous face prevents her from competing for more affection. And while she waits, with gifts she cannot afford, the passing stranger betrays such obvious concern for another with the beauty she will never have. Thoughtless cruelty of the worst type.*

"No. Please do not look for her," Thomas finally croaked his answer. He blocked thoughts of the mute girl and measured his words carefully. "We might ask instead that you honor us with another visit."

The squaring of her shoulders told him he had answered rightly.

Besides, he consoled himself, *even if Katherine found the mute girl, what good would it accomplish?*

The jailer rapped on the door. "Be quick about leaving."

"Tomorrow," Katherine whispered, "we shall talk of escape."

Thomas again woke to the sour taste of heavy sleep. He did not move for several minutes; instead, he stared at the ceiling of the dungeon cell and watched the water drops.

He began going through his never-ending questions. Katherine's visits during the past week had helped to pass the time and to give some hope, but never enough. In her absence, he faced his self-imposed questions.

Who is the knight, and can he be trusted with all secrets? Is the mute girl nearby? Who is the old man? And the most pressing question . . . *With Katherine's help, will our plan for escape succeed?*

The water dripped, uncaring about the fate of humans beneath.

Water. Thomas swallowed and licked dry lips. *Water.* He swallowed the sour taste of sleep again, this time thoughtfully. *Water.* A new realization startled him into sitting bolt upright.

He ran idea after idea through his mind. Much later, he spoke.

"Escape!" he whispered hoarsely.

Sir William muttered from a deep sleep.

"Escape!" Thomas tried again.

Waleran stirred and groaned as he woke. "What's that you say?"

Thomas grinned at Waleran in response, then stepped across the dungeon cell and shook the knight.

"Escape!" He looked over to Waleran. "Yes! I said escape!"

"Back to sleep, you crazed puppy," Sir William said with a thick tongue.

"No. I cannot." Thomas grinned at Waleran, then at the knight.

"I have decided many things," Thomas said. "One is this." He paused and took a deep breath. "Sir William, I have been wrong not to trust you fully. When you threatened my life in the forest, I did not have with me—as you believed—a king's ransom in gold. It was, instead, buried in a safe place. I tell you this now, so that you will trust *me* completely. I need that trust to ensure that our escape plans will not fail."

Sir William nodded.

"The escape is planned for seven days from now. Katherine, as you have noticed, spends much time in conversation with me. She has received instructions that will let her retrieve some of that gold and bribe the captain of the guards to leave the door unlocked as she leaves."

Thomas paused. "We will need on that day the excellence of a knight who can fight as no other."

Sir William warned Thomas with a glance. "Where do we find such a knight?"

"Trust me." Thomas added urgency to his voice. "Listen, you should know the remainder of the gold is buried directly beneath the gallows rope that nearly hung you outside the village of Helmsley."

Thomas looked the knight squarely in the eyes. "Having revealed my secrets thus, I need from you a demonstration of skill."

"You have me thoroughly puzzled, Thomas." Sir William added his own urgency. *Does Thomas not remember the importance of concealing my fighting profession?* "I have no skills to demonstrate."

"Your sword." Thomas ignored the warning in Sir William's voice. "You have my secret now. I wish to see from you what manner of fighter you might be."

Sir William frowned again and gave another quick shake of his head in the direction of Waleran.

Thomas laughed. "Let Waleran witness this. He too will escape with us if he pleases."

"I have no sword," Sir William hissed between gritted teeth.

"Come, come," Thomas laughed. "Such modesty."

Thomas grinned again at Waleran. "He is a knight."

Waleran's jaw dropped. So did Sir William's. Each for a different reason.

"Yes. A knight!" Thomas said. "Something no other person in Magnus knows. And his hidden fighting skills will lead us to safety."

Thomas gestured impatiently at Sir William. "Please. Impress us with your swordplay."

"You are a fool," Sir William growled. He lurched to his feet and wiped sleep from his eyes. "However, if you insist on playing this game . . ."

He yawned, and shook himself awake, much as a dog shakes water. "The basket that Katherine delivered," he said, pointing. "Take from it an apple."

Thomas did as instructed. As Sir William waited, he loosened his shirt, but did not remove it, or the sword.

"Throw it to Waleran," Sir William instructed, from his position halfway between the two.

Thomas shrugged. "As you wish."

He tossed it underhand, slowly, because the distance across the cell was so short.

In a blurring movement that Thomas could not see, Sir William did the impossible. He snapped his hand back and over his shoulders to the sword handle hidden between his shoulder blades. In one motion, he pulled the sword free and slashed the air in front of him just as the apple passed.

"Inconceivable," Thomas breathed.

Waleran could not speak. He merely stared at the apple he had caught in both his hands.

Then Thomas recovered.

"Perhaps few are faster than you," Thomas finally joked. "But your accuracy leaves a little to be desired. That apple passed by unhindered."

"You think so." Sir William's voice had a deadliness that reflected his anger. "You insist in a childish manner on this exhibition, then attempt to mock me. Had you not my sworn pledge, I would strangle you."

He slowly replaced the sword, then spoke to Waleran. None of the deadliness left Sir William's voice. "Drop the apple."

Waleran did.

It landed on the bed of straw and fell apart. Cleanly sliced, each half of the apple wobbled to stillness in the silence that followed.

"I cannot believe in God. Not if you tell me He is a God of love," Thomas insisted in a low voice.

"Why is that, Thomas?" Katherine replied calmly.

Thomas welcomed the sound of her voice, especially since Sir William had refused to speak to him since sheathing his sword that morning. Katherine's cheerful sweetness banished the darkness of the dungeon.

Her voice was so expressive that Thomas did not need to

read her face to enjoy their discussions. By now, he hardly noticed the covering of bandages around her head.

"It is hard to believe," he said, "when there is so much evidence that He does not love us."

With much time to think since morning, Thomas had questions he hardly dared ask Katherine. Questions of escape that he preferred to delay. Moreover, her presence gave such gentle calmness that he wanted to speak of things he had shared with no living soul since the death of his nurse, Sarah.

"Nothing in my life," he said with intensity, "shows such a God. My parents were taken from me—killed by pestilence before I was old enough to remember them. Then Sarah, my nurse, teacher, and only friend, was gone before I was eleven years of age."

Thomas struggled to keep his fists unclenched. "Surely if this God of yours existed, He would have been there in the abbey when all human love failed me. He was not. Instead, there was only corruption by the very men pretending to serve Him."

He described his years in the abbey and the crimes of the four monks.

"And outside of the abbey," he continued. "is a land where most people struggle to live day to day, servants to the very wealthy earls and lords. Beggars, cripples, disease, and death. There is nothing good in this life."

"Thomas, Thomas . . ." Katherine placed a cool hand upon his.

He shook free. "And you," he blurted with anger. "How could you be so cursed if God truly loved . . ." Then he realized what he was saying.

"I'm sorry," he said in a low voice.

"Do not trouble yourself," Katherine said. "I am accustomed to the covering of my face."

She touched her bandages lightly. "This is not a curse. It is only a burden. After all, our time on earth is so short. And God does not see my face."

She moved her hand away from her face and held it up to stop Thomas from protesting.

"Think of a magnificent carpet, Thomas. Thousands and thousands of threads, intertwined in a beautiful pattern. No single thread can comprehend the pattern. No single thread can see its purpose. Yet together, they make the glorious entirety."

She continued with controlled passion. "You and I are threads, Thomas. We cannot see God's plan for us. My scars, your loneliness, the beggars' hunger, and the paths of men in war and peace—all lead to the completion of God's design."

"How do you know this with such certainty?" Thomas almost pleaded, so sure was her voice.

"God grants you peace when you accept Him."

Thomas shook his head slowly. "I wish I could believe. When I left the abbey, I left all pretensions to knowing God. I shall not return."

His statement created a silence between them.

On the other side of the dungeon, Sir William sat in a slouched position, ignoring them. Waleran squatted in his normal position and waited with bread crumbs for the rats.

As the silence between them became uncomfortable, Thomas decided to ask the question he had delayed from fear.

"Tiny John . . . did he succeed?"

"Yes, Thomas. I have made the arrangements."

Gratitude swept warmth across him. For the first time since entering the cell, she replaced in his heart, for a moment, the silent girl with the beautiful face and the haunting eyes.

"Then it is nearly time," he murmured. "Spread the legend among the villagers."

Katherine nodded. "When is it," she murmured in return, "that you wish to escape?"

Thomas thought of the seven days he had promised Waleran.

"In six days," Thomas said. "On the eve of the sixth day from now."

Chapter Ten

Thomas recognized the high pitch of Tiny John's voice echoing in the dungeon hallways long before he could understand the words.

Sir William stopped his silent pacing. "That's—"

"Our pickpocket friend," Thomas finished.

The knight squinted and opened his mouth to ask a question, but was interrupted by the clanging of a key into the cell door.

"Horrid fiend!" the guard shouted. "I hope they tear you into pieces!"

A bleeding hand shoved Tiny John into the cell. He stumbled but did not fall. The door slammed shut.

Tiny John surveyed his new home with his hands on his hips and grinned. "Barely nicked him, I did," Tiny John explained. "If only my teeth were bigger. I'd have bitten those fingers clean through."

Sir William shook his head in mock disgust.

Waleran moved closer, not bothering to hide a puzzled expression. "Who are you? And what did that soldier mean, 'I hope they tear you to pieces'?"

"I'm John the potter's son. Some say I'm a pickpocket. But don't believe everything you hear."

"But this tearing to pieces . . ."

"Oh, that." Tiny John waved away the question. "He was right upset, he was. Losing a chunk of his finger and all." Tiny John paused to elaborately spit his mouth clean, then grinned. "I begged him not to throw me in this cell. Told him these two—" Tiny John gestured at Thomas and Sir William, "were unforgiving about some jewelry I'd lifted from them and that I was sure to be killed if he threw me in the same den.''

Waleran scowled. ''These two would kill you?''

''Of course not,'' Tiny John said in amazement at Waleran's stupidity. ''But how else could I make sure the guard would put me with my friends?''

Waleran sighed.

Tiny John did not notice. He continued in the same cheery voice. ''I'm here now, Thomas. Right at eventide as requested. 'Twas no easy task running slow enough for the soldiers to catch me. Especially with so many of my village friends trying to help me escape.''

''Right at eventide as requested?'' Waleran repeated. He looked to Thomas for help. ''He wanted to be captured?''

Thomas scratched his ear with casualness. ''I promised him he would be out tonight.''

''Tonight? But the escape is tomorrow!'' Waleran blurted.

Thomas ignored that and placed both his hands on Tiny John's shoulders. ''The villagers expect an angel?''

''Some believe. Some don't. But all wait for tonight.''

''Angel?'' Waleran interjected. ''Tonight?''

Thomas did not remove his glance from Tiny John's face. ''And Katherine has spread word among the villagers?''

''They wait for angels,'' Tiny John said. ''No other legend could prepare them so.''

''Angels?'' Waleran almost stamped the ground in frustration.

Thomas removed his hands from the boy's shoulders. ''Well done, Tiny John.'' Then he faced Waleran. ''Yes. Angels. As one born in Magnus you surely recall the legend?''

Waleran opened his mouth and snapped it shut.

Sir William was quick to notice.

''Thomas,'' he said sharply. ''What is it you know about this man?''

Waleran edged away from them both.

Thomas replied with a question. ''Do you not think it strange that one who claims to have been in this cell ten years remains so strong and healthy?''

''The rats,'' Waleran said quickly. ''They provide nourishment when I tire of their friendship."

"Draw your sword, please, Sir William," Thomas continued in a calm tone. "If this man opens his mouth to speak again, remove his head. The guards must not hear him shout for help."

Again, that magical quickness. Almost instantly, Waleran felt the prick of a sword blade pushing the soft skin of his throat.

"Explain," Sir William told Thomas in a quiet voice. "I do not care to threaten innocent men."

"Waleran is a spy," Thomas said. "Each night, as we lay in drugged sleep, he leaves the cell and reports to his master."

"Drugged sleep?"

"Drugged sleep," Thomas repeated. He thought of the mornings he had licked his dry lips and stared at the ceiling. "I believe it is a potion placed into our water each night at supper."

"That explains why you asked me not to drink tonight."

Thomas nodded. "Also, these fetters. I began to wonder why we were not manacled to the walls, as is customary. But Waleran needed to have freedom of movement. We would have suspected too much if we were bound in iron and he were not."

Sir William added pressure to the sword point. "Is the accusation true? Are you a spy?"

Waleran did not reply.

"Answer enough." Sir William held his sword steady and gazed thoughtfully at Waleran. "The foul taste as I woke. The dreamless nights. How did I not suspect . . ."

"It took me some time too," Thomas said. "Do your arms tire, Sir William?"

"Of holding a sword to this scum's throat? I think not."

"Please. Let me sit," Waleran suggested nervously. His Adam's apple bobbed against the sword point. "If the sword slips . . ."

Sir William nodded. "Sit then. But so much as draw a deep breath and you shall be dead."

Waleran burrowed into the straw.

Sir William did not remove his eyes from Waleran's face.

"Thomas, Tiny John said we would escape tonight. Yet nearly a week ago . . . "

"I announced it would happen tomorrow. For the same reason I wanted the demonstration of swordplay for him to see you were a knight. If he thought we trusted him completely, I could plan in safety for escape at a different time."

"You knew then that Waleran was a spy?"

"I suspected as much." Thomas glanced at the ceiling's water drip that had triggered his suspicion. "That night, I poured my water into the straw and pretended sleep. Shortly after, he answered a soft knock on the door and departed. He returned many hours later."

"Does the lord of Magnus believe we escape tomorrow?" Sir William asked with deceptive calm. His eyes had not wavered from Waleran's face.

"You expect me to reply?"

Sir William brought his sword point up again. "These are your choices. You answer to me, and merely risk punishment from him. Or you refuse to answer to me, at the certainty of immediate death. After all, I stand to lose nothing by slaying you."

"Yes," came the quick reply. "He intended to arrest Katherine tomorrow."

"They both know, of course, of the plan to bribe the guards?"

"Yes. Tonight, as you slept, he intended to remove your sword, and tomorrow to arrest Katherine."

"Where," Thomas asked, "will we find Richard Mewburn, Lord of Magnus, tonight?"

Waleran smiled. "If I tell you that, I am no longer merely risking punishment. Should you actually escape and reach him, he will know you could only have discovered that knowledge from one source. And if you don't escape, which is much more likely, then you don't need the knowledge anyway."

"Why were you placed here as a spy?" Sir William asked. Although he knew the answer, Thomas had proven himself too capable at unraveling mysteries. He did not want Thomas to suspect him at all, and he needed to continue to act as if he were merely a knight. "Why would Richard Mewburn think Thomas and I were important enough to need watching in this cell? I came in as a beggar, and Thomas as—"

"And why were you placed here ahead of our arrest?" Thomas asked, as a sudden new thought shocked him.

The answer came as Thomas feared.

"Your arrival and mission were expected."

The old man at the gallows! There was no other way possible for anyone in Magnus to know!

Thomas almost swayed as he fought the rush of adrenaline that swept him. *Why help me and the knight escape, only to imprison us at Magnus! Waleran may hold the answer!*

"Tell me who foretold our arrival!" he said, in a voice hoarsened by urgency. "And where he is now!"

Waleran shrugged and continued his eerie smile. "I am simply a spy. I only know there are many dark secrets in Magnus."

Sir William glowered and rested the blade of his sword against Waleran's throat. "Explain yourself."

"That is all I will reveal. Death itself is a more attractive alternative."

Thomas felt chilled. *Dark secrets of Magnus?* Then he clamped his jaw. *The only magic in any kingdom is the power held by the lords. And if the moor winds continue to blow, morning will find me holding that power.*

"Ignore his blathering," Thomas said, as he focused on the task ahead and his adrenaline subsided. "Sir William, there is much I need to tell you before we leave this cell tonight."

Waleran giggled. "You persist in believing you might leave?"

Thomas nodded at Tiny John.

Tiny John grinned from a dirt-smudged face and pulled from his coat a large key.

"Pickpockets do have their uses," Thomas said.

Sir William frowned. "Any moment the guard will discover it missing and return!"

"Not likely," Thomas said. "Just as Katherine instructed,

Tiny John lifted it three days ago when the guard strolled through the marketplace. Katherine waited at the candle shop, then made a wax impression of it, so that Tiny John could return it within minutes. What you now see is a duplicate."

Sir William began to grin as widely as Tiny John, then stopped abruptly. "How do you propose we silence this spy? We have no rope. No gag. As soon as we leave the cell, he'll call for help."

Thomas smiled. "He should sleep soon. I switched cups during supper. Waleran drank the drugged water intended for me."

They encountered the first guard within ten heartbeats of easing themselves from the dungeon cell.

Startled, he stepped backward and placed a hand on the hilt of his sword.

Sir William was faster. Much faster.

Before the guard could flinch, Sir William's sword point pinned his chest against the wall. The guard dropped his hand and waited.

"Run him through!" Tiny John urged.

"Spare his life," Thomas said, in a voice which allowed no argument.

"Thomas, I'm not fond of killing people, believe me. Yet, this man has been trained to do the same to us. At the very least, he will sound the alarm."

Even in the yellow light cast by smoking torches, the man's fear was obvious by sweat which rolled down his face.

"You have children?" Thomas asked.

The guard nodded.

"Spare him," Thomas repeated. "I would wish a father-less life on no one."

Sir William shrugged. Then in a swift motion, he crashed his free fist into the guard's jaw. The guard groaned once, then sagged.

"We'll drag him back into our cell," Thomas instructed. Then he spoke to Tiny John through a smile that robbed his words of rebuke. "This isn't a game, you scamp. Would *you* care to have a sword through your chest?"

Tiny John squinted in thought. "Perhaps not."

Thomas laughed. "Get on with helping us."

Within moments, they left the guard as motionless as a sack of apples beside the snoring Waleran.

Ten minutes later, they reached the cool night air and the low murmur of a village settling down at the end of evening.

Thomas smiled at the wind that tugged at his hair.

Chapter Eleven

In the early darkness outside the castle walls, Thomas forced away his fear.

Planning in the idle hours, he told himself, *is much too easy. In grand thoughts and wonderful schemes, you never consider the terror of avoiding guards on the battlements and dropping down by rope into a lake filled with black water.*

He shivered in his dampness.

Katherine must be here. Or all is lost.

Sir William must rally the village people. Or all is lost

The winds must hold. Or all is lost.

Thomas shook his head angrily. *"Cast not your thoughts toward the fears,"* Sarah's patient voice echoed in his memory, *"but focus on your wishes."*

At that, Thomas had to grin at the moonlight. *"Focus on your wishes."*

"I want to fly like an angel," he whispered. "Wind, carry me high and far."

As if reading his mind, the wind grew. But with it, his chill in the wet clothing.

Five more minutes, he told himself. *If Katherine doesn't appear within five minutes, then I'll call out.*

He counted to mark time as he walked. *"The winds blow from the north,"* Katherine had said. *"Once you reach the open moors, mark the highest point of the hills against the horizon and move toward it. I shall appear."*

Without warning, she did.

"You have retrieved your bundle?" she whispered.

"Yes. Undisturbed. Everything remains in it."

"Then wrap this around you."

With gratitude, Thomas slipped into a rough wool blanket.

"I've also brought you dry clothing," she said.

Without thinking, Thomas drew her into the blanket, hugged her, and kissed lightly the bandage at her forehead. It surprised him as much as her, and she pulled back awkwardly.

"I'm sorry," he said. "It's just that—"

"Please, dress quickly. Time is short."

Thomas removed his shirt and trousers with numbed fingers. The wind cut his bare skin, but within moments he was fully dressed. Immediately, his skin began to glow with renewed warmth.

"When I am lord," he promised, "you shall have your heart's desire."

"You do not know my heart's desire," she whispered so softly that her words were lost in the wind.

Thomas would not have heard anyway. He was scrambling forward, searching for the sheets and wooden rods he had removed from his bundle. The moonlight aided him.

"I did this as a young child to pass time after my nurse died." Thomas spoke as he worked. This far from the castle walls—several hundred yards—here was no danger in being overheard by a night watchman. "But I confess, it was on a smaller scale."

He tied two rods together at one end, then propped and tied a cross member halfway down, so that the large frame formed an *A*.

"However, I have no fear of this failing." He did, of course, but showing that fear to Katherine would not help. "In a strange land, far, far away, it is a custom for men to build one of these to test the gods for omens before setting sail to voyage."

"How is it you know of these things?" Katherine stood beside him, handing him string and knives and wax as requested.

Surely there is no harm in telling her? Thomas asked of his long-dead Sarah. *I will not mention the books, only what I learned as a child.*

"You must vow to tell no person." Thomas waited until

she nodded. "What I am building comes from the land known as Cathay."

"Cathay! That is at the end of the world!"

Thomas nodded. His hands remained in constant motion. He tested the frame. Satisfied, he moved it to a sheet of cloth, spread flat across the grass.

"It is a land with many marvels. The people there know much of science and medicine. I expect they would be called wizards here."

" 'Tis wondrous strange," Katherine breathed.

Thomas nodded. "Their secrets enabled me to win the services of a knight. And now, through the legend of Magnus, a kingdom."

He kneeled beside the frame. "Needle and thread," he called.

Instantly, she placed it in his hands. He began to weave the sheet to the frame. For the next hour, he concentrated on his task and did not speak.

In silence, Katherine placed more thread in his hands as required. The moonlight, bright enough to cast shadows across their work, hastened their task.

Finally, Thomas stood and arched his back to relieve the strain. He set the structure upright. The wind nearly snatched it from his hands, and he dropped it again.

Satisfied, he surveyed it where it lay on the ground. As wide as a cart, and as high as a doorway.

He found the loose end of the twine and tied it in the middle of the crossbar. There still remained the sewing of bonds that would attach him to the structure. And after that, the flight.

Katherine interrupted his thoughts. Her voice quavered. "You are certain the men of Cathay use such a thing?"

Thomas was glad to speak of what he knew from the books. It took his thoughts from his fears. But he kept his hands busy as he replied.

"There is a man in Italy named Marco Polo," he began. "He spent many years among the people of Cathay." Thomas remembered how he had savored every word of each book, how each page in the dry coolness of the cave soothed the pain of daily living at the abbey. Strange customs and strange men in strange lands.

"This Marco Polo recorded many things. Among them, the custom of sending a man aloft in the winds before a ship sailed from shore. If the man flew, the voyage would be safe. If he did not stay in the air, the voyage was delayed."

Katherine spoke quickly. "There were times he did not stay in the air?"

"Tonight will not be one of them," Thomas vowed. "Too much has happened to bring me this far."

"Then it is God's will that you triumph," Katherine replied.

For the first time since Sarah's death, Thomas permitted a crack in his determined wall of disbelief.

"If that is indeed truth, begin a prayer," he said. "Begin it from both of us."

The winds held steady.

Thomas ignored the cold as he raced to final readiness.

Will my daring attempt to fly succeed? Or will my endless dreams and plans and preparations at the abbey end here with my death?

He tied leather shoulder straps to the cross members of the structure, and another wide leather band that would secure his legs.

Do not think of failure.

He drove a peg into the ground with the hammer Katherine had smuggled out earlier.

My death here would be of no matter. Should I fail, life will not be important to me. I will never have a chance like this again.

To the peg, he attached one end of a roll of twine, the last object from his bundle.

Do not think of failure.

He tied the other end of twine to a belt of leather around his waist. Between both ends, the remaining twine was rolled neatly on a large spool. Small knots every three feet thickened the twine.

Will the knight be inside waiting with the new army? Or has he been captured already?

Thomas looped the handles of a small, heavy bag around his neck. The cord of the bag bit fiercely into his skin and brought tears to his eyes.

Do not think of failure.

Finally, he slipped his hands into crudely sewn gloves of heavy leather.

Will the winds be strong enough? Katherine, pray hard for me.

"I will lie down on this," he said. "Attach the straps around my shoulder. That will leave me movement with my arms. When I am ready, please help me to my feet. Then stand aside. The wind should do the rest."

Moving onto his back relieved some of the pressure of the cords around his neck. Thomas fastened himself securely and took a deep breath.

You have dreamed long enough of this moment. Sarah promised you again and again that this kite was the only way to win Magnus. Wait no longer.

"I am ready."

Katherine reached for his outstretched hand. She braced herself, then heaved backward. Thomas lurched to his feet with the huge structure on his back.

"Wings of an angel," Katherine breathed in awe.

The wind snatched at Thomas. He grabbed the twine where it was secured to the peg. It took all his strength to hold to the ground.

"Thomas!" Katherine pointed behind him at the castle. "Soldiers! At the gate!"

He could not turn to see. That was the worst of it. He was bound to a kite that would let him see only *into* the wind — not where it took him, leaving him driven at a brutally high and hard castle wall which was impossible to watch during his approach.

Two hundred carefully paced steps to reach the walls. Will that give me enough time to soar out of reach?

The wind screamed at the sail on his back.

"Flee, Katherine! Away from the castle. Rejoin me tomorrow!"

She shook her head. "Go! God be with you!" With that, she pushed him, and a gust of wind pulled the twine through his hands.

Airborne!

In the next frenzied seconds, Thomas could not give himself the luxury of worrying about the approaching soldiers. The kite picked up momentum so quickly that the twine sang through his fingers. Even through heavy leather gloves, Thomas felt the heat.

The moon cast his shadow on the ground and from his height, it appeared like a huge darting bat. The soldiers below him shouted and pointed upward.

He dismissed any joy in this sudden flight. He forced the soldiers from his mind. Instead, Thomas concentrated sharply on counting each knot. His mind became a blur of numbers. He reached one hundred once, then began over. At eighty again, he clutched hard and the kite swooped upward even more sharply. His fingers froze.

Katherine!

While he could not see the castle wall, facing into the wind let him glance at Katherine, already far away. The same moon which cut such clear black shadows showed too clearly that the soldiers had reached Katherine.

Why did she not flee?

Thomas understood immediately.

She protected the peg!

Katherine had grabbed one of the remaining sticks of wood to advance on the soldiers. Once the soldiers reached it, a single slash of sword would sever Thomas from the ground. She knew it. The soldiers, if they did not know it now, would almost immediately upon reaching the peg.

Thomas wailed. *Why did I not tell her the twine was needed only briefly?*

"Flee!" he screamed to her. But his words were lost to the wind.

Thomas tore his eyes from the scene below. There was nothing he could do now for Katherine except to get over the castle walls on the wings of an angel. He ached to see behind him. How far was he from the castle walls? He only knew he was not high enough yet to get over the rough stone.

He willed his fingers to release the cord. Eighty-one. Eighty-two. Eighty-three . . .

A scream pierced the darkness. Soldiers had reached Katherine.

Concentrate!

At ninety-nine, he stopped the unraveling by swiftly lashing the twine around his wrist in two loops. It felt as if the sudden stop tore his hand loose. With his other hand, he fumbled with the sack at his neck and pulled free a heavy grappling hook.

It too was attached to twine, and Thomas dropped it, knowing there was ample cord attached to the sack around his neck.

Without the extra weight of the grapple, the kite bobbed upward, high enough to clear the castle wall.

At the same time, the tremendous pressure on his lashed wrist ceased.

The rope at the peg's been cut! Katherine!

"Please, God. Be with us now!" Thomas cried into the black wind.

The grappling hook hit the surface of the drawbridge and bounced upward as the wind took the kite.

Savagely, with all the anger he wanted to direct at the soldiers back with Katherine, Thomas wrapped his fingers around the twine which unraveled from the sack around his neck.

"Please, God. Let it hold!"

The grapple hopped upward again and clacked against the wall of the gate before spinning away.

By then, Thomas was over the walls and in sight of everyone within Magnus.

A great shout arose to meet him. Sir William *had* gathered the army!

Clank. The grapple's first bounce against the lower part of the walls.

Thomas held his breath.

The kite tore upward so quickly that barely any wall remained between the grapple and the night sky. If it did not catch, the wings of an angel would carry Thomas far, far away from Magnus. Without Thomas there, Sir William's army would scurry homeward. Never would Magnus be freed from . . .

Thud.

Despite all the strength he possessed, twine spun through his gloves from the sudden lurch of kite against wind as the grapple dug into the top of the castle wall.

The shout of people below him grew louder.

Thomas still did not dare look downward.

He fought the twine to a standstill, then looped it around his belt. Then and only then did he survey Magnus.

The kite hung as high as the highest tower. Suspended as it was against the moon, people gathered below could only see the outspread wings of white. They roared, "Delivered on the wings of an angel, he shall free us from oppression! Delivered on the wings of an angel, he shall free us from oppression!"

Thomas nearly wept with relief. He pulled his crude gloves free and tucked them among the remaining twine in the sack around his neck.

"Delivered on the wings of an angel, he shall free us from oppression!"

Thomas could see them all armed with hoes and pitchforks, protected by rough shields of tabletops and helmets of pots. As they shouted, they pumped their hands upward in defiance.

That was the secret to conquering Magnus. Not to find a way to bring an army into it. But to form one from people already inside. One knight to lead them. One angel to inspire them.

"Delivered on the wings of an angel, he shall free us from oppression!"

The roar of their noise filled the sky. There were enough to pack the market space and spill into the alleys. Thomas could see no soldiers foolish enough to approach the roiling crowd.

"Delivered on the wings of an angel, he shall free us from oppression."

The pounding of noise almost deafened Thomas. He blinked away tears of an emotion he could not understand.

"Delivered on the wings of an angel, he shall free us from oppression."

It was time to return to earth.

Thomas found the knife in his inner shirt. He twisted against the shoulder straps and reached behind him.

Slash. He tore open a slit in the white cloth. Wind whistled through and the kite sagged downward.

Another slash. Slowly, the kite began to drop, as its resistance to the wind lessened.

Foot by foot it dropped. As Thomas neared the ground, be began to loosen the straps around his shoulders. Then, just before the kite could die completely, he released himself and cut through the twine. The kite bobbed upward as Thomas fell.

He rolled with the impact and stood immediately.

The crowd, with Sir William at the front and Tiny John at his side, advanced in a wave toward him.

"Delivered on the wings of an angel, he shall free us from oppression!"

Thomas held up his right hand.

The instant silence at the front of the crowd rolled backward, as each wave of villagers took its cue from the wave in front.

Within a minute, it was quiet enough for Thomas to hear his own thudding heart. *What do I say? None of my dreams prepared me for a moment like this!*

Sir William rescued him.

"Thomas," he called. "Thomas of Magnus!"

In a great chant, the crowd took up those words. "Thomas of Magnus! Thomas of Magnus!" Like thunder, his name rolled inside the castle walls.

Then Thomas remembered. *Katherine!*

He held up his hand again.

Again, the silence sifted backward from him.

"Sir William," Thomas cried, "the gate is open with half the soldiers outside. If you take the gate now, they will be unable to return inside." Sir William understood immediately. *The army is divided already! The battle is half won!*

It took little urging for him to gather a hundred men.

"Wait," Thomas cried again. "They have the girl Katherine. Bargain for her life."

The knight nodded briskly and moved forward. One hundred angry men followed.

Thomas closed his eyes briefly. What had he seen from his perch in the sky? Soldiers scurrying to their last retreat, the keep itself, four stories tall and unassailable.

Tonight, these villagers were an army, unified by emotion and hope. Tonight, the remaining soldiers would not fight. They knew, as did Thomas, that tomorrow, or the day after, these fierce emotions would fade.

When that happened, these villagers would no longer be a solid army, prepared to die in a fight for freedom. Then, once again a handful of trained fighters would be able to conquer and dominate seven hundred people.

The battle must be won tonight! Thomas thought hard. Then it struck him. *If the soldiers cannot be reached for us to fight them now, they must not be able to reach us later.*

Thomas cast his eyes toward the keep. Unlike the castle walls, it had not been designed for soldiers to fight downward from above. The solution, once it hit him, was obvious.

"Good people of Magnus!"

Whatever shuffling of impatience there was in the crowd stopped immediately.

"Enough blood has been shed within these walls. Enough cruel oppression. Enough pain and bitterness. Tomorrow's dawn brings a new age in Magnus!"

The roar began, "Delivered on the wings of an angel, he shall free us from oppression!"

Thomas held up his hand again. "Our captors, now captive, shall be treated with kindness!"

To this, there was low grumbling.

"Do you not remember the pain inflicted on you?" Thomas shouted. "Then do not double the sin, knowing full well the pain, to inflict it in return."

Immediate silence, then murmurings of agreement. "We have a wise and kind ruler!" a voice yelled from the middle of the mob.

"Wise and kind! Wise and kind!"

Again, Thomas requested silence. "Furthermore," he shouted, "we shall not inflict injury upon ourselves by attempting to storm the keep."

A hum of questions reached him.

"Instead," Thomas shouted, "we shall wait until the remaining army surrenders." Before he could be interrupted again, Thomas picked a large man from the front of the crowd. "You, my good man, gather two hundred. Arm yourselves with spades and shovels and meet me in front of the keep in five minutes."

He pointed at another. "You, gather fifty men and all the tar and kindling in the village."

With that, Thomas turned and strode toward the keep. He did not have to look behind him to know that hundreds followed in a large milling crowd.

A quarter-hour later, the two smaller groups joined Thomas and the main crowd in front of the keep. During that time, not one soldier had even ventured to stick his head outside a casement of the keep.

With the arrival of all the village's men, Thomas quickly began to outline his plan. The men grasped it immediately. Many grinned in appreciation. But Thomas had no time to savor his victory.

Sir William approached him with long strides. "Our men have barricaded the remaining soldiers outside the walls," he said, with a grim furrow across his forehead. "Yet there is no sign of Katherine. Alive or dead."

Thomas beat his side once with his right fist. *This is no time to show pain or mourning,* he told himself. *Those around me must feel nothing but joy.*

He made his face appear expressionless under the bright lights of hundreds of torches.

"We cannot forsake the kingdom for one person," he told Sir William. "Not until this battle is complete shall I begin the search for her." He gave his final command. "The rest must follow me and remain as guards. We do not want to tempt the soldiers to leave the keep and fight. Enough blood has been shed within the walls of Magnus!"

Chapter Twelve

It took until noon the next day—and three shifts of one hundred men each—to complete Thomas' plan for bloodless warfare. When they finished, the keep had effectively been isolated from the rest of the village within the castle walls.

The men had dug a shallow moat around the keep, throwing the dirt to the village side as a barricade. Thomas then had the moat filled with tar and pitch and kindling. Standing guard every twelve paces were men armed with torches. To give them time to lead their normal lives, their duty shifts were to run only four hours each. There was no shortage of volunteers. Day and night, a shift of men would guard the moat.

After the final barrel of pitch had oozed into the moat, Thomas called loudly upward at the keep, "Who wishes to speak to the new lord of Magnus?"

All of the village stood gathered behind Thomas. Tomorrow or the day after they might resume normal village life, if the siege dragged on. Today, however, was a day to behold. A new lord—one who had already shown wisdom and consideration—was about to dictate terms of surrender to the old lord.

Thomas did not disappoint them.

A single face appeared from the third floor. "I am the captain."

Thomas said, "Not a single soldier shall die. But we will not provide food or water. You may surrender when you wish. Be warned, however. Should you decide to counterattack, the moat will impede any battle rush upon the village.

And if you struggle to cross the pitch, it shall be set aflame!"

"We have heard that you deal with fairness," the captain replied.

Thomas frowned in puzzlement.

"One of our men thanks you for his life," the captain explained.

Yes. The prison guard we left with Waleran. And what has become of that spy?

"When you are prepared to surrender," Thomas instructed, "one of your men must deliver all your weapons to the edge of the moat. Then, and only then, will we build you a bridge to the safety of the village and to food and water."

Thomas paused. "Your lord will also be granted his life upon surrender."

The captain said, "That will not be necessary. Nor will a prolonged siege."

"What is that you say?"

"There is a tunnel that leads to the lake. The former lord of Magnus fled with two others during the night. We wish to surrender immediately."

"Fare thee well, Thomas."

"I wish that it were not this way," Thomas replied to Sir William.

The knight smiled his ironic half smile. Beside him, his horse, a great roan stallion given from the stables of Magnus, danced and shook its mane with impatience.

"Thomas," Sir William said, "we are both men of the world. We do not *wish*. We attempt to change what we know can be changed, we accept what cannot be changed, and we always strive for the wisdom to know the difference. In this case, my departure cannot be changed."

Thomas held his head straight. He must fight the lump in his throat. "After a month in Magnus, you still dispense advice."

"Listen, puppy," the knight growled. "You may be lord of Magnus, and a good one, I might add, but you are never too old for good advice."

The new lord of Magnus squinted into the morning sun

to blaze into his memory his last look at the knight. Not for the first time did he wonder from where Sir William had come. Or where he went. Thomas did not voice those questions. Had the knight wanted any of that known, he surely would have revealed it by now.

So Thomas merely stood calmly and fought the sadness of departure.

A breeze gently flapped the knight's colors against the stallion. Behind them, at the other end of the narrow land bridge, lay the walls of Magnus. Ahead, the winding trail that would lead Sir William up into the moors.

"I thank you for all your good advice," Thomas said in a quiet voice. "Without it, I would have foundered."

Thomas knew too well the truth of his words. A month earlier, within hours of forcing the soldiers to surrender, Thomas had discovered that a position as lord meant much more than simply accepting tribute, as he had naively dreamed. The lord of a manor or village was also administrator, sometimes judge, sometimes jailer.

It was more difficult yet for a lord newly established. Sir William had first guided Thomas through the task of selecting his army from the soldiers. Usually those who swore loyalty remained, and those who didn't were skinned alive by flogging, or worse, if the lord chose. Thomas had not. He did not want any men pretending loyalty merely to escape death. As a result, most of the men had been eager to serve a new master of such kindness and common sense.

Day by day, Sir William had taken Thomas through his new tasks as lord. Day by day, Thomas had grown more confident and had earned the confidence of the villagers. If any of them had doubts about their new lord because of his youth, even after his delivery on the wings of an angel and the way he had led them to victory, those doubts quickly disappeared.

Thomas truly was lord of Magnus. And as lord, he hid from public view his grief. Katherine had not been found. Nor was there any trace of the mute girl. Even Tiny John could not find a clue to her disappearance.

Thomas' thoughts must have become obvious in those moments of farewell.

"You brood once more." Sir William's voice interrupted his thoughts. "Perhaps the time is not ready for my departure."

Thomas forced a grin. "So that I must endure more of your nagging? I think not. Be on your way, and may, may . . ."

"May *God* be with me?" Sir William teased. "At least progress has been made. You are now ready to consider Him as a friend?"

Thomas smiled tightly. He *had* spent much time considering Katherine's strong faith. And he could not forget that during his worst moment in the air, he had cried out to the God he thought he did not believe in.

Before the moment could become awkward, Sir William, mounted his horse.

"I thank you for my life," Sir William said with a salute. The drumming of the horse's hooves remained with Thomas all of that day.

One mile past the crest of the hill that overlooked the valley of Magnus, the knight reined his horse to a halt. He hobbled its front feet and let it find grass among the heather and gorse.

Weather changed quickly on the moors, even as spring approached summer. The scattered clouds above him were low, heavy at the bottom with an angry gray, and they moved over the hills in a growing wind he felt more keenly now, outside the protective walls of Magnus. It would not be a good day for travel.

While a few hundred yards farther down there began isolated stands of trees, it was open here, with the long, broad expanse of another valley laid out beneath the sky. Here, against the horizon, he was in plain view. And here, against the horizon, none would be able to approach him without being equally in plain view.

Hawkwood did not keep the knight waiting long enough to begin to shiver. Sir William saw him first as a small black figure stepping out from the trees below, a figure that grew quickly as Hawkwood covered ground with long, vigorous strides.

"My friend," the knight called, "you wear the guise of an

old man, but move as a puppy. Merlin himself would find it a performance sadly lacking."

Hawkwood shook his head and raised his voice to be heard above the moor winds. "Merlin himself would rest beside a fire when the cold begins to move across the hills. If I walked as an old man, I would soon feel as one."

"I feel as one now," Sir William said. "It was no easy task to leave the young lord."

"He does inspire affection," Hawkwood agreed. "Katherine too does not want to believe he serves a different cause."

"Katherine. She is well?" The knight could not keep sharp anxiety from his voice. "All that Gervaise could relay was that she had escaped the soldiers."

Hawkwood nodded. "She suffered one blow, but the bandages softened the club's impact. It helped that I was able to run horses through the midst of them; the commotion from inside the walls accomplished the rest."

Sir William relaxed. "And now?"

"Now we have the luxury of time and privacy so that she can be taught in our ways."

"The luxury of time? You fear not the fate of Magnus?"

"Always," Hawkwood said. The wind plucked at his hood, and he threw it back to expose his silver hair. "But I fear it will be unwise to force whatever happens next. It will serve us better to wait and watch. Gervaise, of course, is there, and I hope to continue to find ways to wander freely throughout Magnus when necessary. Over twenty years have passed; another few months will not hurt."

"No? If Thomas is not one of theirs, they will double their efforts. Who will protect him from an enemy he cannot see?"

Hawkwood leaned forward, both hands on the head of his cane. "If he is not one of theirs, they will assume he is ours and in most likelihood will play the waiting game too. Besides, if they truly wanted him dead, there is nought we could do. As you well know, dealing death is too simple . . . poison, an asp beneath his bed covers, a dart from a passageway."

"Your task is to wait and watch," the knight said heavily, "while I return to exile, to rely on messages which take months to receive. I do not know which is the more difficult."

Chapter Thirteen

The next morning, at sunrise, two soldiers escorted the mute girl into the keep of the castle and she spoke her first words to Thomas.

"My name is Isabelle," she said with a bow.

"Isabelle," Thomas repeated softly. He did not rise from his large chair in the front hall, despite his flood of joy. No lord rose during an audience.

She stood in front of him in the front hall of the keep. Tapestries hung on the walls. The fireplace crackled, for even in the summer, early mornings were cool. Two soldiers guarded the entrance, stiffly unmoving with eyes straight forward.

Tiny John bobbed into the room. All guards knew he had privilege at any time.

"I heard she was back," he blurted with wide eyes. He glanced her up and down and whistled.

"She's a marvel of beauty, she is!"

"She can also hear every word you say," Thomas observed with a dry smile.

"Aaack!" Tiny John spun on his heel and ran.

Tiny John had spoken truth. The mute girl—*no, Isabelle,* Thomas told himself—did not wear rags. Instead, her slim body was covered from neck to ankle in a clean white dress. Her long dark hair now gleamed with health. The same beautifully etched high cheekbones . . . the same mysterious eyes . . . and the same haunting half smile.

She had become as much a woman in the previous month as Thomas had grown toward manhood with his new responsibilities as lord of Magnus.

He wanted to weep with joy. Instead, he dismissed the soldiers. He was too conscious of the dignity required as lord.

When they were alone, he whispered it again. "Isabelle."

"Yes, my lord."

"You speak. And hear."

"Yes, my lord."

"Please, 'Thomas.' "

She lowered her head, looked upward, and said shyly, "Yes, Thomas."

He wanted to throw himself into her arms. His heart pounded at the strange feelings he had tried to forget during the previous month.

Watching her, Thomas somehow knew that she would embrace him gladly in return.

"Isabelle," he started. Although he could will himself to remain in his chair, he could not keep the hushed wonder from his tone. "Your return is a miracle. Yet I am flooded with questions. Where have you been? How is it you prospered while away? And how is it you now speak and hear?"

She straightened her shoulders and looked him directly in the eyes. "There is much to tell. Will you listen, lord?"

He smiled. "Gladly."

Her smile, a promise and a reward all in one, drew from him a silent inward gasp. He managed to keep his face motionless. *Yes,* he exulted, *she is worth as much as a kingdom.*

"I, like you, am an orphan, from a village far south of here. My parents perished in a fire when I was a baby. I am told the villagers did not think it worth their while to preserve me. After all, I was only a girl. But a lonely old woman, one who was truly mute and deaf, defeated them. She fought for me. The villagers, who suspected she was a witch, dared not disagree and so raised me. She died when I was ten. With her gone, the villagers were free to chase me away."

Thomas nodded. His heart ached with growing love for her. *She was an outcast too. Together, they might . . .*

"Because the old lady could not hear, I learned early to

speak with my hands. And when I was forced to travel from village to village, seeking food and shelter, I soon discovered the advantages of posing as mute and deaf. It earned pity. Also, I learned not to trust, and being mute and deaf put me behind walls that no person could break."

Isabelle faltered and looked down at her hands. "Not even you, Thomas, wanted me. You saved us all from death by hanging, and you wanted only the knight."

"That is no longer true," he said quickly and with some guilt.

"So I chose to remain mute and deaf. Yet often, I would see you glancing at me, and my heart would wonder."

Thomas finally moved from his chair. He approached her and took her hands in his. "Perhaps," he said gently, "your heart was hearing mine."

Moments of silence seemed to roar in his ears.

"When you were arrested," she began again, "I fled Magnus. After three days of travel, I reached the dales near the town of York. I had not eaten. I had barely slept. I threw myself at the mercy of the first passing carriage and begged for a chance to work. The lady inside took pity. She fed and clothed me, and arranged for me to work as a maid in her kitchen. When word reached me of the fall of Magnus—"

"Word has reached the outer world?" Thomas interrupted sharply.

She bowed her head again. "Yes."

The earl of York will arrive soon, Thomas realized with a pang of urgency. *Am I prepared to keep this small kingdom against the forces of the larger one?*

He kept his face still. "So you braved the moors and returned."

"Yes," Isabelle said. "My heart could not rest until it discovered the answer."

"Answer?"

She tightened her grip on his hands. "Yes. Answer. Did I belong to you? Or had I been fooling myself about your glances?"

"I am the only fool," Thomas said gallantly. "Not to have searched the world for you."

She did not hesitate. She threw her arms around his neck.

Thomas felt on his neck her warm skin and the cool circle of her medallion.

"Take them with you." The old man's words at the hanging. *"It will guarantee you a safe journey to Magnus."*

Even as Thomas held her, his mind raced with thoughts and questions.

Slowly, ever so slowly, he released her.

A single tear dropped from his eye.

"Isabelle," he croaked, "I wish it were not so."

What had Sir William said upon departure? *"We do not wish. We attempt to change what we know can be changed, we accept what cannot be changed, and we always strive for the wisdom to know the difference."*

"You must answer me these further questions," Thomas continued in the same pained voice. "Who are you? And who placed you among us? Was it the old man at the gallows?"

"I . . . I do not understand."

Do not wish. Attempt to change what you know can be changed.

He forced the words from his mouth. "If you do not answer, you shall spend your remaining days condemned to the same dungeon you arranged for me and the knight."

It took five days for Isabelle to realize that Thomas was not bluffing. Five days of darkness. Five days of solitude. Five days with the endless rustling of rats in the straw.

When she next appeared in front of him in the hall, her hair was matted, and her eyes held a wildness of fear, not of mystery.

Thomas too had dark circles under his eyes. Sleep did not come easily in the anguish of doubt.

Yet there was the medallion. . . .

Thomas again dismissed the guards at the entrance and rose to shut the doors behind them.

He waited for her to speak.

The silence stretched. Still, he waited behind her and said nothing.

Finally, she spoke without turning. Her voice broke upon the words. "How is it you know?"

At that, Thomas sighed. A tiny hope had flickered that he was wrong, that he could still trust her.

"Your medallion," he said. "What a blunder to leave it around your neck upon your return."

She clutched it automatically.

"Do not fear," Thomas said heavily. "I had seen it already, the day that Tiny John lifted it from you on the moors. The strange symbol upon it matches the symbol engraved in the scepter I found below the former lord's bed, now mine. I forgot seeing it, until your return reminded me."

Isabelle shivered and hugged herself.

"Moreover," Thomas continued, "there was the soldier's attack outside the walls of Magnus the night I was delivered on 'the wings of an angel.' How did they know to venture outside the walls? I had not been followed. No sentry could have seen me or Katherine. You or the knight or Tiny John were the only ones to know that I had with me on my way here a bag filled with the means to conquer Magnus. You or the knight or Tiny John were the only ones to know I had left it outside the castle walls."

Isabelle turned to face him.

"And our arrest," Thomas said, "could not have been a coincidence. Or the fact that a spy had already been planted in the dungeon ahead of us. The knowledge of our presence in Magnus could only have come from you, the person who disappeared our first morning here to return with a bowl of porridge to explain your absence."

Isabelle nodded.

The implications staggered Thomas. *Isabelle's nearness had already been planned before the hanging and the rescue of Sir William! Again, it circled back to the old man at the gallows and his knowledge!*

"Why? How?" Thomas said, almost quiet with despair. "My plans to conquer Magnus were a dream, kept only to myself. How did the lord know—"

"Why?" she said calmly. "Duty. I am Lord Richard's daughter."

"Daughter! You were one of the three figures to escape the night of my conquering!" Thomas stopped, puzzled. "No one recognized you here when you arrived with us."

"Do you think the lord of Magnus would dare let his daughter wander the streets among a people who hated him? No one recognized me because I spent so little time among them."

Thomas shook his head. "And duty dictated you return and pretend love for me?"

She nodded.

"How were you to kill me?" Thomas asked with bitterness. "Poison as I drank to your health? A ladylike dagger thrust in my ribs during a long embrace?"

A half sob escaped Isabelle. "Those . . . those were my father's commands. I am still unsure whether I could have fulfilled them."

Thomas shrugged, although at her admission the last pieces of his heart fell into a cold black void. "No matter, of course. I cared little for you."

She blinked, stung.

"Go on," Thomas said with the same lack of tone. "From the beginning. At the gallows."

"As you have guessed," she then said, "it was arranged I would be on the gallows. My father feared a threat to his kingdom. And he did not believe the knight would die."

That was the greatest mystery. From the beginning, the lord of the very kingdom Thomas intended to take had foreseen his every move.

"How did your father know? Did he instruct the old man to appear at the gallows? Or is it reversed—did the old man instruct your father of my intentions?"

"Old man?" Isabelle stared at Thomas for long moments. Then she threw her head back in laughter. When she finished, and found her breath again, she said, almost with disbelief, "You truly do not know."

Thomas gritted his teeth. "I truly do not know *what?*"

"I was not there because of you. You were not the threat my father feared. I was there because of the knight."

Because of the knight with the unknown background!

Isabelle kept her voice flat. "My father sometimes used cruel methods to maintain his power. I did not approve or disapprove. This is a difficult world. I am told that when my father first overthrew the lord of Magnus . . ."

Thomas gritted his teeth again. *Sarah's parents.*

". . . that he publicly branded each opposing soldier and knight. Then he had them flogged to death. One escaped . . . the most loyal and most valiant fighter of them all."

She let those words hang while Thomas grasped the truth.

"Sir William!"

"Yes, Sir William. When my father received word that Sir William had returned to this land, he paid a great sum of money to have the sacred chalices stolen and placed among his belongings."

"You were sent to the hanging to be a spy, should he be rescued. How did your father know it would happen?"

"He guessed it might, and he wanted to be safe. The hangman had instructions to release me if the knight died on the gallows."

Thomas paced to the far side of the room. "Why? Why did he foresee a rescue?" Nothing could be more important to Thomas than this. If Isabelle could explain why, it would lead to the old man, and how anyone knew Thomas would be at the hanging.

"Thomas," she began, "there is a great circle of conspiracy that is much larger than you and I. My father also acted upon the commands of another. And there is much at stake."

"You are speaking in circles."

"I know only what I have guessed after a lifetime in Magnus. Haven't you wondered why this castle is set so securely, so far away from the outer world? Why would anyone bother attacking a village here? Yet an impenetrable castle was founded. And by no less a wizard than—"

The door exploded open.

Time fragmented before Thomas' eyes. Geoffrey the candlemaker! At a full run with short club extended! Startled guards in half motion behind him! Club thrown downward! Thomas beginning to dive! Too late!

Much too late. And Thomas, half-stunned by his full-length dive, raised his head in time to see the first guard with an uplifted sword.

"No! Don't—" Thomas began to roar. "He must not be killed."

Too late again. Geoffrey fell into a limp huddle. Beside him in a smaller huddle, Isabelle.

Geoffrey's arm and hand scraped the floor in a feeble twitch.

Thomas could only stare at the fingers and ring now inches from his face.

He finally rose in the horrified silence shared by both guards.

"My lord, we did not know—"

Thomas waved a weary hand to stop the soldier's voice. He bent and gently took the medallion from Isabelle's neck. Then he matched it to the ring on Geoffrey's hand.

They were identical.

Chapter Fourteen

Dawn found Thomas on the eastern ramparts of the castle walls. The guards knew by now to respect his privacy; each morning the sentry for that part of the wall would retreat at the sight of the new lord of Magnus approaching.

This hour gave Thomas what little peace he could find. The wind had yet to rise on the moors. The cry of birds carried from far across the lake surrounding Magnus. First rays of sun edged over the top of the eastern slope and began to reflect off the calm water. The town lay silent.

It was the time of day that he searched his own emptiness.

"Sarah," he spoke to his long-dead friend, "the castle has been taken from the brutal conquerer who killed your parents. That was my promise to you as you lay dying. Now it is fulfilled. Yet, why do I feel so restless?"

The morning did not answer.

He could keep a brave and resolute face as the new lord of Magnus, and he always did during the busy days with the villagers. Yet in the quiet times, there were too many questions.

There is so little that I know, Thomas thought.

An old man cast the sun into darkness and directed me here from the gallows. The old man knew Isabelle was a spy; the old man knew my dream of conquering Magnus. Who was that old man? Will he ever reappear?

A valiant knight befriended me and helped me win the castle that once belonged to his lord. Then he departed. Why?

A crooked candlemaker and the daughter of the lord we vanquished remain in the dungeons of Magnus, refusing to speak, though long since recovered from the blows which rendered them unconscious. What conspiracy was Isabelle about to reveal? Why is she silent now? And why do they share the same strange symbol?

And what fate has befallen Katherine?

There is so much I must do.

There are the books filled with priceless knowledge, able to give a young man the power to conquer kingdoms. They must be brought safely to the castle.

The earl of York has heard that Magnus has fallen to me. He will arrive to exact tribute or begin a seige. All of Magnus must be prepared.

And I must not cease in searching—without the villagers being aware—for the secrets of Magnus.

Thomas closed his eyes.

For a moment, Katherine's voice echoed in his mind. He kept his eyes closed, desperate for any comfort.

What had she once said? *"You and I are threads, Thomas. We cannot see God's plan for us."*

Thomas opened his eyes. The sun had broken over the top of the faraway hill, spilling rays across the dips and swells of the land.

Thomas smiled. *Oh, that there were a God with enough love and wisdom to watch over all our follies.*

He speculated with wonder on that thought for many long minutes. He thought of Katherine's bravery and conviction. He thought of his own confusion.

Suddenly, Thomas spun on his heels and marched from the ramparts. He strode through the village streets and came to a small stone building near the center market square. There, he banged against the rough wooden door.

A strong voice answered and the door opened to show an elderly man with gray hair combed straight back.

"My lord," he said without fear. "Come inside, please. We are graced with your presence."

They moved to the nave at the front of the church. Sunlight streamed through the eastern windows and cut sharp shadows across both their faces. In the man's eyes, Thomas saw nothing of the greed he had witnessed for many years at the abbey. It was enough for Thomas to finally speak.

"Father," Thomas said. "Help me in my quest."

Chapter Fifteen

Northern England
June 1312

Thrust! Thrust! Slash sideways to parry the counterthrust! Thrust again!

A small group of hardened soldiers watched impassively as Thomas weakened slowly in defense against their captain.

Ignore the dull ache of fatigue that tempts you to lower your sword hand, Thomas commanded himself. *Advance! Retreat! Quickly thrust! Now parry!*

Above Thomas, gray clouds of a cold June day. Around him, a large area of worn grass, and beyond the dirt and grass, the castle keep and village buildings within the walls of Magnus.

Right foot forward with right hand. Concentrate. Blink the salt sweat from your eyes. And watch his sword hand!

A small boy struggled to push his way through the wall of soldiers who blocked him from Thomas.

He can sense you weakening. He pushes harder. You cannot fight much longer. Formulate a plan!

"Thomas!" the boy cried. One burly soldier clamped a massive hand around the boy's arm and held him back.

Thomas began to gasp for air in great ragged gulps. His sword drooped. His quick steps blurred in precision.

The captain, a full hand taller than Thomas, grinned.

The death thrust comes soon! Lower your guard now!

Thomas flailed tiredly and relaxed one moment too long.

His opponent stretched his grin wider and—overconfident because of the obvious fatigue in front of him—brought his sword high to end the fight.

Now!

Thomas focused all his remaining energy on swinging his sword beneath that briefly unguarded upstroke. The impact of sword on ribs jarred his arm to the elbow. He danced back, expecting victory.

Instead, the captain roared with rage as he fell backward onto the dirt and scrabbled to his feet.

"Insolent puppy! Now learn your lesson!"

Among the soldiers, a few faces showed amusement. The small boy among them kicked his captor in the shins, but did not free himself.

The captain rushed forward and waved his sword.

Intent on saving what energy he could, Thomas merely held his own sword carefully in front to guard. He watched the waving sword as a mouse in hiding watches a cat.

"Fool!" the captain shouted, still waving the sword in his right hand as distraction, while his left hand flew upward in an arc that Thomas barely saw. At the top of that arc, the captain released a fistful of loose dirt into the eyes and mouth of his opponent.

Thomas caught most of the dirt as he sucked in a lungful of air. The rest blinded him with pain. The choking retch brought him to his knees, and he did not see the captain's sword flash downward.

Once across the side of the ribs. Then a symbolic point thrust in the center of his chest.

Over.

The soldiers hooted and clapped before dispersing to their daily duties. The small boy broke loose as his captor joined the applause. He darted to Thomas.

"That dirt was an unfair thing for 'im to do, it was!" the boy said.

In reply, Thomas coughed twice more, then staggered to his feet.

"Wooden swords and protective horsehide vests or not, my lord," the captain said to Thomas, "I expect you'll be taking a few bruises to your bed tonight."

Thomas spit dirt from his mouth. "I expect you'll have one yourself, Robert. It was no light blow I dealt to your ribs. By our rules, I thought the fight would end." He wiped his face and left a great smudge of sweat-oiled dirt.

The boy tugged on his sleeve. "Thomas."

"Later, Tiny John."

"Rightfully so. By our rules, you *were* the winner." Robert of Uleran replied. He was a man nearly into his fourth decade of living. Solid and tough, his scarred and broken face was a testimony to the first three decades of rough living. When his face was set in anger, children would run from him. But when he smiled, as he did now, no child would ever be frightened.

"I continued to fight, however, for two reasons."

Thomas spit more dirt from his mouth and waited.

"One, I was angry you had fooled me by pretending tiredness so effectively. A teacher should never misjudge his student so badly. It's been only a month and you've learned far more than most. I should have expected that move from you."

"Thomas!" Tiny John said.

"Later, Tiny John." He turned his attention back to Robert of Uleran. "Anger has never been part of the rules," Thomas observed.

"Neither has mercy. And do not deny it." Robert's eyes flashed beneath thick dark eyebrows. "When you landed that first blow, you should have moved in to finish me. Instead, you paused. That hesitation may some day cost you your life."

Robert drew his cloak aside and began to unbind the thick horsehide padding around his upper body. "I will not impart to you all I know about fighting, only to have you lose to a lesser man with more cruelty. The dirt in your face, I hope, has proved to be a great lesson."

"Thomas!" Tiny John blurted.

Thomas good-naturedly placed a hand over Tiny John's mouth. He knew this was the proper time to make his announcement.

"Robert," he said, "I do not wish for you to remain captain of all these soldiers. Pick your replacement."

"My lord, have I offended you?"

"Pick your replacement," Thomas ordered. As lord of

Magnus, he could not allow anyone to question him lightly.

"Yes, my lord."

Tiny John considered biting the hand over his mouth. But even he recognized the steel in Thomas' voice and decided there would be a better time later.

"David of Fenway, my lord," Robert said. "He shows great promise and the men respect him."

Having said that, Robert of Uleran turned. He had not completed the removal of his fighting gear. Yet because of angry pride, he turned to leave quickly.

"Please remove your possessions from the soldiers' quarters," Thomas said.

For a moment, Robert's face expanded with rage at further insult. His narrow scar-lines flushed with blood, and he drew a deep breath. He wheeled quickly and stared at Thomas.

Neither flinched.

Then Robert's shoulders sagged. "Yes, my lord."

Thomas drew his own breath to speak, but was interrupted by the drumming of horse hooves.

A great white beast rounded the buildings opposite the exercise area. On it, a man in a flowing purple cape, sword sheathed in scabbard. No travel bags were attached to the saddle.

Thomas removed his hand from Tiny John's face and placed it on Robert's shoulder to hold his presence.

"It's the earl of York," Tiny John blurted. "That's what I was trying to tell you. He asked permission at the gates to enter alone and unguarded. Twenty of his men remain outside."

The earl of York! Magnus, tucked as it was in the remotest valley of the North York moors, still lay within jurisdiction of the earl of York. Thomas had always known it was only a matter of time until he faced his next challenge as new lord of Magnus. *Will the earl accept a new pact of loyalty? Or is he here to declare war?*

The horse arrived at their feet within moments, and the man dismounted with an easy grace.

He immediately moved forward to Robert and extended

his right hand to show it bare of weapons. "Thomas of Magnus. I am the earl of York."

Robert was in no mood to enjoy the mistake. "The lord of Magnus stands beside me."

The earl's eyes widened briefly with surprise. He recovered quickly and extended his right hand to Thomas.

"I come in peace," he said. "I beg of you to receive me in equal manner."

"We shall extend to you the greatest possible hospitality," Thomas answered. "And I wish for you to greet Robert of Uleran, the man I trust most within Magnus, and . . ." Thomas paused to enjoy the announcement he had been about to make ". . . newly appointed sheriff of this manor. He may be busy, over the next few hours, as he moves his possessions to his new residence in the keep."

If the earl of York did not understand the reason for Robert's sudden and broad smile of happiness, he was polite enough not to ask.

Thomas, with Robert, led the earl of York and his horse to the stables. There he summoned a boy to tend to the horse.

It took great willpower not to bombard the air with questions. Thomas, however, remembered advice that he had been given by an old friend, now dead. *The one who speaks first shows anxiousness, and in so doing, loses ground.*"

Instead, Thomas contented himself with a very ordinary observation. "The clouds promise rain," he said, as they left the shelter of the stables.

The earl of York looked up from his study of the nearby archery practice range. "I fear much more than rain."

Thomas waited, but the earl said nothing more until their walk brought them to the keep of Magnus.

"A moat *within* the castle walls?" he asked.

In front of them lay a shallow ditch. Had it only been two months since Thomas had filled it with tar and crackling dry wood and threatened to siege to former lord and his soldiers unless they gave up without bloodshed?

"Temporary," Thomas commented, and volunteered no further information.

The earl paused and looked upward at the keep. Four stories high and constructed of stone walls more than three feet thick, it was easily the most imposing structure within the walls of Magnus. Not even the cathedral compared in magnificence.

Thomas also gazed in appreciation. From its turrets, he often surveyed the lake that surrounded the castle walls and stared deep in thought at the high, steep hills of the moors which were etched against the sky. Morning was best, before the wind began and when the heather, that endless low carpet of brush, glowed purple in the sun's first rays.

Each morning Thomas turned and watched Magnus itself as it began to stir. There was the street of shops, each with a large painted sign that showed in symbol its trade. And the narrow, curved streets with houses were so cramped together and leaning in all directions that they were like crooked dirty teeth.

And of course, the cathedral. Thomas would smile to turn his eyes upon the steeple that rose from the depths of the village. Not because of the priest. No, as an orphan, Thomas had seen enough of the dangers of organized religion to learn to hate it. He smiled because of an old man given the task of sweeping the stone floors there, an old man Thomas had once confused for the priest, an old man who truly believed in the God that Thomas struggled to find, and who seemed to live in a manner which showed belief. Not like priests and monks who preyed upon the poor and innocent.

Thomas almost growled at the thought of those priests, then stopped. He was, after all, standing beside the earl of York. He glanced at his guest to see if he had finished his inspection of the keep. The earl nodded.

Thomas almost smiled at the demonstration of power. *Subtle . . . this man appearing to give me permission to allow him to enter my hall.*

They climbed the outside steps with Robert following. The entrance to the keep was twenty feet from the ground, to make it difficult for attackers to gain entrance.

The ground level, reached by descending an inside stairway, contained the food stores and the kitchen on one side, and the open hall for eating and entertainment to the middle and rest of the other side.

Above were the three residential stories, with the lord's rooms on the top. Each level was open in the center and looked down upon the hall, so that all rooms were tucked against the four outer walls. Below, reachable only by a narrow passageway and deep enough below the stone that cries of prisoners would never reach the hall, was the dungeon.

Thomas always shuddered to think of that hole of endless night. He had spent much too long there once, almost doomed before he could even start the events which led to his conquering Magnus. And now—the thought was always on his mind, even as he swung open the great doors of the keep to allow inside the earl of York—the dungeon held two silent and cowed prisoners who were proving to be among his thorniest problems.

Until the arrival of the earl.

"I shall leave, my lord?" Robert asked.

"As you wish," Thomas said. He would have appreciated the man beside him during a discussion with the earl. But the need for help might show weakness. Thomas was glad that Robert knew it too. It said much for the man's thinking.

Thomas gestured at two leather padded chairs near the hearth. Before they had time to sit, a maid appeared with a steaming mixture of milk, sugar, and crushed barley.

"No wine?" The earl raised an eyebrow.

Disdain?

Thomas remembered the instructions from the friend long ago. *"Never show fear. Nor hesitation."*

"No wine. It tends to encourage sloth."

The earl grinned. "There's gentle criticism if I ever heard it. And from someone so young."

They studied each other.

Unlike many of the men in Magnus, Thomas had kept his hair long. Tied back, it seemed to add strength to the impression already given by his square shoulders, high intelligent forehead, straight noble nose, and untrembling chin.

Surely this youth must be frightened, the earl of York

thought. *I have shown much strength by entering his castle alone. He knows I have almost as much power as the king of Britain himself. Yet those gray eyes remain calm, and everything in the way he sits is controlled and relaxed.*

Thomas repeated to himself, *"Never show fear. Nor hesitation."* He wanted to close his eyes briefly to silently thank Sarah, the one who had spent many hours drilling him on how to act. She and she alone had believed he would someday rule Magnus. And now he faced his first great test. *What does the earl want? What is he thinking?*

The earl did not know whether to frown or laugh. *How long will this youth remain silent? Will he not break and utter the first words?*

Thomas lifted his thick clay cup in a wordless salute. The earl responded in turn and gulped the thick, sweet broth.

Still Thomas waited. His eyes did not leave the earl's face. He saw a man already forty years old, but with a face quite different than one would expect of nobility. The chin had not doubled or tripled with good living. There were no broken veins on his nose to suggest too much enjoyment of wine. No sagging circles beneath his eyes, evidence of sleepless nights from poor health or a bad conscience.

Instead, the face was broad and remarkably smooth. Neatly trimmed red-blond hair spoke of Vikings among his ancestors. Blue eyes matched the sky just before dusk. Straight, strong teeth now gleamed in a smile.

"Do you treat all visitors this harshly?" the earl asked.

"Sir! I beg of you forgiveness. Do you wish to dine immediately?"

"It is hardly the food, or lack thereof. Surely you have questions, yet you force me to begin!"

"Again, I beg of you forgiveness."

"If you want me to believe that, you have to stop hiding that smile." The earl laughed at the discomfort he produced with that statement. "Enough," he then said. "I see you and I shall get along famously. I detest men who offer me their throats like craven dogs."

"Thank you, my lord," Thomas said quietly. He coughed. "I presume you are here to inspect me."

The earl nodded.

"I thought as much," Thomas said. "Otherwise, you would not have made such a show of mistakenly greeting my sheriff, Robert."

This time, the earl had enough grace to show discomfort. "My acting was so poor?"

Thomas shook his head. "Only a fool would have entered Magnus without knowing anything about his future ally—or opponent. Between Robert and me, you should have easily guessed which one was young enough to be the new lord of Magnus."

Thomas held his breath.

Yet the earl of York decided to let the reference to ally or opponent slip past them both. He sipped again from his broth.

"Do your men practice their archery often?"

"With all due respect, my lord," Thomas answered, "I think you mean to question me about the distance between the men and their targets."

This time, the earl did not bother to hide surprise.

"You are a man of observation," Thomas said simply. "And a fighting man. I saw your eyes measure the ground from where the grass was trampled to where the targets stand. I would guess a man with experience in fighting would think it senseless to have practice at such great distance."

"Yes," the earl said. "I had wondered. But I had also reserved judgment."

"I am having the men experiment with new bows."

"New bows? How so?"

Thomas showed that the question had been indiscreet by ignoring it. "In so doing, I also wish to let them understand it is my main desire that they survive battles, not die gloriously. Distance between battle lines ensures that."

The earl took his rebuke with a calm nod. "Truly, that is a remarkable philosophy in this age."

Thomas did not tell the earl it was a strategy already fourteen hundred years old, a strategy from a far land, contained in the books of power which had enabled him to conquer Magnus.

"Not one soldier died as Magnus fell," Thomas said instead. "That made it much easier to obtain loyalty from a fighting force."

"You have studied warfare?"

"In a certain manner, yes." Thomas also decided it would be wiser to hide that he could read—a rarity in itself and mostly restricted to the higher ranking priests or monks—and that he could do so as well in French, the language of the nobles, and in Latin.

The earl of York was a man who believed strongly in hunches. And everything told him that Thomas showed great promise.

He said so. "When I arrived," he continued, "I had not decided what I might do about your new status. I feared I might be forced to waste time by gathering a full force and laying a dreadfully long siege."

"Again, I thank you."

"You may not," the earl said heavily.

Thomas raised an eyebrow to frame his question.

"Because of what my heart believes," the earl said, "I wish to seal with you a loyalty pact. You may remain lord here with my full blessing."

Thomas hid his joy. A siege, a protracted war, would not occur!

"That sounds like a reason for celebration, not concern," Thomas said carefully.

The earl pursed his lips, shook his head slowly and spoke with regret. "I am here to request that you go north and defeat the approaching Scots."

Thomas didn't dare blink. To say yes might mean death. To refuse might mean death. He began to formulate a reply.

"Come with me," the earl said, holding up a thick, strong hand to cut Thomas short as he drew a breath. "We shall walk throughout your village."

Thomas, still stunned, managed a weak smile. *At least he calls it* my *village.*

They retraced their steps back through the keep. Within minutes, the crowded and hectic action of the village market swallowed them. Pigs squealed. Donkeys brayed in protest against overloaded carts digging into soft ground. Men shouted. Women shouted. Smells—from the yeasty warmth of baking bread to the pungent filth of emptied chamber pots—swirled around Thomas and the earl.

Despite the push and shove of the crowd, they walked untouched, their rich purple robes as badges of authority. People parted in front of them, as water does for a ship's bow.

"This battle . . ."

"Not yet." The earl held a finger to his lips.

They walked . . . through the market . . . past the church in the center of the village . . . past the white-washed houses.

Finally, at the base of the ramparts farthest from the keep, the earl of York slowed his stride.

"Here," he said. He pointed back at the keep. "Walls tend to have ears."

Thomas hoped his face had found calmness by then. "You are asking me to risk my newly acquired lordship by leaving Magnus immediately for battle?"

"You have no one you can trust here in your absence?"

"Can anyone be trusted with such wealth at stake?" Thomas answered.

The earl shrugged. "It is a risk placed upon all of us. I too am merely responding to the orders of King Edward." Darkness crossed his face. "I pray my request need not become an order. Nor an order resisted. Sieges are dreadful matters."

Unexpectedly, Thomas grinned.

It startled the earl to see that response to his scowl of power, an action which often made grown men flinch.

"That is a well-spoken threat." Thomas continued his grin. "A siege of Magnus, as history has proven, is a dreadful matter for *both* sides."

"True enough," the earl admitted. He thoughtfully steepled his fingers below his chin. "But Magnus cannot fight forever."

Sunlight glinted from a huge gold ring. Thomas froze.

The ring! Its symbol matches those belonging to both prisoners in the dungeon!

The earl did not realize, of course, the ring's effect. He simply kept speaking, as Thomas tried to maintain composure.

"This request for help in battle comes for a twofold reason," the earl said. "First, as you know, earldoms are granted and permitted by order of the king of England, Edward II, may he reign long. The power he has granted me lets me in turn hold sway over the lesser earldoms of the north."

Force yourself to concentrate on conversation.

"Earls may choose to rebel," Thomas said.

Another scowl across the earl of York's wide features. "It has happened. But those earls are fools. The king can suffer no traitors. He brings to bear upon them his entire fighting force. Otherwise, further rebellion by others is encouraged. You have—rightly or wrongly—gained power within Magnus. You will keep it as long as you swear loyalty to me, which means loyalty to the king."

Thomas nodded. That childhood friend and tutor—the one who had given him the plan to conquer Magnus—had long ago anticipated this and explained. *But does loyalty include joining forces with one who carries the strange symbol?*

Once again, Thomas forced himself to stay in the conversation. "Loyalty, of course, dictates tribute be rendered to you."

"Both goods and military support, which I in turn pledge to King Edward," the earl said. "Magnus is yours; that I have already promised. Your price to me is my price to the king. We both must join King Edward in his fight against the Scots."

Thomas knew barely thirty years had passed since King Edward's father had defeated the stubborn, tribal Welsh in their rugged hills to the south and east. The Scots to the north, however, had proven more difficult, a task given to Edward II on his father's death. The Scots had a new leader, Robert Bruce, whose counterattacks grew increasingly devastating to the English.

Reasons for battle were convincing, as the earl quickly outlined. "If we do not stop this march by our northern enemies, England may have a new monarch—one who will choose from among his supporters many new earls to fill the English estates. Including ours."

Thomas nodded to show understanding. Yet behind that nod, a single thought transfixed him. *The symbol. It belongs to an unseen, unknown enemy. One the prisoners in the dungeon refuse to reveal.*

"Couriers have brought news of a gathering of Scots," the earl explained. "Their main army will go southward on a path near the eastern coast. That army is not our responsibility. A smaller army, however, wishes to take the strategic North Sea castle at Scarborough, only thirty miles from here. I have been ordered to stop it at all costs."

Thomas thought quickly, remembering what his childhood tutor had explained of the North York moors and its geography. "Much better to stop them before they reach the cliffs along the sea."

The earl's eyes widened briefly in surprise. "Yes. A battle along the lowland plains north of here."

"However—"

"There can be no 'however,' " the earl interrupted.

Thomas too could match the earl in coldness. "However," he repeated, flint-toned, "you must consider my position. What guarantee do I have this is not merely a ploy to get my army away from this fortress, where we are then vulnerable to *your* attack."

The earl sighed. "I thought you might consider that. As is custom, I will leave in Magnus a son as hostage. I have no need of more wealth, and his life is worth more than twenty earldoms. Keep him here to be killed at the first sign of my treachery."

Thomas closed his eyes briefly in relief. The earl was not lying.

Uncontested by reigning royalty, and given officially by charter, Magnus will now remain mine. If I survive the battle against the Scots. If I survive the mystery behind the symbol on the ring.

Chapter Sixteen

By this time tomorrow, I will be committed to war. Despite a thrill of fear at the thought, Thomas also felt a shiver of joy.

Action. Again.

The earl of York had departed with his twenty men to the main battlecamp—a halfday's ride east—to a valley adjoining the territory of Magnus. Thomas now paced in the privacy of his room on the highest floor of the castle keep.

Action. Again.

Every morning, for seven years as an orphan in a faraway abbey, Thomas had awakened to one thought—*Conquer Magnus.* His childhood nurse and teacher, the only person to show him love, had before her death given him the knowledge to conquer the mighty kingdom. And a reason to do it.

Every night for seven years, the same thought had been his last before entering sleep—*Conquer Magnus.*

Yet, after succeeding in a way that had mesmerized an entire kingdom, Thomas did not feel complete. Was it the need for action, or an emptiness caused by the loss of the two friends who had made it possible for him to become lord?

Action. Again.

And another thrill of fear and shiver of joy. Yet, unlike the battle of Magnus a few months ago, it would be impossible for war against the Scots to succeed without a single loss of life. Would he be numbered among the dead? Or, would he see through the fog that seemed to surround the strange symbol of evil that the earl of York displayed on a ring of gold?

Thomas clenched his jaw with new determination. One answer, he suddenly realized, might wait for him in the dungeon. He reached it a few minutes later.

"Our prisoners fare well?" Thomas asked the soldier guarding the dank passageway to the cells.

"As well as can be expected. Each day, an hour of sunshine. But they are never allowed out together." The guard's voice held faint disapproval at such kind treatment.

A proper ruler would discipline a guard who even in tone questioned orders.

Thomas smiled instead. "Tell me, I pray, who is crueler? The oppressor, or the oppressed people when finally free, who punish the oppressor with equal cruelty?"

The guard blinked, as movement barely seen in the dim light of smoky torches. "The oppressor, my lord. 'Tis plain to see."

"Is it plain? The oppressor, cruel as he may be, cannot feel the effects of his methods. The oppressed, however, know full well the pain of cruelty. To give the same in return, knowing its evilness, strikes me as crueler."

Slow understanding crossed the guard's face. "Your own time in the dungeon . . ."

"Yes," Thomas said. "You will continue, of course, to ensure a fresh bedding of straw each day?"

"Certainly, my lord." This time the guard's voice reflected full approval.

Thomas waited for his eyes to adjust to the hazy torchlight beyond the guard. Then he continued behind the guard through the narrow passageway. He heard the same rustling of bold rats, felt the same feeling of cold air that clung damply. Thomas hated the dungeon, hated the need to use it.

There were four cells, iron-barred doors all facing each other. Two held prisoners. A girl, nearly a woman, in one and a candlemaker who had tried to murder her in the other.

Thomas ignored the instructions directed by his heart and strode past the cell which held the girl.

"I wish to see the candlemaker," he told the guard.

Thomas heard the clanking of keys and the screech of a wooden door protesting on ancient hinges.

"Wait outside," Thomas said as he stepped into the cell. He felt the same despair he did each time he faced a prisoner inside. *So much to know, so little given.*

Geoffrey the candlemaker now sat against the far wall, chained to the rough stone blocks. He was a tiny man, with tiny rounded shoulders and a wrinkled compact face. His cheeks puffed as he grinned mockery at his visitor.

Thomas did not waste a moment in greeting. "Answer truth, and you shall be free to leave this cell."

The mocking grin only became wider.

Thomas began his usual questions. "Why do you and the girl, Isabelle, share the strange symbol?"

The usual reply. Nothing.

"She spoke of a conspiracy before you attempted to stop her through death," Thomas continued. "Who conspires and what hold do they have on you to keep you in silence?"

Only the dripping of water from the ceiling of the cell broke the silence which always followed a question from Thomas.

The test, Thomas told himself. *Now.*

"Your answers no longer matter," Thomas said with a shrug. "Just today, I have pledged loyalty to the earl of York."

Watch carefully.

Geoffrey laughed. The last reaction Thomas had expected. Yet a reaction to give hope. *Either the earl of York did not belong to those who held the symbol, or the candlemaker excelled as an actor.*

"The earl has as little hope as you do, when already the forces of darkness gather to reconquer Magnus," Geoffrey snorted. "You are fools to think Magnus will not return to . . ."

The candlemaker snapped his mouth shut.

"To . . . ?" Thomas pressed. It was as much progress as he had made in the month since capturing Magnus.

That mocking grin shone again in the flickering light. "To those of the symbol," Geoffrey said flatly. "You shall be

long dead by their hands, however, before those behind it
are revealed to the world."

Thomas stood at the rear of the cathedral in the center of
Magnus. Late afternoon sun warmed the stone floor and
etched shadows into the depths of the curved stone ceiling
above.

He waited until the elderly man approached near enough
to hear him speak softly.

"Father, I leave tomorrow. I wish to bid farewell."

That was the joke they shared. Thomas always addressed
Gervaise as a priest, though he was not. Rather, he served
the church as a custodian. Once, during anguish of doubt
and uncertainty shortly after conquering Magnus, Thomas
had finally broken a vow to reject God and the men who
served Him. That morning, he had entered the church and
mistaken Gervaise for a priest.

The questions Thomas had asked that morning, and the
answers which Gervaise had provided in return, proved a
strange but enjoyable beginning for a friendship between a
lord and the man who swept the floors of the cathedral.

"Yes," Gervaise nodded. "You will lead the men of Magnus into battle against the Scots."

"The procession leaves at dawn—" Thomas stopped himself, then blurted, "How is it you knew?"

Gervaise laughed. Deep and rich. His voice matched the
strong lines of humor that marked his old skin. His eyes had
prompted Thomas to immediate trust their first morning.
They held nothing of the greed too often seen in priests
and monks who took advantage of their power among superstitious peasants fearful of God's wrath.

"Thomas, you should not be amazed to discover that men
find it crucial to put their souls in order before any battle. I
have seen a great number enter the church today for con-
fessions. Many whom I haven't seen in months."

Not for the first time did Thomas wonder at the educated
mien of the older man's speech. Why would someone of his
obvious intelligence settle for a lifetime of cleaning duties?

Gervaise saw that doubt flash across Thomas' face and

mistook it for something else.

"Again," he chided with a wry smile, "the disbelief. Simple as these men may be at times, they have the wisdom to acknowledge God. Someday, Thomas, the angels will rejoice to welcome you to the fold."

Thomas summed all their discussions to this point. "I am not convinced there are angels."

The wry smile curved farther upward in response. "Despite the legend you so aptly fulfilled the night you conquered Magnus?"

"Gervaise . . ."

" 'Delivered on the wings of an angel, he shall free us from oppression.' I shall never forget the power of that chant, Thomas. The entire population gathered beneath torchlight by the instructions of a single knight. The appearance of a miracle on white angel wings. Yet you yourself doubt angels?"

"Gervaise!" Thomas tried to inject anger into his voice. And failed.

"Tomorrow you'll be gone, Thomas. Have you any other miracles to astound the Scots?"

"Gervaise! Are you suggesting *I* arranged the miracle of angel wings?"

"Of course. Our Heavenly Father has no need to stoop to such low dramatics."

Thomas sighed. "You would be kind to keep that belief to yourself. As it is, I am able to hold much sway over the rest of Magnus, despite my youth. Leaving this soon would be much less safe for me were it otherwise. I *do* want to be welcomed back as rightful lord."

"Rightful lord? This is indeed news. Has it to do with a certain visitor who entered Magnus earlier in the day?"

"Little escapes you," Thomas commented, then explained much of his conversation with the earl. But Thomas did not mention the symbol, or his fear of it. Some secrets could not be shared.

Gervaise listened carefully. He ached to believe that Thomas was all that he appeared to be, not a tool of the enemy. When Thomas finished, Gervaise spoke with simple grace. "And your prisoners, my friend? Any progress there? Has Geoffrey revealed who instructed him to attempt to murder the former lord's daughter?"

Thomas shook his head. He could not escape the ache in being reminded of the other prisoner. One who had loved, then betrayed him, almost at the cost of his life.

"Time will answer all," Gervaise said. "It was kind of you to visit during a day which demands many preparations."

"I could not have considered otherwise," Thomas replied. The truth in his words surprised him.

Gervaise walked with Thomas to the cathedral doors. "I shall continue praying for you, Thomas. The angels *will* rejoice when you accept His most holy presence in your life."

Thomas almost nodded. Yet how could he believe what he did not see?

Chapter Seventeen

Thomas faced his first challenge before the entire army had assembled in the valley. A council of war had been called. Gathered in a small circle beneath the shade of a towering oak were fourteen of the most powerful earls and barons in the north. Among them, Thomas.

"David, will you permit such a puppy to remain with us in council?" The questioner, a fat middle-aged man whose chubby fingers were studded with massive gold rings, did not hide his contempt and surprise at seeing Thomas.

"Aye, Frederick, the puppy remains," replied the earl of York.

"But these are matters of war!" exploded the fat man, spraying spittle on those nearest him.

Some nodded agreement. Others waited for David, the earl of York, to respond again. All stared at Thomas.

Around these men of power, the army swelled as soldiers marched in from all directions.

Huge war-horses clothed in fighting colors stood patiently, attended by anxious squires. Knights, dressed only in tights and light chain mail, rested in the shade; mules and servants would carry the heavy armor and swords and lances to the battle site.

The bulk of the army, however, did not consist of expensive war-horses and pampered, well-trained knights. Instead, it was formed by the men of farms and villages who owed the knights and lords and earls and barons a set number of days of military service each year.

Many were poorly equipped and carried only crude leather shields and sturdy, sharpened wooden poles called pikes. These men would form stationary front lines of battle—almost like temporary palisades—while the faster moving knights would charge ahead or retreat on their war-horses, according to the earl's command.

More ably equipped than pikesmen were the yeomen, armed with longbows and capable of raining arrows far beyond the opposing front lines with devastating effect. Most lords set aside a practice range within castle walls and demanded regular archery practice from all men over the age of sixteen.

Others carried crossbows, which fired short bolts with enough fury to pierce even a knight's armor. Crossbows were expensive, however, and difficult to reload. Even strong men were forced to brace the bow with their feet and draw the string back with the full strength of both arms. The less expensive longbows, on the other hand, could be reloaded almost instantly; some men could fire two arrows per second. With the much longer arrow length, longbows were also more accurate than a crossbow.

Thomas' own army held six fully equipped knights—a reflection of the moderate wealth of Magnus, since many earls with more property could support only two or three knights. Each war-horse alone was worth five years' wages; each set of armor, two years' wages; and each knight, nearly the ransom worth of a king. As superb fighting machines, knights were held loyal by the reward of estates—many of the outlying valleys of Magnus had been deeded for that purpose.

Thomas' army also held ten men with crossbows, and another forty with longbows. His remaining men, all villagers and farmers with wives and large families, were pikesmen who already sweated with fear, even this far from the lowland plains of future battle.

Most of the earls and barons around Thomas beneath the oak tree had contributed larger armies. The sum of all their armies made for the noise and confusion of thousands of fighting men, plus an almost matching number of cooks and servants and hangers-on. With banners and flags of fighting colors waving like a field of flowers, and with the constant movement of people, the gathering around this council of war gave the center of the valley a carnival-like atmosphere.

Part of Thomas' mind noted the festive hum beyond the circle of barons, but another part of his thoughts held sadness. *Before the army's return, many men will die, to leave behind widows or orphans.*

The fat man yelled to repeat his challenge. "These are matters of war!"

Thomas surveyed the other men in the circle. His only friend—if someone carrying the symbol could be a friend— might be David, the earl of York.

Show no fear. Lose respect here and my own men will never follow me. Lose my men, and I lose control of Magnus.

Thomas fought the impulse to lick his suddenly dry lips. If the earl of York did not vouch for him, he would be forced to prove himself immediately. A fight perhaps. These were solid men, who had scrabbled for power on the strength of steel nerves and iron willpower. Would Robert of Uleran's training be enough to overcome?

The earl of York delayed the answer to that question by replying with the quietness of authority. "Frederick, this 'puppy' you so casually address had the intelligence to conquer alone the ultimate fortress, Magnus itself. Could *you* have done the same, even with an army of a thousand?"

The earl of York laughed to break the discomfort of his rebuke. "Besides, Frederick, this 'puppy' is taller than you already. When he fills out to match the size of his hands, he'll be a terrible enemy. Treat him well while you can."

The others joined in the laughter.

Thomas realized that if this meeting were to end now, he would simply be regarded as a special pet, favored by the earl of York. Yet could he risk the earl's anger?

The laughter continued.

"I need no special treatment," Thomas suddenly declared, then felt the thud of his heart in the immediate silence.

Is it too early to reveal the weapons my men have practiced in secrecy?

Thomas hoped the narrowing of the earl of York's eyes meant curiosity, not anger at the insult of publicly casting aside his approval.

I've gone too far to turn back.

"Tomorrow, when we rest at midday," Thomas said, "I propose a contest."

It took the remainder of the day for all the stragglers to gather. By dusk, the valley was full of men and horses.

As Thomas stood in the growing dusk and watched the countless campfires begin to tremble their light, he felt a hand on his shoulder.

"Friend or foe?" Thomas asked with a laugh.

The earl of York's voice sounded from behind him. "Friend. Most assuredly a friend. And one surprised to hear humor from so serious a man."

"All you and I have discussed is war. It's hard to find humor in the killing of men."

"Spoken well, Thomas," the earl said. "And I'm here to offer apology. You were indeed right to earlier cast aside my vouch for you. I may think of you as an equal, but others choose only to believe what their eyes see, not what is beyond, such as a man's courage or intelligence."

Thomas barely heard the rest of the earl's encouraging words.

"Others choose only to believe what their eyes will see." Must God follow me even among the camps of war?

Dawn broke clear and bright. Despite the cold which resulted from a cloudless night, few complained. Rain would churn into a sucking mud beneath the thousands of feet of an army this size. White mist, common to the moors, would disorient stragglers within minutes. Cold and clear nights were much better for warfare.

Before the sun grew hot, all tents had been dismantled and packed. Then, with much confusion and shouting, the earls and barons directed their men so that the entire army formed an uneven column nearly half a mile in breadth, and so long that the front banners began forward motion nearly twenty minutes before those in the rear.

The army marched only three miles before an eerie noise began. To Thomas, it sounded like the faraway buzzing of bees—once he actually lifted his head to search for the cloud of insects. The whispering became a hum, and the hum gradually became a babble. The noise came from the men and women of the army itself.

Still the army moved its slow pace forward. Finally the babble broke into the pieces of excited conversation.

"Demons upon us!"

"We are fated to doom!"

"Pray the Lord takes mercy upon us!"

Then, like the eye of an ominous storm, the voices immediately in front died. That sudden calmness chilled Thomas more than the most agitated words.

Within sixty more paces, he understood the horrified silence. Thomas felt rooted at the sight, and only the pressure of movement behind him kept him in motion.

To the side of the column stood a small clearing. Facing the column, as if ready to charge, and stuck solidly on iron bars imbedded into the ground, were the massive heads of two white bulls.

Blood had pooled beneath the heads, and swarming flies gorged on the thick brown-red liquid beneath the open and sightless eyes of each head.

The remains of a huge fire scarred the grass between the heads. The charred hooves carefully arranged outward in a circle left little doubt that the bodies of the animals had been burned.

Thomas looked upward. Again a chill of the unnatural nearly froze his steps. At first, it appeared as heavy ribbons hanging from the branches of a nearby tree. Then, as he focused closer, he fought the urge to retch. The entrails of the bulls swayed lightly in the wind.

Carved clearly into the trunk of the tree was the strange symbol of conspiracy, the one which matched the ring of the earl of York.

Thomas closed his eyes in cold fear. Words spat with hatred by Geoffrey echoed through his head. *"Already the*

forces of darkness gather to reconquer Magnus."
Thomas shivered again beneath the hot blue sky.

"This had better be good," growled Frederick. His jowls wobbled with each word. "Anything to make these peasants forget this morning's unholy remains of two white bulls."

White bulls, rare and valuable beyond compare, suggested a special power that appealed to even the least superstitious peasants. What spirits might be invoked with such a carefully arranged slaughter of the animals?

It was a question asked again and again throughout the morning. Now, with the army at midday rest, nothing else would be discussed.

Thomas felt the pressure as he faced the barons and earls around him. "If each of you would please summon your strongest and best—"

"Swordsmen?" Frederick sneered. "I'll offer to fight you myself."

"Yeomen," Thomas stated.

"Bah. An archery contest. Where's the blood in that?"

"Precisely," Thomas said. He wondered briefly how the fat man had ever become an earl. Even a child had a better understanding of war. "How does it serve our purpose to draw blood among ourselves when the enemy waits to do the same?"

The reply drew scattered laughs. Someone clapped Thomas on the back. "Well spoken, puppy!"

The fat man would not be deterred. "What might a few arrows prove? Everyone knows battles are won in the glory of the charge, in the nobility of holding the front line against a countercharge. Man against man. Beast against beast. Bravery against bravery until the enemy flees."

Thomas noticed stirrings of agreement from the other earls and barons. He *did* feel like a puppy among starving dogs. Yet he welcomed the chance to argue a method of warfare which had served generals two oceans away, nearly two thousand years earlier.

"Man against man? Beast against beast?" Thomas countered, as he thought of the books of knowledge which had won him Magnus. "Lives do not matter?"

"*We* command from safety," Frederick said with smugness. "Our lives matter and are well protected. It has always been done in this manner."

Thomas drew a breath. Was it his imagination, or was the earl of York enjoying this argument? It was a thought which gave him new determination.

"There are better methods," Thomas said quickly. He removed all emotion from his voice and the flattening of his words drew total attention.

"The bulk of this army consists of poorly trained farmers and villagers. None with armor. How they must fear the battle!"

"The fear makes them fight harder!" Frederick snorted.

"Knowing they are to be sacrificed like sheep?"

"I repeat," Frederick said, "it has always been done in this manner."

"Listen," Thomas said, now with urgency. He knew as he spoke that some of the earls were considering his words carefully. If he could present his argument clearly . . .

"If these men knew you sought to win battles *and* preserve their lives, loyalty and love would make them far better soldiers than fear of death."

"But—"

Thomas would breach no interruption. "Furthermore, man against man, beast against beast, dictates that the largest and strongest army will win."

"Of course. Any simpleton knows that," Frederick said, his voice laced with scorn.

"And should we find ourselves the lesser army of the two?"

Silence.

Thomas quoted from a passage of one of his secret books. " 'The art of using troops is this. When ten to the enemy's one, surround him; when five times his strength, attack him; if double his strength, divide him; if equally matched, you may engage him; if weaker in numbers, be capable of withdrawing; and if in all respects unequal, be capable of eluding him.' "

The earl of York smiled openly at the slack-jawed response to the quote.

Thomas did not notice. Instead, he searched his memory for the final quote. " 'All war is deception. What is of supreme importance in war is to attack the enemy's strategy. And the supreme art of war is to subdue the enemy without fighting.' "

More silence.

The fat one recovered first. "Bah. Words. Simply words. What have they to do with an archery contest?"

"Let me demonstrate," Thomas said, with much more confidence than he felt. "Gather, each of you, your best archer."

The opposing fourteen bowmen lined up first. Each had been chosen for height and strength. Longer arms drew a bowstring back farther, which meant more distance. Stronger arms were steadier, which meant better accuracy.

Seven targets were set two hundred yards away. People packed both sides of the field, so that the space to the targets appeared as a wide alley of untrampled grass.

Without fanfare, the first seven of the selected archers fired. Five of the seven arrows pierced completely the leather shields set up as targets. One arrow hit the target but bounced off—yet even a good enough feat to be acknowledged with brief applause. The other arrow flew barely wide, and quivered to a rest in the ground behind the targets.

The results of such fine archery drew gasps, even from a crowd experienced in warfare.

The next seven archers accomplished almost the same. Five more arrows pierced the targets. The other two flew high and beyond. More gasps.

Then Thomas and his men stepped to the firing line.

In direct contrast, Thomas had chosen small men with shorter arms. That the contrast was obvious became apparent by murmurs swelling from the crowd.

Thomas stood at the line with his twelve men. He spoke in low tones heard only to them. "You have practiced much. Yet I would prefer that we attempt nothing which alarms you."

He paused and studied them. Each returned his look.

"You enjoy this?" Thomas asked.

They nodded. "We know these weapons well," one said. "Such a demonstration will set men on their ears."

Thomas grinned in relief. "Then I propose this. We will request that the targets be moved back until the first of you says no farther. Thus, none of you will fear the range."

More smile and nods.

Thomas then turned and shouted down the field. "More distance!"

He noted with satisfaction the renewed murmuring from the crowd. The men at the targets stopped ten steps back and began to position them in place.

"Farther!" Thomas commanded.

Louder murmurs. The best archers in an army of thousands had already shot at maximum range!

"Farther!" Thomas shouted, when the men with targets paused. Five steps, ten steps, twenty steps. Finally, one of the archers whispered the range was enough. By then, the targets were nearly a quarter of the distance farther then they had been set originally.

The crowd knew such range was impossible. Expectant silence replaced disbelieving murmurs.

Thomas made no person wait. He dropped his hand, and within seconds a flurry of arrows hissed toward the leather shields. Few spectators were able to turn their heads quickly enough to follow the arrows.

Eleven arrows thudded solidly home. One drove through the shield completely, spraying stripped feathers in all directions. The final two arrows overshot the targets and landed twenty yards farther down.

Thomas wanted to jump with joy and amazement, as were many in the crowd. Instead, he turned calmly to his archers and raised his voice to be heard. He smiled. "Survey the crowd and remember this for your grandchildren. It's not often in a lifetime so few are able to set so many on their ears."

The northward march began again. Memory of the slaughter of two white bulls faded quickly, as all tongues spoke only of the archery contest. But Thomas and his men had little time to enjoy their sudden fame. Barely an hour later, the column of people slowed, then stopped.

Low grumbling rose. Some strained to see ahead, hoping to find reason for the delay. Those older and wiser flopped themselves into the shade beneath trees and sought sleep.

Thomas, on horseback near his men, saw the runner approaching from a distance ahead. As the man neared, Thomas saw his eyes rolling white with exhaustion.

"Sire!" he stumbled and panted. "The earl of York wishes you to join him at the front!"

"Do you need to reach more commanders down the line?" Thomas asked.

The man heaved for breath and could only nod.

Thomas nodded at a boy beside him. "Take this man's message," he instructed. "Please relay it to the others and give him rest."

With that, Thomas wheeled his horse forward and cantered alongside the column. Small spurts of dust kicked from the horse's hooves; the sheer number of people, horses, and mules passing through the moors had already worn the grass to its roots.

Thomas spotted the earl of York's banners at the front of the army column quickly enough. About half of the other earls were gathered around. Their horses stood nearby, heads bent to graze on the grass yet untrampled by the army.

Thomas swung down from his horse and strode to join them. For the second time that day, a chill prickled his scalp. Three men stood in front of the earls. They only wore torn and filthy pants. No shoes, no shirt or cloak. Each of the three was gray with fear, and unable to stand without help.

The chill that shook Thomas, however, did not result from their obvious fear or weakness. Instead, he could not take his eyes from the circular welts on the flesh of their chests.

"They've been branded!" Thomas blurted.

"Aye, Thomas. Our scouts found them bound to these trees." The earl of York nodded in the direction of nearby oaks.

Thomas stared with horror at the three men. The brand marks nearly spanned the width of each chest. The burned flesh stood raised with an angry, dark puffiness.

Thomas sucked in a breath. *Each brand shows the strange symbol.*

"Who . . . who . . ."

"Who did this?" The earl of York finished for Thomas.

Thomas nodded. He fought the urge to glance at the earl's hand to confirm what he didn't want to believe. *The symbol which matched the earl's ring. The symbol burned into the grass between two white bulls' heads. The symbol of conspiracy.*

"It is impossible to tell," the earl of York answered his own question. "Impossible to understand why they have been left for us to find."

"Impossible?" Thomas could barely concentrate. *Already the forces of darkness gather. . . .*

"Yes. Impossible. Their tongues have been removed." The earl shook his head sadly. "Poor men. And of course they cannot write. We shall feed them, rest them, and let them return to their homes."

Can the earl of York be this fine an actor, to stand in front of these tortured men and pretend he had no part of the symbol? Or is his ring simply a bizarre coincidence?

The earl wiped his face clean of sweat.

His ring. Gone.

A tiny band of white marked where he had worn it. Thomas shook off the feeling of being utterly alone.

Chapter Eighteen

Frederick—Frederick the Fat as Thomas silently called him—proved to be a gracious loser.

"This puppy has the teeth of a dragon," he toasted at council of war that evening.

"Hear, hear," the others responded.

Again, the light of countless campfires spread like flashing diamonds through the valley. Still four days away from the lowland plains and any chance of battle, the army had not dug in behind palisades, and tents were still pitched far enough apart so that neighbors did not have to stumble over each other as they searched for firewood or water.

Thomas accepted the compliment with equal graciousness. "As you rightly guessed," he said to Frederick, "the power lies within the bows, not the archers."

"Still," Frederick countered, "and I can say it because he is not here with us, the earl of York has again proven his wisdom. I erred to judge you on size or age."

Thomas shrugged. Not necessarily from modesty, but rather because the idea for the ingenious modification of the bows had simply been taken straight from one of his ancient books.

As a result, running the length of the inside of each bow, Thomas had added a wide strip of thin bronze, giving more strength than the firmest wood. His biggest difficulty had been finding a drawstring which would not snap under the strain of such a powerful bow.

"But such archery will prove little in this battle." An earl sitting beside Frederick interrupted Thomas in his thoughts. "You have only twenty bows with such a capacity for distance."

Thomas laughed. "Do the Scots know that? They will understand only that arrows are suddenly reaching them from an unheard-of distance, far beyond their own range. Even if they know our shortage of these bows, each man on the opposing line still realizes it only takes one arrow to pierce his heart. Surely there is benefit in that."

"Yes." Another earl sipped his broth, then continued in support of Thomas. "You earlier spoke of battle tactics which interest me keenly. I see clearly that even a few of these bows can affect warfare."

The earl of York strode to the campfire as that statement finished. All rose in respect.

"You do well, Sir Steven, to make mention of the tactics of war," the earl of York said grimly in response. "I have just received word from our scouts. It isn't enough to be plagued by the evils of slain white bulls and tongueless men. The Scots' army numbers over four thousand strong."

Silence deepened as each man realized the implications of that news. They numbered barely three thousand. Man against man. Beast against beast. And outnumbered by a thousand. They would be fortunate to survive.

As was his due, the earl of York spoke first to break the silence. "Perhaps our warrior, Thomas of Magnus, has a suggestion."

The implied honor nearly staggered Thomas. To receive a request for council among these men. . . . Yet was the earl of York a friend or foe? And if a foe, why the honor?

"Thank you, sire," Thomas replied, more to gain time and calmness than from gratitude. To throw away this chance . . .

Thomas thought hard. *These men understand force and force alone. This much I have learned.*

Another thought flashed through his mind, a story of war told him by his long dead friend and nurse, a story from one of the books of ancient knowledge.

He hid a grin in the darkness. Each man at the campfire waited in silence, each pair of eyes studied him. Finally, Thomas spoke.

"We can defeat the Scots," he said. "First, we must convince them we are cowards."

Sleep came upon Thomas quickly that night.

He dreamt of Sarah, who had taught him through his childhood, had given him love while he suffered as an orphan, and had prepared him for an earldom before she died of the pox.

He dreamt of Katherine, dirty bandages around the horribly scarred flesh of her face, and how she, at the end, had made it possible for him to conquer Magnus.

It was no surprise, then, that Thomas imagined he was not alone in the tent. And slowly, he woke to perfume and the softness of hair falling across his face.

He drew breath to challenge the intruder, but a light finger across his lips and a gentle shushing stopped him from speaking.

"Dress quickly, Thomas. Follow without protest," the voice then whispered. Thomas saw only the darkness of silhouette in the dimness of the tent.

"Fear not," the voice continued. "An old man wishes to see you. He asks if you remember the gallows."

Old man! Gallows! In a rush of memory as bright as daylight, Thomas felt himself at the gallows. The knight who might win Magnus for him about to be hung, and Thomas in front, through disguise and trickery attempting a rescue. Then the arrival of an old man, one who knew it was Thomas behind the disguise and knew of his quest, one who commanded the sun into darkness, one who had never appeared again.

"As you wish," Thomas whispered in return, with as much dignity as he could muster despite the sudden trembling in his stomach. No mystery—not even the evil terror of the strange symbol—was more important to him than discovering the old man's identity.

The silhouette backed away slowly, beckoning Thomas with a single crooked finger. He rose quickly, wrapped his cloak around him, and shuffled into his shoes.

How did she avoid the sentries outside my tent?

Thomas pushed aside the tent flap and followed. Her perfume hung heavy in the night air.

Moonlight showed that both sentries sat crookedly

against the base of a nearby tree. *Asleep!* It was within his rights as an earl to have them executed.

"Forgive them," the voice whispered, as if reading his mind. "Their suppers contained potions of drowsiness."

He strained to see the face of the silhouette in the light of the large pale moon. In response, she pulled the flaps of her hood across her face. All he saw was a tall and slender figure leading him along a trail which avoided all tents and campsites.

Ghost-white mist hung heavy among the solitary trees of the moor valley.

It felt like a dream to Thomas, but he did not fear to follow. Only one person had knowledge of what had transpired in front of the gallows—the old man himself. Only he could have sent the silhouette to his tent.

At the farthest edge of the camp, she stopped to turn and wait.

When Thomas arrived, she took his right hand and clasped it with her left.

"Who are you?" Thomas asked. "Show me your face."

"Hush, Thomas," she whispered.

"You know my name. You know my face. Yet you hide from me."

"Hush," she repeated.

"No," he said with determination. "Not a step farther will I take. The old man wishes to see me badly enough to drug my sentries. He will be angry if you do not succeed in your mission."

She did not answer. Instead, she lifted her free hand slowly, pulled the hood from her face, and shook her hair loose to her shoulders.

Nothing in his life had prepared him for that moment.

The sudden ache of joy to see her face hit him like a blow. For a timeless moment, it took from him all breath.

It was not her beauty which brought him that joy, even though the curved shadows of her face would be forever seared in his mind. No. Thomas knew he had learned not to trust appearances, that beauty indeed consisted of heart joining heart, not eyes to eyes. Isabelle, now in the dungeon, had used her exquisite features to deceive, while gentle Katherine—horribly burned and masked by bandages—had proven the true worth of friendship.

Thomas struggled for composure. What then drew him? Why did it seem as if he had been long pledged for this very moment?

She stared back, as if knowing completely how he felt, yet fearless of the voltage between them. Then she smiled and pulled the hood across her face once again.

Thomas bit his lip to keep inside a cry of emotion he could barely comprehend. Isabelle's betrayal at Magnus now seemed a childish pain. He drew dignity around him like a shield.

"The old man wishes to see me," he finally answered.

She led him by the hand and picked faultless footsteps through the valley stream.

They walked—it could have only been a heartbeat, he felt so distant from the movement of time—until they reached a hill which rose steeply into the black of the night.

An owl called.

She turned to the sound and walked directly into the side of the hill. As if parting the solid rock by magic, she slipped sideways into an invisible cleft between monstrous boulders. Thomas followed.

They stood completely surrounded by granite walls of a cave long hollowed smooth by eons of rain water. The air seemed to press down upon him, and away from the light of the moon, Thomas saw only velvet black.

He heard the returning call of an owl, and before he could react, he saw a small spark. His eyes adjusted to see a man holding the small light of a torch which grew as the pitch caught fire.

Light gradually licked upward around them to reveal a bent old man wrapped in a shawl. Beyond deep wrinkles, Thomas could distinguish no features; the shadows leapt and danced eerie circles from beneath his chin.

"Greetings, Thomas of Magnus." The voice was a slow whisper.

"Who are you?"

"Such impatience. One who is lord of Magnus would do well to temper his words among strangers."

"I cannot apologize," Thomas said. "Each day I am haunted by memory of you. Impossible that you should know my quest at the hanging. Impossible that the sun should fail that morning at your command."

The old man shrugged and continued in the same strained whisper. "*Impossible* is often merely a perception. Surely by now you have been able to ascertain that the darkness was no sorcery, but merely a trick of astronomy as the moon moves past the sun. Your books would inform a careful reader that such eclipses may be predicted."

"You know of my books!"

That mystery gripped Thomas so tightly he could almost forget the presence of the other in the cave.

The old man ignored the urgency in Thomas' words. "My message is the same as before. You must bring the winds of light into this age, and resist the forces of darkness poised to take from you the kingdom of Magnus. Yet what assistance I may offer is little. The decisions to be made are yours."

Thomas clenched his fists and exhaled a frustrated blast of air. "You talk in circles. Tell me who you are. Tell me clearly what you want of me. And tell me the secret of Magnus."

Again, Thomas' words were ignored.

"Druids, Thomas. Beware those barbarians from the isle. They will attempt to conquer you through force. Or through bribery."

"If I do not go insane because of your games," Thomas said through gritted teeth, "it will be a miracle. Tell me how you knew of my quest that day at the hanging. Tell me how you know of the books. Tell me how you know of the barbarians."

"To tell you is to risk all."

Thomas pounded his thigh in anger. "I do not even know what is at risk! You set upon me a task unexplained and give me no reason to fulfill it! I must have knowledge!"

Even in his frustration, Thomas sensed sadness from the old man.

"The knowledge you already have is worth the world, Thomas. That is all I can say."

"No," Thomas pleaded. *The old man must know more.* "Who belongs to the strange symbol of conspiracy? Is the earl of York friend or enemy?"

The old man shook his head. "Thomas, very soon you will be offered a prize which seems far greater than the kingdom of Magnus."

The torch flared once before dying, and Thomas read deep concern in the old man's eyes.

From the sudden darkness came his final whispered words, "It is worth your soul to refuse."

Chapter Nineteen

In the daylight, Thomas took advantage of the frenzied preparations to break camp. He slipped away and scrambled along the valley stream, searching for the cleft in the rock that had led him to the midnight meeting.

He had no success. The daylight disoriented him and nothing seemed familiar. He walked back, wondering if the night before had been a dream, and hoping it had not. He only had to close his eyes to remember her face and her gently whispered farewell.

Thomas was given little time to ponder the event. Immediately upon his return, a servant led his horse to him. Thomas mounted, trotting alongside his army as the massed march moved forward, creaky and bulky, but now with a sense of urgency. The enemy waited three days ahead.

Repeatedly during the day, the earl of York brought his horse alongside Thomas and relayed new battle information, or confirmed old. It was a clear sign to the other earls that Thomas was fully part of the council of war. Yet Thomas wondered, *Does the earl of York have other reasons for pretending friendliness?*

Thomas also noticed how little laughter and singing there was in the marching column. No one had forgotten the grisly sights of the previous day.

"Druids," the old man had said. *"Beware those barbarians from the isle."*

Were they the ones of the strange symbol and the terrifying acts of brutality?

As Thomas swayed to the gentle walk of his horse, he decided there was a way to find out, even if the old man of mystery never appeared again.

First, however, there was the formal council of war, as camp was made that evening. The earl of York wasted no time once all were gathered. "After tonight, there are only two nights before battle. You have reduced by a third the fires in your camps?" he asked.

In turn, each earl nodded, including Thomas.

"Good, good," the earl of York said. "Already their spies are in the hills. Observing. Waiting."

"You know this to be true?" Frederick asked with slight surprise.

The earl of York snorted. "Our own spies have been reporting for days now. Only a fool would expect the enemy not to do the same."

"Their fires," Thomas said. "What word?"

"The valleys they choose for camp are filled as if by daylight."

Silence, as each contemplated the odds of death against such an army.

The earl of York did not permit the mood to lengthen. He continued his questions in the tone which made them sound like orders. "All of you have brave volunteers ready to desert our army?"

Again, each nodded.

"Tomorrow," the earl of York said, "is the day. Let half of them melt away into the forest. The rest on the following day."

He paused. "Slumber in peace, gentlemen. Dream only of victory."

While all began to leave, the earl moved forward and discreetly tugged on Thomas' sleeve.

"If this battle plan works, friend, your reward will be countless. If not . . ." The earl smiled the smile of a fighter who has won and lost many times. ". . . If not, it shall be man against man, beast against beast. What say you to that?"

"Then I shall fight bravely, milord."

"No, Thomas. What say you to a reward? Let us prepare ourselves for the best. Ask now. What is your wish?"

Thomas thought of the ring. The symbol. And Druids.

Is the earl of York part of the conspiracy to reconquer Magnus? If so, will he still honor a promise made?

"Reward?" Thomas repeated quietly. "I would wish simply that you spoke truth to a simple question."

The earl's jaw dropped. He recovered quickly. "You have my word of honor." Then he dryly added, "My friend, in fairy tales most men ask for the daughter's hand."

Thomas snorted at that unexpected reply. During that moment, he felt at ease with the older man. "I would fear, milord, that the daughter might resemble too closely her father."

The earl slapped his belly and roared laughter. "Thomas!" he cried. "You are a man among men. I see a destiny for the likes of you."

Surely, Thomas told himself, *this man cannot be one of them.*

She was the oldest woman he could find during a hurried search of the other campsites as the last of dusk quickly settled.

Even in the lowered light, Thomas saw the grease that caked deep wrinkles on her hands and fingers. A cook, no doubt. Part of the army which serves an army.

She sat, leaning her back against a stone which jutted from the flattened grass. Her shabby gray cloak did not have a hood, and her hair had thinned enough so that her scalp stretched shiny and tight in the firelight; the flesh on her face hung in wattles from her cheeks and jaw.

"Ho! Ho!" she cackled, as Thomas stopped in front of her. "Have all the young women spurned your company? Tsk, tsk. And such a handsome devil you are."

She took a gulp from a leather bag. "Come closer, dearie. Share my wine!"

Thomas moved closer, but shook his head as she offered the wine. She smelled of many days of squatting in front of a cookfire, and of many weeks without bathing.

She snatched the wine back and gulped again, then cocked her head. "You'd be Thomas of Magnus. The young warrior. I remember from the archery contest." Another gulp. "I'll not rise to bow. At my age, there is little to fear. Not even the displeasure of an earl." She finished her sentence with a coughing wheeze.

The old, instinct had told Thomas, *will know the tales you need, the tales you did not hear the night before.*

So he asked. "Druids. Would you fear Druids?"

The old crone clutched her wine bag, then took a slower swallow and gazed thoughtfully at Thomas. From deep within her face, black eyes glinted traces of the nearby campfire.

"Druids? That is a name to be spoken only with great care. Where would someone so young get a name so ancient and so forgotten?"

"The burnings of two white bulls," Thomas guessed. He was still working on instinct, and the old man in the cave had not connected Druids with those sights. "Three men now tongueless and branded."

"Nay, lad. That's not how you conjured the dreaded name. A host of others in this army have seen the same. Not once have I heard the name of those evil sorcerers cross any lips."

Evil sorcerers!

"So," she continued, "it is not from their rituals you offer that name, although none have guessed so true. Confess, boy. How is it you know what no others perceive?"

He was right. Druids were behind the symbol. That meant then that Druids were behind the conspiracy to take Magnus. What might this old, old woman know of their tales?

Thomas did not flinch at her stare. *Keep her speaking,* he commanded himself. He tried to bluff. "Perhaps one merely has knowledge of their usual activities."

The crone revealed her gums in a wide smile. "But, of course, you're from Magnus."

Thomas froze and every nerve ending tingled. *Magnus . . . Druids. As if it were natural that there was a connection between the two.*

"What," he asked through a tightened jaw, "would such imply?"

"Hah! You do know less than you pretend!" The crone patted the ground beside her. "Come. Sit. Listen to what my own grandmother once told me."

Slowly Thomas moved beside her. A bony hand clutched his knee.

"There have been over a hundred winters since she was a young girl," the old crone said of her grandmother. "When she told me these tales, she had become as old as I am now. Generations have passed since her youth then and my old age now. In that time, common knowledge of those ancient sorcerers has disappeared. Even in my grandmother's youth, Druids were rarely spoken of. And now . . ."

The crone shrugged. ". . . now *you* come with questions." The bony hand squeezed and she asked abruptly, "Do you seek their black magic?"

"It is the farthest thing from my desires."

"I hear truth in your words, boy. Let me then continue."

Thomas waited. So close to answers, it did not matter how bad she smelled. His heart thudded, and for a moment he wondered if she heard it.

Then she began again. Her breath washed over Thomas, hot and oddly sweet from wine. *"Druid* means 'Finder of the Oak Tree.' It is where they gather, deep in the forests to begin their rituals. I was told that their circle of high priest and sorcery began long ago in the mists of time, on the isle of the Celts. They study philosophy, astronomy, and the lore of the gods."

Astronomy! The old man in the cave had known enough astronomy to predict the eclipse of the sun!

Thomas stood and paced, then realized her voice had stopped.

"I'm sorry," he said. "Please, please continue."

"They also offer human sacrifices for the sick or for those in danger of death in battle." The crone crossed herself and swallowed more wine in the same motion. "I remember the fear in my grandmother's eyes as she told me. And the legends still persist. Whispers among the very old. It is said that when the Romans overran our island—before the time of the Saxons and before the time of the Viking raiders—

they forced the Druids to accept Christianity. But that was merely appearance. Through the hundreds of years, the circle of high priests held on to their knowledge of the evil ways. Once openly powerful, they now remain hidden."

Thomas could not contain himself longer. "Magnus!" he said. "You spoke of Magnus."

Her hand clutched his knee one final time, then relaxed. From her came a soft laugh. "Bring me a feast tomorrow. Rich meat. Cheese. Buttered bread. And much wine. That is my price for the telling of ancient tales."

After a cackle of glee, she dropped her head to her chest and soon began to snore.

Thomas washed back the last of his mutton stew with ale as he finished supper. Tomorrow, the army would travel until late afternoon, camp behind hastily constructed palisades, and prepare for battle the following day.

Much was on his mind. The wonderful ache which he could not ignore because of someone who had led him to the old man. The mystery of the old man himself. What he might learn from the old woman. And how the battle against the Scots would end.

His men respected his quiet mood and gave him peace. They stood or sat in small groups around the fire, trading oft-repeated stories which were not as loud as the night before. The older men especially—those who had seen friends die in other battles—said little this close to the lowland plains north of the moors.

"Your provisions, sir," a dirt-streaked servant girl said, with her head down.

"Thank you," Thomas said. He accepted the cloth bag, and noted with satisfaction its heavy weight. The old crone would be well paid for her tales. He walked through the graying light to seek her.

Thomas smiled grimly to see that there were fewer campfires again than the night before. The earl of York's orders had been obeyed with precision.

The area of the camp had been reduced too, and it took little time for Thomas to recognize the banners of the earl whose army held a grumpy, dirty crone with tales that stretched back six generations.

Thomas strode around the fires once, then twice. No one called out to him; his colors clearly marked him as an earl, and avoiding the eye of those in power usually resulted in less work.

Finally, he was forced to attract the attention of a man carrying buckets of water hanging from each end of a pole balanced across his shoulders.

"Tell me, please," Thomas said. "Where rests the old cook?"

"A day's travel behind us, milord." The man grimaced. "Just more duty for some of us now."

Thomas squinted to read the man's face. "She deserted camp?"

"No, milord. She was found dead this morning." The man crossed himself quickly. "Rest her soul."

"That cannot be!"

The man shrugged, a motion that shook both buckets of water. "Too much wine and too much age. It came as no surprise."

Thomas clamped his mouth shut, then nodded thanks to the man.

What had the crone said? *"Druids. That is a name to be spoken only with great care."*

Surely her death was coincidence. Too much wine and too much age and the rigors of daily march. Of course.

Still, Thomas glanced around him often at the deepening shadows as he hurried to his tent and the welcome sentries.

Chapter Twenty

Late afternoon the next day, Thomas joined the earl of York at the head of the army column.

Astride their horses, they overlooked yet another moor valley.

"Thus far, our calculations have served us well," the earl of York said. "Scouts report the Scottish army is barely a half day away. And beyond here, the moors end at the plains."

Thomas nodded and shaded his eyes with one hand. Sunlight poured over the western hills. "This *does* appear to be the perfect place to ambush an army," he said. "High sloping hills—impossible to climb under enemy fire. Narrow entrances at both ends—easy to guard against escape. Your scouts excelled in their choice."

For a moment, both men enjoyed the breeze sweeping toward them from the mouth of the valley.

"Well, then. We have made our choice." The earl of York sighed. "Any army trapped within it is sure to be slaughtered."

He turned and called to the men behind him.

"Send a runner back with directions. We shall camp ahead." He lifted a hand to point. "There. In the center of the valley."

Then quietly, he spoke again to Thomas. "Let us pray the valley does not earn a new name in our honor," the earl of York said with a shudder. "The Valley of Death."

Thomas shuddered with him, but for a different reason. Even after several days of travel, it still seemed too bright, the pale band of skin on his finger where the earl had so recently worn a ring.

A deep drumroll of thousands of hooves shook the earth

and dawn broke with the thunder of impending war.

The screams of trumpets ordered the direction of the men and beasts which poured into both ends of the valley. High banners proudly led column after column of foot soldiers four abreast, every eye intent on the helpless encampment of tents and dying fires in the center of the valley.

It immediately became obvious that much thought had gone into the lightning-quick attack. Amid shouting and clamor, men and horses moved into rows which were hundreds wide.

Like a giant pincer, the great Scottish army closed in on the camp.

When it finished, barely twenty minutes later, the pincer consisted of a deep front row of pikesmen. Behind them, hundreds of archers. Behind the archers, knights on horses.

At first light and with stunning swiftness, it was a surprise attack well designed to catch the enemy at its most vulnerable—heavy with sleep.

Finally, a great banner rose upward on a long pole. Every man in the Scottish army became silent.

It made for an eeriness that sent shivers along the backs of even the most experienced warriors. An entire valley filled with men intent on death; yet in the still air of early morning, the only sound was the occasional stamping of an impatient horse.

Then a strong voice broke that silence. "Surrender in the name of Robert Bruce, king of the Scots!"

The tents of the earl of York's trapped army hung limp under the weight of dew. Not one flap stirred in response. Smoke wafted from fires almost dead. A dog scurried from one garbage pit to another.

"We seek to deal with honor!" the strong voice continued. "Discuss surrender or die in the tents that hide you!"

Moments passed. Many of the warriors found themselves holding their breath. Fighting might be noble and glorious, but to win without risking death was infinitely better.

"The third blast of the trumpet will signal our charge. Unless you surrender before then, all hell will be loosed upon you!"

The trumpet blew once.

Then twice.

And at the edge of the camp, a tent flap opened and a figure stepped outside, to begin striding toward the huge army. From a hundred yards away, the figure appeared to be a slender man, unencumbered with armor or weapons. He walked without apparent fear to the voice which had summoned him.

Thomas could barely comprehend the sight as he walked. Filling the horizon in all directions were men and lances and armor and horses and banners and swords and shields and pikes.

Directly ahead, the men of the opposing council of war. Among them, the man who had demanded surrender in his strong, clear voice.

Thomas tried driving his fear away, but he could not. *Is this my day to die?*

He could guess at the sight he presented to the men on horseback watching his approach. He had not worn the cloak bearing the colors of Magnus. Instead, he had dressed as poorly as a stable boy. Better for the enemy to think him a lowly messenger. Especially for what needed to be done.

There were roughly a dozen gathered. They moved their horses ahead of their army, to be recognized as the men of power. Each horse was covered in colored blankets. Each man was in light armor. They were not heavily protected fighters; they were leaders.

Thomas forced himself ahead, step by step.

The spokesman identified himself immediately. He had a bristling red beard and eyes of fire to match. As he stared at Thomas with the fierceness of a hawk, his rising anger became obvious.

"The earl of York hides in his tent like a woman and sends a lad?"

"I am Thomas. Of Magnus. I bring a message from the earl of York."

The quiet politeness seemed to check the Scot's rage. He blinked once, then said, "I am Kenneth of Carlisle."

Thomas was close enough now that he had to crane his head upward to speak to the one with the red beard.

Sunlight glinted from heavy battle-axes.

"Kenneth of Carlisle," Thomas said with the same dignity, "the earl of York is not among the tents."

This time, the bearded earl spoke almost with sadness. "I am sorry to hear he is a coward."

"Milord, may we speak in private?"

"There is nothing to discuss," Kenneth said. "Accept our terms of surrender. Or the entire camp is doomed."

"Sir," Thomas persisted, hands wide and palms upward, "as you can see, I bear no arms. I can do you no harm."

Hesitation. Then a glint of curiosity from those fierce eyes.

"Hold all the men," Kenneth of Carlisle commanded, then dismounted from his horse. Despite the covering of light armor, he swung down with grace.

Thomas stepped back several paces to allow them privacy.

Kenneth of Carlisle advanced and towered above Thomas. "What is it you can possibly plead which needs such quiet discussion?"

"I mean no disrespect, milord," Thomas said in low tones, "but the surrender which needs discussing is yours."

Five heartbeats of silence

The huge man slowly lifted his right hand as if to strike Thomas, then lowered it.

"I understand." Yellow teeth gleamed from his beard as he snorted disdain. "You attempt to slay me with laughter."

"No," Thomas answered. "Too many lives are at stake."

Suddenly Kenneth of Carlisle clapped his hands down on Thomas' shoulders and shook him fiercely. "Then play no games!" he shouted.

That surge of temper ended as quickly as it had begun, and the shaking stopped.

Thomas took a breath. "This is no game." He looked past Kenneth of Carlisle at the others nearby on their horses. They stared back with puzzled frowns.

"I am here to present you with a decision," Thomas continued. "One you must consider before returning to your horse."

"I shall humor you." Kenneth of Carlisle folded his arms and waited.

Thomas asked, "Did you believe our army was at full strength?"

After a moment of consideration, the Scottish earl replied, "Certainly not. Our scouts brought daily reports of cowards fleeing your army. The deserters we captured all told us the same thing. Your entire army feared battle against us. We saw proof nightly. Your—"

"—campfires," Thomas interrupted. "Each night you saw fewer and fewer campfires. Obvious evidence of an army which shrunk each day, until last night when you may have calculated we had fewer than a thousand men remaining."

Kenneth of Carlisle laughed. "So few men we wondered if it would be worth our while to make this short detour for battle."

"It was the earl of York's wish," Thomas said. He risked a quick look at the tops of the hills, then hid a smile of satisfaction.

"Eh? The earl of York's wish?"

"Again, with much due respect, milord," Thomas swept his arm wide to indicate the valley, "did it not seem too easy? A crippled army quietly camped in a valley with no means of escape?"

Momentary doubt crossed the man's face.

Thomas pressed on. "The deserters you caught had left our army by the earl of York's commands. Each man had instructions to report great fear among the men left behind. We reduced the campfires to give the impression of mass desertion. While our fires are few, our men remain many."

The news startled Kenneth of Carlisle enough for him to flinch.

"Furthermore," Thomas said, "none of those men are here in the valley. Each tent is empty. In the dark of night, all crept away."

Five more heartbeats of silence.

"Impossible," blurted Kenneth of Carlisle. But the white

which replaced the red of flushed skin above his beard showed that he suddenly considered it very possible, and did not like the implications.

Thomas kept his voice calm. "By now," Thomas resisted the urge to look and reconfirm what he already knew, "those men have reached their new positions. They block the exits at both ends of this valley and line the tops of the surrounding hills."

"Impossible." This time, his tone of voice was weaker.

"Impossible, milord? Survey the hills."

This was the most important moment of the battle. Would the huge man be stunned at their desperate bluff?

What he and Thomas saw from the valley floor seemed awesome. Stretched across the entire line of the tops of the hills on each side of the valley, men were stepping into sight in full battle gear. From the viewpoint below, those men were simply dark figures, made small by distance. But the line was solid in both directions and advancing down ward slowly.

The earl of York had timed it perfectly.

"Impossible," Kenneth of Carlisle said for the third time. There was, however, no doubt in his voice.

Murmuring rose from around them as others noticed the movement. Soon word had spread throughout the entire army. Men started shifting nervously.

"The earl of York's army will not advance farther," Thomas promised. "Not unless they have reason."

Thomas also knew that if the earl of York's army moved any closer, the thinness of the advancing line would soon become obvious. The row was only two warriors deep; as many as possible had been sent away from the line to block the escapes at both ends of the valley.

"We shall give them reason," Kenneth of Carlisle swore intensely, as he drew his sword. "Many will die today!"

"And many more of yours, milord."

Kenneth of Carlisle glared, and with both hands buried half the blade of the sword into the ground in front of Thomas.

Thomas waited until the sword stopped quivering. "Milord," he said, hoping his fear would not be heard in his voice, "I requested a discussion in privacy so that you and I could reconsider any such words spoken harshly in the heat of anger."

Kenneth of Carlisle glared harder but made no further moves.

"Consider this," Thomas said. "The entrances to the valley are so narrow that to reach one of our men, twenty of yours must fall. Nor is it possible for your men to fight upward against the slope of these hills. Again, you would lose twenty to the earl of York's one."

"Warfare here in the center of the valley will be more even," Kenneth of Carlisle stated flatly. "That will decide the battle."

Thomas shook his head. "The earl of York has no intention of bringing the battle to you."

Thomas remembered a quote from one of his ancient books, the one which had given him the idea for this battle plan. *"The skilled commander takes up a position from which he cannot be defeated . . . thus a victorious army wins its victories before seeking battle; an army destined to defeat fights in the hope of winning."*

"The earl of York is a coward!" Kenneth of Carlisle blustered.

"A coward to wish victory without killing his men or yours? All your supplies are behind at your main camp. *His* men, however, will be well fed as they wait. In two or three days, any battle of our rested men against your hunger-weakened men will end in your slaughter."

Kenneth of Carlisle lost any semblance of controlled conversation. He roared indistinguishable sounds of rage. And when he ran out of breath, he panted a declaration of war. "We fight to the bitter end! Now!"

He turned to wave his commanders forward.

"Wait!" The cry from Thomas stopped Kenneth of Carlisle in midstride. "One final plea!"

The Scottish earl turned back, his fiery eyes flashing hatred. "A plea for your life?"

Thomas realized again how close he was to death. And

again, he fought to keep his voice steady.

"No, milord. A plea to prevent the needless slaughter of many men." Thomas held out his hands. "If you will permit me to hold a shield."

The request was so unexpected that curiosity once more replaced fierceness. Kenneth of Carlisle called for a shield from one of his men.

Thomas grasped the bottom edge and held it above his head so that the top of the shield was several feet higher than his hands.

Let them see the signal, Thomas prayed. *For if a battle is declared, the Scots will too soon discover how badly we are outnumbered.*

Moments later, a half dozen men broke from the line on the hills.

"Behind you, milord." Thomas hoped the relief he felt was not obvious. "See the archers approach."

Kenneth of Carlisle half turned and watched in silence.

The archers stopped three hundred yards away, too far for any features to be distinguishable.

"So?" Kenneth of Carlisle said. "They hold back. More cowardice."

"No, milord," Thomas said, still holding the shield high. "They need come no closer."

The Scottish earl snorted. "My eyes are still sharp, puppy. Those men are still a sixth of a mile away."

Both watched as all six archers fitted arrows to their bows.

"Fools," Kenneth of Carlisle continued in the same derisive tone. "Fools to waste their efforts as such."

Thomas said nothing. He wanted to close his eyes, but did not. *If but one arrow strays . . .*

It seemed to happen in slow motion. The archers brought their bows up, drew back the arrows and let loose, all in one motion. A flash of shafts headed directly at them, then faded into nothing as the arrows became invisible against the backdrop of green hills.

Whoosh. Whoosh.

The sound arrived with the arrows and suddenly Thomas

was knocked flat on his back.

For a moment, he thought he'd been struck. Yet there was no piercing pain, no blood. And he realized he'd been gripping the shield so hard from fear that the force of the arrows had bowled him over as they struck the target above his head.

Thomas quickly moved to his feet and looked down to follow the horrified stare of Kenneth of Carlisle. Behind him on the ground lay the leather shield, penetrated completely by six arrows.

Thomas took full advantage of the awe he felt around him. "That, milord, is the final reason for surrender. New weaponry. From the hills, our archers will shoot at leisure, secure that your archers will never find the range to answer."

A final five heartbeats of suspense.

Then the huge Scottish earl slumped. "Your terms of surrender?" he asked with resignation.

"The earl of York simply requests that you surrender your weapons. Some of your earls and dukes will be held captive for ransom, of course; but as tradition dictates, they will be well treated. The foot soldiers—farmers, villagers, and peasants—will be allowed to return immediately to their families."

Kenneth of Carlisle bowed his head. "So it shall be," he said. "So it shall be."

"Would that I had a daughter to offer," the earl of York said, under a wide expanse of sky broken by scattered clouds. "She and a great portion of my lands would be yours."

Thomas flushed. The earl believed it was a blush of embarrassment. But mention of marriage simply reminded Thomas of his ache to see again the midnight messenger who had led him to the old man.

"Ah, well," the earl of York sighed, "if I cannot make you my son, at least I can content myself with your friendship."

Another flush of red. The earl believed it was a blush of modesty. Once more, Thomas knew differently. This time, he reddened to remember his suspicions. *Is this man one of the symbol? Will he betray me? Or I him?*

"Yes, yes," the earl of York said, letting satisfaction fill his slow words. "The legend of the young warrior of Magnus grows. Even during the short length of our journey back from the Valley of Surrender, tales of your wisdom have been passed repeatedly from campfire to campfire."

Thomas said nothing. He did not wish credit for strategy taken from the secret knowledge which was his source of power. As well, other worries filled his heart.

Magnus lies over the next hill, he thought. *Will the earl of York now honor his reward promised with victory?*

They rode slowly. Thomas—returning home with his small army in an orderly line behind. The earl—to retrieve his son left at Magnus as a guarantee of safety for Thomas.

All the worries washed over Thomas. *Who are these Druids of the symbol? What games did the old man play—he who, like the Druids, knew astronomy—and where did he gain such intimate knowledge of my life? The castle ahead—will it provide safety against the forces of darkness which left such terrifying sights for all to see on the march northward?*

"Your face grows heavy with dread," the earl of York joked. "Is it because of the question which burns so plainly in your restlessness over the last few days? Rest easy, my son. I have not forgotten your strange victory request."

My son. Surely this man is not part of the darkness. . . .
Thomas steeled himself.

From the marchers behind him, voices grew higher with excitement and anticipation. This close to home, the trail winding through the moors was very familiar to the knights and foot soldiers. Within an hour, they would crest the hill above the lake which held the island castle of Magnus.

There can be no good time to ask, Thomas told himself. He forced his words into the afternoon breeze.

"Your ring, milord. The one which carries the evil symbol burned upon the chests of innocent men, the one you removed before battle. I wish to know the truth behind it."

The earl abruptly reined his horse to a halt and stared Thomas full in the face.

"Any question but that. I beg of you."

Thomas felt his heart collapse in a chill of fear and sadness. "I must, milord," he barely managed to whisper. "It carries a darkness which threatens me. I must know if you are friend or foe."

"Friend," the earl said with intensity. "I swear that upon my mother's grave. Can that not suffice?"

Thomas slowly shook his head.

The earl suddenly slapped his black stallion into a trot. Within seconds, Thomas rode alone.

At the entrance to the valley of Magnus, Thomas saw the earl of York sitting on his horse beneath the shade of a tree well aside of the trail.

The earl waved once, then beckoned. Thomas slowly trotted his own horse to the tree.

The noise of travel faded behind him, and when Thomas reached the earl, he was greeted with a silence interrupted only by the buzzing of flies and a swish and slap as the other horse swung his tail to chase away those flies.

Blue of the lake surrounding Magnus broke through gaps of the low-hanging branches, and dappled shadows fell across the earl's face. It was impossible to read his eyes.

"I suspect you would not force me to honor my vow," the earl finally said. "You have the mark of a man who lets other men live their lives as they choose."

Thomas gazed steadily in return. "The man who betrays another also betrays himself. Often that is punishment enough."

The earl of York shook his head. "From where do you get this wisdom?"

"What little I have was given by a dear teacher, now dead."

More silence.

By then, almost the entire small army had passed along the trail. Then final puffs of dust fell to rest as the last straggler moved on; in the quiet left behind, the earl began again.

"I have waited here in deep thought and anguish," he

said. "The ring is a shameful secret passed from father to son through many generations."

He smiled weakly. "Alas, the debt I owe and a promise made justly demands that now the ancient legend be revealed to one outside the family."

Thomas waited.

"The symbol belongs to a group of high priests with dark power. We know only their name, not the men behind the name," the earl almost whispered.

"Druids," Thomas said.

"Impossible to guess!"

"From the isle of the Celts. Men now hidden among us."

"Thomas, your knowledge is frightening," the earl of York said quickly. "Most who speak that name soon die."

Thomas smiled grimly. "That promise has already been made. Why else do I drive you to answer me all?"

The earl of York sighed. "Then I shall tell all."

He climbed down from his horse and motioned for Thomas to do the same; then he gazed at the far lake of Magnus as he spoke in a flat voice.

"In our family, the ring is passed from father to eldest son, the future earl of York. With it, these instructions: *Acknowledge the power of those behind the symbol or suffer horrible death.* And our memory is long. Three centuries ago, the earl of York refused to listen to a messenger—one whose own ring fit into the symbol engraved upon the family ring. Within weeks, worms began to consume the earl's still living body. No doctor could cure him. Even a witch was summoned. To no avail. They say his deathbed screams echoed throughout the castle for a week. His son—my great-great-grandfather—then became the new earl of York. When he outgrew his advisers, he took great care to acknowledge the power of the ring which had been passed to him."

Thomas felt the chill of the earl's voice. "Acknowledge the power?"

"Yes," came the answer. "A favor asked. A command given. Rarely more than one in an earl's lifetime. Sometimes none. My great-grandfather did not receive a single request. My father . . ."

The earl's voice changed from flat to sad. "My father obeyed just one command. It happened over twenty years ago. I was old enough to understand his pain. Yet he obeyed."

A thought clicked within Thomas. *Over twenty years ago . . .*

"Your father stood aside while Magnus fell," Thomas said with sudden insight. "Despite allegiance and protection promised, he let the new conquerors reign."

The earl of York nodded.

It explained much! Thomas had sworn to his teacher, Sarah, on her deathbed that he would reconquer Magnus to avenge the brutal death of her parents, the former and rightful rulers of Magnus, who had been dethroned over twenty years ago.

Then Thomas drew a deep breath as he realized the implications.

It could not be. But he knew it was.

"Having lost it," Thomas gritted, "these Druids now demand that Magnus be returned. Horrifying rituals plain to see along the march. A message for me, perhaps." Then the implication he dreaded. "Or a message for you."

The earl of York slowly turned to face Thomas. His face showed the gray pallor of anguish.

"Thomas, I call you friend. Yet twice along the march, in the dark of night, I was visited by one of the ring."

Thomas did not blink as he held his breath against the words he did not want to hear.

The earl's voice dropped to little more than a croak. "Each time, Thomas, I received warning to expect that payment for my family's power is soon due."

Chapter Twenty-One

Two others also traveled to Magnus, but with much less fanfare than the triumphant army returning home. These two avoided the main path through the moors, and walked with caution.

Even during the warmth of daylight, the first figure remained well wrapped in black cloth. A casual observer would have aptly blamed it on the old age so apparent by his cane and stooped shoulders, since age often leaves bones aching with chill.

The second figure, however, walked tall and confident with youth. When the wind rose, it swept her long blond hair almost straight back.

They moved without pause for hours, so steadily that the casual observer would have been forced to marvel at the old man's stamina—or urgency. They finally rested at a secluded spot in the hills directly above the lake and castle of Magnus.

"I have no desire to risk you there," Hawkwood said, pointing his cane downward at the village in the center of the lake. "But Thomas will learn both his prisoners have escaped the dungeon. That, I fear, is the bold move which marks the Druid attempt to reconquer Magnus."

"There is little risk for me," the young woman said. "My disguise served me well during my time in Magnus and will continue to do so."

The old man arched an eyebrow barely seen in the shadows that surrounded his face. "Katherine, you were a child during most of your previous time in Magnus, not a young woman now in love."

She blushed. "Is it that apparent?"

Hawkwood shook his head. "Only in little ways. The joy on your face as we discussed a method to reach Thomas during his march to the lowland plains of battle. Your sighs during those days after our midnight meeting, when we followed the army to the Valley of Surrender. And your trembling that morning on the hillside as we waited the outcome of his plan against the Scots."

Her blush deepened. "Thomas is worthy. I had much opportunity to watch him in Magnus. And now, perhaps, my feelings will give me courage to help him as he needs."

Hawkwood suddenly struck a slab of rock with his cane. "No!"

He looked at the broken cane, then at her. His voice softened. "Please, no. Emotions are difficult to trust. Until we are certain of which side he chooses, he cannot know of you, or of the rest of us. The stakes are far too great. We risk your presence back in Magnus for the sole reason that despite all we've done, he is or might become one of them. Love cannot cloud your judgment of that situation."

She ran both her hands through her hair. "You were not there," she whispered, almost to herself, "the day he attacked a man for insulting a poor, hideous freak. You did not see the rage in his eyes that someone so helpless should suffer. Thomas will not sell his soul. He will not be seduced by a promise of Druid power."

Hawkwood sighed. "Beneath your words, I hear you saying something else . . . that you don't want to be his executioner."

Four tall trees cast shadows along the the main path where it became a narrow bridge of land leading across the waters of the lake to Magnus.

She approached the water alone, and instead of continuing across to the drawbridge of Magnus, walked to the base of the trees and bound her hair into a single tail, then slowly bowed to her knees out of sight of the path.

Grass pressed lines into her knees through the fabric of her dress. A travel bag weighed against her hips. She cleared her mind of awareness even of the sounds of insects in afternoon sun or of the breeze which swayed the leaves above her.

There, she began to pray silently. *Lord of love, You are infinitely wise, the Creator of this universe. Please guide my steps to Your divine plan. Please give strength to Thomas, so that he chooses the path of good.*

A stab of fear distracted her from her contemplation. She took the fear and placed it with trust into her prayer.

Dear Father, I am selfish to wish for his love when so much is at stake. Yet if it is Your will, please spare both our lives in the madness which might overcome Magnus. And should he choose the evil of that madness, please help me with my terrible task. In the name of Your Son, our Savior, I pray. Amen.

She stood, and for long minutes simply stared across the water at the cold stone walls of Magnus. Despite the peace of her trust, she shivered.

Then she fumbled with the wide tongue of leather which held her travel bag closed. She reached inside and pulled loose a bundle of filthy bandages.

With practiced movements, she flipped her hair upward and pushed the long tail into a flat bundle against her head and held it there as she wrapped the cloth around her jaws, then her nose and eyes and forehead.

When she finished, only a large, black hole for her mouth and two dark, narrow slits for her eyes showed any degree of humanity.

Katherine drew a deep breath for the strength to imprison herself in the role of a pitiful freak about to return to Magnus.

She woke in the gutter to hands reaching roughly within her blanket. Sour breath, heavy garlic, and the odor of unwashed skin pressed down.

Katherine almost screamed in rage, then remembered her role—burned and scarred too horribly to deserve any form of kindness.

Her voice became a low, begging moan instead.

"Awake? Bad luck for you!" From the darkness, a broad hand loomed to block out the light of the stars, and the blow that followed shot white flashes through her closed eyes. Her left cheek swelled immediately tight beneath the bandage.

Katherine bit back a yelp of pain and resigned herself to being robbed of what little she owned.

Another voice interrupted the figure above her.

"My good man," it called cheerfully from just down the street, "you show kindness to assist strangers during this dangerous time of night. Here, now, let me help you get this poor woman from the gutters."

"Eh?"

The voice from behind its candle moved closer. "And probably not a moment too soon. Why, any common gutter thief might have swooped in like a pest-ridden vulture. And then where would this poor woman be without our help?"

The startled man above Katherine swore under his breath, then fled.

She drew herself upright into a sitting position and hugged her knees. Through the narrow slits of the constricting bandages, it was difficult to see her rescuer as he approached. It was easy, however, to hear his warm chuckle.

"Like a rat scurrying away from a torch. And with not a shred of good humor."

The candle flared and moved downward with the man's slow, stooping motion. Katherine, still wrapped and hidden in a thin blanket, flinched at his touch.

"Come, my child," said the voice. "I am one of several town guards, under hire to the lord of Magnus himself. I mean you no harm. I will bring you to the church where you will be fed and kept warm."

"I have no money," Katherine replied. "Surely that must be obvious at my choice of accommodation."

Another warm chuckle. "You are a stranger here."

"No, I—"

"Otherwise, you would know the lord of Magnus provides a generous allowance to the church for the purpose of sheltering those in need."

His hand found her elbow and guided her to her feet. She could not see his face behind the candle. But she heard his gasp as he pushed aside the blanket which covered her face.

That familiar sound tore at her heart. It reminded her again of the nightmare of living as a freak. Freedom from that life—traveling with the old man and watching the joy in his eyes as he drank in the youth and beauty of her uncovered face—had been so precious after years imprisoned beneath the filthy bandages. And for a moment, she could not sponge away the bitterness inside.

"Horror?" she mocked his gasp. "You were expecting an angel perhaps?"

Long silence. Then words she would never forget. "Not horror, my child. Surprised relief. Thomas of Magnus has spoken often of his friend Katherine. It will give him great joy to see you."

Katherine woke again to the touch of hands. These ones, however, were gentle, and plucked at the bandages on her face.

"No!" Her terror was real, not feigned as so much of her life beneath bandages had been.

The servant woman misunderstood the reason for that terror.

"Shhh, my child. Thomas has instructed that you be bathed and given fresh wraps and new clothing."

"No!" Katherine clutched the servant woman's wrists. "My face!"

"Hush, little one. You shall not be mocked in the lord's home."

Katherine did not have time to appreciate the irony; after a lifetime of abuse, kindness itself finally threatened the secrecy of her disguise. Should those of the darkness discover she had been among them all these years . . .

Katherine pushed herself into an upright position. "Please, milady. Lead me to the bath. Leave the fresh wrap nearby. But I beg of you, grant me the solace of privacy. To inflict my face upon others . . ."

The servant woman felt the urgency in Katherine's plea, and compassion almost rendered her speechless. *This poor child, to have a face so hideously burned and scarred that her entire life must be spent in hiding . . .*

"Of course," the woman said softly.

Katherine let strong, calloused hands guide her from the warmth of the bed. Before she could barely notice the coldness of the floor, the servant woman stooped and fitted on her feet slippers of sheepskin.

As Katherine relaxed and turned to accept help into the offered robe, she smothered a cry of delighted surprise. The previous night had been too dark for her to see her new sleeping quarters in the castle. What she saw explained why sleep had been so sound.

Her bed was huge, and canopied with veils of netting. Her mattress of straw—what luxury!—hung from the canopy on rope suspenders. The mattress was covered with linen sheets and blankets of wool and fur. Feather pillows too!

Such softness of sleep. Such softness of robe against her skin. Katherine suddenly realized how she must appear to a servant accustomed to waking royalty instead.

Katherine's arms and legs were smeared with grease and dirt. The pile of clothes beside her was little more than torn rags. And, in the cool freshness of the room, she suddenly became aware of the stink of the streets upon her body.

She faltered slightly. The servant woman ignored that.

"Come, milady," the woman said. "Your bath awaits. And you shall greet Thomas of Magnus like a queen."

He appears so serious, she thought. *Already, the weight of his power bends him.*

She began with an awkward bow. As her heart thudded, she wondered in the anguish of knowing she could never ask. *Does he feel for me the way I do for him? Or was that simply wishful imagination during those few moments he stared at me beneath the moonlight?*

Katherine forced herself to remember she was beneath bandages, not the midnight messenger, and began to speak as she finished her curtsy. "You overwhelm me with these gifts of—"

Thomas frowned and shook his head slightly.

Katherine stopped.

Thomas stared straight ahead, every inch of his seated body the ruler of an earldom. Behind Katherine, each side of the huge double wooden door slowly swung closed under the guidance of the sentries just outside the room.

The doors thudded shut.

Thomas let out a great sigh.

"They seem to prefer it when I am solemn," he grinned. "Apparently earls are not allowed to have fun. Especially when dispensing wisdom and justice from this very chair."

Thomas stepped down lightly.

"Katherine, you've returned." He knelt, took one of her hands, and kissed the back of it. He stood and placed both his hands on her shoulders. "I missed our conversations."

Katherine smiled beneath her bandages. *To go from formidable man to a sweet boyishness in such a short time. Not bragging about the Valley of Surrender. Not boasting of his new wealth. But to spend effort setting me—a person he believes to be a freak—at ease. It would not be difficult to remain in love with such a person.*

Keeping those thoughts to herself, she replied, "Thank you, milord."

"Milord! Not 'Thomas'? After you rescued me from the dungeon? After you made it possible to conquer the walls of Magnus? You gravely disappoint me with such an insult."

Grave disappointment, however, did not show on his face. Only warmth.

Would that I could tear these bandages from my face, Katherine thought. *Only to watch his eyes and hope he would recognize me.*

She tried to keep the conversation safe so that nothing in her actions might betray her thoughts. And that her questions would reflect ignorance. "How fares that rascal Tiny John? Or the knight Sir William?"

A complex expression crossed Thomas' face—a mixture of frown and smile. She soon understood why.

"Tiny John still entertains us all," Thomas told her, as the smile triumphed.

The smile then lost to the frown and darkened. "The

knight bid farewell too soon after Magnus was conquered. There was much about him which cannot be explained."

He tried a half smile in her direction. "Much, also, is a mystery to me here in Magnus. Perhaps you have not heard. I left Magnus to battle the Scots. During my absence, two prisoners escaped, including the evil man Geoffrey who purchased you as a slave when he became a candlemaker. Impossible that they could escape without help from someone within Magnus. I feel there is no one here I can trust."

He looked at her strangely. "Even your disappearance the night we conquered Magnus—"

Katherine bowed her head. "Thomas—"

"No," he said, as if coming to a quick decision. "I was not seeking an explanation. You assisted me to this earldom. I am happy that you have returned. Furthermore, urgent matters press upon me."

"Oh?"

"Strange evil generated by an ancient circle of high priests known as Druids. And worse."

Thomas stared into space. "News has reached me. Barely days after returning to his home, the earl of York again leads an army into the moors. His destination is Magnus."

"No!" Katherine's surprised horror was not feigned. *Does Hawkwood know of this? What action must we take now?*

"As you know," Thomas said, "when I first arrived in Magnus, the former lord, Richard Mewburn, had me arrested and thrown into the dungeon because of the deaths of four monks. My explanation to you was truth. They had killed themselves by eating the food meant for me, food they had poisoned to murder me."

Katherine nodded.

Thomas responded to her nod by starting to pace back and forth across the room . . . brows furrowed, hands clenched behind his back.

"After Mewburn fled in defeat," he continued, "all in Magnus accepted that the charges of murder had been false, merely an excuse to imprison me and the knight."

Katherine nodded again.

"Yet," Thomas said, "messengers now bring me word

that the earl of York has sworn an oath of justice, that he is determined to overthrow Magnus and imprison me for those same murders."

"That is an impossible task!" Katherine finally spoke. "You are lord within these walls. Over hundreds of years, Magnus has never been taken by force alone."

"Only by treachery," Thomas agreed. "Or, as I did, with the help of the people of Magnus."

"So," Katherine asked quietly, "why are you worried?"

"A prolonged siege will do neither side any good," he answered, "and another matter, more subtle, also disturbs me."

Katherine waited. She was grateful that her old bandages had been changed to new, because even so, it was hardly possible to bear her prison of freakishness while near Thomas.

"There was enough time during the march to the battle against the Scots for the earl of York to accuse me of murder. There was enough time then for him to arrest me. Why did he not?"

"His son was being held captive as a guarantee of your safety?" Katherine asked.

Thomas glanced at her briefly, then shook off a strange expression.

"No," he said a moment later. "If the charges were as true as the earl of York obviously now believes, no one inside Magnus would have harmed his son to protect a murderer."

Long silence.

"Had the earl of York heard of the deaths before the march?" Katherine started.

"That is what puzzles me. If so, why suddenly decide to act upon them later?" Thomas stopped pacing and stared directly at Katherine.

"However," he said, "the monastery of my childhood was obscure, and I as an orphan even more so. Thus, it is easy to think that the earl of York had not heard of the deaths."

Thomas frowned. "But why then did Mewburn, the former lord of Magnus in those isolated moors, know of those deaths soon enough to cast me into the dungeon, while others in power remained uninformed until much later?"

Chapter Twenty-Two

The chamber was so narrow and tight that Katherine was forced to stand ramrod straight. Even so, the stone of the walls pressed painfully against her knees and elbows.

She had stood like this, fighting cramps of pain, in eight-hour stretches each of the previous two days. In the tight confines of darkness and ancient stone, the slightest movement chafed the bandages against her face.

Raw skin and rigid muscles was the price she paid to spy on Thomas.

Necessity of concealment made the chamber so small, hidden as it was in a hollowed portion of the thick rear wall of the throne room. Tiny vents in the cracks of stone—at a height barely above Katherine's waist and invisible to anyone inside the room—brought air upward into the space.

The vents did not allow light into the chamber, only sound, carried so perfectly that any word spoken above a whisper reached Katherine's ears.

She had no fear of being detected. Whenever Thomas left the throne room, she abandoned the hiding spot, with enough time to return to her bedchamber to clean away the dirt smudged into her by the walls, before he might invite her for conversation or a meal.

And, as Hawkwood had instructed before sending her back to Magnus, the entrance to the chamber was fifty feet away, hidden in the recesses of a little-used hallway. To slip in or out, she need simply stand in the recess until enough quietness had convinced her that entry or exit was safe.

More difficult, however, was the twisting blackness of the tunnel which led through the thick castle walls to the chamber behind the throne room. More than once, she had felt the slight crunch of stepping on the fur and bones of dead and dusty mice and bats. Her first time through, two days earlier, had been a gagging passage through cobwebs that brushed her face in the darkness with no warning and clung to her like lace.

Remember Hawkwood and his instructions, she told herself as yet another cramp bit into her left thigh. *This is a duty we have performed for generations.*

Two days of petitions and complaints. Two days of the slowly considered words given in return by the earl, Thomas of Magnus. Two days of exquisite torture, listening and loving more the man who might never discover the secret of her hidden face. But not once, the expected Druid messenger.

Yet the Druid would arrive. Hawkwood had so promised, and Hawkwood was never wrong.

Katherine snapped herself away from her thoughts, and listened to another verdict delivered so crystal clear into the chamber.

"No, Gervaise, there will not be any more money supplied from the treasury for church charity."

"My lord?"

His sigh reached her with equal clarity. "Gervaise, much as you pretend surprise, you expected that decision from me. You know, as I do, that many are now tempted to forsake work for the easiness of charity meals and sound sleep."

Gervaise chuckled. "What do you propose? Every day, one or two more appear at the church doorsteps."

"Get the Father to deliver long sermons. Ones which must be heard before the meals arrive."

Laughter from both.

Then a more sober tone from Thomas. "I jest, of course. Instead, find work on the church building or its grounds," he said. "Any work. Let those who are able contribute long hours, enough so that it is more profitable for them to seek employment elsewhere. You will soon discover who is truly needy."

"Excellent," Gervaise said. "I look forward to our evening walk and discussion. You may tell me more about Katherine.''

In the chamber, her ears began to burn from embarrassment. It was one thing to spy for noble purposes, another to listen to a private conversation. Yet she found herself straining to catch every word. .

"Yes. Katherine. If she were another, my world might be perfect.''

Katherine could not help but feel a warm flush of hope at *those words. Another . . . did he mean her? Or did he still dream of Isabelle?*

She was given no time to ponder.

"Milord. One waits outside,'' a sentry called into the throne room.

Katherine, of course, could only imagine the silent good-bye salutes between Thomas and Gervaise. The voice she heard moments later sent an instinctive fear deep inside her.

"Thomas of Magnus.'' Not a question, but almost a sneer. The voice was modulated, and had no coarse accent of an uneducated peasant.

"Most extend courtesy with a bow,'' Thomas replied, immediately cold.

"I will not prolong this through pretense,'' the voice replied. "I am here to discuss your future.''

A pause. Then the voice spoke quickly. "Don't! You draw breath to call for a guard, but if you do, you will never learn the secrets of this symbol, or of Magnus.''

The Druid messenger.

Katherine no longer felt the ache of stiff limbs, no longer noticed the wraps of cloth which muffled her breath. Every nerve tingled to listen further.

"I grant you little time,'' Thomas replied.

"No,'' came the triumphant voice. "I have as long as I like. Dread curiosity is plain to read on your face.''

"Your time slips away as you speak. What is your message?''

The sneering voice came like a soft caress. "The message is simple. Join our circle, remain earl, and gain great power beyond comprehension. Or deny us and lose Magnus.''

"Why should I not have you seized and executed?" Thomas asked after a long silence.

"For the same reason that you still live. After all, we have a thousand ways to kill you. An adder perhaps—that deadly snake slipped into your bedsheets as you sleep. Undetectable poisons, a dagger in the heart. You still live, Thomas, because your death does not serve our purpose. Just as my death now would not serve yours."

"No?" Thomas asked.

"No. You and I, of course, are merely representatives. Your death would only end your life. It would not return to us the power over the people of Magnus who, before your arrival, were sheep to be handled at our whims."

Short silence. Then from Thomas, "And you represent?" He said it with too much urgency.

The messenger laughed. A cruel sound to Katherine in her hiding spot. "Druids. The true masters of Magnus for centuries."

"Not possible," Thomas said. But Katherine heard enough of a waver in his voice to know he did think it possible.

"Not possible?" the voice countered. "Ponder this. Magnus is an incredible fortress. A king's fortune ten times over could not pay for the construction of this castle and the protective walls. Yet to all appearances, Magnus is located far from the bases of power. Why go to the expense, if not for a hidden purpose?"

No! Katherine wanted to scream. *Lies!*

"And," the voice moved like an arched finger slowly scratching a cat's throat, "why has Magnus existed so long without being seriously challenged by the royalty of England? The earl of York leaves it in peace. So have the Norman kings. And the Anglo-Saxons before them. Would not even a fool decide great power lies within Magnus, great enough to deflect kings for centuries?"

No! Katherine raged. *Thomas must not believe this!*

"Why did the former lord, Richard Mewburn, take Magnus by the foulest treachery?" Thomas said with hesitation. "If you speak truth, it would seem to me that your circle would control this castle's destiny."

"Of course," came the snorted reply. "That's exactly why Mewburn was *allowed* to conquer Magnus. He was loyal to us. The earl before him . . ."

"Yes?" Thomas asked with ice in his voice.

"Don't be a child! We certainly know that his daughter raised you at that forsaken monastery. Can you not consider the possibility it was she who lied to you, not us?"

Katherine almost needed to force herself to breathe. She dimly felt her nails biting into her palms but still did not unclench her fists.

Thomas, don't accept their lies! Please, don't force me to be your executioner!

In the heartbeats that followed, Katherine agonized. Thomas did not know enough to make a decision, yet there was no way it could have been risked that he be given the truth.

"I have considered the possibility that she lied," Thomas said finally. "And logically, there is no reason against it. I was an orphan and depended on her for much. It would be difficult for a lost child to recognize the difference between truth or falsehood."

If Katherine could have slumped in that cramped hollow, she would have. Instead, it felt as if her blood drained into a pool at her feet.

I now wish he had never looked into my eyes, she told herself, *and had never raised hopes of love.*

"Good, good," the voice said, now as if it were the cat satisfied with a finger soft against its throat. "We much prefer that you choose to live as one of us. You will share the mysteries of darkness with us, and anything you wish will become yours."

"It must have a price," Thomas said, almost defeated. "The rewards may be plain to see, but loyalty has its demands."

"Thomas, Thomas," the voice chided. "We wish only one thing as a test of your commitment."

"Yes?" Now the pleading of total defeat.

"Your hidden books of knowledge. We must have them."

If he agrees, Katherine told herself, *nothing will ease the pain of my duty. Yet he cannot lead them to the books. I must force my hands to betray my love for him, and to-night he will die.*

"Go," Thomas said with sudden strength and intensity. "Go back to the isle of the Celts!"

Katherine blinked in her darkness.

"Yes!" Thomas raged. "Report back to your murdering barbarian masters that Thomas of Magnus will not bend to those who brand the chests of innocent men."

"Yet—"

"Yet it appeared I might pledge loyalty? Only to see what it was you truly wished. Now, I shall do everything in my power to prevent you from that desire."

"Fool!" The word sounded as if it was molten iron, spat bright red from a furnace. "Magnus shall be taken from you as it was given. By the people."

"That remains to be seen," Thomas said in a steady voice.

Behind her mask of bandages, tears of relief filled Katherine's eyes.

Chapter Twenty-Three

The first howl began while Katherine and Tiny John walked the streets of Magnus. Then another, from farther away.

"Listen." Tiny John cocked his head. As usual, a grin shone bright from dirty and smudged skin. No matter how often the clucking castle servants managed to hold him long enough to wipe him clean, he found a way to crawl or scamper through a hole or passageway barely wide enough to make their efforts useless. It was amazing that he had slowed down long enough to escort Katherine to the market.

"Two dogs," Katherine said. Her mind was not on the streets bustling with early morning activity, activity which no longer bothered her. Her bandages were a badge of distinction, since all knew she had helped Thomas dispose of Lord Mewburn. Nor were her thoughts on Tiny John's happy prattling. A single night had passed since the Druid visitor had proclaimed his warning to Thomas, and Katherine's stomach still churned with fear. She knew the power of the barbarian Druids.

Worse, the earl of York was expected to arrive in the valley with his army sometime in midafternoon. Katherine, better than anyone in Magnus, knew Thomas faced enemies both inside and outside the fortress of Magnus.

What would be the first attack? The Druids? Or a conquering army?

Then Katherine's skin prickled. Another unearthly howl.

Within moments, the shrieking chorus filled Magnus.

Dogs—in the streets, under carts, in sheds—all moaned and howled and barked. People stopped and stared around in amazement and superstitious fear. The howling grew louder and more frenzied.

An unease filled Katherine, an unease which had nothing to do with the almost supernatural noise of the dogs. She wanted to hold her head and shake away the grip of something she couldn't explain.

Now cats. The high-pitched scream of yeowling cats gradually became plain above the yipping and howling of dogs. All people stood where they were, frozen in awed dread. Rats scurried from dark hiding places, from the corners of market stalls, from the holes among stone walls, and in dozens of places ran headlong and uncaring across the feet of shopkeepers and market people.

Then, unbelievably, bats! Dozens fell from the sky. A great swarm circled frantically a hundred feet above Magnus, each bat dipping and swooping a crazed dance to exhaustion.

Bats do not fly during the daytime, Katherine told herself, as she struggled to accept what her eyes told her. *They do not drop like a hailstorm of dark stones.*

Still the bats fell. Onto thatched roofs. Onto the carts of shopkeepers. Onto the packed dirt of the streets.

The thud of their landing bodies was lost among the howling and shrieking of cats and dogs.

And into the noise came the screams of terrified peasants.

Then, like a snuffed candle, it stopped.

A final dozen bats dropped from the sky to quiver and shake in death throes. The dogs stopped howling. The cats stopped shrieking. And, stunned by the sudden end of noise, the terrified peasants stopped screaming.

Whispers began.

"A judgment from God," someone said.

"Yes," said another, more clearly. "We allow a murderer of monks to remain earl of Magnus!"

"The earl of York brings justice with his army!"

"God's judgment!"

"Yes! God's judgment upon us!"

The whispers around them in the marketplace became shouts of anger and fear. Tiny John reached up and held Katherine's hand. She squeezed comfort in return. The boy needed it. Bats lay strewn in all directions.

"We'll . . ." She forced herself to swallow, her mouth was so dry. "We'll return immediately. Thomas must hear of this . . . if he hasn't been informed already."

Katherine, her face hidden in bandages, joined Thomas on the top of the wall.

"The earl of York makes no effort to hide the size of his army," she observed.

"He has no need," Thomas replied. "Magnus, of course, cannot flee."

They shared the silence as they watched the faraway blur of banners and horses as the army approached.

Still at least two miles away, the mass of men and beasts was plain to see as it wound its way through the valley.

Katherine ached to tell Thomas more, to tell him that he was not alone in his struggle against the Druids. But she could not. Hawkwood's remembered warning echoed stronger than the inner voice which urged her to remove the bandage from her face.

Yet tonight, she would slip away from Magnus and speak again to Hawkwood.

"Will you see the earl of York?" she asked.

Thomas shook his head. "We will deal through messengers."

Unspoken was the thought neither could avoid. *Already, division weakens Magnus within. Thomas can ill afford to leave to conduct negotiations himself.*

"Whom do you trust?" Katherine asked several minutes later. "Robert of Uleran?"

"His dismay at the escape of the prisoners in my absence seemed real," Thomas said. "Upon my return, he offered his resignation. Now . . . now I have no other choice but to trust him. After the unnatural happenings, it is only his strong insistence that keeps many of the superstitious soldiers faithful to our cause."

Despite the afternoon sun, Katherine shivered at her memory of the uncanny events of the morning. Not a single peasant in Magnus believed any longer that Thomas was innocent of the murders. Not for the first time did Katherine consider the harm that a few well-placed rumors from Druid sources might cause. Yet how could they have called bats from the sky to add strength to the rumors?

She had nothing more to say and wanted only to place her hand on his arm. But Thomas stared with rigid anger at the approaching army.

Shortly after, the sounds of that army drifted upward to them . . . grunting beasts . . . the slap of leather against ground as men marched in unison . . . and the rise of voices behind Thomas and Katherine, as villagers heard of the army's progress.

When the army reached the narrow bridge of land that connected the island fortress to the land around the lake, one man on foot detached himself from the front of the army.

Thomas watched briefly, then spoke more to himself than to Katherine as the man walked alone slowly toward the castle.

"He holds paper rolled and sealed. I have little faith the message is a greeting of friendship."

Katherine reached the secluded grove long after the bells of midnight had rung clearly across the valley from within Magnus. She blamed it on caution generated by the necessity to avoid an entire army camped around the lake of Magnus.

Bent and covered in shawls, to get by a sentry she had more than once played the role of a disoriented servant, seeking her tent in the darkness. And each time she had faced a sentry, she had gripped tightly beneath her shawl a dagger. *Nothing must keep me from Hawkwood.*

The long walk along the valley bottom through the black of night had not been simple. Each rustle of leaves, each sway of branches, each tiny movement seemed a falling bat or a scurrying rat. Before, the night had held nothing to frighten her. Now, after the horror of those brief moments in Magnus, it was difficult to recover her lack of fear.

Her nerves, however, had not prevented her from making steady progress. Step by step, tree by tree, clearing by clearing, she had moved toward the prearranged meeting place.

As always, Hawkwood was waiting.

He wasted no time with greetings. Nor in seeking identification. Only Katherine would know of this place, or that he would be here each night at this time.

"What happens in Magnus?"

She felt a brief pride that he trusted her enough to assume she succeeded in her mission.

"As you foresaw," Katherine said, "those of darkness sent a messenger."

"And as *you* predicted," the old man said after some thought, "he refused to be bullied or bribed."

"Yes, but how do you know of—"

"Katherine, had you been forced to be his executioner, nothing could have hidden it in your voice. Thus, I know he is alive. And alive only because he wants no part of the Druids."

"There is more," she said, and explained the morning's happenings, and the rumbles of fear within Magnus.

The old man mused for several moments. "Your fear is legitimate, my child. No matter what they wish to believe, kings rule only by the consent of the people. History is scarred by revolutions against fools who believed otherwise. Thomas may indeed lose Magnus."

"And Thomas grieves," Katherine told the old man. "He is bewildered by the earl's declaration of war and by his fierce anger. Thomas once believed they were friends as close as brothers."

Katherine explained the savage message delivered late that afternoon by scroll. *Unconditional surrender or unconditional death.* She told how Thomas wondered why the former lord of Magnus had heard of the monks' deaths so much before the earl of York had.

"That, at least, is not a mystery," Hawkwood said. "On their journey to Magnus, Isabelle would have learned from Thomas of the monks' deaths and reported them accordingly."

Hawkwood paused. "Then, I'm sure it was convenient for the Druids that only the reigning lord of Magnus know. Now, of course, it is convenient for the earl of York to know. It will be much easier for the Druids if the earl fights their battle in a misguided pursuit of justice."

Katherine nodded. "The dogs. The cats. Bats falling dead from the sky. Now that the people within Magnus believe justice must be served against Thomas, he may lose his earldom the same way he gained it."

"I catch doubt of his innocence even in your voice, child."

Katherine sighed. "Slight doubts only. How could our enemies be capable of calling bats to hurl themselves from the sky?"

"It is a question not easily answered," Hawkwood agreed. "Let me think."

Katherine knew better than to speak again.

He sat cross-legged and arranged his mantle over himself to fend off the cold night air. He seemed to slip into a trance.

Katherine waited, and knew too well how long that wait might be. She waited as the cold seeped into her. She waited as her tired legs grew to feel the soreness even more. She waited in silence broken only by the distant muttering of owls and the light skipping of mice across leaves.

Not until the gray fingers of false dawn reached into the valley did Hawkwood stir.

When he finally spoke, it was a question.

"Close your eyes," he said to Katherine. "Do you recall if you saw the smoke of a fire as the creatures howled in Magnus?"

She did as instructed. Eyes closed lightly, at first she saw only the frantic movement of bats against the morning sky. Then, dimly, something snagged in her memory because it did not belong against that sky.

"Yes," she said with triumph. "Smoke from the bell tower of the church!"

Hawkwood let out held breath. "And you say you felt like shaking your head free from a grip you couldn't explain."

Katherine nodded. In the cold dawn, slight wisps rose white from her mouth with rise and fall of her chest. Even in summer, the high moors and valleys could not escape chill.

Did she imagine that a smile appeared in the shadows of his cowl?

"I believe I understand their methods. I would have done the same were I they. As would Merlin himself." Hawkwood spoke slowly. "And I believe there is a way that Merlin would have countered those actions. So speak to Thomas tonight. As yourself, unencumbered with bandages. If he has courage, he can defeat the Druids."

She hoped for, watched for — and with thudding heart — saw the startled flare of recognition in his eyes.

"You!"

"Yes, Thomas. I bring greetings from an old man. One saddened to hear of your troubles."

"You! Impossible! Soldiers are posted at every turret."

Katherine repeated her greetings from Hawkwood — she was cool on the outside, but glad inside that her sudden presence had shocked him into not hearing her first words.

They stood in nearly the same position she had stood beside him, disguised in her bandages a day earlier, on the outside walls of Magnus. Fifty yards farther along the top of the wall a soldier stood posted at a square stone turret. Fifty yards behind, another.

Below and across the water were campfires of the sieging army, so close they heard the pop and saw the sparks whenever a log exploded in the heat.

Thomas groaned and laughed in the same sound.

"Why must I be tortured so? Is it not enough that Magnus rumbles with rebellion? That the most powerful earl in north Britain camps on my doorstep? That the sorcery of Druids threatens? That you haunt my dreams?"

His dreams are haunted.

The groan deepened. "And with all of that, you place in front of me the never-ending mystery of the old man."

He shook his head, and in light, joking tones said, "I pray thee tell me all."

"I cannot," she said. *Although I wish to.*

"For example," he said, "tell me how you arrived here, during a siege, on these walls during the night?"

She shook her head.

"Perhaps why you and the old man dog my footsteps?"
She shook her head.

"The identity of the old man?"
Another shake.

"The mission he wishes me to pursue?"
Again, Katherine shook her head silently.

In one quick, almost angry motion, he stepped across the space between them, and pulled her close enough to kiss her squarely on the lips. Then he pushed her away.

"And tell me if you enjoyed that."

Katherine's first response—and one too immediate to stop —was to slap him hard—open palm against open face—for taking such action without permission or invitation. Her second response was regret at the first response.

A woman should not value lightly her first kiss, she thought. *Not if it is one never to be forgotten.*

"Milord?" One of the sentries had heard the noise of the slap.

Katherine could not help but giggle. "I didn't intend to hit *that* hard," she whispered.

"It's nothing," Thomas called back to the sentry. Then to Katherine. "Punishment justly deserved."

They stared at each other. Thoughts and impressions crowded Katherine's mind . . . his now grave and steady eyes, clearly seen in the light of the moon . . . the skin which had tightened across his cheekbones from worry.

Stop, she told herself. *It is duty which brings you here.*

So she spoke. "You talk of rebellion within Magnus, of the army across the water, and of the sorcery of Druids."

Thomas nodded without taking his eyes away from hers.

Will he have the courage?

She plunged ahead. "The old man wishes for me to tell you that there is a way to overcome all three."

He must have the courage.

"How is that?" Thomas asked.

She paused before answering, then said, "Ask for God's judgment. Trial by ordeal."

Chapter Twenty-Four

Thomas, Robert of Uleran, Tiny John, and the disguised Katherine stood and waited at the end of the drawbridge.

At the other end of the narrow strip of land that reached the shore of the lake, the earl of York and three soldiers began to move toward them.

"Are you sure they'll not run us through with those great swords?" Tiny John asked, not for the first time that morning.

"Yes," Katherine whispered. "The earl will not risk losing honor by dealing in treachery. Not after Thomas requested a meeting such as this."

Her answer did not stop Tiny John from fidgeting as the earl of York moved closer.

Beside her, Thomas and Robert of Uleran stared straight ahead. Each wore a long cloak of the finest material in Magnus—this was not a time to appear humble.

For Katherine, the earl of York's march across the land bridge seemed to take forever. How badly she wanted it to still be the previous night, with Thomas listening so carefully to her words, half his attention on her face, the other half on the instructions from Hawkwood. How badly she wanted it to be that single moment of farewell, with the awkwardness of Thomas not daring to hold her, yet hoping she would not disappear again. And how badly she wanted to be free of the bandages which now disguised her from Thomas.

The earl of York was now close enough for Katherine to observe the anger set in the clenched muscles of his face.

She heard that anger moments later.

"What is it that you want, you craven cur of yellow cowardice?"

A quick, surprised intake of breath from Thomas.

"An explanation, perhaps, of this sudden hatred," Thomas said shortly after. "I understand, if you truly believe me guilty of those murders, that duty forces you to lay siege. But you called me brother once. Surely that—"

"Treacherous vulture. Waste no charm on me," the earl said in thunderous tones. "Were it not for honor, I would cleave you in two where you stand. You called me here for discussion. Do it quickly, so that I may refuse your request and return to the important matter of bringing destruction to Magnus."

Thomas stiffened visibly and kept his voice level and polite. "I ask for a chance to prove my innocence."

"Surrender the castle then. Submit to a trial."

Thomas shook his head. "I ask for trial by ordeal."

The earl of York gaped at him. "Ordeal!"

That had been Katherine's reaction to Hawkwood's instructions.

"Ordeal!" the earl of York repeated, for the first time showing emotion other than anger. "The church outlawed such trials more than a hundred years ago."

"Nonetheless," Thomas said, "I wish to prove to you and to the people of Magnus that I am innocent."

The earl rubbed his chin in thought. "Tell me, shall we bind you and throw you into the lake?"

That had been one of the most common ways of establishing guilt. Bound, and often weighted with stones, a person was thrown into deep water. If the person did not drown, innocence was declared. None, of course, were found innocent.

"Not by water," Thomas said. "Nor by fire."

Some chose the hot iron. The defendant was forced to pick up an iron weight still glowing from the forge. If, after three days in bandages, the burns had healed, it was taken as a sign of innocence.

"What then?" the earl of York demanded. "How are we to believe you are innocent?"

"Tomorrow, I will stand alone on this narrow strip of land," Thomas said. "Stampede toward me twenty of the strongest and largest bulls you can find. If I turn and run, or if I am crushed and trampled, then you may have Magnus."

Katherine stood among the great crowd at the base of the castle because she wanted to hear and watch Thomas, and there was no way for her to remain beside him as he addressed the people from the top of the castle stairs.

When he appeared, the rustling undercurrents of speculation immediately stopped. Thomas held their complete attention.

Katherine was grateful for her bandages. She smiled in admiration, and she wasn't sure she wanted Thomas to know how he impressed her.

"People of Magnus," Thomas began, "today I face death."

Whispered and excited chattering.

Thomas held up his hand for silence. He wore a brown cloak and no jewels.

"Because of you I undergo trial by ordeal. Magnus can withstand any siege, but only with your support. Some of you have chosen to believe I am guilty of the charges laid against me. Today, then, I will prove my innocence so that Magnus might stand."

Now his face darkened, the face of nobility angered. "And I tell you now, dogs will howl and bats will fall from the sky at the injustice of these false accusations."

Thomas said nothing more. He spun on his heel and marched back into the castle.

Surely he feels fear.

From Katherine's position among the hundreds of men and women of Magnus lined along the top of the fortress wall, Thomas appeared small, standing alone halfway across the land bridge.

He stood completely still and faced the opposing army. Between them, and where the land bridge joined the shore of the lake, a hastily constructed pen, made from logs roped together, held huge and restless bulls. From the castle wall, they seemed dark and evil.

Katherine frowned as the tension of the spectators began

to fill her too. Dried bushes had been heaped at the back end of the pen.

Dear God, she prayed, *let Hawkwood be correct in his calculations.*

Soldiers moved to the front of the pen.

A sigh from the crowd along the fortress wall swept like wind down the valley hills.

Thomas crossed his arms and moved his feet apart slightly, as if bracing himself.

If he turns and runs, he declares his guilt. Yet it will take great courage to remain there as the bulls charge. The land is too narrow. Unless the bulls turn aside, he will surely be crushed.

A sudden muttering took Katherine from her thoughts. She looked beyond Thomas and immediately understood.

The bushes at the rear of the pen! Soldiers with torches! They meant to drive the bulls into a frenzy with fire! Thomas had not agreed to this!

The vulnerable figure that was Thomas remained planted. Katherine fought unexplainable tears.

Within moments, the dried bushes crackled, and high flames were plain to see from the castle walls.

Bellows of rage filled the air as the massive bulls began to push forward against the gate. Monstrous black silhouettes rose from the rear and struggled to climb those in front as the fire surged higher and higher.

Then, just as the pen itself bulged outward from the strain of tons of heavy muscle in panic, the soldiers slashed the rope which held the gate shut.

Bulls exploded forward toward Thomas in a massed charge.

Fifty yards away, he waited.

Does he cry for help? Katherine could not watch. Neither could she close her eyes. Not with the thunder that pounded the earth. Not with the bellowed terror and fury and roar of violence of churning hooves and razor-sharp horns bearing down on him like a black storm of hatred.

Thirty-five yards away, Thomas waited.

Men and women around Katherine began to scream.

Still, he did not move.

Twenty-five yards. Then twenty.

One more heartbeat and the gap had closed to fifteen yards.

Screams grew louder.

Then the unbelievable.

The lead bulls swerved and plunged into the water on either side of Thomas. Within moments, even as the bellows of rage drowned out the screams atop the castle walls, the bulls parted as they threw themselves away from the tiny figure in front of them.

Katherine slumped. It was over.

No bull remained on land. Each swam strongly for the nearest shore.

Another sigh from the crowd atop the castle walls. But before excited talk could begin, the first of the bulls reached shore. As it landed and took its first steps, it roared with renewed rage and bolted away from the cautiously approaching soldiers.

Small saplings snapped as it charged and bucked and bellowed through the trees lining the shore, through the tents and campfires beyond, and finally to the open land beyond.

Each bull did the same as it reached land, and soldiers fled in all directions.

And behind the people, dogs began to howl in the streets. The men and women of Magnus turned in time to see bats swooping and rising in panic in the bright sunshine, until moments later, the first one fell to earth.

Chapter Twenty-Five

Katherine did not see Thomas anywhere on the streets of Magnus during the celebration which traditionally followed the end of a siege. Merchants and shopkeepers, normally cheap to the point of meanness, poured wine freely for the lowliest of peasants and shared the best cakes and freshest meats freely.

Around her was joyful song, much of it off-tune because of the wine, and the vibrant plucked tunes of six-stringed lutes and the jangle of tambourines.

People danced and hugged each other as long-lost brothers—even the most bitter of neighbors. Today, the threat of death had vanished, and their lord, Thomas of Magnus, had been proven innocent. How could they have ever doubted?

Only the most cynical would have observed that much of the celebration was desperation. Not a single person in Magnus wanted to remember the uncanny howling of dogs and the death of bats that had followed Thomas' trial by ordeal. No, that was something to be banished from memory, something that, if possible, all would pretend had never happened.

Katherine moved aimlessly from street to street. Never in her life as a freak in Magnus had she felt like she belonged. This celebration was no different. Few offered her cakes, few offered her wine, and no one took her hand to dance.

Does it matter? she wondered. All those years of loneliness, years serving a greater cause. She thought she had become accustomed to the cruelty of people who judged merely by appearance.

Yet today, the pain drove past the walls around her heart.

Because of Thomas. Because she could remember not wearing the bandages. Like a bird freed from its cage, then imprisoned again, she longed to fly.

Now, walking along the streets among the crowds, thoughts of Thomas darkened her usual loneliness.

Yes, Thomas had proven his courage. Yes, Thomas had defeated the Druid attempt at rebellion within Magnus. And yes, Thomas had also turned away the most powerful earl in the north.

But the Druids had not been completely conquered. As well, the earl of York had departed as a sworn enemy—a mystery she knew both bewildered and tormented Thomas. Magnus was not free from danger.

Katherine was disappointed in her selfishness. So much was at stake, as her duty to Hawkwood proved day after day. Yet, she could barely look beyond her feelings—a frustrating ache—and beyond the insane desire to rip from her face the bandages which hid her from Thomas.

She sighed, remembering Hawkwood's instructions. *"Until we are certain of which side he chooses, he cannot know of you, or of the rest of us. The stakes are far too great. We risk your presence back in Magnus for the sole reason that—despite all we've done—he might become one of them. Love cannot cloud your judgment of that situation."*

Head down and lost in her thoughts, Katherine did not see Gervaise until he clapped a friendly hand upon her shoulder.

"Dear friend," he said, "Thomas wishes you to join him."

"The Roman caltrops worked as the old man predicted," Thomas said in greeting. He stood beside the large chair in his throne room and did not even wait for the guard to close the large doors.

Strange. Thomas trusts me enough to reveal how he survived the charge of the bulls?

Katherine kept her voice calm. With only the two of them in the room, she could bluff. "Predicted? Forgive my ignorance, milord." After all, the person behind the bandages should have no understanding of caltrops or of Hawkwood.

"Katherine," Thomas chided. "Caltrops. Small sharp spikes. Hundreds of years ago, Roman soldiers used to scatter them on the ground to break up cavalry charges. Certainly you remember. After all, the old man gave you instructions for me. 'Go the night before and seed the earth with spikes hidden in the grass. Bulls are not shod with iron. The spikes will pierce their feet and drive them into the water.' "

"Milord?"

Behind her bandages, beads of sweat began to form on Katherine's face.

"Katherine . . ." He used the patient exasperation, a parent humoring a dull child. "We are friends, remember? You need not keep the pretense. After all, you're the one who told me how to bring dogs to a frenzy. How to force bats to their deaths in daylight."

Yes, but it was me unfettered with bandages. Not me hidden as I am now. How can you know we are both the same?

"Milord?"

"Come here," Thomas said sharply.

Katherine did not move. Not with legs frozen in shock.

So Thomas stepped toward her and lifted a hand to her bandaged face.

"No!" she cried. "You cannot shed light upon my face! It is too hideous."

Thomas dropped his hand. "These are your choices. Unwrap it yourself. Let me unwrap it. Or, if you struggle, the guards will be called to hold you down. They will also be witnesses . . . something I'll wager you do not wish."

Impossible he should have guessed!

Katherine whimpered, something she had learned to do well over the years. "Milord . . . the humiliation. How can you force me to—"

"I shall count to three. Then I call the guards."

He stared at her, cold and serious.

Katherine firmed her chin. "I shall do it myself."

It seemed a dream, to be within Magnus and finally removing the hated mask. Wrap by wrap, she removed the cloth around her face. When she finished, she shook her hair free. And waited, defiant.

"You did that in the moonlight, once," Thomas said, with wonder in his voice. "You loosed your hair and gazed at me directly thus. I shall never forget."

Do I feel anger or relief? She showed neither. Merely waited.

"Please," Thomas said gently. "Sit and talk."

She remained standing. "How long did you know?"

He shook his head. "How long did I *suspect?* Since you arrived back as Katherine beneath those bandages. That is your name? Katherine?"

She nodded. He smiled.

He is not raging at the deception?

"Your disappearance the night after I conquered Magnus," Thomas began. "At first, I thought the soldiers had killed you and hidden the body. There could be no other explanation. After all, I had promised you anything if Magnus was won."

I remember that well, Katherine thought. *I remember wishing for something you could never give to a freak behind bandages—the love between a man and woman.*

"When you returned unharmed much later, I could not think of a reason why you would remain away from Magnus so long, knowing I had conquered it. But I did not want to ask."

"Yes," Katherine said. "You cut me short when I tried to explain."

"I had been lied to already," Thomas said, "by someone whose beauty nearly matches yours."

"Isabelle. You thought of her often while waiting in the dungeon."

"I did," Thomas said. "She was a lesson well learned. Mere admiration of beauty does not make love. Mere beauty does not make a person whole. I confess, however, to having learned feelings for you as the Katherine behind the mask. . . ."

He stopped himself and his voice hardened slightly. "I had been lied to by one person whose face could deceive.

With your beauty, there was no way to know if you would do the same."

"Thomas—"

He did not let her finish. "And there was your unexplained entrance into Magnus. Since the night you disappeared, all guards at the drawbridge had instructions to watch for one whose face was hidden by bandages. I hoped always for your return. Yet, when you finally arrived, no guard noticed. Thus, I was forced to conclude you had entered as you are now. Unmasked."

Katherine did not protest. *Better that he did not know the truth.*

"So," Thomas said, "I pretended trust. I wanted to learn more about you, and playing the fool seemed the best way. The dungeon, as you know, had little effect in getting the truth from Isabelle. I thought honey would work better than vinegar."

He held up a hand to forestall her reply. "Finally," Thomas said, "as the midnight messenger, unhidden by bandages, you were able to appear within Magnus, even during a siege. Since it would be impossible for you to leave or enter with an army camped around us, I decided you had been here before the siege began. As Katherine."

Once again, she managed not to betray her thoughts. *He cannot know the truth about my escape, or my visit, then, to Hawkwood during the siege.*

So she asked, "You are not filled with anger at my deception?"

Thomas smiled. "Not yet."

Katherine felt a skip in her chest. *Not yet.*

Sadness and joy tinged his smile as he spoke again.

"Katherine," he said, "I learned to know you before you spellbound me beneath a midnight moon. You are courageous, you love truth, you love God. And you brought me instructions which saved Magnus. It is much easier to believe you are not an enemy."

"I am not," she said quickly. "How can I convince you of that?"

"Tell me about the old man. Tell me about the mission

he has placed upon my shoulders. Tell me why you endured endless years in the horror of disguise." His voice grew urgent, almost passionate. "Tell me the secret of Magnus!"

Many long moments of silence. Many long moments of wanting to trust, wanting to tell him everything.

But she could not. There was Hawkwood and his instructions. *Love cannot cloud your judgment of that situation.* And too much was at stake.

Finally, and very slowly, she shook her head. "I cannot."

Thomas sighed. "As I thought. Even now, I cannot find anger."

She moved toward him and placed a hand on his arm. "Please . . ."

"No," he said with sadness. "I know so little. All I can cling to is the memory of someone who gave me the key to Magnus, and the reason to conquer. More important to Sarah than winning Magnus, was a treasure of . . . of . . ."

Books, Katherine thought. *Knowledge in an age of darkness.*

"Books," Thomas said. "You know that because I told you the night I conquered Magnus. It is a mistake I now regret."

"Regret?"

"I should have kept my secret. How I am to know you are not one of the Druids? Perhaps, by appearing to help save me from the earl, you deceive me into revealing what the Druids want most."

"Thomas, no!"

Still sadness as he spoke. "No? The Druids first caused dogs to howl unnaturally by rubbing crystal into sounds so high-pitched that the animals writhed in torment. The Druids first caused bats to leave their roosts by lighting a fire beneath, and poisoning them with the smoke of yew branches thrown on the fire. Then you reveal to me those secrets so that I can cause the villagers to believe in my innocence once again."

"No!" she pleaded again.

"How is it then you know what the Druids do? Even

astronomy, as the old man proved with his trickery at the gallows? If you are not a Druid, who are you?"

That was the question she wanted to answer more than any other. But she could not.

Tears streamed down her cheeks as she shook her head again.

"I am sorry, milady," Thomas said. He lifted her hand from his arm, then took some of her hair and wiped her face of tears. "I cannot trust you. This battle, whatever it may be, I fight alone."

He lifted her chin with a finger. "Know this, Katherine. The God of whom you spoke, He let me find Him."

Katherine opened her mouth to ask. He placed his finger against her lips.

"No more," he said. "Remember, I shall not forget the Katherine—the real Katherine—who comforted me in the depths of a dungeon and told me of God. Because of her, I cannot and shall not hold you, the deceiving Katherine, against your will."

He turned away from her as he spoke his final words. "Please depart Magnus."

Chapter Twenty-Six

Magnus, Northern England
May 1313

Each morning, the guards on the castle walls expected Tiny John to appear shortly after Tierce, the ringing of the bells which marked the nine o'clock devotional services. By then, Tiny John would already have visited half the shopkeepers' stalls in Magnus.

The guards had good reason to watch for him; few were the ones who had not been plucked of loose coins by the rascal pickpocket. A temporary loss of silver—because Tiny John would return it without fail the next day—meant nothing. It was the ribbing of other guards which always left the victim red-faced and huffing with indignation. After all, how could any military man keep self-respect if robbed by an eight-year-old?

None, however, were the guards who could carry a grudge against Tiny John. He had been in Magnus since Thomas arrived the previous summer; yet that lopsided grin which flashed from his smudged face was still welcomed like the bright colors of a cheerful bird in every corner of the village, especially throughout an exhausting and long winter.

And, even without the charm of a born rascal, Tiny John was always safe within Magnus. Thomas, who ruled with unquestioned authority, considered him a special if untamable friend.

Before the bells of Tierce stopped echoing this spring morning, Tiny John had already scampered from the first castle wall turret to the next. He dodged the two gruff guards like a puppy whirling with glee among clumsy cattle.

"'Tis a fine kettle of fish, soldier Alfred!" Tiny John shouted through his grin at the second guard. "All the tongues in town waggle about the sly looks you earn from the tanner's daughter. And with her betrothed to a mason at that!"

Tiny John waited, hunched over with his hands on his knees, ready for flight after the delivered provocation.

"Let me get a grasp 'a you," soldier Alfred grunted, as he lunged at Tiny John. "Then we'll see how eager you might be to discuss these matters."

Tiny John laughed, then ducked to his right and made a rare mistake. He misjudged the slipperiness of the wet stone below his feet, and fell backward.

"Ho! Ho!" A moment later, soldier Alfred scooped him into his burly arms, grabbed him by the scruff of his shirt and the back of his pants and hoisted him halfway over the castle walls.

"Scoundrel," Alfred laughed. "Tell me what you see below."

"Water," Tiny John gasped. A weak sun glinted gray off the waves of the small lake which surrounded the castle island.

"Water, indeed. Perhaps for a fine kettle of fish?"

"Wonderful jest," Tiny John managed to say. The fall had winded him, and it was still difficult for his lungs to find air. "'Tis easy to understand why the tanner's daughter would be taken with such a man as yourself."

"Aaargh!" Alfred grunted. "What's to be done with you?"

"A reward perhaps?" Tiny John asked.

Alfred set him back down on his feet and dusted off the boy's back.

"Reward, indeed! Be on your way."

"I speak truth," Tiny John protested. "Because of me, you shall be the first to sound alarm."

"Eh?" Alfred squinted as he followed Tiny John's pointing arm to look beyond the lake.

"There," Tiny John said firmly, "from the trees at the edge of the valley. A progression of fifteen men. None on horseback."

It took several minutes for Alfred to detect the faraway movement. Then he shouted for a messenger to reach the sheriff of Magnus.

Moments later, Alfred shouted again. This time in disgust. His pouch no longer carried any farthings.

Tiny John, of course, had disappeared.

Rich, thick tapestries covered the walls of the royal chamber. Low benches lined each side, designed to give suppliants rest as they waited each morning for decisions from their lord on his throne.

At the rear of the chamber, Thomas leaned casually against the large, ornate chair which served as his throne. He waited for the huge double doors at the front to close behind his sheriff, Robert of Uleran.

Thomas' last glimpse was of the four guards posted out front, each armed with long pike and short sword. As usual, it irritated him to be reminded that double guard duty remained necessary.

"The arrival of fifteen men?" Thomas asked, to break their solitary silence.

"Exactly as Alfred spoke," Robert of Uleran replied to his lord. "Although I confess surprise at his accuracy, and the earliness of his warning. He is not known for sharp eyes."

Thomas smiled in agreement, pulled one of the long, padded benches away from the wall, and sat down. With a motion of his hand, he invited Robert of Uleran to do the same.

"Have the visitors been thoroughly searched?" Thomas asked.

Robert of Uleran froze his movement halfway into his sitting position, and without lowering his body further, turned his head to frown at Thomas. When he smiled, warmth spread from him as from a hearth. But when he set his face in anger—as it was now, ladies would gasp and children quiver.

Despite his worries, Thomas suddenly laughed.

"Relax, Robert. You'd think I had just pulled a dagger!"

"You may as well have, milord," Robert of Uleran grumbled. "To even suggest my men might shirk their duty."

Thomas continued to laugh. "My humblest apologies. How could I *not* think they had been searched."

Mollified, the big man finally eased himself onto the bench. "We searched them thrice. There is something about their procession which disturbs me. Even if they claim to be men of God."

Thomas raised an eyebrow. "Claim?"

Robert of Uleran nodded once. "They carry nothing except the usual travel bags. A sealed vial. And a message for the lord of Magnus."

"Vial," Thomas repeated thoughtfully.

"I like it not," Robert of Uleran said with a scowl. "A vial which they claim holds the blood of a martyr."

Thomas snorted. "Simply another religious miracle designed to draw yet more money from even the most poverty-stricken. To which martyr does this supposed relic belong?"

The sheriff stood and paced briefly before spinning on his heels. He looked directly into the eyes of Thomas, lord of Magnus.

"Which martyr?" Robert of Uleran repeated softly. "The man who listened to the cock crow on the dawn of the crucifixion of Christ. The man Christ called the rock of the church, St. Peter himself."

Thomas called for the doors to the royal chamber to be opened. Normal chaos reigned in the large hall. The huge fire to one side crackled and hissed as the fat dripped down from the pig roasting on a spit, and servants and maids scurried in all directions to prepare for the daily meal. The high table, set across the far end of the hall on a raised platform, was ready with pewter plates in place. The rough wooden tables down the entire length of the hall were crowded with people, some resting as they waited to see Thomas, some there because of the liveliness of the hall. There were men armed with swords, bows, and large wolfhounds; some women were in fine dress, and others in rags.

Standing to the side of all this activity, aloof to the world, were fifteen men garbed in simple gowns of brown. They did not bother to look up when the doors opened. When summoned by Robert of Uleran, two of the men broke away from the group, but walked as if they were bestowing a favor in agreeing to the summons.

Thomas noticed the posturing and gritted his teeth. Too often, holy men were blatantly arrogant. Thomas wrapped his purple cloak around him, crossed his arms, and waited for their approach.

He said nothing as the doors swung shut again, leaving the two monks alone in the chamber with him and Robert of Uleran.

The silence hung heavy. Thomas made it no secret that he was inspecting them, although their loose clothing hid much. He could not tell if they were soft and fat, or hardened athletes. He could only be certain that they were large men.

The first, who stared back at Thomas with eyes of flint, had a broad, unlined forehead and a blond beard cropped short. His nostrils flared slightly with each breath, an unconscious betrayal of restrained anger at the deliberate lack of civility from the lord of Magnus.

The second appeared slightly older, perhaps because his face above his scraggly beard was etched with pockmarks. His eyes were flat and unreadable.

The tops of their skulls were shaved. Because the tight skin gleamed, Thomas guessed it was a very recent shave, or that they spent time each day to reshave.

Thomas fought a shiver and then forced calmness upon his own features, hoping his eyes seemed as cold and as gray as the North Sea only thirty miles to the east.

Thomas had spent the entire winter learning and practicing swordplay. The hall outside had rung each day with the clang of steel against steel, and no man could handle a broadsword for hour after hour without developing considerable bulk. Thus, he was no longer the unseasoned puppy who surprised others with unnoticed strength. He now had the presence of a formidable man. That and his well-fitted, expensive clothing added to the poise earned from the responsibilities which he carried as lord of Magnus, and made him an imposing figure when he decided to withhold even the slightest of smiles.

He did not smile now.

Finally, the younger of the two men in front of him coughed. It was enough of a sign of weakness for Thomas to finally speak.

"You wished an audience."

"We come from afar, from—" the younger man began.

Thomas held up his hand and slowly and coldly stressed each word. "You wished an audience."

The older man coughed this time. "Milord, we beg that you might grant us a brief moment to hear our request."

"Granted." Thomas smiled briefly and without warmth. "Make introduction."

"I am Hugh de Gainfort," the dark-haired man said. "My fellow cleric is Edmund of Byrne."

Thomas stepped backward slowly until he reached his throne. He then sat upon it, leaned forward, and steepled his fingers below his chin in thought.

"Clerics?" he said. "You appear to be neither Franciscan nor Cistercian. And representatives of Rome already serve Magnus."

Hugh shook his head. "We are from the true church. We are priests of the Holy Grail."

"Priests, I presume, *in search* of the Holy Grail?" But even as he asked, Thomas felt suddenly chilled by their smug certainty.

Hugh's next words confirmed that chill and came on the edge of his disdainful smile. "No. We *guard* the Holy Grail."

"Impossible!" blurted Robert of Uleran. "One might as well believe in King Arthur's sword in the stone."

For a moment, Hugh's eyes widened.

In shock? The moment passed so quickly that Thomas immediately doubted he had seen any reaction.

"The Grail and King Arthur's sword have much in common," Hugh replied with scorn. "And only fools believe that the passing of centuries can wash away the truth."

Robert of Uleran opened his mouth and drew a breath. Thomas held up his hand again to silence any argument.

"I am told that your procession brings a saint's relic,"

Thomas said. "Are you here among the people of Magnus—" Thomas raised his top lip in distaste "—to squeeze from them money and profit from the blood of St. Peter? Or have you requested audience merely to siphon directly from the treasury of Magnus?"

Edmund clucked as if Thomas were a naughty child. "We are not false priests. *They* shall be punished soon enough for their methods of leeching blood from the poor. No, we are here to preach the truth."

"Yes," Hugh added, as humorlessly and dryly as if they were discussing a transaction of business accounts. "Our only duty is to deliver our message to whoever has a hunger for it. We have coin for our lodging in Magnus, so we beg no charity. Instead, we simply request that you allow us to speak freely among your people during our stay."

"If permission is refused?" Thomas asked.

Hugh bowed in a mocking gesture.

"Enough of your villagers have already heard rumors of the martyr's blood that you dare not refuse." The priest's voice became silky with deadliness. "If you do, our miracles will become your curses."

Chapter Twenty-Seven

The priests of the Holy Grail waited until the afternoon of their second day to demonstrate their first miracle.

The low, gray clouds of the previous week had been broken by a sun so strong it felt almost like summer. To the villagers of Magnus, it was a good omen. These priests, it seemed, had banished the dismal spring chill.

Now the streets were alive with men and women and children anxious to be out in the bright sunshine. Shopkeepers shouted good-natured abuse at each other across the rapidly drying mud of the streets. Housewives forgot to barter down to the last farthing, often accepting the stated price with absent smiles, as they enjoyed the heat of the sun on their shoulders. Servants shook bedding free of the winter's accumulation of fleas and dirt. Dogs sprawled at the sides of buildings, too lazy in the promise of summer to nose among the scraps.

The priests of the Holy Grail were quick to take advantage of the joviality.

There were only five now, speaking at the corner of the church building which dominated the center of Magnus. The others rested quietly within nearby shadows. They took turns, constantly calling out and delivering selected sermons, answering questions, and warding off insults from the less believing.

Hugh de Gainfort was leading this group of five into the hours of the early afternoon. His brown robe made him swelter in the heat; that much was obvious by the oily sweat which poured down his shaven skull.

Still he spoke with power. It was not unusual for twenty

or thirty of the village people to be gathered in front of him.

He looked beyond the crowd into the shadows of the church, then nodded so quickly that any observer would have doubted the action had been made.

"Miracles shall prove we are the bearers of God's truth." Hugh raised his voice without interrupting his sentence as he completed that slight nod. "And as promised for two days, one shall now appear."

His raised voice and his promise drew murmurs from the crowd in front, and attention from passersby.

"Yes!" Hugh continued in a near shout. "Draw forward, believers and unbelievers of Magnus! Within the quarter hour, you shall witness the signs of a new age of truth!"

Hugh swept his arms in a circle. "Go," he urged the crowd. "Go now and return with friends and family! Go forth and bring back with you all those to be saved! For what you see will be a sure sign of blessing!"

The other four priests, all garbed in brown and with skulls shaven, began chanting, "The promised miracle shall deliver blessings to all who witness. The promised miracle shall deliver blessings to all who witness."

For several seconds, none in the crowd reacted.

Hugh roared, "Go forth into Magnus! Return immediately, but do not return alone! Go!"

An old man hobbled away. Then a housewife. Finally, the rest of the crowd turned and spread in all directions. Some ran. Some walked and stumbled as they looked back at Hugh, as if afraid he might perform the miracle in their absence.

Almost immediately, Edmund of Byrne left the shadows. He carried a statue nearly half his height and set it down carefully in front of Hugh.

"Well spoken, my good man." He patted the top of the statue. "Remember, Hugh, not until they are nearly in a frenzy should you deliver. Thomas of Magnus must suffer the same fate as the once-proud earl of York."

Edmund smiled with a savage gleam as he finished speaking. "After all, there is a certain sweetness in casting a man into his own dungeon."

Within half an hour, a great noisy crowd had filled the small square in front of the stone church. It was not often that such unexpected entertainment broke life's monotony and struggle.

Hugh de Gainfort raised his arms to request silence. Beneath the bright sun, his pockmarks formed pebbled shadows across his face.

"People of Magnus," he called, "many of you doubt the priests of the Holy Grail. Some of you have ridiculed us yesterday and today, but we, the speakers of truth, forgive. After you witness the miracle of the Madonna, such insults will not be forgiven as those delivered from ignorance. After today, none of you will be excused for not following our truth!"

Excited and disdainful murmurings from the crowd.

Hugh lifted the statue, and with seemingly little effort, held it high above him.

"Behold, the Madonna, the statue of the sainted Mother Mary."

The murmurings stopped instantly. All in the crowd strained for a better view.

The sun-whitened statue was of a woman with her head bowed behind a veil. A long flowing cape covered most of her body. Only her sandaled feet and her folded hands appeared beneath the cape.

The Madonna's face captivated with carved details of exquisite agony. Her eyes were even more haunting than the pain etched so clearly in the plaster face. Those eyes were deep crystal, a luminous blue which seemed to search the hearts of every person in the crowd.

"The Mother Mary herself knew well of the Holy Grail," Hugh said in deep, slow words, as he set the statue down again. "She blessed this statue for our own priests those thirteen centuries ago, our own priests who already held the sacred Holy Grail. Thus, we were established first as the one true church!"

A voice from the entrance to the church interrupted Hugh. "This is not a story to be believed! Only the Holy Pope and the Church of Rome may make such claim!"

Hugh turned slowly to face his challenger.

The thin man at the church entrance wore a loose, black robe. His face was white with anger, his fists clenched at his sides.

"Ah!" Hugh proclaimed loudly for his large audience. "A representative of the oppressors of the people!"

This shift startled the priest. "Oppressors?"

"Oppressors!" Hugh's voice gained in resonance, as if he were a trained actor. "You have set the rules according to a religion of convenience! A religion designed to give priests and kings control over the people!"

The priest stood on his toes in rage. "This . . . is . . . vile!" he said with a strained scream. "Someone call the lord of Magnus!"

No one in the crowd moved.

Hugh smiled, a wolf moving in on the helpless fawn.

"The truth shall speak for itself," Hugh said. He turned back to the people. "Shall we put truth to the test?"

"Yes!" came the shout. "Truth to the test!"

The priest felt the trap shut. He knew he could not defy such a large crowd, and he felt fear at Hugh's confidence.

Hugh held up his arms again. Immediate silence followed.

"What say you?" Hugh queried the priest, without deigning to glance back. "Or have you fear of the results?"

More long silence. Finally the priest croaked, "I have no fear."

Hugh smiled at the crowd in front of him. He noted their flushed faces, their concentration on his words.

Yes, he mentally licked his lips, *they are ready.*

"This Madonna," he said with a theatrical flourish, "blessed by the Mother Mary herself, shall tell us the truth. Let us take her inside the church. If the priest speaks truth, the Madonna will remain as she is. However, if in this church resides falseness against God, the Madonna will weep in sadness!"

Even as Hugh finished speaking, those at the back of the crowd began to push forward. Excited babble washed over all of them. None wanted to miss the test.

Once again, Hugh was forced to request silence.

"And," he continued in those confident, deep tones, "when the truth is revealed, the new and faithful followers of the priests of the Holy Grail will soon be led to the Grail itself!"

At this, not even Hugh's upraised arms could stop the avalanche of shouting. The legendary Grail promised blessings to all who touched it!

Knowing nothing more could be said above the tumult, Hugh took the statue into his arms, turned to face the church, and marched forward.

Without pausing to acknowledge the priest, Hugh walked through the deep shadows of the church's entrance, and into the quiet coolness beyond. He kept walking until he reached the altar at the front. He moved the lit candles and set the statue down so that it faced the gathered people.

Soon the church was full, every eye straining to see the Madonna's face, every throat dry with expectation.

"Dear Mother Mary," Hugh cried to the curved ceiling above, "is this a house worthy of your presence?"

The statue, of course, remained mute. So skillful, however, was Hugh's performance, that some in the audience expected a reply.

Hugh fell to his knees and clasped his hands and begged at the statue's feet.

"Dear Mother Mary," Hugh cried again, "is this a house worthy of your presence?"

For a dozen heartbeats, he stayed on his knees, silent, head bowed, hands clasped high above him. Then he looked upward at the statue and moaned.

He stood in triumph and pointed. "Behold," he shouted, "the Madonna weeps."

Three elderly women in the front rows fainted. Grown men crossed themselves. Mothers wept in terror. And all stared in horror and fascination at the statue.

Even in the dimly filtered light at the front of the church, all could see tears glistening in the Madonna's eyes. As each second passed, another large drop broke from each eye and slowly rolled downward.

Chapter Twenty-Eight

Thomas made it his custom to greet each dawn from the eastern ramparts of the castle walls, before the wind swept the moors. Often, a mist would rise from the lake that surrounded Magnus; and behind Thomas, the town would lie silent as he lost himself in thoughts and absorbed the beauty of the sun's rays breaking over the tops of the faraway hills to cut sharp shadows into the dips and swells of the land.

There, on the ramparts in the quiet of a new day, Thomas found great solace in prayer—not the rituals intoned by priests who insisted only they could mediate between man and God, but the opening of his heart to the God who listened directly to each man and woman who called upon His name.

Yes, Thomas now took comfort in his faith, something he would not have believed possible a year earlier; but he still could not overcome his suspicion of the priests and monks who used religion as a battering ram for their own selfish purposes.

For many, the church was more of a career than a way to serve God. Thomas knew that his society was classified in three orders: those who work, the peasants; those who fight, the nobility; and those who pray, the clergy.

Since praying was easier than working, and safer than fighting, it was an attractive career. Because of this—as Thomas remembered too well from his days as an orphan in the supposed care of monks—many abused their positions. The leaders in the church were as prone as the nobles to eat from plates of gold and silver. Clergy, using the hard-earned money of their peasant charges, often wore jewels and rings and kept fine horses and expensive hounds and hawks.

It was not difficult to claim shelter in the wings of the Roman church. A test for clerical status was simple; because literacy and education was so rare, any man who could read a Latin text from the Bible—even if it was memorized and repeated as if read—could claim "benefit of clergy." This was especially valuable, for those in the church who had committed any crime from simple theft to blatant murder were given complete exemption from the courts of the land and tried instead by the church. In this manner, clergymen escaped the king's judges. And, since the laws within the church forbade the use of mutilation and the death sentence, and since it was too expensive for the church to maintain its own prisons, it relied on spiritual penalties for punishment. At the very worst, a cleric might face a fine or a light whipping for even the most terrible of crimes.

Thus, Thomas lived in uneasy alliance with the priests of Magnus. No matter how powerful any ruler, the power of the church was equal. More dreaded to an earl or king than a sieging army was the threat of excommunication. After all, if the mass of people believed that a ruler's power was given directly by God, how could that ruler maintain power if the church made him an outcast?

Each Sabbath, Thomas entered the church to worship, as expected by tradition. Too often, however, his mind wandered. Unlike most of the people of Magnus, Thomas could read and write. He understood Latin in its written form, and winced at the biblical inaccuracies spouted by priests too willing to deliver whatever message it took to ensure that ignorant peasants remain cowed by the threat of God's punishment.

It was with relief, then, that Thomas pursued the knowledge of God through his own reading and prayers.

And without fail, each morning following his prayers and each night before falling to sleep, Thomas would silently ask himself the questions which haunted him in empty hopes that the asking might one day receive an answer.

*An old man once cast the sun into darkness and direct-
ed me here from the gallows where a knight was about to
die, falsely accused. The old man even then knew my
dream of conquering Magnus. Who was that old man?
How did he know?*

*A valiant and scarred knight befriended me and helped
me win the castle that once belonged to his own lord. Then
he departed. Why?*

*A crooked candlemaker and Isabelle, the daughter of the
lord we vanquished, captured and imprisoned in the dungeons of Magnus, escaped in a manner still unknown.
How?*

*And the midnight messenger, Katherine. She spent all
those years in Magnus disguised beneath bandages as a
scarred freak. Was she one of the false sorcerers who nearly won Magnus from me? Or was she truly a friend, now
banished unfairly by my command from this kingdom?*

What is the secret of Magnus?

The early rays of sun which warmed Thomas on the eastern ramparts had never replied to these silent questions.

On this day, less than a week after the arrival of the
priests of the Holy Grail, Thomas now had other urgent
questions and problems to occupy him as he walked the
ramparts.

Not even the enthusiastically squirming burden left in his
throne room yesterday—Thomas smiled as he recalled how
Tiny John had deposited a clumsy puppy on his lap—was
enough of a distraction during these terrible days.

His only comfort was in knowing that there was one man
in all of Magnus who had a gentle wisdom. It took little for
Thomas to decide that this day required another visit and
discussion.

"Five days of nonsense about the Holy Grail!" exploded
Thomas. "Blood of a martyr which clots and unclots as
directed by prayer! I am at my wits end, Gervaise. It is
almost enough for me to sympathize with the priests of
Rome."

"Then the matter *must* be grave." The elderly man, on

his knees in the rich dirt of the garden, chuckled without looking up from his task. "Brave would be the man to gamble that you would ever side with Rome."

Thomas paced two steps past Gervaise on the stone path which meandered through the garden, then whirled and paced back. "Jest if you will, but do not be surprised if you find yourself without gainful work when the priests you serve are cast from this very church."

Gervaise merely hummed in the sunshine which bathed his stooped shoulders in pleasant warmth. His gray hair was combed straight back. His voice was deep and rich in tone, and matched in strength the lines of humor and character etched in his face. He had thick, gnarled fingers, as capable of threading the most delicate needles as of clawing among the roots of the roughest bush, which he did now with great patience.

Carefully pruned bushes stood tall among wide, low shrubs, and lined in front of these were rows of flowers almost ready to bloom. The greatest treasures among these for Gervaise were his roses. He would coax forth each summer the petals of white or pink or yellow, all considered prizes by the noble women of Magnus.

Gervaise gently snapped another weed from the roots of a rose bush. He placed the weed on a rapidly drying pile an arm's length away. "The sun proves itself to be quite hot these days," he said in a leisurely tone. "It does wonders for these precious plants. Unfortunately, it also encourages the weeds."

Thomas sighed. "Gervaise, do you not understand what happens within Magnus? With these signs of miracles, the priests of the Holy Grail have almost the entire population of Magnus in their grip."

Gervaise straightened with effort, then finally turned to regard the young master of Magnus.

"I understand it is much too late to prevent what surely must happen next. The horse has escaped the stable, Thomas. Therefore, I will not worry about closing the gate." Gervaise swept his arms in a broad motion to indicate the garden. "So I shall direct my efforts where they will have effect."

Thomas stopped halfway through another stride. "So you agree with me," he accused. "And what do *you* believe will happen next?"

"The priests of the Holy Grail will replace those within the church now," Gervaise said mildly. "Then, I suspect they will preach sedition."

"Sedition? Rebellion against the established order?" Thomas exploded again. "Impossible. To set their hand against the church is one thing, but against the royal order is yet another!"

Gervaise shook the dirt from his knees and walked to a bench half hidden by overhanging branches.

Thomas followed.

"Impossible?" Gervaise echoed softly as he sat. "Last summer you conquered Magnus and delivered all of us from the oppression of our former master. Yet how have you spent your winter? Relaxed and unafraid?"

Thomas sat alongside the old man. He did not answer immediately. Around them, the joyful, caroling birds were oblivious to the matters of state in discussion between an old caretaker and a young lord.

"You know the opposite," Thomas said slowly, realizing where his answer would lead. "Day after day, each meal, each glass of wine tasted first for poison by the official tester. Each visitor searched thoroughly for daggers or other hidden weapons before an audience with me. Double guards posted at the door to my bedchamber each night. Guards at the entrance to this garden, ready to protect me at the slightest alarm. I am a prisoner within my own castle."

"Thus," Gervaise said with no trace of triumph, "you are no stranger to rebellion. Why, then, do you persist in thinking it may not come from another source?"

"Mayhaps," Thomas countered. "Yet these are priests against priests, Holy Grail against those from Rome, each seeking authority in religious matters, not matters of state. . . ."

Thomas let his voice trail away as Gervaise shook his head and pursed his lips in a frown. "Thomas, these new priests carry powerful weapons! The Weeping Madonna. The blood of St. Peter. And the promise of the Holy Grail."

Gervaise paused, then said, "Tell me, Thomas, should the priests of the Holy Grail become your enemy, how would you fight them?"

Thomas opened his mouth to retort, then slowly shut it as he realized the implications.

"Yes," Gervaise said. "Pray these men do not seek your power, for they cannot be fought by sword. Every man, woman and child within Magnus would turn against you."

Thomas leaned on the ledge near the window and waited until Robert of Uleran entered and closed the door to the bedchamber.

"Attack, beast!" Thomas called out. "Attack!"

With a high-pitched yip, the puppy bolted from beneath a bench and flung itself with enthusiasm at Robert's ankle.

"Spare me, milord!" cried Robert of Uleran in fake terror. "Spare me from this savage monster!"

The puppy had a firm grip on Robert's boot, and no shaking could free him.

Thomas laughed so hard that he could barely speak. "Tickle him behind the ears, good Robert. He's an easy one to fool."

Robert of Uleran reached down, then stopped and glared at Thomas with suspicion. "He'll not piddle on my boot instead?"

"You guessed my secret weapon," Thomas hooted. Tiny John's gift had already proven itself dangerous.

"Bah." Robert of Uleran reached down, soothed the puppy with soft words and a gentle touch, then scooped him up and quickly dropped him in Thomas' arms.

"Go on," Robert of Uleran said to the puppy. *"Now* discharge your royal duties. Then we'll see who has the last laugh."

"Rich jest," Thomas said, and cradled the dog in the crook of his right arm, rubbing the top of its head. "Would that all of Magnus could be tamed this easily."

Robert of Uleran nodded, then spoke above the panting

of the puppy. "You seem far from ill, milord. The reports had led me to believe I would find you half dead beneath the covers of your bed."

Thomas smiled. "I was that convincing, was I? Of course, to lie fully dressed beneath those covers is enough to put the sweat of fever on any person's brow."

Thomas became serious very quickly. "Do not let the rumor rest. It serves our purpose for all to believe the fever grips me so badly that I cannot leave this room."

"Milord?"

"Robert, three days ago, with the miracle of the weeping statue, the priests of the Holy Grail won the mantle of authority in the church of Magnus. They now preach openly from the pulpit itself, and the former priests have been banished from the church. It is not a good sign."

"It cannot be so bad," Robert protested. "Let the religious orders fight among themselves."

"I wish I could agree," Thomas said. The puppy chewed on the end of his sleeve and sighed with satisfaction. "But I must be sure that there is no threat to the remainder of Magnus."

Robert of Uleran raised his eyebrows in a silent question.

"All winter," Thomas continued, "we have been hidden in these towers, away from the people. Aside from the servants in this keep, and those who request audience, I have almost been a prisoner."

"The Druids, milord," Robert of Uleran said in a whisper. "You cannot be blamed for precautions."

"Perhaps not. But now I have little idea what concerns these people in everyday life. For certes, I hear their legal problems in the throne room, but little else."

"But—"

"How do they feel about these new priests?" Thomas interrupted. "Someone must go among them and discover this."

Robert of Uleran straightened. "I will send someone immediately."

"A guard?" Thomas asked. "A knight? Do you believe such a man will receive the confidence of housewives and beggars?"

Robert of Uleran slowly shook his head.

Thomas grinned. "I thought you might agree. Therefore, someone must spend a day on the streets in disguise, perhaps as a beggar himself."

"But who, milord? It must be someone we trust. And I am too large and well known for such a task."

"Whom do I trust more than myself?" Thomas countered. His grin widened. "And it has been a long and terrible winter cooped inside these walls."

Thomas rejoiced to be a beggar.

Gone, indeed, was the long, flowing purple cape he wore as lord of Magnus. Gone were the soft linen underclothing, the rings, and the sword and scabbard that went with his position.

In their stead were coarse, dirty rags for clothing, no jewelry, and—as Thomas had copied from his long-departed knight friend—a short sword ingeniously hidden in a sheath strapped between his shoulder blades. To pull the sword free, Thomas would only have to reach over his shoulders as if scratching his back.

With Robert of Uleran's help, Thomas had dyed his skin several shades darker with the juice of boiled bark. He hoped this would give him the rough texture of a person who spent too much time in the bitter, cold wind or the baking sun.

Thomas had cut his hair short in ragged patches, and also had carefully scraped dark grease beneath his fingernails. It was his plan to spend at least two days among the peasants of Magnus, and only the blindest of fools would fail to notice the improbability of clean hands on a street beggar.

But how would Thomas disguise his features?

Robert of Uleran had suggested an eyepatch. Many in the land were disfigured or crippled and forced to beg or die. It would not be unusual for another strange beggar with only one eye to appear among the poor.

Thus disguised, Thomas let his shoulders sag and added a limp as he slipped unnoticed through the great banquet hall among the crowds of morning visitors.

He stepped into the spring air outside and rejoiced at his

freedom as a beggar. For with his purple cloak and scepter of authority, he had also left behind his responsibilities and the constant vigil against Druid assassination.

It took less than a minute for some of that joy to be tarnished.

"Step aside, scum!" bellowed a large man guiding a mule loaded with leather. When Thomas did not react instantly—indeed, he was wondering with amusement which poor scum was intended—the man shoved him rudely back into a crowd of people on the side of the street.

"Watch yourself!" another shouted at Thomas. Hands grasped and pulled at him, while others pushed him away in disgust. One well-placed kick inside the back of his knee almost pitched Thomas forward, and when he stood upright again, he knew it would not be difficult to pretend his limp for the rest of the day.

Thomas moved ahead, handicapped by the lack of depth vision because of the eye patch.

Still, he refused to be downcast. He was, after all, temporarily free. In two days, he would resume his position of authority—without regrets; for now, he could wander much as he did the first time he set foot in Magnus as a powerless orphan.

He smiled to remember that day. The streets, of course, looked identical. Shops so crowded the streets that the more crooked buildings actually touched roofs where they leaned into each other. Space among the bustling people was equally difficult to find.

Thomas did not let his renewed sightseeing stop him from carefully placing his steps. The streets were filled with the stench and mess of emptied chamberpots and the waste of sheep or calf or pig innards thrown there by the butchers.

Pigs squealed, donkeys brayed in protest against heavy carts, and dogs barked, all a backdrop of noise against the hum of people busy in the sunshine.

Thomas sighed and turned backward to squint against that sunshine, as he gazed at the large keep of Magnus dominating the center of the village. It was easy to rejoice in his new role as beggar, knowing he would be back in its quiet and safety by the next evening, and knowing he would not need to beg to feed himself.

To confirm that, Thomas reached for his hidden pouch which contained two silver coins. Beggar or not, he did not relish going hungry in the evening or on the morrow—

Thomas groaned.

Those grasping hands in the crowd! Only five minutes away from the castle and I have been picked as clean as a country fool.

Thomas then sighed and resigned himself to a long two days among his people.

Chapter Twenty-Nine

"'Tis our good fortune the weather holds so well," the old lady cackled to Thomas. "Or the night would promise us much worse than empty bellies. The roof above us leaks horribly in any rain at all."

Thomas grunted.

The old lady chose to accept his grunt as one of agreement. She moved herself closer to Thomas and snuggled against his side in the straw.

Thomas grunted again, then fought the urge to laugh.

Which was worse? The cloying barnyard smell of the dirty stable straw, or the stale, unwashed odor of the old woman who sought him for warmth. His skin prickled; already he could feel the fleas transferring from the woman to him.

Besides, Thomas did not know if he agreed with her. It had been so long since he had felt this hunger, he almost would have preferred a rainy, cold night for the sake of being fed.

He stared into the darkness around him. Vague shapes moved; the horses, at least, were content.

The old woman burped, releasing a sour gas which did little to help Thomas sleep.

"I wonder," he asked, "why there are not more of us seeking shelter here in the stables. Do they fear the soldiers of Magnus?"

Thomas, however, knew well they did not. As lord, he had commanded his men not to harry the poor who commonly used the stables as a last resort. *So why are the stables empty?*

The old woman snorted. "The others choose the church as sanctuary."

"Ah," Thomas said. He maintained his role as a wandering beggar, freshly arrived in Magnus. "I hear the priests of Magnus will give food and a roof to any who pledge to work the following day."

Thomas smiled quickly to himself as he finished his words. After all, he and Gervaise had set that policy themselves, to allow the penniless their pride, and to stop the abuse of charity by the lazy.

Much to his surprise, the old woman laughed cruelly. "No longer! Have you not heard? Those priests have been replaced by the men of the Holy Grail."

"Indeed?" Thomas replied.

"Indeed." The old woman explained the miracle of the weeping statue and its effect on the people of Magnus, and how the priests of the Holy Grail had ruthlessly used that newfound power to banish the former priests from their very own church building.

"I understand little, then," Thomas admitted. "You say the priests of old are not in the church. Where, then, do the less fortunate stay each night, if not here in the stables or at the church?"

The old woman shifted, heedless of the elbow which forced a gasp from Thomas.

"I did not say the church was empty," she told him. "Only that the poor need not pledge a day's services in exchange for food and lodging. Instead, the priests of the Holy Grail demand an oath of loyalty."

"What!" Thomas sat bolt upright and bumped the woman solidly. He almost forgot himself in his outrage and forced himself to relax again.

"Lad," the old woman admonished, "I pray thee might give warning the next time. My old bones cannot take such movement."

"I beg pardon," Thomas said, much more quietly. "It seems such a strange requirement, this pledging an oath." He must keep his voice wondering instead of angry. "I had thought, however, an oath of loyalty could only be pledged to those who rule."

The old woman cackled again. "Are you so fresh from the

countryside that your eyes and ears are still plugged with manure? These priests have promised the Holy Grail to their followers. With such power, how could they not rule soon?"

Once again, Thomas fought frustration at the invincibility of his unreachable opponents. When he felt he could speak calmly again, he pretended little interest.

"What do you know of this Grail?" he asked casually. "And its power?"

The old woman clutched Thomas tighter as the evening chill settled upon them.

"Had you no parents, lad? Anyone to instruct you in common legends?"

She reacted instantly to his sudden stillness.

"It is my turn to beg pardon," she said softly. "There are too many orphans in the land."

"'Tis nothing." Thomas waved a hand in the darkness, as if brushing away memories. "You spoke of the Holy Grail."

"The Holy Grail," she repeated. "A story to pass the time of any night."

Her voice became singsong, oddly beautiful as it dropped into a storytelling chant. As Thomas listened, the stable around him seemed far away. He no longer sucked the air carefully between his teeth to lessen the stench. The straw no longer stabbed him in tiny pinpricks. And the burden of the woman leaning against him lessened. Thomas let himself be carried away by her voice, back through lost centuries to the Round Table of King Arthur's court.

"Long ago," she said softly, "at Camelot, there was a fellowship of knights so noble . . ."

So the story began.

It was a quest for the eternal, she explained, this legendary search by King Arthur's knights for the Holy Grail. The tiny, wrinkled woman recounted the legend which so many in the land wanted to believe.

The Holy Grail, she told Thomas, was the cup which Christ had used at the Last Supper, the night before He was crucified. This cup was later obtained by a wealthy Jew, Joseph of Arimathaea, who undertook to care for Christ's body before burial. When Christ's body disappeared after the third day in the tomb, Joseph was accused of stealing it, and was thrown into prison and deprived of food. But he was miraculously kept alive by a dove which entered his cell every day and deposited a wafer into the cup.

"Yes," the old woman breathed, "it was in that prison cell that Christ Himself appeared in a blaze of light and entrusted the cup to Joseph's care! It was then that Christ instructed Joseph in the mystery of the Lord's Supper and in certain other secrets! It is these secrets which make the Holy Grail so powerful!"

"These secrets?" Thomas interrupted.

"No one knows," she said, "but it matters little. How can these secrets help but be marvelous!"

Yes, Thomas thought sourly, *despite the profound lack of truth in this legend, it is something to which the people want to cling. And oddly, again, I find myself sympathizing with the difficulties of the church as it struggles to counteract the ignorance around it in this age of darkness.*

Thomas did not betray that almost bitter reaction. He wanted the old woman to continue, wanted badly to know if the priests of the Holy Grail had managed to poison the people of Magnus entirely.

She told him the rest of the legend in awed tones, as if whispered words in the black of the stable might reach those priests of power.

After Joseph was released, he was joined by his sister and her husband, Bron, and a small group of followers. They traveled overseas into exile, careful to guard the cup on their journey, and formed the First Table of the Holy Grail.

"This table was meant to represent the Table of the Last Supper," the old woman said with reverence. "One seat was always empty, the seat which represented Judas, the betrayer. A member of the company once tried sitting there and was swallowed up!"

Thomas marveled at the woman's superstitious belief. Yet, he told himself, if one cannot read, one cannot combat the evils of ignorance.

"Go on," he said gently. "This takes place long before King Arthur, does it not?"

"Oh, yes" she said quickly. "Joseph of Arimathaea sailed here to our great island and set up the first Christian church at Glastonbury, and somewhere nearby the Grail Castle."

She sighed. "Alas, in time the Grail Keeper lost his faith, and the entire land around the castle became barren and known as the Waste Land, and strangely, could not be reached by travelers. The land and the Grail remained lost for many generations."

The woman settled farther. Her silence continued for so long that Thomas suspected she had fallen asleep.

"Until King Arthur?" he prompted.

"No need to hurry me," she said almost crossly. "I had closed my eyes to see in my mind those noble knights of yesteryear. Too few are the pleasant thoughts for a forgotten old woman."

Then, remembering the impatience of youth, she patted Thomas' knee in forgiveness. "Yes, lad. Until King Arthur. At the Round Table the Holy Grail appeared once, floating veiled in a beam of sunlight, and those great knights pledged themselves to go in search of it."

Thomas settled back for a long story. Many were the escapades of King Arthur and his men, many the adventures in search of the Holy Grail, and many the hours passed by people in its telling and retelling.

Thomas heard again of the perilous tests faced by Sir Lancelot and his son, Sir Galahad, by Sir Bors, Sir Percival and the others. Thomas heard again how Sir Percival, after wandering for five years in the wilderness, found the Holy Grail and healed the Grail Keeper, making the Waste Lands once again flower. Thomas heard again how Percival, Galahad, and Bors then continued their journey until they reached a heavenly city in the East, where they learned the mysterious secrets of the Grail and saw it taken into heaven.

She told it well, this legend which captured all imaginations. But she did not finish where the legend usually ended.

"And now," she said, "these priests offer to us the blood of a martyr of ancient times, blood which clots, then unclots after their prayer. They offer us the weeping statue of the

Mother Mary. And they speak intimately of the Holy Grail, returned rightfully to them, with its powers to be shared among their followers!"

Thomas felt his chest grow tight. Indeed, these were the rumors he had feared. "These followers," he said cautiously, "what must they do to receive the benefits of the Holy Grail?"

The old woman clucked. "The same as the poor must do to receive shelter. Pledge an oath of loyalty, one that surpasses loyalty to the lord of Magnus, or any other earthly lord."

Open sedition, open rebellion! These were the rumors which had not yet reached him, the rumors he had sought by leaving his castle keep. How much time did he have left to combat these priests?

Another thought struck Thomas.

"Yet you are here," Thomas said to the woman curled against his side, "in the stable and not at the church. Why have you not pledged loyalty to this great power for the benefits of food and lodging?"

The old woman sighed. "An oath of loyalty is not one to be pledged lightly. And many years ago, when I had beauty and dreams, I pledged mine to the former lord of Magnus."

"Yet . . . yet . . ." Thomas stammered suddenly at her impossible words, "was that not the lord which oppressed Magnus so cruelly, the one which Lord Thomas so recently overcame?"

"You know much for a wandering beggar," she said sharply. "Especially for one ignorant of the Holy Grail."

"I have heard much in my first day here," Thomas countered quickly.

"So be it," the old woman agreed, then continued. "I did not swear an oath to *that* tyrant. No, my pledge of loyalty was given to the lord who reigned twenty years earlier, a kinder lord who lost Magnus to the tyrant."

Thomas marveled. This woman showed great loyalty to the same lord Thomas had avenged by reconquering Magnus. *Yes,* Thomas thought, *I will reward the old woman later, when I leave my disguise and resume my duties as lord of Magnus.*

He was given no time to ponder further. The nearby horses stamped nervously at a sudden rustling at the entrance to the stable.

"Hide beneath the straw!" the old woman hissed. "We'll not be found!"

She began to burrow.

While Thomas did not share her fear, he wanted to maintain his role, and a half-blind beggar in a strange town would do as she instructed. So he burrowed with her until they were nearly covered.

Many moments passed. Strangely, a small whimpering reached them.

Straw poked in Thomas' ears and closed eyes. Despite his curiosity, he held himself perfectly still.

Somehow, a patter of light footsteps approached their hiding spot directly and with no hesitation. From nowhere, a cold wet object bumped against his nose, and Thomas nearly yelped with surprise. Then a warm tongue rasped against his face, and Thomas recognized the intruder was nothing more alarming than a friendly puppy.

Can it be—

"Thomas?" a voice called.

Tiny John! What meaning did this hold?

Thomas sat up and shook the straw free from his clothes. Yes, it was his puppy wriggling against him in joy.

"I am here," Thomas said from beneath the straw. He ignored the surprised flinch of the old woman. "What urgent business brings you in pursuit?"

"I followed the puppy to you," Tiny John explained. "Exactly as Robert of Uleran predicted in his last words to me."

Thomas stood quickly, with a cold fear in his stomach.

"His *last* words? What has occurred?"

Tiny John's voice trembled. "The castle has fallen without a fight, milord. Few were those who dared resist the priests of the Holy Grail."

"That . . . cannot . . . be," Thomas uttered. He felt weak on his legs.

"I recognize you!" the old woman cried, as she stood beside Thomas.

"The deception could not be helped," Thomas muttered, as his mind tried to grasp the impossible.

The old woman clouted Thomas. "Not you, ragamuffin! The boy. Dark as it is, I know his voice. Tiny John. He is a friend of the lord of Magnus! And a friend to the poor. Why, more than once he has raided the banquet hall and brought us sweet meats and flagons of wine. The boy could pick a bird clean of its feathers and not wake it from its perch. Why, he . . ."

The old woman's voice quavered, then faded. "What deception? You spoke of deception?" Then a quiet gasp of comprehension. "The boy called you Thomas! Not our Thomas? The lord of Magnus?"

"Aye, indeed. I am Thomas. And by Tiny John's account, now the *former* lord of Magnus."

The old woman groaned and sat heavily.

"Milord," Tiny John blurted. "The priests appeared within the castle as if from the very walls! Like hordes of rats. They—"

"Robert of Uleran," Thomas interrupted with a leaden voice. He wanted to sit beside the old woman and, along with her, moan in low tones. "How did he die?"

"Die?"

"You informed me that he spoke his last words."

"Last words to *me*, milord. Guards were falling in all directions, slapping themselves as they fell! The priests claimed it was the hand of God, and for all to lay down their arms. It was then that Robert of Uleran pushed this puppy into my arms and told me to flee, told me to give you warning not to return to the castle."

Thomas shifted the puppy into the crook of his left arm and gripped Tiny John's shoulder fiercely with his right hand. "You know not the fate of Robert of Uleran?"

"No, milord. There was great confusion."

Thomas then covered his face with his free hand, and bowed his head in sorrow.

Chapter Thirty

The shadows of the castle spires had hardly faded in the rising sun, yet the news was already old.

"Magnus has fallen to the priests of the Holy Grail!"

Some rejoiced, almost in religious ecstasy. After all, there had been the miracles of the weeping statues! The blood of the martyr! And now, stories of how the guards had fallen without a fight! Surely, the Grail must appear next!

Others were saddened. Wisely, they did not show this sadness, for who could guess the intentions of Magnus' new masters? Yet they grieved for the loss of Thomas, who had mysteriously vanished as the castle fell to the priests. These mourners were those who understood how Thomas had ruled with compassion and intelligence. These mourners were those who still had gratitude for the manner in which Thomas had released them from the bondage of a cruel lord less than a year before.

And a few were those whose eyes glinted with greed to hear that Thomas had been deposed. For the priests of the Holy Grail had offered a brick of the purest gold to the man who might capture Thomas.

Thomas limped along the edge of the streets. It took little effort to add that limp to his step; yesterday's brutal kick was this day's growing bruise, and a sleepless chilled night had stiffened his leg considerably.

Beneath his rags, he carried the puppy in the crook of his left arm. There was comfort in the warm softness of the animal against his skin. Occasionally, the puppy would lick Thomas' arm, something which each time brought a small smile, despite his troubles.

The smile did not reach anyone, however. Thomas kept his gaze lowered on each halting step along the street. Whispers of the massive bounty placed upon his head had reached his ears. *If the wrong sharp pair of eyes recognizes me, despite the rags and eyepatch . . . if the old woman does not keep her vow of secrecy . . . if Tiny John is captured by bounty hunters . . .*

Yet Thomas could not remain hidden, cowed in a dark shadow somewhere within Magnus. If he were to survive, he must escape the castle island. To escape, he needed help from the one person he might trust.

And to reach that person, he must enter directly the lion's den. So Thomas limped to the church and prayed no Holy Grail priest would inquire too closely of the business of a starving beggar.

At the rear of the stone building, Thomas followed the same garden path he had walked only two days before in his purple cape as lord of Magnus.

He rounded a bend of the path and saw the familiar figure of Gervaise kneeling in the soil, pulling weeds with methodical delicacy. Thomas almost straightened and cried aloud in relief, but something stopped him.

What is this strangeness?

Not weeds, but piled in neat bundles beside Gervaise were the rose bushes, roots already wilting in the sun. These were the most precious plants in the garden. *Why does Gervaise pull them out?*

Thomas sucked in his breath. Was this a message? It disturbed him enough that instead of a joyful call, Thomas continued to limp, and in that manner slowly reach the old man.

"Good sir," Thomas croaked. "Alms for the poor? I've not eaten in two days."

Gervaise yanked another rose bush free from the soil without looking up. "Gervaise," Thomas hissed. "It is I!"

The old man laid the bush on the nearest bundle and shuffled sideways on his knees to an unworked patch of soil.

"Of course it is you, Thomas. And not a moment too soon," Gervaise grumbled, without looking up. "Removing these roses has robbed me of five years of toil. This price counts little, however, for indeed you noticed and took it as warning."

Gervaise paused, then said, "Ask your question, again, as if I am deaf. And add insult to your words."

Thomas hesitated a moment, then raised his voice. "Are you deaf, you old cur? I've not eaten in two days."

"Do as the other beggars," Gervaise instructed equally loudly with acted impatience. "Enter the church and pledge allegiance to the priests of the Holy Grail."

"Within the church?" Thomas said quickly. Shock raised his voice another level. "Why would—"

Thomas stopped abruptly as Gervaise turned his head to look upward in response.

The mangled right side of the old man's face was swollen purple. Lines of dried blood showed the trails of cruel, deep slashes. His right eye was swelled shut, and his nose was bent and pushed sideways at an angle which made Thomas gag.

"The priests of the Grail know you and I are friends," Gervaise said calmly without moving his head. "This was done to encourage me to deliver you into their hands. And as you may have guessed, they observe me now from the church windows and from the trees behind you."

Thomas blinked back tears.

"If you do not go into the church shortly," Gervaise said in a low voice, "those watchers will suspect you and hunt you down. They may be within hearing distance. Ask me now which priest to see. Do not forget the insults."

Thomas hoped his voice would not choke as he forced the words into a scornful snarl. "Worthless donkey! Instruct me well the priest to seek, ere I add to the scars on your face!"

"Enter the church without hesitation," Gervaise commanded quietly. "You *must* reach the altar. Then—" Gervaise looked past Thomas, then back at Thomas. "Spit upon me. Curse me as if I have not replied!"

"I cannot."

"Thomas, anything to deceive our watchers. It will purchase a few precious moments."

The old man's eyes compelled Thomas.

"May the pox blind you and your children." Thomas finally blurted, then spat downward. "Feed my belly, not my ears, you miserable old man. May worms rot your flesh as you sleep if you do not help me."

Gervaise recoiled and bowed his head as if afraid.

But his voice continued strong. "Thomas, the panel beneath the side of the altar which holds the candles—kick it sharply near the bottom. Twice. It will open. Use the passage for escape."

"But—"

Gervaise then looked Thomas squarely in the eyes. Exhaustion and strain marked the other side of the old man's face. "After sixty steps, you must make the leap of faith. Understand? Make the leap of faith. You will find the knowledge you need near the burning water."

Thomas began to shake his head. "Burning water? What kind of madness do you—"

"Strike me across the face," Gervaise urged Thomas. "You must reach the altar. If they suspect who you are, Magnus and all its history is lost."

"Gervaise—" Thomas pleaded.

Gervaise sighed. "Show courage, my young friend. Strike me."

Thomas raised his right hand.

Gervaise nodded slightly without turning away. "God be with you, Thomas," he whispered.

Thomas swung down. The impact of hand against swollen face sickened him. And the grunt of pain from the old man brought a whine from the covered puppy in Thomas' other arm.

Gervaise crumpled beneath the blow.

Will that convince the unseen watchers?

Thomas stepped over Gervaise, then limped toward the entrance of the church. He kept his head low and wept.

At the wide doors to the church, Thomas discovered some of his fears had been unfounded. Instead of being a lone and highly noticeable figure, he was only one of many entering and leaving the building.

Once inside, he stopped to let his stinging eyes adjust to the sudden dimness.

Gervaise, Thomas sorrowed, *what evil has forced itself upon us?*

Men and women stood in a long line down the center of the nave, the main chamber of the church. In the chancel near the altar stood a priest who briefly dipped his hands in a vessel, then touched the forehead of the person bowed before him.

"Move on, you bag of scum," a fat man growled at Thomas from behind. "This is no place to daydream. Not with blessings to be had."

Thomas told himself he could not spare any thoughts of grief, only thoughts of action. He fell in behind two women and slowly limped toward the front of the church.

The measured pace of the line provided Thomas time to look around. Vaulted stone ceilings gave an air of majesty and magnified the slightest noise, so that all inside spoke in careful whispers. The nave where Thomas stood was, of course, clear of any objects except support pillars. While rumors had once reached Magnus from London that churches there actually built long bench seats called pews for the worshipers, no one bothered believing such nonsense; people had always stood to worship.

There were at least four priests of the Holy Grail in the church—one at the front and three on the sides of the nave. Thomas tried to study their movements without betraying obvious interest.

Was it fear, or did he imagine they in turn studied him?

Thomas also wondered at his own lunacy. How much trust should he have placed in Gervaise? Had the blows to the old man's head addled him? What could exist beneath the altar? And how would the altar be reached—and kicked—without the notice of the four priests of the Holy Grail?

Yet Thomas moved forward. He had no choice. Those behind him pressed heavily.

And even if he could turn away, what good would it do?

There was no place to hide in Magnus; and if he bolted now, surely the watchers would decide he was more than a cruel-hearted beggar sent inside by Gervaise.

His heart pounded harder as step by step the line advanced to the priest at the front. Thomas recognized him as Hugh de Gainfort. Garbed in royal purple robes, he dipped his hand in the liquid.

"Partake of the water of the symbol of the Grail," Hugh de Gainfort intoned, "and henceforth be loyal to the Grail itself and to its bearers. Blessings will be sure to follow. Amen."

The woman kissed his hand. "Thank you, father."

The line moved ahead.

"Partake of the water of the symbol of the Grail," said Hugh de Gainfort without acknowledging the woman's adoration, "and henceforth be loyal to the Grail itself and to its bearers. Blessings will be sure to follow. Amen."

The next person moved up.

Would the puppy in Thomas' arms remain quiet? Or would it draw unwanted attention?

"Partake of the water of the symbol of the Grail . . ."

Thomas wondered if the priest would hear the thumping of his heart long before he reached the front. Only ten people stood between him and Hugh de Gainfort, and Thomas could see no way to reach the altar beyond without drawing attention to himself.

What trouble had Gervaise cast him into?

". . . and henceforth be loyal to the Grail itself, and to its bearers. Blessings will be sure to follow. Amen."

The light of the sun through the reds and blues of the stained-glass windows cast soft shadows upon Hugh de Gainfort, so that if Thomas did not look closely, he would not see hatred glittering in those eyes, hatred he had felt during their brief audience in the castle keep.

Will I be recognized during the blessing? Thomas worried. *And if not, how to reach the altar? And even at the altar, what truth can there be to the old man's instructions? And if the passage reveals itself, how can I enter unnoticed?*

Thomas swallowed in an effort to moisten his suddenly

dry throat. This was madness, and he was only one step away from a blessing which . . .

"Partake of the water of the symbol of the Grail . . ." Hugh de Gainfort's hand dipped automatically into the water. Wet fingers brushed against Thomas' forehead. ". . . and henceforth be loyal to the Grail itself and to its bearers. Blessings will be sure to follow. Amen."

Thomas started to turn away. The movement drew Hugh's eyes briefly. Suddenly those black eyes widened.

"It is you!" the priest hissed. He opened his mouth to shout.

Thomas reacted with a fighting move he had been taught by Robert of Uleran, but had never been forced to use. He twisted his shoulders away from the priest, then spun them back to drive forward his right hand in a shortened swing. In that blink of an eye, Thomas managed to hit his target with his clenched fist, middle knuckle slightly protruding. The point of the knuckle found its target, a small bone between the ribs, just above the priest's stomach.

The air left the priest's lungs with an audible pop. He clutched himself and began to sway. It happened so quickly those behind Thomas were not sure what they had seen.

Before Thomas could decide how best to flee, a terrifying crash shattered the quiet church. One of the arched windows fell inward, burying a nearby priest. A large stone clattered across the floor. White light from sudden sun flooded the church and danced off rising dust.

Hugh de Gainfort dropped to his knees, still winded so badly he could barely breathe, let alone draw enough air to shout.

Then another crash as the window farther down tumbled inward.

The destruction—it can only be Gervaise!

Thomas did not hesitate. Whatever sacrifice the old man had just made to create the diversion must not be wasted.

All eyes were focused on the western arm of the church building, and the third window cascaded inward, as if riding the high scream that entered with it.

Thomas darted to the altar.

What did the old man say? The panel beneath the candles—kick it sharply near the bottom. Twice.

Thomas glanced to see if Hugh de Gainfort had seen him, but the priest had sagged into a limp bundle. All others stared in horror at the sight of priceless stained glass in pieces. *If there truly is a passage, I may escape without witnesses.*

Thomas kicked once. Twice.

Soundlessly, the panel swung inward. It revealed a black square beneath the altar, wide enough for a large man.

Then another scream from outside the building. *What price has Gervaise paid?*

Thomas bit his lower lip. He must ensure the sacrifice was not made in vain. Thomas ignored the pain in his leg and sat quickly, so that his feet dangled over the edge. He pulled the puppy from beneath his arms.

"My friend, if you go to your death, so do I."

Thomas put both arms around the puppy to shield it, then let himself fall into the darkness.

Chapter Thirty-One

Thomas dropped for half a heartbeat. He closed his eyes and braced for the crush of impact to splatter him against the black unknown.

Then, incredibly, it felt as if arms began to wrap him, as a great resistance began to slow his fall. Thomas felt growing friction against his body and realized these were not the arms of a savior, but a giant sleeve of cloth tapered into a narrowing tube.

It slowed him almost to a standstill as the tube grew so narrow that the fabric squeezed even against his face. Then, just as it seemed he had more to fear from suffocation than from splintered bones and shredded flesh, his feet popped into open air, and he slid loose from his cloth prison.

Even though the final fall was less than the height of a chair, Thomas was not able to see the ground in time to absorb the impact; the jarring of his heels against hard ground forced a grunt of pain.

He recovered his breath quickly and strained to see around him.

"Wherever we are, puppy," Thomas said, glad in this darkness for the company of his whimpering friend, "let's pray it is a better alternative than what was in store for us above."

Thomas reached around to explore for walls. In the darkness, he could not even see the movement of his own arms. He pulled his eyepatch loose, but that did not help his vision.

Thomas forced himself to smile. "Ah, puppy, you do not answer. That is a good sign. For if I were mad, or dreaming, you would speak."

The puppy whined at the gentle sadness in Thomas' tones and squirmed in his arms as it tried to reach upward to offer comfort with well-placed licks of a tongue much too wet.

"Enough!" Thomas said through a laugh. "Next, you'll punish me by wetting yourself."

He set the puppy down and sobered immediately.

So much had happened so quickly. Only yesterday, he had ruled the island castle of Magnus, and by extension, the kingdom around it. Today, he was a fugitive, marked for death by the offer of a brick of gold for his head. Because of him, his friends had suffered equally. Robert of Uleran's fate was unknown; Gervaise was surely dead for his sacrifice of distraction; and Tiny John could only wander the streets and hope the priests of the Holy Grail would not place any importance on his freedom.

And now?

Thomas took a deep breath to steady himself.

Now he was in pitch blackness, somewhere below Magnus in a pit or passage he had never known existed.

To return to Magnus would endanger his life. Yet how long could he remain within the bowels of the earth?

A new thought struck Thomas with such force that he sucked air in sharply.

Gervaise knew.

Gervaise knew of the trapdoor below the altar.

More thoughts tumbled upon Thomas. Warnings and whispers of evil and secrets within Magnus he had heard more than once. Warnings he had tried to ignore throughout a long winter of isolation within the castle keep. Warnings that had plagued him since first conquering the kingdom.

Surely this must be part of the mystery of Magnus. Yet if Gervaise knew, why did he not reveal it much earlier, before the arrival of the priests of the Holy Grail? And if Gervaise knew but said so little, was he a friend or foe? And if he was a foe, what lies ahead?

Thomas stopped his whirlwind of thoughts. *No, if Gervaise were foe, he would not have ensured this temporary escape.*

Thomas must believe. He had no choice.

He strained to remember the old man's words.

"After sixty steps, you must make the leap of faith. Understand? Make the leap of faith. You will find instructions near the burning water."

Somewhere in this darkness, he would find the answer. But if there ever was a moment to delay the search, it was now.

Several minutes later, a sharp yipping drew Thomas from his quiet repose.

"Puppy," he admonished in mock severeness, "can a man not pray in peace?"

Despite the chill stillness of darkness so deep that not even fifteen minutes of adjustment had brought the faintest gray of light to his eyes, Thomas spoke in a conversational manner, as if he and the puppy were in bright sunshine, sharing the warmth of the spring day.

"Faith is difficult to explain, puppy. But with it, prayer eases the mind much. How do I know He listens? That I cannot explain."

A light patting reached Thomas as the puppy's tail thumped the ground to reflect contentment.

Thomas drew himself ramrod straight in the darkness as he imitated Gervaise during a serious discussion. The puppy remained pressed against his feet. Thomas tucked his chin into his chest and mimicked the old man's voice. " 'You have a mind, Thomas. How can you remain so unwilling to learn? Religion—the organized church much as you distrust it—is the necessary structure on earth for faith in God and His promises.

" 'Because *some* men have twisted this structure for their own purposes is no reason to choose to cast away faith. Because the monks in your boyhood abbey showed such little faith is no reason to reflect falseness upon an essential truth.' "

Thomas squatted and scratched the puppy's head. He reverted to his own voice and spoke almost absently, because his mind was already on the problems ahead. "Puppy, we are here now because of false priests making false claims of truth."

Thomas straightened and finished thinking out loud.

"There was more, of course. And should you care to listen later, it will be my delight to recount those long hours of conversation with Gervaise. Because as much as I did not want to believe, puppy, twice I faced death, and twice I cried to the God I did not want to believe. Explain that."

Instead of answering, the puppy shifted its weight and settled for a nap.

"Not so soon," Thomas warned his small friend. "Our journey begins."

Thomas took his first halting step with a courage which resulted from three things—the calm from prayer, the promise of an explanation should he find the burning water, and, strangely, from the puppy which blundered into his legs each step he took. A companion, no matter its size, made the eerie silence easier to bear.

Thomas took his second step into a rough stone wall. His groping hand prevented any injury to his face, yet Thomas recoiled as if he were struck. Any sudden contact, gentle or not, created awesome fear in this pitch darkness.

Thomas pushed himself away, then thought against it, and brought his right shoulder up to the wall again.

"I'll feel my way along," he told the puppy, simply as a way to break the tension which brought sweat in rivers down his face, despite the damp chill. "It will give me warning of twists and turns."

Thus, his fingers became his eyes.

Thomas patted the wall as he followed it, grimacing at real or imagined cobwebs. He stubbed his fingertips against outcrops of stone and stumbled occasionally against objects on the ground. Twice he patted empty air—as much a fright as the original contact against stone—and each time discovered another turn in the passage. He counted every step, remembering the strange message about a leap of faith. The puppy stayed with him and did not complain.

Upon his sixtieth step, Thomas paused. There was nothing to indicate a leap of faith. *What did the old man mean?*

Two steps later, Thomas reached for the stone wall ahead of him and for the third time found nothing.

"Another turn," he muttered to the puppy. "Is this what he meant? Then why not warn me of the previous two? The shock of many more will kill me more surely than those priests."

He slowly began to pivot right, when a low angry noise froze him.

It took a moment, but Thomas identified the echoes as growls of the puppy at his feet.

Thomas relaxed.

"Hush," he spoke downward, then moved to take his step.

The puppy growled again, with enough intensity to make the skin ripple down Thomas' back.

"Easy, my friend." Thomas knelt to hold the puppy. The growling stopped.

Thomas stood and moved again. This time the puppy bit Thomas in the foot and growled louder.

"Whelp! Have you gone crazy?"

Thomas reached down to slap the puppy for its insolence, but couldn't find it in the dark.

He groped farther, patting the ground. First behind him, then to his side, then—

Ahead! The ground ahead has disappeared.

Thomas forgot the puppy. He patted the wall on his right, found the edge of the corner, and slid his hand downward, finally kneeling to reach as low as possible. Where the corner met the ground, it was no longer a corner, but a surface which continued downward below the level of his feet.

The skin on his back now rippled upward in fear.

"Puppy," he cried softly. A whimper answered him.

Thomas, on his knees and blind in the darkness, crawled backward two more paces, then eased himself onto his stomach.

Feeling safer on his belly, Thomas inched forward again, feeling for the edge of the drop-off with his extended right hand. When he reached it, he kept his hand on the edge, but shuffled to his left, determined to find the width of the unseen chasm.

Seconds later, he found it, joined to the left wall.

Thomas was too spent with the jolts of fear to react with more than a moan of despair.

"How deep?" he asked the puppy. "How far ahead to the other side?"

Thomas crawled ahead as far as he dare. With his dangling hand, he reached down into the blackness. *After all, perhaps this drop is a mere foot or two. I could be stuck here forever, afraid to step downward.*

Thomas slumped. His exploring hand had found nothing. Even after drawing his sword and extending it to reach farther, he could not prove to himself that the drop was only a shallow ditch.

Long minutes later, he raised his head from the ground. He knew he had three choices. *Leap ahead and trust the chasm was narrow enough to cross. Drop into the chasm and trust its bottom was just beyond his reach. Or retrace his steps.*

He chose to reverse direction.

Sixty-two counted steps and two turns later, he was back to his starting point. Thomas looked upward, half expecting to see light where the priests might be peering downward from the trapdoor beneath the altar. But he knew that would not be. No one had seen his escape. And now he was trapped here, unless the other direction yielded better results.

He patted the ground and crawled ahead. Since he had passed his original beginning point, he did not know whether he should expect another sudden chasm ahead in the opposite direction.

Thomas did not travel far before the wall turned sharply, then sharply again.

By now, as blind as if both eyes had been covered with patches, Thomas was accustomed to thinking with his fingers. He knew he had reached the end of the passage and was proceeding in his original direction, except along the left wall.

"Are you with me, puppy?" Thomas called. He wanted to be reassured by a familiar sound in the blackness. The puppy whined and Thomas smiled through his misery. He had no choice but to proceed sixty-two steps back to the chasm and from there, debate his bleak prospects in a silence louder than any noise he had ever heard.

Unless . . .

Unless the passage split! After all, he had only traced the right-hand side of it. Perhaps the left-hand side broke into another passage and all he need do was find it by patiently continuing his blind groping.

Thomas called the puppy closer and tried to find its ears in the darkness. The puppy found his hand first and gently licked Thomas' fingers.

It was then Thomas realized the rawness of his broken skin and that the puppy was trying to lick away blood. In his fears, Thomas had not noticed the damage done by the walls to his fingers.

He took a deep breath and moved ahead. Yes, the left wall must split into a new passage somewhere before the chasm. *It must.*

It did not.

Sixty-two steps and two turns later, Thomas was again on his belly, feeling ahead in the terrifying darkness for that drop-off.

He found it, retreated slightly, and with his palm banged the ground in frustration, uncaring of the new pain.

How could he possibly overcome this barrier?

Then a tiny flicker caught his eye. Thomas almost missed it, so much had he given up on using vision to aid his senses.

He blinked, then squinted. Five minutes passed. Another minute.

There! The flicker again. It brightened, then dropped to nothing. Thomas strained to focus and pinpoint its location. Ten agonizing minutes later, another flare, hardly more than a candle, suddenly snuffed.

It dawned slowly upon Thomas.

Burning water.

He was seeing the light of a far-off flame, light he had missed the first time here because it flared so rarely and softly, light which reflected and bounced through one or two more turns of the passageway.

Thomas lowered himself and sat, knees huddled against his chest. The puppy leaned against him, whining occasionally and then growling for no apparent reason.

A phrase echoed through his head. *"Understand? Make the leap of faith."*

Why had the old man been so urgent with those words? Why had he repeated them and no other part of his intructions?

"Make the leap of faith."

It reminded him of a part of a conversation once held with Gervaise. To pass time, Thomas spoke aloud to the puppy.

"During the quiet of an early morning," Thomas said, "Gervaise told me, 'No matter how much you learn or debate the existence of God, no matter how much you apply your mind to Him, you cannot satisfy your soul.' "

The puppy rested his chin on Thomas' upper thigh as he listened.

"Then the old man said, 'There must come a time at the beginning of your faith when you let go and simply trust, a time when you make the leap of faith, something much like a . . .' " Thomas faltered as he suddenly realized the significance of Gervaise's repeated words.

He finished the thought silently. *"Something much like a leap into the darkness."*

That entire conversation flooded Thomas' mind. They had talked often, usually in the early hours after Thomas had walked the ramparts of Magnus. This conversation had taken place barely a month after Thomas had conquered Magnus. Gervaise had talked simply of faith in answer to all of Thomas' questions.

"It is a leap into the darkness, Thomas," he had said. *"God awaits you on the other side. First your heart finds Him; then your mind will understand Him more clearly, so that all evidence points toward the unshakable conclusion you could not find before; and after that leap your faith will grow stronger with time. But faith, any faith, is trust and that small leap into the darkness."*

"No, Gervaise," Thomas said aloud. "I cannot do this. You ask too much."

Damp chill settled on Thomas.

"Make the leap of faith. Understand? Sixty steps and make the leap of faith." Thomas had no doubt that Gervaise had meant he should do this now. Yet how could he blindly jump ahead? What lay on the other side? What lay below?

An encouraging thought struck him.

Magnus was surrounded by lake waters. Indeed, the wells of Magnus had to go very little depth before reaching water. And this passage was already below the surface. How far down, then, before reaching water from this passageway?

Might he drop his sword to test the depth of the chasm? An immediate clatter, after all, would tell him the water was shallow.

"Make the leap of faith."

No, he could not venture weaponless.

Might he drop the puppy ahead to test the depth of the chasm? Or cast it ahead to test the width?

"Make the leap of faith."

No, not when the creature had first warned him of the chasm. Not when it trusted him so.

"Make the leap of faith."

Thomas frowned. *Did I not regard Gervaise with trust? And if I now show such concern for the puppy, would not Gervaise show that much more concern for me?*

"Make the leap of faith."

Thomas finally allowed himself to decide what he had known since recalling the old man's words about faith.

He must leap into the darkness.

Ten times Thomas paced large steps backward from the edge of the chasm. Ten times he repaced them forward again, careful to reach down and ahead with his sword on the eight, ninth and tenth steps to establish he had not yet reached the edge.

"Puppy," he said, as he retraced his steps backward yet again, "if leap we must, I shall not do it from a standstill.

Faith or not, I doubt our God or Gervaise enjoys stupidity."

Thomas had debated briefly whether to take the puppy. But only briefly. The extra weight was slight, and he could not bear to make it across safely and hear forever in his mind abandoned whimpers of a puppy left for dead.

Thomas squatted and felt for the line he had gouged into the ground to mark the ten paces away from the edge.

He rehearsed the planned action in his mind. He would sprint only eight steps, for he could not trust running paces to be as small as his ten carefully marked paces. On the eighth step, he would leap and dive and release the puppy. His hands would give him the first warning of impact—he prayed for that impact—and at best he might lose his breath. The puppy would travel slightly farther, and at best tumble and roll. At worst, neither would reach the other side of the unknown chasm in this terrible blackness.

Thomas drew a deep breath. He hugged the puppy once, then tucked it into the crook of his right arm.

"Make the leap of faith."

"God be with us," he whispered. Then he plunged ahead.

Chapter Thirty-Two

On the eighth step, at full sprint, Thomas drove upward and left the ground.

In the blackness around him, he had no way to measure the height he reached, no way to gauge how far forward he flew, and no way to know how much he dropped.

It seemed to take forever, the rush of air in his ears, the half sob of fear escaping his throat, and the squirm of the puppy in his outstretched hands.

The puppy! In midair, Thomas pushed him ahead and released him from his hands. Before he could even think of praying for safety, the heels of his hands hit solid ground, and he skidded onto his nose and chin; then, as his head bounced upward, onto his chest and stomach. He could count his heartbeats thudding in his ears.

Was he across? Or at the bottom of a shallow ditch?

The puppy's confused whimper sounded nearby.

Thomas coughed and rolled to his feet.

"My friend," he said, "we seem to be alive. But across?"

Thomas answered his own question by turning around and crawling back. Moments later, his hands found an edge!

Thomas grinned in the darkness.

The next two turns in the passageway and the next eighty-eight steps took nearly an hour. Although the occasional flare of reflected light grew stronger, it provided little illumination, and Thomas dared not risk another unseen chasm.

When he reached the final turn, his reward was another flicker of light, this time, the flame itself! Not a reflection! It was straight ahead and far down the passageway.

As Thomas walked closer, the rising and falling light provided him more clues about the passage.

The walls were shored up with large blocks of stone, unevenly placed. He understood immediately why his groping fingers had received such punishment in the total darkness.

The passage was hardly higher than his head, and wide enough to fit three men walking abreast. Other than that, nothing. No clues to the builders. No clues to its reason for existence. No clues to its age.

Thomas half ran the final few steps to the light. The leg he had managed to forget in the previous few hours ached again with the extra movement, but he did not mind.

Gervaise promised the knowledge I needed. It can only mean a message. And if Gervaise managed to leave the message, he also managed to leave here again, and there is hope in that.

Thomas noted the source of the light. It was imbedded in the wall, as if a hand had scooped away part of the stone. A wick of cloth rose above a clear liquid, and from it came the solitary tongue of flame.

Burning water!

He did not examine the light for long, because the puppy whined and sniffed at a leather sack barely visible in the shadows along the wall below the flame. Thomas pulled the sack away before the puppy could bury its nose in it entirely.

He understood the puppy's anxiousness as soon as he opened it.

Cheese. Bread. And cooked chicken legs. All wrapped in clean cloth.

Thank you, Gervaise.

Thomas suddenly realized how hungry he was. He ripped into a fat chicken leg, chewed a mouthful, then tore pieces free with his fingers to drop to the puppy.

More objects remained in the bag. Thomas pulled free a large candle. He dipped the end into the flame in the wall and immediately doubled his light. Next from the bag came a candleholder, hooded so the bearer could shed light without fear of killing the flame.

Finally, Thomas pulled free a scrolled parchment, tied shut with a narrow ribbon.

He wiped his hands of chicken grease, set the candleholder on the ground, and sat down beside it.

The puppy nosed his palms for more food.

"Later," Thomas said absently. His fingers, no longer bleeding and suddenly without pain as he focused on the parchment, trembled as he pulled the ribbon loose and unscrolled the parchment.

The ink lettering was bold and well spaced, as if the writer had guessed Thomas might be forced to read it in dim light.

Thomas, if you read this, it is only because the Druids, guised as priests of the Holy Grail, have conquered Magnus. Yet, if you read this, it is because you dared make the leap of faith I requested, and in so doing have proved you are not a Druid.

Druids! The shock was as of an arrow piercing his heart. Then Thomas rubbed his forehead in puzzlement. *To suggest I might be a Druid—how could Gervaise even dare to think the unthinkable? I have spent the entire winter in fear of their return.*

Yes, my friend, the chasm you leaped was a test. Were you one of the Druids, you would have known that these passages and halls—

Passages and halls? Thomas sighed. This message created more mystery than it solved. Did Gervaise imply that all of Magnus was riddled with secret tunnels?

—passages and halls are buried so deep in the island that anything more than several feet below their level would fill with water. As a Druid, you would already be familiar with this. As a Druid, you would have confidently stepped down and walked across, even without a light to guide you.

That you are reading this means you are not a Druid, for in that shallow, dry moat, I placed a dozen adders.

Adders! Snakes with venom so potent that only a scratch of poison could kill. *A dozen adders!* In the darkness, the puppy had not growled at the drop-off, but at what his nose had warned him about.

Thomas scratched the puppy behind the ears, and shuddered at what might have happened had Gervaise not urged him to make the leap of faith.

Thus, you now have my trust, Thomas. I regret I could not give it earlier. There is much to tell you, my friend, and I fear by the time you return to Magnus, I will not be alive to reveal to you the epic struggle between the Druids and Merlins.

Merlin! Mention again of the ancient days of King Arthur. For Merlin, King Arthur's adviser, had become a legend equaling the king himself!

I cannot say much in this letter, for who is to guess what others may stumble across it, should you not take the leap of faith. Let me simply ask you to consider the books of your childhood. It was not chance that they were placed near you, those books of ancient knowledge from faraway lands. It was not chance that one of us was there to raise you, to teach you, to guide you, to urge you to reconquer Magnus, to show you the way. It was not chance that I spread the legend of the angel shortly before your birth.

These new words were not the piercing of an arrow, but the bludgeoning of a club. *Gervaise knew of those precious books hidden near the abbey? Impossible!* At the significance of the message, Thomas could hardly breathe. He remembered the night he had conquered Magnus on the wings of an angel, how the entire population of Magnus had gathered enough strength from his arrival to overthrow its evil lord, simply because of a legend which all believed. *This had been planned before I was born?*

Yet none of this knowledge could I share, Thomas, much as I treasured our conversations. For too many years passed with you alone in the abbey. We did not know if they had discovered you and converted you. We did not know if you were one of them, allowed to conquer in appearance only, so that we might reveal the final secrets of Magnus to you, secrets so important I cannot even hint of them now.

You trusted me this far. I beg of you to continue that trust. Your destiny has grown even more crucial. We did not expect the Druids to act so boldly, so soon. Even now, perhaps, they have the power to conquer completely. As a born Merlin, you must stop them.

Thomas wanted to protest aloud. *A born Merlin. I a born Merlin? Gervaise, how can you reveal so much, yet reveal so little?*

Follow this passage, Thomas. It will take you to safety. Return to the abbey of your childhood. Search for the answers among your books. Trust no person. Our stakes are too high. The Druids must not prevail.

Chapter Thirty-Three

Paris, France
May 1313

Katherine looked up, startled as a shadow crossed the pages of her open book.

"I'm sorry, my child," a soft voice reassured her. "The thoughts I interrupted, they must have been enjoyable. Your face showed such pleasure. And I was clumsy to—"

She blushed. "Frere Dominique, it is I who should apologize for daydreaming. The progress I have made with this Latin has not been remarkable. With all due respect to the author, it is . . . it is . . ."

Katherine fumbled for a tactful way to express how boring she found eleventh-century German philosophy. Her French failed her, however, and all she could do was shrug and look down modestly.

"Katherine," Frere Dominique admonished, "is it not enough you have won an old priest's heart? And now you take advantage of it with beautiful helplessness that is merely acted?"

Katherine laughed. Little escaped the old priest. He moved with the energy of a far younger man. Although he was plump and graying and always wore a jolly smile, his eyes gleamed sharp in unguarded moments, or during the rough-and-tumble arguments in logic he and Katherine enjoyed to pass the time throughout the long winter.

The priest smiled indulgently. How peaceful it was here in the library of the royal palace. On days like this, with the sun casting its golden warmth through opened windows, with the quiet of the large room broken only by the birds in the royal garden, Frere Dominique's thoughts often strayed to heaven.

Yes, he would tell himself as he did now, *heaven shall be the peace of precious books arranged in order and the solitude of one free to seek more and more knowledge, always aware of Him the highest, and*—Frere Dominique sighed because of the news he must deliver and how he would miss Katherine—*with angels of sweetness such as this one nearby.*

Frere Dominique studied Katherine's face. These might be their final moments together. He would miss the joy of admiring her fine, high cheekbones, the curve of her smile, the depth and innocence of her gaze.

"Yes, father?" Katherine asked his searching eyes. "Is something wrong?"

Frere Dominique nodded. "Only for me," he said. "You see, when I tell you my heart has been stolen, it is not merely the flattery of a man who enjoys too much—" the priest patted his stomach "—your touch with our French recipes. I shall truly miss your presence here."

Katherine stood quickly. She took one of the priest's hands in hers and squeezed it tight. "He has returned?"

Frere Dominique nodded, then shook his head mournfully. "After an absence of six months, he refuses to accept the hospitality of a night's stay here. Even now, that scoundrel is in the stable, preparing a horse for you."

Katherine dropped the priest's warm hand. "Travel? So soon? Did he mention—"

Once again, Katherine blushed.

"England?" Frere Dominique finished for her.

Katherine nodded, watched the priest's face, and waited.

"Yes," Frere Dominique finally said. Then he smiled at her unconcealed expression. "Your face again carries the look I interrupted moments ago. Who has captured your thoughts, Katherine? Were I three decades younger, I would be smitten with jealousy."

Katherine and Hawkwood rode for two days to reach the harbor town of Dieppe on the French side of the English Channel.

She knew Hawkwood was anxious. He did not question the price offered for their horses in Dieppe, although it was scandalously low. And half an hour later, he did not barter with the ship's captain for passage across the Channel.

Three days on a pitched and gray North Sea brought them to the cliffs of Scarborough. Once again, Hawkwood did not waste time searching for the fairest price of horse-flesh, and paid double what he should have.

They rode thirty miles, directly to an obscure abbey north and east of the town of York, stopping only when the sun went down.

"Patience," Hawkwood said, "is well known as a virtue."

"Then I shall be nominated for sainthood," Katherine replied. "For nearly a week now, I have waited for you to inform me of the reason for our mad haste."

She waved at the land around them. "And now you ask me to sit here for hours, perhaps days, on the mere chance that Thomas might arrive in this remote valley."

"Keep your hands still," Hawkwood admonished. "He must have no hint of our presence."

"He will not arrive."

Hawkwood chuckled. "Your voice betrays your hope."

To that, Katherine did not reply, for Hawkwood spoke truth.

His earlier promise had been that Thomas would arrive. And Hawkwood had never been wrong, at least not in her memory.

They had settled into the side of this hill barely half an hour earlier, just as the morning sun rose to show that the valley below was narrow and compressed, with more rock and stunted trees on the slopes than sweet grass and sheep.

Although they were near the exposed summit of the valley, Hawkwood had shrewdly chosen a vantage point among the shadows of large rocks. Downstream, trees guarded the tiny river which wound past the abbey.

Hawkwood had pointed at a jumble of rocks and boulders on the river, some as large as a peasant's hut. "There," he had said, "is hidden a dry, cool cave, invisible except to those who have been led to its narrow entrance among the granite and growing bush. That is his destination."

And now, long enough later so that the prickling of the sun's first heat had brought forth the ants which played in the dust in front of her, Katherine turned the discussion back to the questions she wanted answered.

"Not only shall I receive a sainthood for patience, but if ignorance is bliss, I shall be the happiest saint to have walked this earth."

This drew another chuckle.

"Yes," Hawkwood said. "I tell you little, but for your own protection."

"No," Katherine corrected. "For the protection of Magnus." She then repeated the oft-heard words. "After all, I cannot divulge what I do not know."

That drew a sigh.

"Katherine," he said, "not even I know the entire plan. We all have our tasks, and we must trust to the whole."

Would it be fair, she wondered, *to push him now for more?*

She hesitated. *Was it fair,* she countered, *to know so little?*

So she decided to ask, almost with dread at his anticipated anger. "Yes," she said softly. "There is truth in that. You fear that I might be taken by the Druids and be forced to betray us. But if something should happen to you . . . how could I carry on our battle without more knowledge than I have now?"

Hawkwood dropped his head. Instead of anger, sadness filled his voice. "There is truth in that. And I've wondered how long it would take for you to use my sword of defense upon myself."

She waited, sensing victory, but feeling no enjoyment in it.

He continued. "In the cave below are books. In Latin, French, even Italian. But mostly Latin. Once, as you know, those of us in Magnus had the leisure to translate from all languages into that universal word."

"Books?" Katherine was incredulous. "Here in this valley. But that is treasure beyond value! Why here?"

"Indeed," he said, "treasure beyond value. More than

you know. These are not books coveted by the wealthy for beauty and worth. In that cave lies knowledge brought from lands as far away as the eastern edge of the world. All for Thomas to use in his solitary battle."

"That is why you are so certain he will return," Katherine breathed.

"The messenger told me that Magnus had fallen. With no money and no army, Thomas has no choice but to seek power from the knowledge in that cave."

"Much as he did to first conquer Magnus," Katherine said absently.

A sharp intake of breath from Hawkwood. "You know that?"

"Wings of an angel," she said simply. "How else could he have had such a secret?"

"Of course," he said. "You would not fail to see the obvious."

Should she feel guilty? Her answer was not a lie, but she had not told Hawkwood that Thomas had once hinted to her of these books. And that he had regretted it later as he banished her from Magnus.

Katherine now realized the immensity of the secret Thomas had held, not knowing she was one of his watchers. But her new information led to more questions.

As Katherine puzzled through more thoughts, she changed the direction of her query. "Why must we continue to watch? Surely he now needs our help."

Hawkwood shook his head. "Not until we are certain to which side he belongs. Our only word was that Magnus had fallen. Nothing else arrived from Gervaise to guide us further. In this game of masks behind masks, we can only wait."

Katherine finished for Hawkwood. It was a familiar argument. "For if he were a Druid, he would act as if he were not. Now, perhaps, it was convenient for them to assume open control of Magnus. And equally convenient for them to send him forth as bait."

He in turn finished her oft-used argument. "Yet, if he is not one of them, we can do so much good by revealing ourselves. Together, our fight will be stronger."

They both sighed. It was an argument with no answer they could trust. Too much depended on Thomas.

When he arrived, they almost missed him.

He still remembered every secret deer path in the surrounding hills from his years of avoiding the nearby harsh monks. At times, Thomas would approach a seemingly solid stand of brush, then slip sideways into an invisible opening among the jagged branches, and later reappear farther down the hill.

His familiarity with the terrain, however, did not make him less cautious. It was only the loud caws of a disgruntled crow which warned Katherine and Hawkwood. Even then, it took them twenty minutes to see his slow movement.

From above, they watched Thomas circle the jumbled rocks near the river. Then he slipped into a nearby crevice and surveyed the area.

"He was taught well," Hawkwood whispered approval. "He has no reason to be suspicious, yet he still remains disciplined."

Minute after minute passed.

"He counts to one thousand," Hawkwood explained. "He was taught that this cave is the most important secret of all. Taught never to let anyone discover the entrance."

Thomas circled slowly once more, sometimes visible, sometimes not.

Katherine ached to see him, to discover if she still felt as she remembered. But she too had been taught discipline, and she held herself motionless, with none of these thoughts crossing her face.

Then she noticed something.

"He walks awkwardly," she whispered. "Not from the bag he carries, but as if hunched."

Then she gasped as that hump on his back moved. And just before Thomas disappeared into the cave, she saw his burden poke its nose out from the back of his shirt.

"A puppy," she said in amazement. "An entire kingdom rides on his shoulders, and in its place he carries a puppy."

Chapter Thirty-Four

Two days passed. During the long hours of waiting, Katherine could satisfy little of her curiosity through discussion, for Hawkwood insisted on silence. He also insisted on alternating watch duty. One must sleep while the other observed the rocks of the entrance.

The few moments they were both awake were spent sharing the sack of breads and cheeses they had carried with them.

At night, they moved closer to the rocks by the river and settled into a nearby crevice in the hill. They could not trust the light of the moon to remain unclouded, and Thomas might leave at any hour. Twice already he had alarmed them with sudden appearances, only to fill a leather bag with water and return to the cave.

At night then, Hawkwood had told Katherine, their ears must serve as their eyes, for if they failed to follow Thomas to his next destination, the plan would surely be doomed.

Tell me more of the plan, Katherine had wanted to ask, but she did not. What Hawkwood knew of the plan would be revealed only when he deemed it proper.

In the early hours of the third day, despite her coldness, the discipline Katherine had been taught since birth did not leave her. She did not let the shivers shake her body; she sat so still that once a fox almost blundered across her feet. At the last moment, it caught her scent and leapt sideways to disappear into the dark jumble of trees and rocks. That was the only break in the monotony. Yet, except for the shivering, she did not mind. In these quiet moments, she felt at peace.

Soon, the rhythms of approaching day would begin, telling her that God's order still remained in nature, in spite of the confused affairs of men which had brought her to this quiet valley. Faint gray would brush the horizon first. Then tentative and sporadic chirps of faraway birds, as if each hardly believed they were to be granted the gift of another day. The rustling of the small night creatures would stop in response.

Each minute of growing light brought her unexpected pleasures. Yesterday, it had been a spider as it delicately stepped across large beads of dew on its web, woven on a branch so close to Katherine's face that she could see each drop of water bend but not quite break with the weight of the spider. The day before, she'd seen a rabbit trailed by six tiny bundles of fur tumbling in their mother's footsteps.

Part of Katherine knew that she chose to focus on the hill around her because she wanted relief from the questions she could not yet ask Hawkwood.

She knew his urgency stemmed from reports that Magnus had again fallen, and she understood the need for action. *Without Magnus . . .* now she had been fully taught the history and tradition of the Merlins and hardly dared contemplate how many centuries of careful guidance were on the brink of destruction.

But why the importance of Thomas?

Deep as her feelings for him might run, warm as the skin on her face might flush as she remembered him, Katherine *could* force herself to remain objective enough to wonder why so much rested upon his shoulders.

Where are the other Merlins of this generation? Must Thomas combat the Druids alone and unaware of battles which have been fought for centuries?

And why the extreme urgency now? After all, until Thomas recaptured the kingdom, Magnus was under the control of the Druids for twenty years. Surely the passing of one month, two months, cannot determine the battle now.

Surely —

"Katherine."

She turned her head slightly to acknowledge Hawkwood's voice.

"Day is nearly upon us."

So it was. Despite her determination to contemplate the beauty of creation, those faint licks of gray had been banished by pale blue while her thoughts had wandered to areas that Hawkwood refused to discuss.

Katherine stirred, ready to pick her careful way back to the observation point.

"Wait!" came the soft whisper.

She froze. And immediately understood.

Below her, Thomas had finally moved out of the cave, and without the sack of food he had carried inside. Without the leather bag for water. Without the puppy.

He wore the plain brown garb of a simple monk.

They followed him along an isolated path in the forest south of the small Harland Moor abbey. Hawkwood went first, melting into the trees and keeping Thomas in sight. Katherine, a hundred yards behind and less adept at stealth, simply kept Hawkwood in her line of vision.

At times, she lost sight of him completely. She marveled again and again at how silently he flitted from tree to tree, bush to bush.

An hour later, Hawkwood held up a hand of warning, then settled into a crouch. Katherine responded by doing the same.

Five minutes later, Hawkwood was up and moving ahead. This march of three continued for another half hour until they reached the road leading into the town of Helmsley.

Hawkwood waited for her at the side of the road.

"He is ahead of us," he told Katherine. "I have no doubt he is going to town."

Katherine raised an eyebrow in question. "His detour?"

"Gold," Hawkwood replied. "He has retrieved some of the gold he had buried before leaving here with the knight for Magnus last summer. The gold he had earned from the gallows in Helmsley. And gold can only mean he has purchases in mind."

Hawkwood's prediction proved correct.

They next saw Thomas near the Helmsley stables where

they had left their own horses a few days earlier. Watching discreetly proved no problem, with the usual crowds around the market stalls.

Thomas engaged himself in conversation with the ruddy-faced man who tended the stables.

After five minutes, both nodded. The man disappeared inside the stable and returned with a middle-sized gray horse.

Thomas shook his head. The stableman shrugged. Another five minutes of conversation, this time with much animation.

The man again entered the stable, this time returning with a large roan stallion. Even from their vantage point, Katherine could appreciate the power suggested by the muscles that rippled and flinched as the horse occasionally shook itself of flies.

A few more minutes of conversation. A snort of derisive laughter from the stableman reached them. And yet again, he entered the stables. He brought out not a horse, but shabby blankets and saddlebags customarily placed on donkeys.

Thomas nodded and the man departed. Instead of swinging onto the horse, Thomas threw a blanket over it and cinched on the saddlebags. He remained on foot and led the horse away by its halter.

As soon as he was safely out of sight, Katherine and Hawkwood approached the stableman.

Hawkwood flashed a bronze coin.

The stableman grunted recognition. "The two of you." He looked at the coin and sneered. "I thought you'd both died. I've kept both your mounts in oats for three days. You expect bronze to pay the fare?"

"No," Hawkwood said. He pulled a tiny gold coin from deep within his cloak and handed that to the man, who bit the coin to test for softness, then said, "It's barely enough, but I'm not one to take advantage of strangers."

"It's a third more than you expected," Hawkwood said quietly. He then showed the bronze coin again. "And this is yours if you tell us what the little sparrow heard."

"Eh?"

Hawkwood fluttered his hand skyward. "The little sparrow flitting around as you spoke to that monk's assistant. What harm could there be in telling us words from a sparrow's mouth."

The fat man leered comprehension. "Ah, that sparrow. Now I recall." He leaned forward and widened his leer to show dark stumps for teeth. "Unfortunately, that sparrow's a shy one."

A second bronze coin appeared in front of the stableman.

"The monk's assistant told me he wanted a horse that could outrun any in York," the stableman said quickly. "That was all."

"You spent ten minutes in conversation," Katherine protested.

The stableman looked at her darkly, then back at Hawkwood. "It's a sad day when a woman interrupts the business of men."

Katherine rose on her toes to answer, but caught the slight warning wave of Hawkwood's hand.

"I'll see she learns her lesson," Hawkwood said. He then stroked his chin. "York? Hasn't its earl fallen from power?"

"It's what I said too," the stableman nodded. "I told him what even the deaf and blind know, that the earl of York now rots in his own dungeon."

The man paused.

"Yes?" Hawkwood prompted.

"It's peculiar. When I said that, he told me that's exactly why he needed the horse."

Katherine knew Hawkwood had no appreciation for foolishness, so she waited an hour to ask her question. By then, they had traveled five miles along the road to York, and she had sifted through enough of her thoughts to know which question to ask, even if she would not start with it.

"We have not reached or passed Thomas yet," she began. "This means one of two things."

"Yes?" Hawkwood asked in good humor. It always lifted his spirits when Katherine applied her training.

"Either he mounted his horse as soon as he was out of

sight of the town, and has ridden it fast enough to keep the distance between us as he travels to York. Or—"

"How do you know it will be the second and not the first?" Hawkwood interrupted.

Katherine smiled. "Because he wants to appear as a lowly monk's assistant leading a master's horse from one town to the next. He doesn't dare ride, because too many travel this road, and many would wonder at someone dressed so poorly mounted on such a fine horse. Since we have not yet reached him, he does not first travel to York."

Hawkwood clapped approval. "Instead, he has—"

"Thomas has undoubtedly returned to the abbey to retrieve what he needs from the cave to fill those saddlebags." Katherine paused at the thought and at what it meant. "He is arming himself."

"Yes, my friend." Hawkwood said nothing more, and they passed the next hundred yards with only the clopping of the horses' hooves to break their companionable silence. A breeze at their backs kept the dust from rising, and Katherine let it lull her thoughts away from her question.

She turned her gaze downward as the minutes passed. Not for the first time did she stare at the road and wonder at the Roman soldiers who had set these stones more than a thousand years earlier, even before the time of Merlin himself. York had been an outpost in the wild interior— Hawkwood had explained five days previous—while Scarborough forty miles to the east had been the coastal watchpost. From the high cliffs of Scarborough, the Roman sentries could easily spot enemy ships; the efficient road to the interior made it easy to shuffle legions of soldiers back and forth between Scarborough and York. And now, hundreds of years later, the road carried the everyday traffic between the two towns.

"Katherine."

She pulled away from her thoughts.

"What question do you have?"

"You can read me that well?" Katherine said.

"You had no need to impress me with your guesses. Except that I am sometimes impatient with meaningless prattle, and it seemed as if you sought to discuss Thomas more."

Katherine felt her face color as she noticed Hawkwood's tiny grin of comprehension and the twinkle in his eyes. He read her too well.

She also knew Hawkwood did not like false modesty or coy games, so she simply asked her question with no further hesitation.

"Why York?" she blurted. "Thomas knows—as do all—that the priests of the Holy Grail rule York as surely as they rule Magnus. Moreover, the earl of York, in chains or not, is a sworn enemy to Thomas. Why enter the lion's den?"

Hawkwood spoke so softly she could barely hear. "I've wondered that myself. Perhaps he has decided that if he frees the earl of York, they will swear a pact of allegience and together fight the priests. Perhaps he simply wishes to observe the priests without fear of recognition by the townspeople, as would happen to him in Magnus. After all, he knows that the first maxim of warfare is simple. 'Know thine enemy.' "

Another hundred yards.

The riders swayed to the rhythm of the slow plodding. With less urgency now than during their previous travels, there seemed little purpose in taxing the horses.

The leaves of the oak trees lining the road had already burst forth, and dappled shade covered the two as they moved steadily along the road. Soon the leaves would be full and the road entirely covered from the sun.

Have only four seasons passed since Thomas first entered Magnus? Only four seasons since I first spoke to him in a candlemaker's shop? Only four seasons since his long-predicted arrival captured my heart?

Another thought haunted her. *In another four seasons, will Thomas still be alive and the battle continued?*

"Your face is an open book, my friend." The gentle voice once again took her from her thoughts.

"Even if Thomas frees the earl," Katherine blurted, "or if he knows the priests of the Holy Grail as well as they know themselves, how can he prevail against their miracles?

Blood of the martyr? The weeping statue?" Katherine resisted the urge to cross herself even as the peasants did to speak of such sacred things.

"The blood and statue I can easily explain," Hawkwood said. "How he is to prevail, I cannot tell."

"Please," Katherine said quietly. "I have great curiosity. The blood of the martyr . . . the weeping statue."

"Simple," Hawkwood said. "The blood is nothing holier than a mixture of chalk and water from rusted iron, sprinkled with salt water."

He snorted. "Those false priests pray for the congealed blood to turn to liquid, but they help their prayers by gently shaking the vial. That's all it takes. And when it settles, it appears like thickly clotted blood."

"And the weeping statue?"

Another snort. "Those stone eyes weep water only when brought from the warmth into the coolness of the church. More sham and trickery."

"We too could duplicate those miracles?"

"And prey upon ignorant superstition? Never. And we choose to always remain hidden from the people."

"Thomas could expose those tricks for what they are!" Katherine said. "Surely, if enough see the truth, the priests would be known as frauds and lose their power to rule."

"No, Katherine. There is only one Thomas, and thousands upon thousands to convince. People treasure their misconceptions, cling to them, and never look beyond. Besides, how long could Thomas travel as a free man during his demonstrations against the priests?"

Katherine puzzled for several moments. "An army, then. Thomas can observe the priests, discover their weaknesses, and muster an army to strike as he sees best."

The old man shook his head. "With what money might he raise an army? With what allegiances? Moreover, the priests now maintain rule because all believe they are spokesmen for God. What man, what knight, dares raise a sword against the Almighty, when false miracles are so eagerly believed?"

They traveled much farther before Katherine spoke again. "There seems to be little hope for him. And for us."

Hawkwood snorted. "Perhaps Thomas is not meant to prevail. We still have no certainty to which side he belongs. They must know he is watched by us, even if they do not know the watchers. An apparent defeat of Thomas will lead us to trust him, and with trust, we might impart to him the final secrets they need so badly."

Katherine could only set her chin stubbornly as a means to hold back a sigh of sadness.

The never-ending logic of argument.

She closed her eyes and spoke to the sky. "This waiting is a cruel game."

Chapter Thirty-Five

The next morning their wait at the massive gates to the town wall was rewarded as the bells rang Sext to mark midday.

Unlike Magnus, the walls around the town of York did not have the advantage of a protecting lake. But they were much thicker, to better protect against battering rams. Indeed, so wide were these walls that atop were large chambers built from equally massive stone blocks.

Katherine and Hawkwood were so close to the west gate that almost directly above them, and built into the high arch above the entrance to the town, was one of York's prisons.

An open window had been cut into each of the four walls of the prison, hardly large enough for a small boy to crawl through. Despite the thirty-foot drop to the ground, iron bars had been placed into the windows as a final barrier to prisoners with dreams of escape.

When Katherine looked up, she imagined the occasional dark shadow of movement through the window closest to her. She did not look up often, however. Imbedded into the stone walls were iron pikes. Upon three of them were impaled the heads of men who stared their silent horror on the town, as warning to others who might also become rebels.

Katherine watched as a stream of peasants and craftsmen entered the town beneath those gateway prisons. The air was noisy with curses at stubborn donkeys, the cackles of geese, and the grunts of pigs.

This steady stream disappeared quickly once inside York, as the cobbled road twisted and turned its way into dozens of side streets. Some strangers, new to the wonders of York, stopped almost immediately at one of the shops on the side of the road. Others, more experienced and unwilling to be fleeced immediately, continued for the markets.

Katherine and Hawkwood stood among the jostling people bartering for the wares of the cook shop. The aromas of the food did not make their waiting easy. Katherine could smell roasted joints and meat pasties—for a price double what one could expect to pay closer to the town center.

To amuse herself as she waited, Katherine tested her powers of observation by scanning the crowd for pickpockets. She saw two. One particularily clever pickpocket played the role of a drunk. He staggered and bounced into people, enduring their abuse and leaving with the coins he had dipped during the confusion of his fall against them.

Katherine hoped the jugglers would return. Yesterday, a half-hour had passed in the space of a drawn breath, so adept were these men with whirling swords and flames. Even Hawkwood had coughed admiration and thrown small coins in their direction.

Perhaps the man with the wrestling bear would entertain again. What a treat that had been. Of course, sights like this were to be expected in York. After all, with its ten thousand inhabitants, only London exceeded it in size.

Katherine lapsed into her favorite daydream, the one where she was able to explain as much as she knew to Thomas. She formed an image of his face and tried not to hear his last words to her as he banished her from Magnus. She tried to picture his smile on the day he might finally understand why she had withheld the truth.

Hawkwood nudged her just as the last of the Sext bells rang. "He approaches," came his whisper. "Hide your face well."

Thomas went no farther than the town gates. Hawkwood and Katherine were close enough to see the expression of surprise on his face as the guard shrugged and pointed upward. They were close enough to see the discreet transfer of a gold coin from Thomas' hand to the guard's. They were close enough to hear Thomas' instructions to a boy standing just inside the town walls.

He left the boy holding the horse's reins and guarding it just inside the gate. Thomas then spun on his heels and half-sprinted back to the guard beneath the arch of the wall.

The guard nodded upon his approach, brought Thomas to the side of the arch, and led him through a door.

"Can it be?" Hawkwood said in hushed tones, as they watched from the shadows near the cook shop. Then conviction entered his voice. "It must be. Why did I not realize it before?"

"Yes?"

He pointed upward. "The earl of York is held there." He pointed upward. "Not in the sheriff's prison. I should have asked the same question he did upon entering York. . . ."

Katherine caught the trace of self-doubt. "No," she said, as she patted his arm, "you should not have inquired. We do not want to draw attention to ourselves."

Hawkwood sighed. "Of course."

His sadness disturbs me, Katherine thought, as they resumed their watch in silence. *He has never allowed me to see it before.*

Following that sigh, none of her former distractions seemed enjoyable, and the waiting and watching passed very slowly.

Three-quarters of an hour later, Thomas stepped outside again, nodded at the guard, and marched back to his horse. He took the reins from the small boy and, without looking back, led the horse into the center of York.

Even before Thomas was lost to sight in the swirling crowds, Hawkwood pressed two coins into Katherine's hand.

"One to bribe the same guard he did," he explained. "The other to bribe the guard above."

He spoke with renewed vigor. An effort to restore her confidence?

She did not comment but merely waited for more instructions.

"Reach the earl," he said next. "We must hear what Thomas plans."

"If the earl does not speak?" Katherine asked.

"Tell him it is the only way for him to remove the curse from his family."

Katherine paused. "I do not understand."

"He will," came the reply. "All too well."

Damp stone steps led upward in a tight spiral. The guard's leering cackle still echoed in Katherine's mind as she began to climb.

"'Tis money poorly spent for an audience, my sweet duckling," he had said. *"The earl's as powerless as a new-born babe."*

Knowledge is power, Katherine told herself firmly, *and if the earl shares his, it will be worth every farthing.*

She reached the open chamber at the top of the stairs. The ceiling was low, and its only furniture was a crude wooden chair for the upper guard, as he watched the doors of the four cells which opened into the chamber.

As she arrived, the guard was unlocking one of the doors.

It startled Katherine. *How does he know I wish to visit the earl? I have not yet placed a bribe in his hand, nor stated my request.*

Her silent question was answered within moments as she saw a prisoner step through the low, opened doorway. That prisoner was not the earl of York.

"You've done well," the prisoner said to the guard. "It is no surprise that Thomas—"

He stopped suddenly as he noticed Katherine. The guard turned too, and they both stared at their quiet visitor.

The black eyes of the prisoner studied her sharply. His cheeks were rounded like those of a well-stuffed chipmunk. Ears thick and almost flappy. Half-balding forehead, and shaggy hair which fell from the back of his head to well below his shoulders. A thoroughly ugly man.

And she recognized him.

His name was Waleran. He had once shared a dungeon cell in Magnus with Thomas, placed there as a spy to hear every word he spoke. Katherine had been there too, but as a visitor, disguised beneath a covering wrap of bandages around her face.

Katherine bit her tongue to keep from blurting out her surprise at his presence.

Surely Waleran has seen Thomas, has already discovered him, within the hour of arriving in York!

Katherine fumbled for words, wanting to look as flustered as she felt. "I've brought this for the . . . the former earl," she said, extending the wrapped food that Hawkwood had insisted she carry. "To repay a kindness he once did my father."

Katherine bowed her head in a humbleness which she hoped hid her flush of fear. As she waited, her heart pounded a dozen times.

How can I warn Thomas? If I leave now, they will suspect!

The prisoner finally spoke to the guard. "Help this pretty creature. I need no escort. And time presses me."

It is Waleran who orders the guard!

The guard grunted agreement and began to unlock the adjacent door.

Katherine let her pent-up breath escape as the prisoner brushed past her and began to descend the stairs. She willed herself to move forward slowly, despite the sudden urgency.

The guard blocked her movement. Her heart leapt into her throat, but then he held out a grimy hand, and she understood. She had forgotten the bribe. With concealed relief, she placed a coin in his palm. He bowed a mock bow and and made room for her to enter the cell.

Before the door had latched firmly behind her, she started in a rushed whisper.

"My good lord," she began, "there is—"

The former earl of York understood why she halted her words. He touched his face lightly with exploring fingertips of his left hand. "The penalty of losing an earldom. It appears much more terrible than it is," he told her. "There are days I do not feel any pain, and without a mirror . . ."

He shrugged.

This was not the proud warrior who had stood beside Thomas in battle against the northern Scots. This was not the confident man of royalty who had later decreed that

Thomas surrender himself and Magnus. Gone was the red-blond hair that spoke of Viking ancestors. His face was still broad but no longer remarkably smooth. The blue eyes that matched the sky just before dusk were now dimmed. And gone was the posture of a man at ease with himself and the world he commanded.

Instead, below his shaved skull, his face was crisscrossed with half-healed razor cuts, so that it appeared a giant eagle had raked him with merciless talons. His right shoulder nung limp at an awkward angle, popped loose from the collarbone. And his feet were still in splints wrapped with bandages gray-red from dried blood.

"Please, my dear, smile," he encouraged her. "It would be a small gift well received."

Katherine did so, hesitantly.

He waved her to speak. "You had something to impart, and, it seemed with great speed."

Katherine nodded. She did not yet know if she could trust her voice. She swallowed a few times, then spoke.

"Your visitor, Thomas," she said. "Would you still wish him dead as you did when he ruled Magnus?"

The earl leaned forward with a suddenness that made him wince in pain. "You knew the monk's assistant was Thomas of Magnus?"

"Yes, milord. And I fear so shall those who now hold York."

"Impossible," the earl said.

Katherine pointed to a vent in the wall. "Impossible that your voices might carry to the prisoner beside you?"

"Hardly," the earl snorted. "My conversations with him have kept me from losing all sanity here. Yet, even if he eavesdropped, there is nothing he can do."

"Unless he were a spy named Waleran." Katherine explained those days with Thomas in the dungeon beneath Magnus.

The earl clenched his fists. "The prisoner across the wall was one of them? A Druid?"

Katherine replied softly, "Then I need not explain the Druid circle of conspiracy?"

The earl shook his head. "No. Nor the darkness they have placed upon my family for generations. You know of the Druids too? What madness is this?"

Katherine nodded at his first question, and shrugged at his second. She wanted to learn what Thomas intended, but she dared not press the earl too quickly.

He shuddered. "Druids. We have always been at their mercy."

He darted a sharp look at Katherine. "This is strange, your sudden appearance. You are not one of them?"

She shook her head. "The Druids have already imprisoned you."

The earl gaped in sudden comprehension. "These priests of the Holy Grail are . . . are . . . Druids?"

"And Thomas, I pray, is not," Katherine replied, "Yet you swore his death. Until today."

"I swore his death because the Druids had forced it upon me, had threatened my sons would die a horrible death of worms eating their flesh as they lived, as once happened to a former earl of York. And now you tell me Druids pose as these priests who rule my kingdom?"

The earl shook his head weakly. "First Thomas with his rash promises. And now you. I feel so old."

Time. So little time remains. Those heads on spikes are a reminder of the price of failure.

"Rash promises?"

"He offered my kingdom back," the earl said.

"What does Thomas ask of you in return?" Katherine asked quickly. "How will he attempt this? Where goes he next?"

The earl stared strangely at Katherine. "It dawns upon me that you are privy to much, yet are a stranger. Why should you have more of my trust? Why should I believe the story of a spy in the opposite cell? Perhaps you are here to prevent Thomas from succeeding. After all, only a Druid could know what you do."

The earl gained more strength as his thoughts became more certain. "Only a Druid watcher placed at the gates would have known of Thomas' arrival so soon."

Time. Too little time remains. Yet can I betray a secret which has been kept from outsiders for centuries?

She thought of Thomas, of the heads outside this very prison. Even as she spoke in this prison cell, did Thomas walk unknowingly to his doom? Katherine made her decision.

"Few know of the Druids and the evil they pursue," she whispered. "None know there are those who seek to counter them."

The earl's eyes widened. "Another circle?"

Anguish ripped through Katherine for even hinting at that. Since birth, she had been trained to keep what secrets she knew, and had been permitted to grasp only the edges of the truth. It was a secret so precious that not even she knew much more than the existence of the Merlins, only that she was one of them and had been given much of their teaching.

The earl repeated himself, almost impatiently. "Another circle?"

How could she bring herself to go beyond that hint and betray even more? But there was Thomas. If he were not a Druid but, as she hoped, one like her, mere observation was no longer enough. Thomas now needed help.

Finally, Katherine forced herself to nod. "Another circle."

Those words hung while she waited until she could remain silent no longer. "Please. Thomas is in danger."

The earl made his decision based on the pain in Katherine's eyes.

"I gave Thomas my ring," he said, unconciously twisting his now empty finger. "He was to offer it at the castle keep to gain an immediate audience with the man who now holds York for the priests—the new earl of York."

"That is insane," Katherine blurted. "For what reason would he seek audience with the enemy?"

The earl's reply stunned her.

"Thomas believes he will be able to escape York with a ransom hostage."

Chapter Thirty-Six

The sunlight blinded Katherine after the dimness of the prison, and she almost stumbled in her rush to rejoin Hawkwood.

For a moment, she felt panic, for she could not see him in the crowd. Then the familiar black cape appeared as he stepped from a nearby doorway.

His face, always difficult to read, was no different as he approached. Yet Katherine knew he was troubled. Instead of waiting for her information with calmly folded arms, he was reaching out to grasp her shoulders and search her face.

"It is not good," Katherine answered his questioning eyes. "Thomas, it seems, seeks his own death."

She explained quickly. Later, she would tell Hawkwood what she had had to reveal to the earl of York to get her news.

"We have little choice but to follow, watch, and pray," Hawkwood said. "Too much happens too soon." He did not elaborate, but turned to march down the street which led to the castle of York.

Katherine remained close behind. Although she did not cast a final look backward, she could not escape the feeling that her every step was watched by those sightless heads of the men who had dared to rebel against the priests of the Holy Grail.

They reached the outer courtyard of the castle burdened with a sack of flour that Hawkwood had hurriedly purchased as they passed by the market stalls.

Wolfhounds lazed in the dirt. Servants scurried determined paths through the steady flow of noblemen and ladies who paraded in and out of the entrance with the assured arrogance that money and title provide. Squires stood in conversation with knights, casually alert and leaning against stone benches. More humbly dressed squires held the reins of their masters' horses.

Of Thomas or Waleran there was no sign. Within seconds, however, Katherine noticed Thomas' now familiar stallion tethered to the trunk of a sapling in the far corner of the court. Tending the horse was the same boy Thomas had hired near the town gate.

She tugged on Hawkwood's arm and whispered, "Thomas is already inside. Do we follow?"

He shook his head, and kept his voice low. "If he succeeds, he must come this way. If not, we will bribe servants to tell us the story of his failure and make our plans in accordance."

"How can he hope to succeed?" Katherine asked.

"That is my question too," Hawkwood said softly. He motioned with his head for Katherine to stay at his side, and walked to the boy who tended Thomas' horse.

"The monk's assistant," Hawkwood said to the boy. "Has he promised to return soon?"

"He made a jest," the boy replied. "He said soon or not at all."

Katherine shivered. It seemed so futile, this direct attack by a single person. What could Thomas accomplish without an army?

"We have business to complete," Hawkwood continued, as he pointed at the sack of flour that Katherine held. "Yet if he trusted you with his horse, he most surely will trust you with his purchase that we now deliver."

The boy shrugged.

"Place it in one of the saddlebags," Hawkwood instructed Katherine. "We shall leave it there as he requested."

Katherine complied, as puzzled now as when Hawkwood had bought the flour. When she finished, Hawkwood moved beside her to inspect.

"Keep the boy's attention," he said quietly.

That task was easy. Katherine's beauty was uncommon, even in her modest clothing and beneath a bonnet which shaded much of her face. A slight smile was enough to encourage the boy's full stare, and Katherine had no need to further distract him with conversation.

Less than a minute later, Hawkwood rejoined her and they strolled to another portion of the court. Little attention fell upon them. The noblemen and ladies were much too full of themselves and their gossip to look at mere townspeople.

"All that remains is the wait," Hawkwood said. "And the longer it takes, the poorer his chances."

Katherine closed her eyes and summoned the vision of her last meeting with Thomas. *"I am sorry, milady," Thomas said before banishing me. He lifted my hand from his arm, then took some of my hair and wiped my tears. "I cannot trust you. This battle—whatever it may be—I fight alone."*

Those were the words which echoed. *"I fight alone."*

It was at least five minutes before Hawkwood spoke again. "He leaves the entrance."

Katherine opened her eyes wide and drew her breath sharply.

For at Thomas' side was another, a person she recognized instantly.

Long, slim body, long, dark hair, haunting half-smile of arrogance now touched with fear. Isabelle Mewburn. The daughter of the former lord of Magnus. Isabelle Mewburn who had proclaimed love for Thomas as a means to assassinate him. Isabelle Mewburn, once held prisoner by Thomas himself.

Katherine could not help but feel a stab of jealousy. She knew that Thomas had been captivated by that royal grace and the stunning features of a finely pale face. And now, clothed in a dress which made the ladies around her look like shabby peasants, Isabelle seemed more heart-winning than ever.

To a casual observer, it might appear that Isabelle merely

accompanied the lowly monk's assistant. Yet, as Thomas descended the steps at Isabelle's side, Katherine could see strain etched across her face and the falseness of the smiles she offered passersby. For Thomas discreetly had hold of her elbow with his left hand. His right hand was hidden beneath his cape.

Katherine guessed he held a dagger, and that he had threatened her life at the slightest attempt of escape, the slightest attempt of obstruction by any of the castle guards. Yet, with her dead, Thomas would surely be killed as well.

They reached the courtyard ground.

At the top of the stairs, two guards watched closely every move that Thomas made, and followed them both from ten yards behind.

Thomas guided Isabelle to his horse. The boy removed the reins from the tree and placed them across the horse's neck.

Isabelle balked as Thomas gestured upward, then slumped as he said something Katherine was unable to hear. A renewed threat to plunge the dagger deep?

She swung up onto the horse. At that, the idle chatter in the courtyard stopped as if cut by the knife Thomas most certainly held.

"How strange, how crude," the whispers began. "A royal lady mounting a horse in full dress."

Some pointed, and all continued to stare.

Isabelle remained slumped in defeat, until Thomas moved to climb up behind her. At the moment his grip shifted on the unseen dagger, she kicked the horse into sudden motion.

Thomas slipped, then clutched at the saddle. His dagger fell earthward.

The next moments became a jumble. Thomas strained to pull himself onto the now galloping horse. Isabelle kicked at his face and both nearly toppled from the horse. People threw themselves in all directions to avoid the thundering hooves.

And the following guards noticed the dagger was now lying in the dust; Isabelle was no longer threatened. The first one shouted. "Stop him. He kidnaps the lord's daughter!"

Knights scrambled to their horses. Screaming and shouting added to the general panic.

Thomas now had his arms around Isabelle's waist. The horse was galloping in frenzied circles, once passing so close to Katherine that a flying pebble struck her cheek.

The speed of the horse was its only saving grace. Had its panic not been so murderous, Isabelle could have thrown herself free of the horse and of Thomas. Instead, she could only cling to the horse's neck.

Thomas finally reached a sitting position in the saddle and roared rage as he reached for the the flapping reins. His hands found one, then the other.

"Raise the drawbridge!" the other guard shouted. "Call ahead and tell them to raise the drawbridge."

Thomas pulled the reins. The horse responded instantly to the bit. Thomas spun the horse in the direction of the courtyard entrance, then spurred it forward amid the shouting and confusion.

People once again scattered, except for a solitary knight with a two-handed grip on a long broadsword. The knight braced to swing as the horse approached him.

That iron will cleave a leg! Katherine wanted to scream.

As the horse reached and then began to pass the knight, arrows flew, three above Thomas and into the stone wall of the courtyard. The last struck the knight's right shoulder and he dropped in agony. The sword clattered, useless.

Thomas swept through the gateway and thundered toward the drawbridge.

Katherine scrambled with all the other people in the courtyard to catch a glimpse of what might happen next.

Thomas and the horse passed into the shadows of the gateway.

Already, the bridge was a third of the way raised!

Yet Thomas did not slow the horse. A clatter of hooves on stone, then on wood. Then silence as the horse leapt skyward from the rising bridge. In the hush of disbelief that followed, that sudden silence became a sigh.

Almost immediately, the thundering of more hooves broke the sigh of silence.

Four knights had finally readied their horses, and the first charged through the courtyard gate toward the drawbridge.

After seeing Thomas escape, Katherine had relaxed. Now, with a deadly group of four in pursuit, she clenched her fists again and for the first time felt the pain. In her fear, she had driven two fingernails through the skin of her palm.

She forced her hands to open again and ignored the tiny rivelets of blood; but she could not stop the urge to draw huge lungfuls of air, as if she, not Thomas, were in full flight.

Thomas must escape. Yet we are so helpless.

She spun sideways in shock to hear Hawkwood softly laughing.

"Look," he pointed from their vantage point at the front of the gathered crowd. "The drawbridge."

All four horses skidded and skittered to a complete stop in the archway at the drawbridge. One bucked and pawed the air in fear.

For the huge wooden structure was still rising!

Loud bellows of enraged knights broke the air.

"Fools! Winch it down!"

Hawkwood's delighted chuckle deepened. "Such a bridge weighs far too much to be dropped. They'll have to lower it as slowly as it rose. With three roads to choose on the other side, and open fields in all directions, Thomas will have made good his escape!"

Five minutes later, when the drawbridge was finally in place again, they saw the obvious confusion of the knights as they waltzed in hesitant circles at the crossroad beyond the moat.

Hawkwood touched her arm.

"Much has yet to be done," he said. "But if he truly is one of us, we could not ask for more."

Katherine tried to smile.

Yes, she could exult that Thomas still lived. And still lived in freedom.

But he was not alone. Another was at his side.

Chapter Thirty-Seven

"Our friend Thomas is free," Hawkwood said. "Yet, there is much that troubles me."

Katherine turned her face to watch his features closely. *There is much that troubles me too. I cannot shake my last vision of him. The reins in his hands. The stallion in full flight. And she . . . far too beautiful, and Thomas holding her far too close.*

Katherine did not voice those thoughts. Instead, she said simply, "I am sorry you are troubled."

They stood at the crossroads outside the town walls of York. Behind them lay the confusion and chaos of an entire population buzzing with the incredible news. *The lord's daughter has been taken hostage! Kidnapped in daylight beneath the very noses of the courtyard knights!*

Those same knights had already scattered in all directions from the crossroads where Hawkwood and Katherine and a handful of travelers now stood, each knight engaged in useless pursuit of a powerful horse long since gone on roads which would carry no tracks.

One of the nearby travelers pausing at the busy crossroads might have found the picture of Hawkwood and Katherine bent in conversation together to be warmly touching.

Katherine shone with the innocent loveliness given only to those who pay little heed to their own beauty. Her long, blond hair was tightly braided. Pulled back as it was from her face, it showed more fully the smoothness of her soft skin and the deep blue of eyes which seemed luminously aware of every detail around her.

She stood nearly as tall as Hawkwood, and when she

leaned forward to listen to his quiet words, it was with a gentle grace that promised much for the woman she would become.

Hawkwood, however, would not have seemed exceptional to that same traveler. Despite the warm spring afternoon, he was draped in a loose black cloak that exposed only his hands and sandaled feet. With the stoop that forced him to lean heavily on the cane, his height dropped to match that of the woman beside him.

Yet, had that traveler been able to see into the shadows cast over the man's face by his hood, he would have been met by fierce eyes that burned with strength. Had that traveler taken away Hawkwood's cane, he would have seen the stoop disappear, and would have found no shakes or trembles in the gnarled hands. And had that traveler stolen Hawkwood's cloak, he would have been amazed at its weight and the objects hidden inside.

Katherine and Hawkwood, of course, paid little heed to any stranger's glance, and, with greater matters of concern, would have cared nothing of that stranger's impressions of their conversation.

Hawkwood's head was bent even lower now, as he searched the hard ground of the well-traveled roads.

"Stay with me," he said softly. "We shall talk as we follow Thomas."

"Follow Thomas?" Katherine echoed with equal softness. "Half an army runs in circles of useless pursuit. If he has escaped them, most surely he has also escaped us."

Hawkwood laughed quietly. "Hardly, my child. Do you not remember the puppy he left behind with his secret treasure of books?"

Of course. In the excitement of his escape, Katherine had forgotten that Thomas must soon return to the cave which held those books.

"Yes," she said quickly. "We shall find him there. We know he'll have to get back to his books within several days. And, regardless of his plans, he will not let the puppy die of starvation."

Hawkwood continued his low chuckle. "That only demonstrates that once again when you think of Thomas, you think with your heart. You wish him to have the nobleness of mind that would not let an innocent animal die a horrible death."

"It is otherwise?" Katherine challenged, even though her face flushed at Hawkwood's remark.

"Perhaps not. But others might believe Thomas will return to his puppy merely because of the more valuable books nearby."

Katherine ignored that. "So we proceed back to the valley of the cave and wait."

"Not so," Hawkwood replied. "That is far too long, and time is now precious."

"Until then?" Katherine asked. She did not want to think about the days which Thomas would pass in the company of such an attractive hostage, one who had once claimed a true love for him.

"We will find Thomas by nightfall," Hawkwood promised. His head was still down, as he still examined the ground carefully.

"That shows much confidence."

"No," Hawkwood smiled. "Foresight."

They hurried ahead on the road which led east to Scarborough on the North Sea. Neither found it unusual that several of the strangers behind them followed the same road.

Several minutes later, Hawkwood stopped and dropped his voice to a whisper.

"Speak truth now," he warned. "An hour back, in York, you were convinced I had lost my mind to purchase that sack of flour. After all, we had need to reach Thomas in the lord's courtyard before he could attempt to take his hostage."

Katherine hummed a noncommittal comment.

"Answer enough."

Hawkwood tapped the ground at his feet with the end of his cane.

"There," he said. "Our trail to Thomas."

He rubbed the tip of his cane through a slight dusting of coarse, unmilled flour.

Katherine nodded, unable to hide her own sudden smile at Hawkwood's obvious delight in himself and the implications of that flour.

"Yes," Hawkwood said, as if reading her mind, "I cut a small hole in his saddlebag and, of course, in the sack of flour. Unmilled and coarse, the flour that falls through is heavy enough to leave a trail wherever he goes."

A mile farther, Katherine remembered Hawkwood's words at the crossroads.

"What troubles you about the freedom Thomas so dangerously earned?" she asked.

Hawkwood's eyes searched ahead for the next traces of flour. He answered without pausing in his search.

"Thomas should never have escaped York."

"God was with him, to be sure," Katherine agreed.

"Perhaps. But I suspect instead the Druids in York provided earthly help."

"He nearly lost his life," Katherine protested.

"Are you certain? Describe the events you recall."

Were the subject matter less serious, Katherine might have enjoyed this test of logic. Somewhere in those events were clues Hawkwood had noticed and now wanted her to find.

"He left the castle with Isabelle, a dagger hidden beneath his cloak and pressed against her ribs."

"Before that," Hawkwood said, with a trace of impatience.

"A boy watched his horse at the side of the courtyard."

"Katherine . . ." Now his voice held ominous warning.

Suddenly, she understood. And understanding brought a pain, as if her heart had twisted in her chest.

"On his arrival," Katherine said slowly, "he met with the earl of York. A spy named Waleran in the neighboring cell overheard their entire conversation. That spy then hurried away as I entered the prison."

"Continue," Hawkwood said. Satisfaction in her perception had replaced his rumblings of vexation.

"Much time passed as the earl of York told me what Thomas intended," Katherine said. "Enough time for Waleran to reach the castle and provide warning."

Katherine's heart twisted more at the implication.

With that much warning, how had Thomas succeeded? Unless those at the castle had not feared his actions. Unless he were one of them.

Another memory flashed. Of a knight blocking escape, with his huge broadsword raised high to cleave Thomas dead as the horse and its two riders galloped toward him. Until a stray arrow slammed through the knight's shoulder.

"It was no accident, then," she said slowly, "that those arrows missed Thomas and instead struck the one knight able to stop him."

"Nor," Hawkwood added, "that the drawbridge was *not* raised soon enough to hold him inside the town. Then raised high enough to keep the knights from immediate pursuit."

"Yet why?" Katherine moaned. Her words were meant as release for the sorrow which gripped her. She already knew the answer.

"Our much-used argument," Hawkwood said. "The unseen Druid masters play a terrible and mysterious game of chess. Would they not prepare for any of us who had followed Thomas? The only thing they could not know is that you would recognize Waleran. And neither, of course, could he know. For bandages no longer cover your face. And had you not seen Waleran and known they had been warned, this escape would not have been suspicious."

"I've always said it could not be," Katherine murmured. "I could not argue with my heart. But a contrived escape can only prove he is one of them."

Hawkwood stopped and touched her arm in sympathy. It was a touch as light as the breeze which followed them down the road.

"Against the Druids, nothing is what it appears to be," Hawkwood said. "They know we watch, even if they know not who we are. The more it would seem Thomas is not one of them, the more likely we might finally tell him the truth."

They walked farther in silence.

"What shall we do?" Katherine despaired.

"We shall play this mysterious chess game to the end," Hawkwood said grimly. "We shall tell Thomas enough for him to believe we have been deceived. And then arrange a surprise of our own. He shall soon be a pawn which belongs to us."

That night, Katherine paused in the edge of darkness just outside the glow of light from a small fire in front of Thomas and his captive.

Thomas had chosen his camp wisely. He was flanked on two sides by walls of jagged rock, and protected but not trapped. The light of his fire was low enough that intruders passing even within twenty yards would not notice; and his horse, tethered to a nearby tree, had been muzzled.

Katherine had prepared herself to remain cold of heart for this moment. She had told herself again and again since leaving York that she would not care how Thomas chose to react to his hostage. What would it matter if she would step into the firelight and find the two gathered together side by side to seek warmth against the night chill, Isabelle's long hair soft against Thomas' face as she leaned on his shoulder?

It would matter, Katherine discovered. Her heart soared upward as she surveyed their makeshift camp. As much as she was forced to suspect Thomas was one of the false sorcerer Druids, it filled her with relief to discover them far apart.

Thomas was seated on a log, leaning with two hands on the hilt of a sword propped point first into the ground, and staring into the flames. He seemed oblivious of Isabelle on her blanket near the fire. Her hands were tied together and her feet hobbled no differently than might have been done to a common donkey.

Hardly the signs of romance!

Katherine smiled, then felt immediately guilty for rejoicing in someone else's misfortune. *Besides,* she reminded herself severely, *we are forced to believe Thomas is one of them. Even if he is one of us, there is no surety that his heart belongs to me, as mine already does to him. Did he not once banish me from Magnus?*

So she set her face into expressionless stone and stepped forward. He would not get the satisfaction of seeing any delight in her manner.

At her movement into the light, Isabelle shouted. "Flee! He has set a trap!"

In the same moment, Thomas stood abruptly and slashed sideways with his sword.

Both actions frozed Katherine, and a thought flashed through her mind. *A warning from Isabelle. They expected an intruder!*

Katherine was given no opportunity to ponder. A slap of sound exploded in her ears, and a giant hand plucked her feet and yanked her upward. Within a heartbeat, Katherine was helpless, upside down and her hands flailing.

She bobbed once, then twice, then came to a rest, her head at least five feet from the ground.

She swung upside down gently, and Thomas came forward to examine her.

Wonder and shock crossed his face.

"You!" he said.

"This intruder is an acquaintance?" Isabelle asked, her voice laced with scorn.

Thomas turned and replied, as if instructing a small child, "Your voice is like a screeching of saw blades. Please grace me with silence, unless you choose to answer my questions."

He turned back to Katherine. His face now showed composure.

"Greetings, my lady." He bowed once, then gestured above her. "As you can plainly see, an arrival was not entirely unexpected. My traitorous captive, however, hoped to give you warning."

Katherine crossed her arms to retain her dignity. It was not a simple task, given the awkwardness of holding a conversation while blood drained downward to fill her head. "You may release me," she said. "I have no harmful intentions."

"Ho, ho," Thomas said. A smile played at the corners of his mouth. "You just happened by? It was mere coincidence that my saddlebag is nearly empty of flour?"

Thomas tapped his chin in mock thought. "Of course. You found a trail of flour and hoped to gather enough to bake bread."

"Your jests fall short of humor," Katherine snapped. "Are they instead meant as weapons in your bag of tricks?"

"You approve, then, of the hidden noose attached to a young sapling?" He savored her helplessness. "All one needs do is release the holding rope with a well-placed swing of the sword, and the sapling springs upward."

The expression on his face became less jovial, and his voice slightly bitter. "Another weapon from the faraway land of Cathay. Surely you remember our discussion of that matter in better times. Times of friendship."

Katherine regarded Thomas silently and bit her tongue to keep from replying. This oaf knew so little about the risks she had taken and the sacrifices she had made on his behalf. How could she ever have dreamed of confiding in him? Even if he offered her half a kingdom, she would not tell him the truth.

"Without speech, now?" Thomas suddenly became serious with anger. "Magnus has fallen, and like magic, you appear, dogging my footsteps when I have avoided all the soldiers of York. From you too I demand answers."

"Thomas, Thomas," another voice chided from behind him. "Emotion clouds judgment."

He whirled to face a figure in black, head hidden by the hood of the dark gown.

"And you! The old man at the gallows!" Thomas said hoarsely. He raised his sword. "I shall end this madness now."

The figure said nothing.

"Before, I had questions," Thomas continued, the strain of holding back his rage obvious in his voice. "And you spoke only of a destiny. Then you disappeared."

Thomas advanced and threatened the figure with his sword. "Now speak. Give me answers or lose your head."

Still no reply.

Thomas prodded the figure with his sword. It collapsed into a heap of cloth.

"You have much to learn," Hawkwood said from the nearby darkness. "Had I chosen, you would have died a dozen times already."

Thomas sagged.

Katherine felt stirrings of pity for what must be going through him. Anger. Confusion. Desperation. An entire guantlet of emotions. He must feel intensely weary.

"By the knowledge that you are still alive, accept that we come in peace," Hawkwood's voice drifted upon him. "Cast your sword aside, and we will discuss matters that concern us both. Otherwise, the crossbow I have trained upon your heart will end any discussion."

Thomas straightened and regained his noble bearing. Then he dropped his sword.

Hawkwood stepped into view. Unarmed.

He shrugged at the expression that crossed Thomas' face. "No crossbow. A bluff, of course. You are free to grasp your sword. But I think your curiosity is my best defense."

Thomas sighed. "Yes." He pointed to the clothes on the ground. "How was it done?"

Katherine coughed for attention. Men! Her eyeballs might pop from her head at any moment and they were more concerned with boasting of techniques of trickery.

"Simple," Hawkwood replied. "It is merely a large puppet, a crude frame of small branches within the clothes, extended from string at the end of a pole, with the darkness around it to hold the illusion."

Katherine coughed louder.

Thomas ignored her and nodded admiration at Hawkwood. "A shrewd distraction."

Hawkwood shrugged modestly. "You are not the only one with access to those books."

Thomas froze at the implications. "Impossible that you know!"

"Perhaps. Perhaps not." Hawkwood moved to a log near the fire and sat down. "Please release poor Katherine. And I shall tell you more."

Thomas retrieved his sword, stepped out of the low firelight and approached Katherine where she hung.

He brought his sword back quickly, as if to strike her. A half smile escaped him at her refusal to flinch.

Barbaric scum. To think I once dreamt of holding you. Katherine did not give Thomas the satisfaction of letting him see her thoughts cross her face.

He slashed quickly at the rope holding her feet and she dropped, head first.

It forced from her a yelp of fright.

Yet somehow, he managed to drop his sword and catch her in one swift movement that cost him a grunt of effort.

For a heartbeat, she was in his arms, face only inches from his. And for that heartbeat, she understood why dreams of him had haunted her since her banishment from Magnus.

She could not, of course, see the calm gray of his eyes in the darkness of night, but the depth of those eyes remained clear in her memory. She could feel the warmth of his breath as he tightened with the effort of holding her aloft.

Even in the shadows, the face that looked upon her was as she had remembered each morning upon waking. Her right arm had draped around his shoulder as she fell, and the back of her hand brushed his dark hair.

In the heartbeat of stillness between them, she sensed a strength of quiet confidence. The total impression in that brief moment was much too enjoyable, and the rush of warmth she could not prevent as he held her became an anger. After all, he had joined the Druid cause. She should not feel as she did to be in his arms.

Her response at the anger she felt toward herself—almost before she realized her left arm was in motion—was to slap him hard across the open face.

He blinked, then set her down gently, but did not take his eyes from her face.

"On this occasion," he said softly, referring to the portion of an evening they had once shared on the ramparts of the castle Magnus, "there was no stolen kiss to deserve such rebuke."

Katherine glared at him, shook the cut rope lose from her ankles, then strode over to rejoin Hawkwood.

Side by side, they faced Thomas across the tiny fire.

"You promised to tell me more," Thomas said. "And for that, I would be in your debt." He rubbed his face before continuing. "Although it will take much to convince me of your good intentions. And your arrival here was not coincidence. Little encourages me to believe you will speak truth."

How can he pretend to be innocent? What monstrous deceit!

Just once, Katherine wished she had not been taught to hold her emotions in control. Just once, she wished she could stamp the ground in frustration and scream between gritted teeth.

She was conscious, however, that Isabelle was watching her closely. Too closely. So Katherine composed herself to stand in relaxed grace.

Hawkwood answered Thomas.

"We do have much to explain," he said. "There was our first meeting at the gallows—"

Thomas interrupted. "Timed to match the eclipse of the sun. I wish, of course, an explanation for that."

Hawkwood nodded. "Then our midnight encounter as you marched northward to defeat the Scots—"

"With your vague promises of a destiny to fulfill. That too you must answer."

"And finally," Hawkwood continued, as if Thomas had not spoken, "Katherine's return to Magnus and her delivery of my instructions which resulted in the trial of ordeal that you survived so admirably."

Thomas shook his head slowly.

"You did not survive?" Hawkwood said in jest. "I see a ghost in front of me?"

"Hardly," Thomas answered with no humor. "You spoke the word 'finally.' There is much more I need to hear. How do you know of my books? What do you know of the priests of the Holy Grail? Why the secret passages which riddle Magnus? How did you find me in York?"

Thomas paused and delivered his next sentence almost fiercely. "And what is the secret behind Magnus?"

Hawkwood shrugged. "I can only tell you what I know."

"Of burning water?" Thomas asked.

Neither Katherine nor Hawkwood were able to hide surprise, even in the low light given by the small flickers of flame.

Thomas pressed. "Of Merlin and his followers?"

Hawkwood sprang forward over the fire and grabbed Thomas by the elbow.

"We have nearly said too much," he whispered in a hoarse voice. "Your hostage is not as deaf as you once believed."

Chapter Thirty-Eight

How many times have I done this? Katherine wondered, as she stirred her gruel over the open fire. The small pot before her was dented from dozens of similar mornings over similar fires, during her previous travels with Hawkwood.

Only this morning was different. Instead of Hawkwood resting in thoughtful contemplation of the day, it was the captured daughter of a powerful earl who stared at her with open hostility.

Katherine smiled to herself. At least she was not the only one who received those angry stares. Thomas too was marked for hatred by Isabelle's sullen rage.

Not for the first time since rising with the sun's light did Katherine glance at Thomas as he rested against a tree. *Even in the lowly clothes of a monk's assistant, he still appears as noble as the lord of Magnus he once was.*

She quickly turned her head back to the fire. *Stupid child,* she told herself. *Appearances are deadly illusions.*

Absentmindedly she tried to lift the pot away, then sucked in a breath of pain as the hot metal punished her for her lack of concentration.

How much does Thomas know? If only Hawkwood had not insisted on speaking with him privately last night. If only Isabelle had not been nearby, forcing Thomas and Hawkwood to walk far from camp and leave me behind as her guard.

Katherine consoled herself with the thought that it would all be explained later, when Thomas was fully in their control. For as Hawkwood had promised, a surprise for that coldhearted deceiver truly did wait ahead.

"The girl is expensive baggage," Hawkwood said, as Thomas began to roll up the blankets of camp and pack his saddlebags.

"I agree," Thomas snorted, knowing full well that Hawkwood meant Isabelle. "However, it was your decision to travel with *Katherine*. And mine to depart from you both."

He looked sideways to see if his jest had struck the mark. Katherine said nothing, but could not hide the tiny flushed circles of anger on her cheeks.

Isabelle laughed, but a dark look from Thomas cut her short.

"Merely as a hostage," Thomas said, answering Hawkwood's original question, "the earl's daughter is worth a fortune. To me, however, she is even more valuable. Little as the chance is, her captivity is my only hope to reclaim Magnus."

"Oh?" Hawkwood queried politely.

It was a deceptive tone, for Katherine had often discovered his mild words were only a prelude to slashing observations which would destroy the most carefully laid argument.

"Soon she will tire of her silence."

"Oh?"

"Her father rules York only by permission of the priests of the Holy Grail, so I am not fool enough to believe that the possibility of her death will frighten them into relinquishing power. But she has knowledge of those priests, and knowledge of the secret circle of Druids. When Isabelle tells me all, I can seek to find their weakness, or a way to begin to fight."

"Alone?"

"Despite what you said last night, despite the book you gave me, I cannot place my trust in anyone."

Hawkwood shrugged. "You still need help."

"After Isabelle speaks, she will then be ransomed for gold. That, along with what I have now, will fund a small army. And, as you know, I am not without hidden sources of strategy."

"She is still expensive baggage," Hawkwood commented.

"Whatever knowledge she gives you is useless. Whatever army you build is useless. And whatever means of fighting you devise is useless."

Thomas tied down the last saddlebag. "For what you told me in privacy last night, I am grateful, if indeed it was truth. As for your advice this morning, I thank you too. But I must respectfully disagree."

He pulled Isabelle roughly to her feet and tied a rope from her bound wrists to the saddle.

"I am to walk?" she asked in disbelief.

"There are times when chivalry must be overruled by common sense," Thomas said. "You once planned to kill me. I hardly intend to let you control the saddle while I walk."

Thomas swung upward into his saddle. They were ready to depart. Thomas looked at Hawkwood and studiously ignored Katherine.

"Thomas," Hawkwood said, "no amount of force will defeat the priests of the Holy Grail. Not now. As kings receive their power because the people believe they have a divine right to rule, so now do these priests begin to conquer the land. By the will of the people they deceive."

Thomas froze briefly, but enough to show he had suddenly comprehended.

"Yes," Hawkwood continued. "Is it not obvious? Think of how Magnus fell. By consent of the people inside. None dared argue with signs which seemed to come from God, no matter how false you and I knew those signs to be. First York, then Magnus. Word has reached me that four other towns have been infiltrated, then conquered by these priests. Soon all of this part of England will belong to them. How long before the entire land is in their control?"

Hawkwood paused.

What did they discuss last night? Katherine wondered. *This sounds like a plea for Thomas to return to us, to join with us and learn the truth behind Magnus, to help in a final battle against the Druids.*

Katherine did not discover the answer, for the cry of a loud trumpet shrilled through the forest. Within moments, dozens of men, on foot and on horseback, were crashing toward them with upraised swords.

She relaxed.

The surprise has arrived as arranged, she thought in triumph. *Thomas will now be our pawn, regardless of his answer.*

Then she cried with horror. These were not the expected visitors! The attackers plunging toward camp wore the battle colors of York. These were knights of the priests of the Holy Grail.

Two lead horses galloped through the camp, scattering the ashes of the fire in all directions. Each rider reined hard and pulled up abruptly beside Thomas and Isabelle.

Within moments, the rest of the camp was flooded with men, some in full armor, some merely with protective vest and sword.

Katherine felt rough hands yank her shoulders. She knew there was little use in struggle, and she quietly accepted defeat. A man on each side held her arms.

Her attention had been on Thomas. Now she squirmed slightly to look around her for Hawkwood. The slight movement earned her an immediate prod in the ribs.

"Pretty or not, milady, you'll get no mercy from this sword," came the warning in her ear.

Katherine stared straight ahead and endured the arrogant smile that curved across Isabelle's face. Isabelle opened her mouth to speak, but the knight interruped.

"Greetings from your father," the first knight said to Isabelle. "He will delight to see you safe."

"And you, I am sure, will delight in the reward," she said scornfully as her attention turned to the warrior on his horse.

The knight shrugged.

"Shall my hands remain tied forever?" Isabelle asked.

The knight nodded to one of the men on foot, who stepped forward and carefully cut through her bonds.

Thomas, still in his saddle, had not yet spoken, nor moved. His eyes remained focused on Katherine.

Rage and venom. She could feel both from Thomas as

surely as if he had spoken the words.

Yet it was she who should be filled with rage and venom. He had lured them here and sprung this trap to capture them. But the shock of the sudden action had numbed her and she was still far from the first anger of betrayal. A part of her mind wondered about Hawkwood somewhere behind her, surely just as helpless as she.

Their capture might end whatever hope there had been to defeat the Druids. Would Hawkwood see this as a total defeat? Was he also just beginning to realize the horror that waited ahead? For neither would reveal their secrets willingly. And both knew well the cruelty of torture which delighted the Druids. Katherine prayed she would die quickly and without showing fear.

"We have them all," the second knight grunted to the first knight beside him. "The girl and her old companion."

He then spoke past Katherine's shoulder. "Someone see that the old man reaches his feet. We have no time to waste."

Reaches his feet?

This time Katherine ignored the point of the sword in her ribs and turned enough to see a heap of black clothing where Hawkwood lay crumpled and motionless.

"Sire, he does not breathe!" protested a nearby foot soldier.

"Who struck him down!" the second knight roared. "Our instructions were—"

The first knight held up a hand to silence him.

"It was I," the first knight said quietly. "He leapt in my path, and my horse had no time to avoid him. I believe a hoof struck his head."

No! Katherine wanted to scream. *Impossible!*

Until that moment, she still had held no fear. Hawkwood had been her hope. He would devise a means of escape, even from the most secure dungeon. *He cannot be dead. For if he is, so am I.*

The second knight dismounted, walked past Katherine and knelt beside Hawkwood. He leaned over and checked closely for signs of life.

"Nothing," the knight said in disgust. "We shall be fortunate if our own heads do not roll for this."

He straightened, then glared at the men holding Katherine. "Bind her securely," he said, "but harm not a single hair. Her life is worth not only yours, but every member of your family."

Katherine could not see beyond the blur of her sudden tears. Rough rope bit the skin of her wrists, but she did not feel the pain. Within moments, she had been thrown across the back of a horse, but she was not conscious of inflicted bruises.

Hawkwood is dead. And Thomas is to blame.

"Sit her up properly," barked a voice that barely penetrated Katherine's haze of anguish. "She'll only slow our horses if you leave her across the saddle like a sack of potatoes."

Fumbling hands lifted and propped her in a sitting position and guided Katherine's hands to the edge of the saddle. She was too deep in her grief to care or to fight.

Her mind and heart were so heavy with sorrow that when her tear-blinded eyes suddenly lost all vision, it took her a moment to realize that someone had thrown a hood over her head. Now she had no chance to escape on the horse they had provided her.

Then came a sharp whistle, and her horse moved forward. Slowly, it followed the lead horses in single file down the narrow trail which led back to the main road.

Each step took her farther away from the final sight she would carry always in her mind, that of Hawkwood silent and unmoving among the ruins of camp.

Eventually, the tempo quickened and the steady plodding of her horse became a canter. Katherine had to hold the front edge of the saddle tight with her bound hands and sway in rhythm to keep her balance.

She could hear own breathing rasp inside the hood, as she struggled to keep her balance in the darkness.

By the drumming of hooves she knew other horses were now beside her, which meant that the trail had widened.

Soon they would be at the main road which led into York.

How far then?

She and Hawkwood—she felt sharp pain twist her stomach to think of him—had walked several hours along the main road yesterday. *That means less than an hour on horseback to York. There* . . . she shut her mind. To think of what lay ahead was to be tortured twice—now and when it actually occurred.

Would she have a chance to make Thomas pay for his treachery? Even if it was only an unguarded second to lunge at him and rake her nails down his face? Or a chance to claw his eyes?

As the horses picked up pace her own anger and venom started to burn. Thomas had arranged this. He had trapped them and led Hawkwood to death. If only there might be a moment to grab a sword and plunge it—

Without warning, the lead horse screamed.

Even as the first horse's scream died, there were yells of fear and the thud of falling bodies and then the screams of men.

Because of the hood over her head, Katherine's world became a jumble of dark confusion as her own horse stumbled slightly, then reared with panic. The sudden and unexpected motion threw Katherine to the ground at the side of the horse.

A roar of pounding hooves filled her ears and she felt something brush the side of her head. The horses behind her! Would she be trampled?

Dust choked her gasp of alarm. More thunder of hooves, then a terrible crack of agony that seemed to explode her head into fragments of searing fire.

Then nothing.

Chapter Thirty-Nine

The light tickle of an butterfly woke Katherine as it settled on her nose. By the time she realized the identity of the intruder, it had already folded its wings.

Despite the deep throb in her head, Katherine suppressed a giggle. Her eyes watered from the effort of crossing them to focus on the butterfly, and even then, the butterfly was little more than a blur of color a scant inch away.

In any other situation, she thought, *this would be a delight. Such a gentle creature honors me with a visit.*

Her memory of the immediate past events returned slowly as the terrible throbbing lessened.

Hawkwood dead. The procession of horses back to York. Then a terrible confusion. The fall. Unconsciousness. And now—

And now she could see. The hood no longer blocked her vision. Katherine turned her head slowly. Not because of the resting butterfly on her nose, but because dizziness filled her stomach at the slight movement.

She was sitting against a tree, rough bark pressing against her back. Her hands were free.

She brought them up, almost in amazement at the lack of pain. That movement was enough to startle the butterfly into graceful flight.

"The woman child wakes," a voice said, "and with such fairness, it is no surprise that even the butterflies seek her attention."

Katherine tensed. The voice belonged to a stranger behind her. Before she could draw her legs in to prepare to stand, he was in front of her, offering a hand to help her rise.

"Milady," he said. "If you please."

If the man means harm, he would have done so by now, she told herself. *But what occurred to bring me here in such confusion?*

When she stood—aware of the rough callouses on the man's hand—she saw the aftermath of that confusion beyond his shoulders, on the trail between the trees.

Two horses, unnaturally still, lay on their sides in the dust. Several others were tethered to the trunks of nearby trees. She counted four men huddled at the edge of the trail. Their groans reached her clearly.

"It's an old trick," the man apologized, snapping her attention back to him. "We yanked a rope tight across the bend, knee high to their horses. These fools were traveling in such a tight bunch that when the leaders fell, so did all the others, including you. I offer my apologies for the bandage across your head. We did not know you would be hooded."

Katherine gingerly touched her skull, and found, indeed, a strip of cloth bound just above her ears.

"It is not serious," the man said quickly. "The bandage is merely a precaution."

"Of course," Katherine murmured.

The man shrugged and grinned at her study of his features.

His eyes glinted good humor from beneath shaggy, dark eyebrows. His nose was twisted slightly, as if it had been broken at least once, but it did not detract from a swarthy handsomeness, even with a puckered, X-like scar on his right cheek. His smile was proof he was still young, or had once been noble enough to enjoy a diet and personal hygiene which did not rot the teeth before the owner was thirty years of age.

Indeed, traces of nobility still showed in his clothes. The ragged, purple cape had once been exquisite, and his balance and posture showed a confidence instilled by money and good breeding. His shoulders, however, were broad with muscles borne of hard work, and the callouses on his hands had not come from a life of leisure. Altogether, an interesting man.

He interrupted her inspection.

"Your friend Hawkwood, I presume, escaped?"

His smile faltered as a spasm of grief crossed Katherine's face.

"That," he said gently, "is answer enough."

Katherine nodded. She was spared the embarrassment of showing a stranger unconcealed tears, because someone was calling him from behind.

"Robert, come hither."

He beckoned her to follow, and turned toward the voice. Together, they moved deeper into the trees and moments later entered a small clearing.

Katherine blinked in surprise. The remainder of the enemy horses were gathered. Isabelle sat on one, two enemy knights on others, Thomas on the fourth. Each was securely bound with ropes around their wrists. A dozen other men stood in casual circles of two or three among the horses.

"Robert, it is high time we disappeared into the forest," the voice said.

Katherine identified its owner as an extremely fat and balding man in a brown monk's robe.

"Yes, indeed," Robert replied. "The lady seems fit enough to travel." He paused. "Those by the road . . . they have the ransom note?"

The fat man nodded. "Soon enough they will find the energy to mount the horses we have left for them."

"They're lucky to be alive," spat another man. "I still say we should not bother with this nonsense about the earl's gold."

Robert laughed lightly. "Will, the rich serve us much better when alive." Robert motioned at Isabelle who sat rigidly in her saddle. "The daughter alone is worth three years' wages."

Robert turned to Katherine.

"Yes," he said in a low voice. "We did promise to help Hawkwood by capturing Thomas. But we made no promise about neglecting profit, did we? And although the arrival of these men of York has complicated matters, there is now much more to be gained by selling these hostages for ransom."

He lifted his eyebrows in a quizzical arch. "After all, as the king's outlaws, we can't be expected to be sinless."

Their southward march took them so deep into the forest that Katherine wondered how she might find her way back to any road.

The man she knew as Robert led the silent procession of outlaws and captives on paths nearly invisible among the shadows cast by the towering trees.

It was a quiet journey, almost peaceful. Sunlight filtered through the branches high above them and warmed their backs. The cheerful song of birds seemed to urge them onward.

Twice they crossed narrow rivers, neither one deep enough to reach Katherine's feet as she sat secure on the horse Robert had provided. The men on foot merely grinned and splashed through the water behind her. Each time, Katherine hoped that Thomas would topple from his own horse and flounder in the water, with his hands bound as they were.

Never will that traitor be forgiven.

Again and again as they traveled, she reviewed the morning's horror. *How did Thomas accomplish it? By prearranging his campsite so that the enemy knights knew exactly where to appear?*

Again and again, she fired molten glances of hatred at Thomas' back. *Of course he knew the saddlebag was leaking flour. To be followed so easily made his task of flushing us out that much easier. How he must have chuckled as he waited for us in his camp!*

Katherine needed to maintain the hatred. Without it she would have to face the numbness of the loss of Hawkwood. Without the hatred to consume her, she would have to focus on the struggle ahead. Yet even with the hatred to distract her, questions still troubled her.

With Thomas captured, what am I to do next? Without Hawkwood to guide me, what hope is there of carrying on the battle against the Druids?

Each time those questions broke through, she moaned

softly in pain, and forced herself to stare hatred at Thomas' back.

It was after such a moan that the outlaw Robert halted the lead horse. He dismounted, then walked past all the others to reach Katherine.

"Milady," he began, "we will leave all the horses here and move ahead on foot."

He answered the question without waiting for her to ask it. "A precaution. We near our final destination. The marks of horses' hooves are too easy to follow." Robert gestured at the outlaw named Will. "He will lead the horses to safer grounds."

Katherine nodded, then accepted the hand that Robert offered to help her down from her horse.

"My apologies again," Robert said. "For you and the others must be blindfolded during the final part of our journey."

His grin eased her alarm. "Another precaution. As the king's outlaws hiding within the king's forests, it is only natural that we are reluctant to show hostages—or visitors—the paths to our camp."

Although none of the outlaws hesitated to call to each other across the camp, their voices were muted with caution. But it could have been the hush of the forest. Great trees in all directions blocked whatever wind there might be; the air in their shade was a blanket of stillness.

As the shadows deepened with approaching dusk, small campfires appeared. At some fires, there was low singing of ballads. At others, the games of men at rest—arm wrestling, storytelling, and quiet laughter.

The fire at the center of the camp was much larger than any other. Beside it, turning the spit which held an entire deer, was the fat and half-bald man in a monk's robe. His face gleamed with sweat in the dancing firelight. In his free hand he held a jug of beer which he replenished often from the cask beside him. A steady parade of men approached with jugs of their own for the same purpose.

Katherine leaned against the trunk of a tree and watched the proceedings with fascination.

How had Hawkwood known of these outlaws? How had he contacted them? And why had they agreed so readily to help?

At the thought of Hawkwood, her tears—now always so near—began to trickle again. She blinked them away, then jumped slightly. The outlaw Robert had appeared in front of her in complete silence. *Surely in this darkness he cannot see my grief.*

"I would bid you join us in our eventide meal," he said. "I am told our venison will be ready soon."

"Certainly," Katherine replied in a steady voice. She did not feel any hunger.

"There is a message I have been requested to relay to you first, however," Robert told her.

Katherine waited.

"Thomas seeks a private audience with you."

The outlaw noticed her posture stiffen.

"Do not fear, milady. He is securely bound, and a guard is posted nearby."

Katherine noted with satisfaction that her tears had stopped immediately at the prospect of venting her hatred upon Thomas. "Please," she said, "lead me to him."

The outlaw took her to a small fire a hundred yards away. As promised, a well-armed guard stood discreetly nearby.

"He is now yours," Robert said. Before departing, he added loudly enough to make sure Thomas received the message, "Milady, don't hesitate to call if he disturbs your peace. A sound whipping shall teach him manners."

Katherine nodded, and the outlaw Robert slipped away with the same silent steps he had used to approach her.

She then turned to Thomas. He sat on a log, hands bound in front, a chain around his waist and attached to the log. Nothing about his posture indicated captivity, however. His nose and chin were held high in pride.

"You requested my presence," Katherine stated coldly.

"Yes, milady," Thomas said in a mocking voice. "If it doesn't inconvenience you too much."

Katherine shrugged.

As Thomas raised his bound hands and pointed at her,

his voice lost all pretense of anything but icy anger.

"I simply want to make you a sworn promise," he said in quiet rage.

"You seem in a poor position to make any promise," she answered with equally calm hatred.

"That will change," Thomas vowed. "And then I will seek revenge."

"Revenge?" she echoed.

"Revenge. To think that I almost believed you and Hawkwood might be friends instead of Druids." He half stood and the chain around his waist stopped him short. "Hawkwood has already paid for his lies with death. And you too will someday regret the manner in which you betrayed my trust."

For a moment, Katherine could not get air from her lungs. She opened her mouth once, then twice, in an effort to speak. The shock of his audacity had robbed her of words.

"You . . . you . . .," she barely managed to sputter.

She looked about wildly and then saw in the nearby underbrush a heavy stick. Rage pushed her onward. She stooped to the stick, pulled it clear, and raised it above her head.

She advanced on Thomas.

He did not move.

"Barbaric fiend!" she hissed. "His life was worth ten of yours!"

She slammed the short pole downward. Thomas shifted sideways in a violent effort to escape and the wood crashed into the log, missing him by scant inches.

It felt too good, the release of her pent-up anger.

She slammed the stick downward again. And again. Each blow slammed the log beside Thomas. He was no longer her target, as she mindlessly directed her rage into the sensation of total release. Again and again she pounded downward.

A strange sound reached her through her exhaustion. She realized it was her own hoarse breathing and half-strangled cries of despair between gasps. The heavy pole was now little more than a slivered pulp in her hands. Thomas was staring at her in a mixture of fear and awe.

She poked the splintered pole at his face and stopped it just short of his eyes.

"You craven animal—" she began, then whirled as the guard's hand gripped her shoulder while he spoke in concern. "Milady—"

"This is none of your concern!" Her rage still boiled, and the guard stepped away in surprise.

She turned back to Thomas and jabbed the wood toward his face again. "How dare you slur Hawkwood's name! He was the finest Merlin of this generation! He was the last hope against you and the rest of the evil you carry! He was—"

Katherine had to stop to draw air. She wavered in sudden dizziness. Then as the last of her rage drained with her loss of energy, she began to cry soundlessly.

She had nothing left inside her but the grief of Hawkwood gone. After forcing back her sorrow for an entire day, she finally mourned Hawkwood's death. The tears coursed down her cheeks and fell softly at her feet.

Blindly, she turned away from Thomas.

His voice called to her. It contained doubt.

"A Merlin?" he asked. "You still insist on posing as a friend?"

"As *your* friend? Never." She could barely raise her voice above a whisper, yet her bitterness escaped clearly. "What you have betrayed by joining them is a battle beyond your comprehension. Yet you Druids shall never find what you seek. Not through me."

"*You* Druids!" His voice began to rise again with rage. "I am exiled from Magnus. A bounty on my head! And you accuse *me* of belonging to those sorcerers?"

Katherine drew a lungful of breath to steady herself. "You knew we watched," she said. "Your masters sent you forth from York with the earl's daughter as bait for us."

"Sent me forth? Your brains have been addled by the fall. I risked my very life to take her hostage."

Katherine managed a snort. "Pray tell," she said with sarcasm. "How convenient, was it not, that the drawbridge remained open for you, and not the pursuing knights? And explain how you managed to reach the earl inside the castle, even though he had been forewarned. "

Thomas gaped. "Forewarned? You speak in circles."

Another snort. "Hardly. You pretend ignorance."

They stared at each other.

Finally Thomas leaned forward and asked in a low voice, "Who then forewarned the earl, if not you, the people who managed to follow me when none other knew my plans?"

Had it been less dark, Thomas would have seen clearly the contempt blazing from Katherine's eyes. "I was a fool for you," she said. "Caring for you in the dungeon of Magnus when even then your master, Waleran, was there. Then to discover him nearby in York—"

Thomas gasped. "Waleran? In York? How did you know?" He stiffened in sudden anger. "Unless," he accused, "you are one of them. Leading those knights to my camp."

More moments of suspicious silence hung between them.

"Why?" Katherine then asked softly. "Why do you still pretend? And why did you betray us so badly? Is it not enough you were given the key to the secret of Magnus at birth?"

Thomas spoke very softly. "I pretend nothing. I betray no one. And this secret of Magnus haunts me worse than you will ever know."

He continued in the same gentle, almost bewildered tones. "Katherine, if we fight the same battle, whoever betrayed us both would take much joy to see us divided." He shook his head. "And if you are one of them, may God have mercy on your soul for this terrible game of deceit you play."

"Milady, what plans have you for the morrow?" Robert asked. With dawn well upon them, lazy smoke curled upward from the dying fires.

Katherine huddled within her cloak against the chill. She had remained motionless for the last four hours, staring at the embers of the campfire nearest her. Now she stood.

"Milady?"

With visible effort, Katherine pulled herself from her thoughts and directed her gaze at the outlaw Robert.

"Plans? I cannot see beyond today."

It was said with such despair that Robert gently took her elbow and guided her to the main campfire where the fat outlaw, still with a jug of beer in his free hand, now stirred a wooden paddle in a large iron pot.

"Broth," Robert directed the fat man. "She needs broth."

With catlike grace that showed surprising nimbleness for such a large man, a bowl was brought forth and filled to the brim from the pot.

Robert helped Katherine lift the bowl to her mouth. When she tried to set it down after a tiny sip, he forced it to her mouth again. And again. Until finally, enough warm salty soup had trickled down her throat to make her realize that she was famished.

Greedily, she gulped the soup, then held the bowl out for more.

Robert smiled in satisfaction. He waited until she had finished two more bowls before leading her to a quiet clearing away from camp.

"Tell me," he said, "what plans have you for the morrow?"

Katherine stood straighter now, and much of the wild hopelessness had disappeared from her eyes.

"None." She smiled wanly. "Not yet."

"I have discovered," Robert said slowly, "that to make plans, one must first decide one's goal. Then it is merely a matter of finding the easiest path to that goal."

Despite herself, Katherine chuckled. "Knowing the goal, my friend, presents little difficulty. The path to that goal? One might as well plan a path across open sky."

The outlaw shrugged. "The task is not that impossible. After all, birds fly."

"They are not armed with weapons to destroy."

"Milady, what is it you want?"

Katherine thought of the secrets she had shared so long with Hawkwood. With sadness, she said, "I cannot say."

The outlaw studied her face, then said quietly, "So be it.

But if I or my men can be of service . . ."

Katherine studied his face, as if seeing it for the first time. "Why is it that you offer so much? First to rescue me and capture Thomas? And now this?"

"Hawkwood never told you?"

Katherine shook her head.

"We had been captured once," the outlaw said. He rubbed the scar on his cheek. "Captured and branded like slaves. Held in the dungeons of York . . . the rats and fleas our only companions. The night before our execution, all the guards fell asleep."

Robert's face reflected wonderment. "Each guard, asleep like a baby, and suddenly Hawkwood appeared among them. One by one, he unlocked our doors and set us free. When he sent word to us to arrange your capture, we were glad to pay our debt."

Katherine hid her smile. Child's play for a Merlin. A tasteless sleeping potion in food or wine. It did not surprise her that Hawkwood might release innocent men, nor that he would know how to reach them later. His foresight had almost been perfect. Had he not died at the unexpected appearance of the knights of the Holy Grail, he and Katherine could have pretended surprise at the outlaws' appearance and lulled Thomas into revealing more.

"When?" Katherine asked. "When did this happen?"

"Some years ago," the outlaw replied. "We learned our lesson well. Since then, the sheriff's men have not so much as seen a hint of us."

He grinned. "Except, of course, through the complaints of those we rob."

He went on quickly at Katherine's frown. "Only those corrupted by power," Robert explained. "Those who will never face justice because they control the laws of the land."

"You will continue to be a thorn in the sides of those who reign now, the priests of the Holy Grail?"

"It will be our delight to provide such service."

A new thought began to grow in Katherine's mind. She spoke aloud. "My duty," she said, "is to fight them also. No matter how hopeless my cause might seem, I must strive against them."

Robert nodded. He understood well the nobility of effort.

"I have little chance to succeed," Katherine continued. "But what chance there is, I must grasp it with both hands."

"Yes?" Robert sensed she had a request.

"Offer to battle Thomas. Set the stakes high. His life to be forfeit if he loses or his freedom if he wins."

"Milady?"

Katherine spoke strongly, more sure each passing second of what she must do in the next weeks. "Then," she said, "make certain that you lose the battle."

"As you wish, milady," the outlaw bowed, "or my name is not Robert Hood."

Chapter Forty

English Channel
July 1313

"I've already said it once. Board this vessel alone or not at all." Thomas, in reply, merely shifted the puppy to his other arm. It was a deliberate act, done slowly to show he had no fear for the loud sailor. It was also a difficult act. The cloak Thomas wore did not encourage movement. Yet he would not ever consider traveling without the cloak. He understood well why Hawkwood had always worn such a garment. It concealed much of what he must always carry with him.

The sailor facing him jabbed a dirty finger in the air to make his point. "You and a dog with all its fleas. Hah! Might you be thinking this is Noah's Ark?"

The sailors around him, always eager to watch a confrontation, laughed loudly.

"Aargh! Noah's Ark!" The laughter continued in waves as the joke was passed from crewman to crewman.

Silence finally settled upon them, broken only by the constant screaming of gulls as they dipped for the choicest pieces of refuse on the swelling gray water.

"This puppy once saved my life," Thomas said quietly. "You will receive full passage for the creature."

The sailor squinted. "Eh? You'll pay double just to keep the mongrel beside you on the North Sea?"

Thomas nodded.

They stood on the edge of a great stone pier that jutted into the Scarborough harbor. Because of his history lessons in the abbey from his childhood nurse, Thomas knew how ancient this harbor town was.

More than twelve hundred years earlier, Roman soldiers had built a signal post behind a rough, wooden pallisade, on the edge of steep cliffs directly north of the harbor. From there, they could see approaching warships and send messages forty miles inland to York for reinforcements.

In later centuries, Scarborough had suffered—as had most of the coastal towns—under the lightning-quick raids of the bloodthirsty Vikings. Time and again the Norsemen had sailed into this harbor, forcing the townspeople to scurry up the paths to the castle walls which now lined the edge of the cliff above them. Time and again the people had watched helplessly while the Vikings looted the houses clustering the harbor, killing and torturing those too slow to reach the castle in time.

Those Vikings had found the English land so rich that it defeated them with its luxury—eventually they began to settle and intermarry. Then, in the year 1066, the Anglo-Saxons suffered defeat by the Norman invasions. Through it all, Scarborough had served well as a harbor town, nearly as important as the major coastal city of Hull, a few days' travel to the south.

Now, as Thomas' nostrils informed him, Scarborough thrived through fishing and merchant boats. Around him, the stench of rotten fish, their entrails discarded carelessly in the water, and the equal stench of salt-encrusted wood forever soaked with fish blood, and of mildewed nets.

He prayed his thanks again for finding the *Dragon's Eye,* a merchant ship which was already near full with bales of wool from the sheep grown on the hills of the inland moors, and for finding one of the few ships not owned by the Flemish or Italians. Now he could at least barter his passage in English.

He looked directly into the sailor's eyes, bloodshot and bleary above a matted beard.

"Double passage," Thomas repeated firmly. To prove his point, he dug into his small purse for another piece of gold.

The act of keeping the puppy beneath his arm while using the same hand to hold the purse proved tricky, however, and as the puppy squirmed slightly, it knocked the purse loose.

A dozen gold coins spilled across the stone.

Thomas knelt quickly and scooped them into his free

hand. But it was much too late. When he stood, he faced greedy stares from all directions.

The sailor in front of him coughed politely.

"We welcome you aboard. And your companion." The sailor smiled, but there was no kindness in his eyes. "It would appear you both deserve to be treated like kings."

A deckhand led Thomas to the rear of the *Dragon's Eye,* and chattered like a man who was far too accustomed to lonely weeks at sea with a crew of only eighteen, none with anything new to discuss.

"You picked a fine ship, you did," the deckhand said. "A cog like this handles the roughest seas."

The cog was over a hundred feet long, with a deep and wide hull to hold the bulkiest of cargoes. Thomas stepped around the bales of wool. Above him, he saw the single sail furled around the thick, high, center mast. Thomas had seen cogs leaving the harbor with open sails and knew the square sail was large enough to drive the boat steadily in front of any wind.

"It's not a fast or easy boat to maneuver," the deckhand continued, in the voice of one happy to have the chance to finally impart knowledge to someone who knew less than he. "But it's almost impossible to capsize."

He lowered his voice. "And its high sides make it difficult to be boarded at sea by pirates."

He smiled at the result he had hoped to achieve. Thomas' face had darkened with sudden concern.

"Look about you," the deckhand waved. "The castle at the prow—" His voice became smug. "Fighting tower at the front—how I explain it proper for you land people—lets us fire arrows and such from above at any raiders who draw close."

He then waved at their destination on the cog, ahead of them by some fifty feet. "The sterncastle—the tower at the rear—is for important guests."

The deckhand sighed. "A bed and privacy. What gold can't buy!"

Then he remembered he had superiority because of his

knowledge and immediately began lecturing again. "We've got oars—we call them sweeps—should the gales be too rough or should we need to outrun pirates. You might be asked to man one."

Thomas said nothing to stop the flow of words which he barely heard.

Dangerous gales and pirate attacks. What folly brought me here? Hawkwood's advice—words from one who betrayed me. And some vague references in my secret books. Such madness to begin the journey, let alone hope in its success.

Yet what else is there to do? The reward on my head has been increased, and with the priests of the Holy Grail controlling town after town, there soon will be no safe place left for me in northern England—unless I choose to live the uncertain life of an outlaw. My contest for life and freedom against that wily Robert Hood showed how dangerous that might be—

The deckhand interrupted his thoughts. "Here you are. The sterncastle. My advice is that you tie the dog inside. There'll be enough grumbles about a dog enjoying the shelter denied the crew without his presence outside as a daily reminder."

Thomas nodded.

The deckhand hesitated, an indication he knew he should not ask. But his curiosity was too strong. "Our destination is Lisbon. Do you intend to go beyond Portugal?"

The scowl he received from Thomas was answer enough.

You and your friends stared at my scattered coins like wolves at a lamb. And I'm fortunate if we depart before you hear about the gold offered for my head. The less you know the better.

The deckhand stumbled back awkwardly to make room for Thomas to enter the dank and dark sterncastle.

Thomas finished his thoughts as he ducked inside. *Most certainly the Druid spies will someday discover I escaped England on the* Dragon's Eye, *and eager will be the sailors to impart that information for the slightest amount of gold. They cannot know my destination is that of the last crusaders—Jerusalem, the Holy City.*

If the deckhand believes this to be luxury, Thomas thought with a sour grin, *then he and all the crew have my sympathy.*

As if in agreement at the squalor of the dark and cramped quarters—hardly more than walls and a low roof—the puppy beneath his arm whined.

"You don't like it either?"

Thomas set the puppy down on the rough wood floor. It shivered, then crawled beneath a crude bed.

"They said two weeks to Lisbon if the weather is favorable," Thomas told his companion. "And crossed themselves when I asked how long if the weather isn't."

Another answering whine.

Thomas smiled. A week earlier, the puppy had first growled fearlessly as Thomas entered the cave after the absence of several days, the time spent captive among Robert Hood and his outlaws. But fearless growls had changed to yips of total joy as the puppy recognized the scent of Thomas returning.

Thomas had responded to the barking and jumping with equal joy, something which surprised him greatly. True, he had indeed worried upon his capture that the puppy would die the slow lingering death of starvation; yet, he did not want to be burdened with concern for anything except his goal of winning Magnus. Until that joy at their reunion had so surprised him, he intended to leave the puppy somewhere with peasants.

Instead, he decided not to abandon it, then spent two days in the cave, poring through the ancient pages of knowledge, or staring in thought at the natural rock chimney which allowed sunlight to enter, uncaring of the aches which still battered his every move because of the fierce fight against the outlaw Robert Hood.

During those two days he puzzled his next move. Yes, Magnus seemed out of reach. But the quest for Magnus had been instilled almost before he had learned to run, by the childhood nurse who replaced the parents he had never seen.

Without Magnus to pursue, what else had he in life? So, despite the near impossibility of his task, he could not let it go.

And at the end of the second day of silence in the cave near the abbey, Thomas decided that the one chance of victory would be in uncovering the very reason that the books had been hidden where they were. The only clues he had were vague references to the last Crusade, written in the margins of two of the books. And simply because those were too similar to what Hawkwood had said during their midnight discussion before the betrayal, he realized he could not ignore what it meant.

A sudden wave nearly pitched him against the far wall of his quarters. He recovered his balance, but realized the wave was a brutal reminder of the obstacles ahead. Had he chosen the right direction for his search? Or was Hawkwood's advice merely bait? To be wrong meant a year wasted, one more year for the priests of the Holy Grail to add strength to their hold over the area around Magnus.

Despite the swaying of the boat, Thomas knelt and poured out his troubles in prayer. That quiet moment brought him peace. After all, in the face of the Almighty, the One who counts years as seconds and who promises love beyond comprehension for eternity, what mattered a man's gravest troubles when that promised eternity made any life on earth the briefest of flashes?

"Strive to do your best here on earth," Thomas could hear a patient voice echo in his mind. *"Yet in all your pursuit, remember and take heart that it is only the first step toward something much greater."*

At that thought, Thomas' eyes watered. Gentle and kind Gervaise, the calm speaker of that lesson, like his childhood nurse, had now passed from this life. And in efforts to save Magnus.

"God rest their souls," Thomas finished his prayer with a sudden determination to continue his quest, if only because of the sacrifices others had made. "And God be here on these cold gray waters with mine."

He opened his eyes and prepared himself for the beginning of a voyage which gave him little hope of return to England, let alone a victory over the Druids who held Magnus.

Chapter Forty-One

Shortly after dawn on the third morning at sea, Thomas wanted to die.

"Carry your own bucket out," snarled the sailor into the cramped quarters, as Thomas sat hunched over his knees on the edge of his bed. "We've no time for softheaded fools around here."

The sailor half dropped and half threw the bucket in Thomas' direction, then slammed the door in departure.

Thomas could not even lift his head to protest. A small part of his mind was able to realize that the deckhand's prediction about resentment because of the puppy had been proven right. For two days, food had been brought to his quarters. For two days, each visitor bearing that food—except for a small, dirty cook's assistant who had stooped to let the puppy lick his hands—had grumbled about the waste of good food and valuable space for anything as useless as a dog.

The larger part of his mind, however, thought nothing about the puppy or the obvious resentment among the crew.

Thomas truly wanted to die.

The cog rode the rough seas with no more danger of sinking than if it had been a cork. However, like a cork, it tossed and bobbed on top of the long, gray swells of water, as the winds slowly took it south, through the English Channel, and into the vast Atlantic Ocean.

Only once had Thomas been able to stagger to the door of his quarters to look out upon those green-gray waves. The waves had seemed like small mountains, bearing down on the vessel without mercy, lifting it high, then throwing it down again, only to be lifted by the next rushing surge of tons of water.

That sight had propelled him back into his quarters where he had fallen to his knees and emptied the contents of his stomach into a bucket. It did not help that the food offered with such little grace consisted of biscuits and salted herring and weak beer.

The puppy seemed oblivious to the sea. Indeed, it seemed to delight in the pitches and rolls of the ship, and bounded around the small quarters with enthusiasm.

"Traitor," Thomas muttered, as the puppy now attacked the food. "It is no wonder you grow like a weed, taking my portion with such greed." The puppy did not bother to look up.

A vicious wave slammed the side of the cog and knocked Thomas a foot sideways.

He groaned as the nausea overwhelmed him, and prepared for the now familiar tightening and release of his stomach and ribs racked with renewed pain.

The cold wind bit the skin of his face and throat and provided Thomas a slight measure of relief, as he lurched from his quarters at the rear of the ship.

Below him, in the belly midship, was the crude, tentlike roof of cloth that sheltered the crew from the wind and inevitable rain. Men moved in and out of the shelter, all intent on their various duties.

Thomas carried the slop bucket to the side of the ship and braced his legs to empty it over the side. He was so weak that it took all of his energy and concentration to keep his balance and not follow the contents overboard.

As he turned back to retrace the few steps to his quarters, he nearly stumbled into the large sailor who blocked his path.

"By the beard of old Neptune," the sailor said with a nasty grin, "you would favor us all by becoming food for the fish yourself."

Thomas saw something as cold as the ocean in the man's

eyes, and beyond the man's shoulder he saw that two other sailors were entering his quarters in his absence. He understood the implications immediately.

"I had feared pirates at sea," Thomas said. He had to swallow twice to find the strength to continue and was angry at the weakness it showed so clearly. "But I did not expect them aboard this vessel."

The sailor leaned forward, yellow eyes above a dirty beard. "Pirates? Hardly. We saw the color of your gold and know the ship's captain charged too little by far for us to bear the insult of living so poorly while a dog lives so well."

Thomas sucked in lungfuls of cold air, hoping to draw from it a clearness that would rid him of his nausea.

"Rate of passage is the captain's realm," he finally said.

The sailor took Thomas' hesitation as fear, and laughed. "Not when the captain sleeps off a night's worth of wine!"

There was a loud yelp from the quarters, then a muffled curse. The other two sailors backed out. One held his hand in pain. The other held the puppy by the scruff of his neck.

"No signs of coin anywhere inside," the sailor with the puppy said. He dangled the puppy carelessly and ignored its small whines of pain.

The other sailor grimaced and squeezed his bleeding hand. "That whelp of Satan took a fair chunk from my thumb."

The yellow-eyed sailor turned back to Thomas. He dropped his hand to his belt and with a blur of movement, pulled free a short dagger.

He grinned black teeth.

"Consider your choices, lad. 'Tis certain you carry the gold. You'll hand it over now. Or lose a goodly portion of your neck."

In the sailor's yellow eyes Thomas saw a gleaming coldness which could belong to no sane man. He knew the sailor was lying. Once they had the gold, he would die anyway. Alive, he would later be able to complain to the captain, or once ashore, seek a local magistrate. The sure solution for them was to make sure no one was watching this far corner of the ship, and toss him—alive or dead—

overboard. Then, no person aboard the ship would be able to prove their crime.

Show weakness, Thomas commanded himself. *Your only chance against three is to lull them into expecting no fight at all.*

He sagged, an easy task considering the illness that seemed to bring his stomach to his throat.

"I beg of you," Thomas cried, "spare my life! You shall receive all I have!"

The evil grin of blackened teeth widened.

"Of course, we'll spare your life," the yellow-eyed sailor promised. He jabbed his knife forward. "Your coin!"

All three laughed at how quickly Thomas cowered in reaction to the movement of the knife.

Then Thomas fumbled with his cloak. "I keep it in a pouch hanging from my neck," he said, not needing much effort to place an extra quaver in his voice. "'Twill take but a moment."

Thomas had learned something about swordplay in the dungeon cells of Magnus with Sir William. *"Reach for your neck, as if scratching a flea,"* the knight had said. *"Then in one motion, lean forward, draw it loose, and slash outward at your enemy."*

"The knot is awkward," Thomas explained in a stammering voice, as he fumbled with his right hand at his throat. He bent forward slightly, as if reaching behind his neck for a knotted string of leather. "But it will only take—"

He did not finish. The hours of training had not been wasted.

In one smooth move, the sword drew free beneath his ducked head. Head still down, he struck at the spot he had memorized before bending—the knife hand of the yellow-eyed sailor.

A solid thunk and squeal of pain rewarded him, even as he raised his head to give him a clear view of all three.

The sailor's knife bounced off the wooden deck.

Without pause, Thomas kicked fiercely, sinking his foot solidly into the man's groin. Then, even as the man fell forward in agony, Thomas charged ahead, slashing sideways and cutting steel into the flesh of the second sailor's shoulder.

The third sailor managed to step back half a pace, but even in that time he had brought his arm back to cast the puppy overboard.

He froze suddenly.

"I think not," Thomas grunted.

The sailor did not disagree. He slowly lowered the puppy, careful not to move in any way that might encourage Thomas to press any harder with the point of the sword pressed into the hollow of his throat.

"Let the puppy fall," Thomas said softly. "He'll find his feet. And you might not find your head."

The sailor could not even nod, so firmly was the sword lodged against his flesh. He simply opened his hand. The puppy landed softly, then growled and bit the sailor's ankle. Tears of pain ran down the man's face, but no sound could leave his throat.

"Obey carefully. This sword may slip," Thomas warned. "My balance on these pitched waves has proven difficult."

The sailor's eyes widened in agreement.

Thomas pointed left with his free hand, and the sailor slowly shuffled in that direction. Thomas kept the sword in place and shuffled right, and in that manner of a grotesque dance, they continued until Thomas had half circled and now faced the other two.

The puppy stood directly between his legs and growled upward at all three sailors.

"Listen to him well," Thomas said. All three were bleeding, the yellow-eyed sailor with the bones showing on the back of his hand, the second one with a gash through sleeve and shoulder, and the third from a torn ankle.

"Listen to my friend well," Thomas repeated. "The next time, your greed will cost you your lives."

Even as the next words left his mouth, however, Thomas knew by the hatred in their eyes that they would return. Yet he was helpless, for he would have to betray every instinct to kill them now in cold blood.

God help me, he prayed silently, *if they catch me unawares again.*

Chapter Forty-Two

Thomas could only guess the time when he next left his quarters, for low and angry gray skies hid the sun's location.

He grinned despite the bleakness of the forbidding sky and endless swells of water, for the dizziness and nausea had finally left him. After days without food, he was famished.

He carried the empty food bucket and swayed in rhythm to the motion of the ship, as he walked to the edge of the rear deck. From there, he slowly studied the movements of the crew below.

Nothing seemed threatening.

For a moment, he considered seeking the ship's captain to set forth his accusations against the three. Then he dismissed the idea. Whose side would the captain choose? Certainly not his. With a crew of eighteen men — most of them unhappy with Thomas because of the puppy's comfort — the captain would never risk becoming the focus of anger by trying to discipline one-sixth of the crew.

Thomas could only pray that he had shown enough willingness to fight that the crewmen would not feel it worth the effort to provide more trouble.

Yet, Thomas felt that the sailor with the yellow eyes would return. And probably when all advantages were his. It would be a long, long journey, Thomas told himself, even if the cog were to reach Lisbon in the next hour. And there were weeks ahead.

A slow, small movement below demanded his attention and tore him from his thoughts. Yet, as he had been taught, Thomas refrained from glancing immediately at its source.

No, by yawning and stretching and swiveling his head as if he had a sore neck, he was able to direct his gaze at the movement without showing any interest.

Only the cook's assistant. Hat over eyes, shifting in sleep in a corner away from the constant menial work of preparing food.

Thomas looked elsewhere only briefly. The weight of the empty bucket was an unnecessary reminder of his intense hunger.

Thomas whistled, low and sharp.

The boy sleeps soundly.

Thomas whistled again. This time, the cook's assistant raised his head and opened bleary eyes.

Thomas waved for him to approach the short ladder that led up to his quarters from the main deck of the cog.

"I beg forgiveness for waking you," Thomas began, for he could remember his own days of back-grinding labor and little rest. "But I grow faint with hunger."

Thomas lifted his empty bucket and smiled. "You could earn yourself a friend."

The cook's assistant shrugged, face lost in shadows beneath the edge of the battered, leather cap, and took the offered bucket. When he returned, Thomas climbed down the ladder, reached into the bucket, and used his teeth to tear apart a hard biscuit. He swallowed water from a jug in great gulps, and then filled his mouth with the salted herring.

Thomas ate frantically in silence, half grinning in apology between bites. When Thomas finally finished, he wiped his mouth clean with the sleeve of his cloak.

"You have my gratitude," Thomas said with good-natured fervor.

Once again, the cook's assistant shrugged, then held out his hand for the bucket.

"A moment, please," Thomas asked. "Have you any news of three crewmen in foul tempers?"

Raised eyebrows greeted that question. *What face I can see is so dirty,* Thomas thought, *hair so filthy that he is fortunate it is cut too short to support many fleas. And his clothes are hardly more than layers and layers of rags.*

"Of course." Thomas laughed at the silent response to his question. "All sailors have foul tempers."

A guarded smile greeted his joke.

"Three men," Thomas prompted, "with wounds in need of care. Has any gossip regarding their plans reached your ears?"

Another shrug. Then the cook's assistant touched his forefinger to his own lips.

Thomas understood. *Mute.*

The cook's assistant set the bucket down and cupped his hands together, palms upward, He then stroked with one hand the air above the other.

"Puppy?" Thomas asked. "You inquire of its well-being?"

The cook's assistant nodded, almost sadly.

"Its belly is fat with the food I could not eat." Thomas smiled lazily, happy to be seasick no longer. "At least only one of us needed to suffer."

The cook's assistant opened his hands wide.

"Why?" Thomas interpreted. "Why so much trouble for a worthless puppy? That small, worthless creature saved my life."

Then, speaking more to himself than to his audience, Thomas said very softly, "And it is the only living thing I dare trust."

They attacked when the moon was at its highest.

The clouds had broken early in the evening, some six hours before, and the water had calmed shortly after. The dark of night provided peace to the weary crew. While the constant creaking of the ship continued, no longer did it groan and strain with every wave.

Thomas saw every move of their advance. Crouched low, and silent with stealth, they slipped from bale to bale until reaching the ladder. There were only three.

Thomas smiled. Whatever code sailors had, it probably contained some of the rules of knighthood. Since Thomas had shown bravery by fighting earlier in the day, the other sailors had probably decided he should be left alone.

If the other crew members had refrained from joining the attack, however, they had done nothing to prevent these three from waiting until the stillest hour of the night to finish their crime.

Thomas smiled again.

The sailor at the rear limped with each step. *Ah, the puppy's teeth left their mark.*

Thomas could enjoy their deadly approach because he was far from his quarters, hidden in the shadows of bales of wool. Far too easy for an unwary sleeper to be trapped inside those quarters, and for a knife of revenge to be drawn across his throat. So he had chosen the discomfort of the open ship.

Seek what treasures you will, Thomas thought merrily. *Seek it until dawn. For what you desire rests safely with me.*

Within his cloak lay his gold. Warm against his side lay the puppy, squirming occasionally with dreams.

I shall rest during the day, Thomas silently promised the three sailors, *and spend my nights on constant guard among these shadows.*

Much to his satisfaction, angry whispers reached Thomas. There was a light bang of the door shutting and a grunt of pain. More angry whispers.

Then silence. Minutes of silence.

It began to stretch his nerves, knowing they were above him, out of sight, about to appear in silhouette at the top of the ladder at any moment.

Thomas wanted the warning, wanted to know as soon as possible when they were about to descend. But he did not look at the top of the ladder.

Instead, he chose to focus on a point beyond it. Night vision, he knew, caught movement much more efficiently at the sides of the eyes.

Silence continued. Now the creaking of the ship seemed to be the low, haunting cries of spirits.

Suddenly, Thomas' heart leapt in the terror of shock.

Directly above him, the edge of the deck detached itself!

He managed not to flinch, then forced himself to be calm; slowly, very slowly, he turned his head to see more clearly.

The black edge of the deck had redefined itself to show the black outlines of a man's head and shoulders.

These men are shrewd. They have decided I must be hidden nearby. Instead of choosing the obvious — the ladder — they now watch from above, hoping I will not notice and will betray myself with a movement.

Thomas told himself he was safe as long as he remained still. After all, he had chosen a deep shadow.

Yet, his heart continued to hammer at a frantic pace. *This is what the rabbit fears, hidden among the grass. I understand now the urge to bolt before the hounds.*

But Thomas did not bolt. What betrayed him was the only creature he trusted. The puppy, deep in dreams, yelped and squirmed. And within seconds, two of the sailors dropped to the belly of the ship. One from each side of the upper deck.

The puppy yelped again, and they moved with unerring accuracy to the bale which hid Thomas.

Moonlight glinted from their extended sabers. Thomas barely had time to stand and withdraw his own sword before they were upon him.

"A shout for help will do no good," came the snarl with the approach of the first. "The captain's drunk again, and the crew have turned a blind eye."

"For certes," a harsh whisper followed, "none take take kindly to the manner in which you crippled my hand."

Thomas said nothing, waiting with his sword in front.

The puppy, now awake, pressed against his leg in fear.

Another movement as the third sailor, the one with the limp, scuttled down the ladder from the upper deck. He too brandished a saber.

I have been well trained, thought Thomas, *by Robert of Uleran, the man who fell in my defense at Magnus. I shall not disappoint his memory by falling without a worthy fight.*

The sailors circled Thomas, shuffling slowly in the luxury of anticipation. The silver light of the moon made it an eerie dance.

Impossible to watch all three at once. From where will the first blow come?

Thomas heard the whistle of steel slicing air and instinctively stepped back. He felt a slight pull against the sleeve of his cloak, then—it seemed like an eternity of waiting later—a bright slash of pain and the wetness of blood against his arm.

"Ho, ho," the yellow-eyed sailor laughed. "My weaker hand finds revenge for the damage you did the other!"

The sailors circled more. One dodged in and back, daring Thomas to attack, daring him to leave the bale behind him and expose his back. The others laughed in low tones.

This is the game. Cats with a cornered mouse. They are in no hurry.

"Gold and your life," the second sailor whispered. "But only after you beg to be spared."

The other two chortled agreement.

Until that moment, Thomas had felt the deep cold of fear. He knew his blood would soak the rough wood at his feet. But their taunts filled him with anger, and his fear became distant.

"Beg?" Thomas said in a voice he hardly recognized as his. "If I die, you will die with me. This is a fight which will cost you dearly."

The yellow-eyed sailor mimicked his voice with a high-pitched giggle. " 'This is a fight which will cost you dearly.' "

That growing anger suddenly overwhelmed Thomas. He became quiet with a fury that could barely be restrained.

He lifted his sword and pointed it directly at the yellow-eyed sailor and spoke with compressed rage. "You shall be the first to taste doom."

The yellow-eyed sailor slapped his neck. As Thomas lowered his sword to a protective stance, the sailor sank to his knees, then fell face forward onto the deck.

What madness is this?

Thomas had no time to wonder. As the second sailor betrayed himself by a movement, Thomas whirled to face him. Still carried by that consuming rage, he pointed his sword at the man's eyes.

The man grunted with pain, eyes wide and gleaming with surprise in the moonlight. Then he too dropped to his knees and tumbled forward, to land as heavily as a sack of fish.

What madness is this?

Thomas answered his own bewilderment. *Whatever it might be, this is not the time to question.*

He spun on the third sailor, who now staggered back in fear.

Thomas raised his sword and advanced.

"Nooo!" the man shrieked loudly in terror. "Not me!"

Then the sailor gasped, as if slapped hard across the face. His mouth gaped open, then shut, before he too pitched forward.

That shriek had pierced the night air, and from behind Thomas came the sounds of men moving through the ship.

He gathered his cloak about him, scooped the puppy into his other arm, and fled toward the ladder.

Chapter Forty-Three

Thomas had fourteen nights and fifteen days to contemplate the miracle which had saved his life, fourteen nights and fifteen days of solitude to puzzle the events. For not a single member of the crew dared disturb him.

The three sailors had risen the next day from stupor, unable to explain to the crew members who dragged them away what evil had befallen them, at the command of Thomas' sword.

Each day, the cook's assistant came with food and then darted away, without even the boldness to look Thomas in the eye.

While fourteen nights and fifteen days was enough time for the shallow slice on his arm to heal, it was not long enough for Thomas to make sense of those scant minutes of rage beneath the moonlight.

Many times, indeed, he had taken his sword and pointed it at objects around him, disbelieving that it might have an effect, but half expecting the object to fall or move, so complete was his inability to understand how he in his rage had been able to fell three sailors intent on his death, without touching one.

And for fourteen nights and fifteen days, he fought the strange sensation that he *should* know what had happened. That somewhere deep in his memory, there was a vital clue in those strange events.

On the sixteenth day, he remembered. Like a blast of frigid air, it struck him with a force that froze him midway through a troubled pace.

No, it cannot be!

Thomas strained to recall words spoken to him in near panic the night Magnus fell to the priests of the Holy Grail.

He had been hidden in a stable, saved from death only because of his guise as a beggar.

As Thomas projected his mind backward, the smells and sounds returned as if he were there again. The pungent warmth of horses and hay, the stamping of restless hooves, the blanket of darkness, a tired, frightened old woman clutching his arm, and the messenger in front of him.

"Milord," Tiny John blurted. *"The priests appeared within the castle as if from the very walls! Like hordes of rats. They—"*

"Robert of Uleran," Thomas interrupted *with a leaden voice. He wanted to sit beside the old woman and, along with her, moan in low tones. "How did he die?"*

"Die?"

"You informed me that he spoke his last words."

"Last words to me, milord. Guards were falling in all directions, slapping themselves as they fell! The priests claimed it was the hand of God, and for all to lay down their arms. It was then that Robert of Uleran pushed this puppy into my arms and told me to flee, told me to give you warning so that you not return to the castle. . . ."

No, it cannot be, Thomas told himself again. Yet the Druids had posed as priests of the Holy Grail. They had mysteriously appeared within the castle—undoubtedly through the secret passages which only in his last hours there had Thomas discovered riddled Magnus—and had somehow struck down the well-armed soldiers within.

Guards were falling in all directions, slapping themselves as they fell.

Yellow-eye had slapped himself, then fallen.

Impossible that a Druid was aboard this same ship.

Thomas had little time to search or wonder. An hour later, a shout reached him from the watchtower at the top of the mast. The port of Lisbon had been sighted.

To present myself as bait would be dangerous under any circumstance, thought Thomas. *But to be bait without knowing the predator, and to be bait in a strange town with no idea where to spring and set the trap, is sheer lunacy. Especially if that strange town is a danger in itself.*

Lisbon sat at the mouth of the wide and slow River Tagus, a river deep enough to bring the ships in and out of the harbor area. The town itself was nestled between the river and two chains of hills rising on each side. It was one of the greatest shipping centers of Europe, for the Portuguese were some of the best sailors in the world.

Thomas stood at the end of a crowded street that led to the great docks of Lisbon. He shifted from one foot to the other, hoping to give an appearance of the uncertainty he felt.

Which eyes follow me now? Impossible to decide.

Hundreds, nay, thousands of people flooded the docks of Lisbon. Swaggering men of the sea, cackling hags, merchants pompously wrapped in fine silk, soldiers, bellowing fishmongers.

Seagulls screamed and swooped. Wild and vicious cats, fat from fish offal, slunk from shadow to shadow. Bold rats scurried up or down the thick ropes which tethered ships to shore.

It was confusion driven by a single purpose. Greed. Those canny enough to survive the chaos also thrived in the chaos. Those who couldn't survive were often found in forgotten alleys, never to receive a proper burial.

Thomas needed to find such an alley, to finally expose his follower. And he had only a few hours of sunlight left. For he knew he would need the protection of a legion of angels, should he be foolish enough to wander these corners of hell in the dark.

He moved forward, glad once again for the comfort of the puppy beneath his arm.

It took half of the remaining daylight to find a proper place for ambush.

He had glanced behind him occasionally, but only during the moments he pretended to examine the merchants' wares—spices from Africa, exquisite pottery from Rome, and strange objects of glass called spectacles which the bulky merchant had assured him were the latest rage among highbred men and ladies all across Europe.

Not once had Thomas spotted a pursuer during his quick backward glances. Yet he dared not hope that meant he was alone or safe. Not after the strangeness of men collapsing because of an upraised sword.

During his wanderings, he noticed a side alley leading away from the busy street. He discovered that it led—after much twisting and turning—onto another busy street. The alley itself held many hidden doorways already darkened by the late afternoon sun.

So Thomas circled, an action which cost him much of his precious time. In the maze of streets, it was no easy task to find the original entrance to the alley again.

Once inside that tiny corridor between ancient stone houses, he smiled. Here, away from the bustle of the town, it was almost quiet. And, as with the first time through, it was empty of passersby. He could safely assume any person who traveled behind him was his follower.

Thomas rounded a corner and slipped into a doorway. He set the puppy down and fumbled through his travel pouch for a piece of dried meat, then set it on the cobblestone.

"Chew on that, you little monster," Thomas whispered. "I have no need for your untimely interference again." The puppy happily attacked the dried meat in silence.

Will it be flight or fight? Thomas wondered. His heart hammered against his ribs as each second passed. He knew he was well hidden in the shadows of the doorway. He could choose to let his follower move on and in turn stalk the stalker, or he could step out and challenge his unknown pursuer. *Which will it be?*

More seconds passed, measured by the rapid beats of his heart.

Thomas did not hear footsteps. His pursuer moved along the cobblestone so quietly that only the long shadow of afternoon sun behind him hinted at his arrival.

When the figure appeared in sight, head and neck straining ahead to see Thomas, his decision was instant.

Fight. For the figure was barely the size of a boy.

Thomas reached out and grasped for the shoulder of the small figure. His reaction was so quick that Thomas only managed a handful of cloth as the figure spun and sprinted forward. But not before Thomas recognized the filthy face and hat.

The cook's assistant.

Thomas bolted from the doorway in pursuit.

The cook's assistant? Surely he is a mere messenger or spy. Yet his capture is my only link to his masters.

Thomas ignored the pain of his feet slamming against the hard and irregular cobblestones. He ducked and twisted through the corners of the tiny alley, gaining rapidly on the figure in front.

Behind Thomas, the frantic barking of the puppy as he joined in this wonderful game.

Thomas closed in, now near enough to hear the heaving breath ahead.

Three steps. Two steps. A single step away. Now tackle!

Thomas dove and wrapped his arms around the cook's assistant. Together, they tumbled in a ball of arms and legs.

Get atop! Grasp those wrists! Prevent the reaching for a dagger.

Thomas fought and scrambled, surprised at the wild strength of this smaller figure. For a moment, he managed to sit squarely on his opponent's stomach. A convulsive buck threw him off and Thomas landed, dazed.

The cook's assistant scuttled sideways, but Thomas managed to roll over and reach around his waist and pull him back close into his body.

Then Thomas froze.

This is not what I should expect from a cook's assistant. Not a yielding softness of body that is more like...

Angry words from this mute cook's assistant interrupted his amazement and confirmed his suspicion.

... more like that of a woman.

"Unhand me, you murderous traitor."

Katherine's voice!